Night of the Bear

**William Smethurst
& Julian Spilsbury**

First published in 1993
by HEADLINE BOOK PUBLISHING

First published in paperback in 1994
by HEADLINE BOOK PUBLISHING

A HEADLINE FEATURE paperback

10 9 8 7 6 5 4 3 2 1

ISBN 0 7472 4239 9

Typeset by CBS, Felixstowe, Suffolk
Printed and bound in Great Britain by
HarperCollins Manufacturing, Glasgow

HEADLINE BOOK PUBLISHING
A division of Hodder Headline PLC
338 Euston Road
London NW1 3BH

To Diane

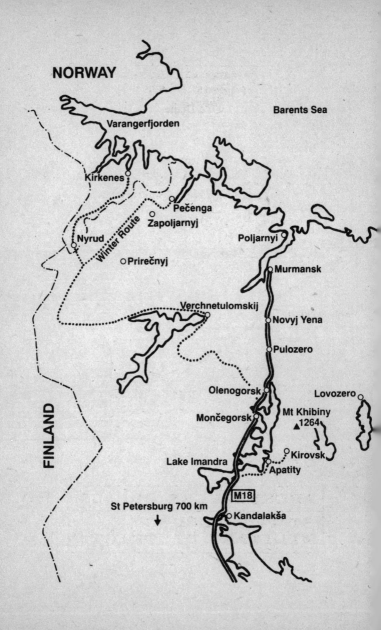

Stop line Puma
5k East M18

Kola Peninsula

ARCHANGELSK OBLAST

ST PETERSBURG
MILITARY DISTRICT

PART ONE

KIRKENES

Let storms of indignation rage
And righteous wrath outpour.
This is a sacred war we wage,
A people's sacred war

Red Army Song, 1941-45
War

Back once more to the sins of men,
To the Land of the Midnight Sun,
I go to spend a worthy end
For the North is calling 'Come!'

'Eskimo Nell' as recounted by
Lance-Corporal Leech

Now the Bear is dying.

Ethnic civil war rages in Kazakhstan and Georgia. There are food riots in Petersburg and Moscow. The Baltic states, Belorussia and the Ukraine have long been free, but Third Shock Army masses on the borders of Latvia as the Russian Federation tries to renegotiate a barter deal on oil-shale and manufactured goods.

In the far north the sparsely populated, poor and insignificant Karelian Autonomous Republic has lapsed into near anarchy.

It is rumoured that in Murmansk the Navy will refuse to take to sea for winter manoeuvres. There are reports of gun battles in the streets between deserters, Militia, and Federation MVD troops.

As the first snows of winter coat the tundra, it is clear that Moscow's writ no longer runs inside the Arctic Circle. Federation army units have pulled back to Arkhangelsk. The massed armour that once loured over the Norwegian/Finnish border now rusts in abandoned tank parks. Norwegian Army's elite Brigade North has to cope, instead, with a pathetic trickle of refugees.

ONE

Mount Kirovsk, Karelian Autonomous Republic,
19 October

This could only end one way. The man knew it now, as he
lay panting at the forest edge, fighting the urge to stuff his
mouth with snow, to freeze his core temperature, to kill his
heartbeat.

A lifetime's training had taught him to always believe
himself a victor, to discount the possibility of failure. But
the time comes when training gives way to instinct. And
instinct told him the end was close.

Night had brought him this far, almost within reach of
some kind of safety. Dawn had brought a greasy yellow
sun – no source of warmth here, fifty miles inside the
Arctic Circle – and the helicopters.

Mi-28s, successors to the 'Devil's Chariot' so feared by
the mujahideen, with their rapid-fire cannon and rocket
pods, the demented drumming of rotors alternating with
the shriek of twin turboshafts as they swept the open
tundra and combed the finger valleys that snaked down to
the Murmansk highway.

As the sun rose, his ski tracks would show like a trail of
golden thread.

* * *

His plan had been simple – as last resorts are. Set off in the dead of night at the end of eight hours' duty. Another eight hours, sixteen with luck, before he was missed. By then he would have reached his contact point with the English Spetznaz team, the SAS infiltrators.

The guards must have missed him within the hour.

A mile ahead, perhaps, lay the road; but above him, over him now, were the Mi-28s, the nearest flying fifty yards ahead and so low that he could see the crewmen, encased in steel and titanium, faceless behind their black visors.

They would be men he knew. Men he would recognise, faces glimpsed once or twice through the miasma of cabbage, potato soup and tasteless Uzbekistan coffee in the soldiers' canteen.

Soon they would find him. The range detection radar would target him, a bloodheat spot on its screen.

He could see the gunner in the turret, the nose-gun slaved to his command helmet so that, as he moved his head, the eight 12.7mm barrels rose and fell, traversing left then right as his eyes roamed along the edge of the wood.

Wherever the gunner's right eye rested, death lay at the touch of a thumb.

From the open ground to his right, four more helicopters swept in and formed a line a hundred metres apart, noses towards him, tails swaying in the air. Suddenly they dropped to earth like hawks, and through the snowstorm of their rotors he saw men spring fully armed from their bellies. Men and dogs.

He rose to his feet, stiff and clumsy, and floundered back into the wood. Back on his tracks. Away from the rendezvous with the English, who would be watching, perhaps, from their *dnovka*, their snowcave. A last desperate bid to win through to one of the mining settlements under Mount Kirovsk, although the helicopter above must have seen him by now; its pilot must be whispering instructions into his throat-mike.

Crouching for lower wind-resistance, he let his skis take him to the bottom of a stream bed, then toiled painfully up the other side. From here he could see the northern edge of the wood and a long slope of virgin snow.

It came from nowhere. No bark, no warning growl: just ninety-eight pounds of iron-hard bone and muscle, hammering his left side, knocking the breath from his body – a compound dog, the sort even handlers fear, the sort they feed over the compound wall. Once, twice, the concertina bite tearing open his left arm as his right hand drew the Spetznaz knife from his boot, and in the same movement swept it upwards in a gutting stroke.

It missed. This dog had learned to fight the hard way: in prison yards against condemned men who had been given a knife and one last chance to serve the state. It was dragging him round to the left, keeping clear of his right arm as it dragged him down.

His thumb found the safety-catch on the knife's handle, flicked it off, and found the button beside it. As the dog released his left arm and leapt for his throat he pressed the button. The blade shot from the hilt. The dog fell back on the snow, yelping for a moment, and then still.

He would have liked to rest, to sit with his back to a tree, to look at the sun, to think and reflect.

But the small plastic capsule was in the palm of his hand. 'Spetznaz are never taken prisoner,' they had always said in Afghanistan. He had cracked the same old joke when he had signed for it, and Ilich the storeman had smiled the same old smile.

The capsule lay on his tongue – a little snow to wash it down – and he felt nothing at all when the dog-handler's boot clubbed into the side of his face.

'Bastard!'

The M1-34 Scout dropped the regimental commander on the frozen lake below the wood. The soldiers had loaded the body on to a pulk, and were standing round smoking, waiting for the helicopter transports.

The senior lieutenant began to stammer an apology – the orders had been to secure the man alive at all costs – but the commander shook his head. It was to have been expected.

He begged a cigarette from one of the soldiers, lit it and looked round at the lakeside and surrounding forests.

'Beautiful,' he said. 'I don't get above ground as much as I should.'

'Good fishing in summer,' said the senior lieutenant, awkwardly: the guard company did not see the commander all that often.

'We'll come in the spring – you and I. Remind me!'

The soldiers were pulling the pulk towards the place where the helicopter would land.

'Do we know who he was?' asked the lieutenant, made bold by the moment of intimacy.

There was a moment's pause. 'KGB – Fourth Directorate,' said Colonel Vasili Aleksandrovich Kvatov.

He looked again at the lake, and the snow-covered trees sparkling in the sunshine; wistfully, like a condemned man.

TWO

The RAF bus sped across the tarmac through the rain and the dead, gusting leaves, circled the plane and came to a halt. Passengers tumbled out and hurried to the metal steps that led into the vast jaws of the C-130 Hercules. Getting there slightly ahead of the pack, Nick Chard, a captain in the Royal Mercian Regiment, stood back to give precedence to a lieutenant-colonel in the Light Infantry, an air commodore, and a stout middle-aged major in the Royal Artillery. There followed a dozen Queen Alexandra's nurses who had been drinking Pils in the mess for three hours, and four Dental Corps personnel who had spent the same time attempting, with some success, to beguile them with a description of the commander-in-chief's molars. One dentist said, 'Cheers, mate,' to Nick as they hurried up the steps. Another said: 'What happened to the air-bus?'

Left standing in the rain was a young major, about Nick's age, in the Devon and Dorset Regiment.

'After you,' said the young major politely.

'No, no,' said Nick, 'after *you*.'

The major grinned and went quickly up the steps. Nick followed him into the body of the plane. It was

11

bitterly cold inside and smelled of rubber and oil. The nurses and dentists were settling themselves on canvas seats lashed to the cabin struts, facing inwards towards the cargo. Nick and the major squeezed past them. They found seats next to the air commodore who had grabbed, or been cunningly allocated, a seat by the heating duct. Before them were pallets of white field medical kits, perhaps five thousand in number. To the right, in front of where the lieutenant-colonel was sitting, the medical kits gave way to cardboard boxes marked 'NATO standard' and the name of a Middlesex plastics company.

Nick and the major from the Devon and Dorset Regiment looked at them thoughtfully.

'You know what those are?' said the major.

'Yes,' said Nick. 'I saw them in Kurdistan.'

'I was walking in a government warehouse,' said the major:

> 'Where the daylight never goes
> 'I saw fifteen million plastic bags
> 'Hanging in a thousand rows.'

'Adrian Mitchell, isn't it?' said Nick. 'I'm more of a seventeenth-century man myself.'

The lieutenant-colonel had shown the whites of his eyes when the major started reciting verse. Now he gave Nick a despairing look and took papers from his briefcase.

'Peter Griffiths-Jones,' said the major, extending a hand.

'Nick Chard,' said Nick. 'You lot joining ACE Mobile Force?'

'No,' said the major, but did not elaborate.

A few minutes later the C-130's jaws closed with a whine of hydraulics, and the plane began its long manoeuvring before take-off. Nick remembered his first flight in a Hercules. Ten minutes after it first started to move, he had looked out expecting to see the Oxfordshire countryside some fifteen thousand metres below, and been severely shocked to find that they were still on the tarmac.

He turned up the collar of his greatcoat and settled down to try to sleep. He was dog-tired. He had left Leintwardine at dawn, his mother rising, despite his protests, to cook him eggs and bacon; his sister Julia driving him to RAF South Cerney in her MGB; everyone worrying about his father's stroke, the chances of a full recovery, the things they could do with drugs and physiotherapy these days.

'Nobody wants to push you into a decision,' his sister had said as she gunned the car through Herefordshire lanes, 'but Daddy's going to have to give up work and the business won't run itself, and you do keep talking about leaving the army.'

'Captain's menopause,' said Nick, looking out at the dripping hedgerows. 'They say you get over it. You could go into the business yourself if you wanted to.'

Julia did not want to. She was twenty-five, four years younger than her brother. She and a friend ran a patisserie and sandwich shop in Ludlow. She drove on in silence. They stopped for coffee in Hereford, and, after she had scathingly condemned a Danish pastry, she said:

'I saw Emma. At a party at the Phippses'. She asked after you.'

13

Nick had been engaged to Emma.

'She's really beautiful, that girl. Everybody says you must have been mad to let her go.'

'Julia . . .'

'Everybody says you were mad to chuck the most beautiful—'

'I think we ought to get moving,' said Nick firmly.

They reached RAF South Cerney at 10.50, ten minutes before he was due to report. Julia parked in a layby fifty yards from the entrance to the base.

'Oh well, off you go again,' she said.

Her retriever dog, Harold, who had travelled in the luggage space behind their seats and wanted to be let out, rested his jaw on Nick's shoulder and breathed heavily in his ear.

'Harold doesn't want you to go.'

'Come on, Julia,' said Nick.

'It's just that it's so bloody for me. Daddy's got no heart left for the business, Mummy's worried sick about you being sent to the Baltic – I mean, what's going on, for God's sake? Is NATO really going to use tactical nuclear weapons? Nobody can understand what's going on. Why don't we just cut off the Russians' food aid or something?'

'I know as much as you do,' said Nick. Two weeks previously, on orders from HQ ACE Mobile Force, Narvik, he had doubled his company's Nuclear, Chemical and Biological Weapons training programme. 'Anyway, I'm not in the Baltic. I'm in the Arctic.'

'But for how long?'

They sat in silence. Ahead of them lights blazed down

on the entrance to the base. There was a full guard. The wooden sign by the gates said 'Bikini Red', as did an identical sign outside every army base and RAF base in the UK. 'Bikini Red' was the highest degree of readiness alert for UK land forces.

'All those lights on in broad daylight, taxpayers' money, that is,' said Julia suddenly, sniffing and fumbling for a Kleenex.

Two RAF Regiment guards, rifles slung in the crooks of their arms, left the guardhouse and walked, unhurried, along the road towards them.

'You'd better go. They're coming to check us out.'

'They needn't try and check me. I'm on a public road,' said Julia rattily.

'Look, it's going to be all right,' said Nick. 'He's out of intensive care. He's off the danger list. There's no need to worry.'

'It's not Daddy we're worried about, you idiot,' said Julia. She turned the ignition and drove out of the layby, past the two guards who turned to watch, and pulled up by the entrance to the base.

'Bye, kid,' said Nick. 'Bye, Harold.'

'Bye,' said Julia miserably.

He slept – to be awakened an hour or so later by an RAF orderly with coffee. Next to him the major was working at a word-processor. His case was open, and Nick saw the cover of a red MoD high-security file. He slept again, and only woke as the plane was descending over Oslo.

'This is my stop,' said Griffiths-Jones. 'You going on?'

'Narvik and then Kirkenes.'

'Isn't that near Nyrud?'

'Nyrud's down on the Finnish border. Norwegian Army's Brigade North have a refugee post.'

'I've been reading the intell reps. What's it like up there?'

'Minus-30.'

Griffiths-Jones smiled and nodded. 'Have a good journey,' he said. When he had gone, Nick wondered what a major in the Devon and Dorsets was doing working with Norwegian Brigade North intelligence reports and MoD high-security files.

They had to wait at Oslo while part of the cargo was unloaded. Half the cardboard boxes were left on the plane.

'You're taking bodybags up to Narvik?' he asked an RAF youth, who replied, 'Refuse sacks, chief. Keep Norway tidy.'

The Queen Alexandra nurses and the dentists had departed. Nick was the only passenger on the last leg.

'Don't leave the plane, for Christ's sake,' grumbled the RAF youth, 'I'm not coming looking for you.'

Nick left the plane, and stood on the tarmac, stretching his legs, thinking about his father in hospital, his mother's distress, the total inadequacy of a seventy-two-hour compassionate leave pass.

Then, moving a few metres from the plane and the fumes of aviation fuel, he suddenly smelled the clean, cold air of the north, the conifer-scent of the taiga. He felt his spirits rise. He started to think about his command, 'B'Company Royal Mercians, and he forgot about his family worries, and bodybags, and majors with high security clearances.

THREE

A moving image flickered on a white wall. Amateur video: sailors and naval infantry, some of them tearing off their insignia and rank badges. Filing cabinets outside a burning building, documents spilling out into the slush. BTR-70 troop carriers in a suburb, two tank men dancing a *gopak* for the camera. A civilian on a roadblock, waving a Kalashnikov pistol, emptying a magazine into the void.

The video ended.

'Poljarnyi, two days ago. That's it for the general summary, sir,' said Griffiths-Jones, G2 officer to Joint Intelligence Committee, Northern Command.

'Right, let's move to item five,' said Generalleutnant Hoepner, Commander-in-Chief NATO Forces Northern Europe. 'An unusual one, this.'

Griffiths-Jones opened a file.

A dozen men were in the Secure Room. Four armies were represented, as well as the Luftwaffe, the RAF, and the Royal Navy. One civilian was present. He was a man in his forties, a diplomat from the European Commission in St Petersburg.

19

Everyone drank coffee. Hoepner smoked small black cheroots. Overhead the anti-bugging and air-conditioning systems hummed in discreet unison.

Griffiths-Jones started to read.

'Maria Lewandowska crossed the border at Nyrud three days ago. At the moment around four hundred and fifty refugees a day are being processed up there by Norwegian Army Brigade North. She had travelled with some nickel miners and their families from Novyj Yena, and was suffering from exposure and exhaustion. It was several hours before she saw a senior officer, and then only by insisting that she had a personal message for a particularly important person.'

Griffiths-Jones touched a pad. On the huge video screen appeared a picture of the Princess of Wales.

There was a buzz of interest.

'Photo courtesy of *Hello* magazine, taken just over two years ago when the hospital opened. Nurse Lewandowska is on the far right.'

The Princess of Wales was surrounded by smiling nurses. A small girl in some sort of national costume was presenting a bouquet. The child was perhaps nine years old, her face thin, the bone structure starkly revealed, her eyes darkly smudged, her smile uncertain.

'An English rose,' said Hoepner. 'Diana I mean. Never seen the nurse before.'

'A Polish rose perhaps,' said his chief-of-staff, Brigadier Grenfell. A man not noted for his sense of humour.

Griffiths-Jones said: 'You have Norwegian Intelligence's debriefing in front of you. According to Nurse

20

Lewandowska, the hospital has enough coal to run the heating boiler for another ten days at most. The local commune in Mončegorsk is believed to be sympathetic but helpless. Telephone lines are not working, electricity from the Kandalakša hydrostation is spasmodic. The biggest problem, however, is food. This is an allergy clinic. There are children who cannot eat potatoes, for example, without physically choking. Children who need special foods in order to live. Another week and Nurse Lewandowska believes these children will start to die.'

Hoepner turned to the diplomat from Petersburg. The diplomat said: 'We have heard nothing. It is impossible to find out what is happening north of Arkhangelsk.'

The senior RAF officer said: 'Can we use a C-130 transporter, Hamburg to Murmansk, then ship supplies down the M18 to Mončegorsk?'

The Joint Services Strategic Intelligence officer, an American, said: 'According to Norwegian Intell there have been gun battles in the suburbs between deserters, militia, and MVD troops. We believe the airport has been closed since yesterday.'

'The hottest landing zone since Arnhem,' said Grenfell, and Hoepner smiled slightly.

The diplomat from St Petersburg said: 'There is another point. The Russians are happy for us to resupply the hospital, but they don't want air traffic – fixed-wing or helicopter – over Karelia.' He added: 'You can see their point of view.'

The Strategic Intelligence officer said: 'I'm not quite certain about ours. JS Intell predicts that half a million will die of disease or hypothermia or civil war in the Federation this winter. I've seen a report saying the average energy intake in Karelia will be less than 1800 calories a day by January. There must be fifty thousand children at risk between Murmansk and Arkhangelsk.'

'But not in a European Community hospital,' said the diplomat from Petersburg patiently. 'Not in a hospital we sent the Princess of Wales to open less than two years ago.'

'Of course,' said the American. 'Why didn't I think of that.'

'OK,' said Hoepner. 'It's overland through Finland or Norway. What's the best route?'

'Lotta, then along the Winter Route,' said Grenfell, 'but the best unit available is further north at Kirkenes. "B" Company Royal Mercians, doing trials on the Snow Leopard oversnow vehicle.'

'We're going to risk the new Snow Leopard?' said a Bundeswehr representative, startled.

'That's what it's for,' said Grenfell curtly.

The diplomat from Petersburg said: 'We are very grateful. Can you supply a medical team? If you have any problems I think we could get the French to help.'

'You're cleverer than we are in that case,' said Grenfell. 'Anyway, field medics is a Luftwaffe responsibility.'

Hoepner was Luftwaffe commander as well as Commander-in-Chief NATO Forces Northern Europe. 'Get on to them, Peter,' he said. 'Tell them this is not a request. Right, gentlemen, item six. Sitrep on Third Shock Army on the Latvian border . . .'

* * *

The daily intelligence review ended. Left in the Secure Room were Hoepner, Grenfell, Griffiths-Jones and a major called John Biggin, who had been introduced to the committee as an observer from the Cabinet Office, London. The triple-thickness door closed with a gentle thud. Hoepner lit another cheroot. Griffiths-Jones took a file from his briefcase.

It was the file on Operation Terrier.

'So, it's overland,' said Hoepner. 'What do we know about "B" Company Royal Mercians?'

Griffiths-Jones said: 'Funnily enough, sir, I met their OC yesterday on the flight from South Cerney.'

'Seem OK?' said Hoepner.

'Yes, sir.'

'Major Nicholas Chard,' said Biggin, who was, in fact, an officer in 22 SAS Regiment.

'Acting major actually,' said Grenfell. 'Substantive rank is captain. Twenty-nine years old.'

'One lucky soldier,' said Hoepner.

FOUR

Kirkenes, northern Norway, 24 October

Nick gently squeezed his nose between his thumb and forefinger, waiting for the sensation of crushing ice in his nostrils. Nothing happened. The temperature had not yet fallen to minus-30: it just felt as if it had.

He slid his hand back into its glove-and-waterproof outers, leaned his elbows on the roof of the Land-Rover, and scanned the snowscape through his binoculars.

The vedda: endless, dreary, isolated. Home of the troll and, along its coast, the maelstrom.

A grey sky merged into a white landscape. In the far distance he could see the sulphur cloud from the smokestacks of Nikel, and the lights of the border post where Norwegian Army's Brigade North was processing refugees from Karelia.

Beneath him was a shallow valley of birch scrub and frozen tundra pools. On the valley floor a solitary Snow Leopard over-snow vehicle – a million pounds sterling worth of advanced electronics, manoeuvrability and firepower – was barely distinguishable against its background.

There was no movement. No sound but that of the wind

25

that had been blowing in from the Barents Sea now for four days, its wind-chill reducing the temperature by twenty degrees, grounding all helicopter flights north of Narvik.

Nick said: 'Ask him if he's ready.'

The HQ Land-Rover driver, Private Collins, spoke into the microphone strung round his neck. A moment later a voice said: 'Waiting for a signal from Decoy One.'

Nick leaned down and said into the microphone: 'I'm not hanging around all day. What's the matter with him?'

'I think he's a perfectionist.'

'Jamie, let's just get on with it, shall we?'

'Moving now,' said the voice.

Nick raised his binoculars. Faintly on the wind came the cry, 'Rapid fire!'

Suddenly flashes of yellow sparkled along the tree-line, and the valley cracked with sound as five machine-guns and thirty assault rifles opened up. Seconds later, ski-troops advanced in half sections through the stunted birches, dropping on one knee to fire, then rising to lope forward through the powdery snow.

Close behind them came the new Snow Leopards, inching forward in support of the infantry, their turret-mounted twin machine-guns blazing as they raked the scrub-covered ridge on the far side of the valley.

'Stop! Cease fire!'

The command was taken up by sergeants and corporals along the skirmish line. The valley fell silent; skiers and vehicles skewed to a halt in flurries of snow. Men rose from fire positions, applied safety-catches, brushed themselves off, and slung their rifles.

Nick spoke into the microphone: 'Jamie, ask him if it was OK, will you.'

There was a pause, then: 'He says his camera wasn't set.'

Nick said: 'Say that again.'

'He says we were a bit premature.'

'Right. Take them back up.'

He watched the vehicles turn, and the soldiers begin to trudge back up the slope. They were tiring, and they would be sweating. Soon the sweat would start to freeze, tentacles of ice forming inside their clothes, moisture transformed to frost.

'Collins?' he said.

'Sir?'

'Where did that stupid bugger come from?'

'Don't know, sir.'

'He wasn't here when I went away.'

'No, sir.'

The stupid bugger had been sneaked in when his back was turned.

'I'm going down there.'

'Sir,' said Collins, and grinned to himself as Nick skied vigorously down the slope.

'I think we got our wires crossed,' said Sergeant Worembrand, Army Public Relations photographer, emerging from the front seat of the Snow Leopard, rotund as a Michelin Man in his layers of military and non-military kit, a tartan scarf round his chin.

'And do you know what I think?'

'Sir?' said Worembrand cautiously.

Experience had taught him to be wary of keen young officers, and in his view Chard was super keen, the kind of bastard that had sent Worembrands and their ilk to death and destruction over many centuries.

'I think you were inside, on your fat arse, with the heater on full blast,' said Nick. 'No, just listen.'

Worembrand had not been going to speak.

'My men have been up that slope five times so that you can get your picture. *Five times!* Now, I know you are not enjoying life with us, sergeant, I know you are not a happy PR man, I know they had to prise you out of your cosy Rheindahlen office with a spanner, but I will not have my men fucked about because you are too idle to do your job. You understand what I'm saying?'

'Well, yes . . .' said Sergeant Worembrand.

'We are going to give it one more go, and you are going to stay out here with that camera if I have to weld you to it. Do you understand?'

'Well, yes—'

'And you are not to get into that vehicle again without my express permission. Do you understand?'

'Well, yes—'

'Don't say "Well, yes" to me, for Christ's sake.'

'It's the light. I can't do anything about the light!' Worembrand yelped, adding after a moment, 'Sir.'

Nick looked up to the tree-line. Although it was barely 15.00 hours the light was going fast. By 16.00 it would be pitch dark and minus-30.

'It's a bugger, I know,' said Worembrand.

28

Nick unhooked his personal radio. 'Jamie?'

He was using a spare frequency as a chat net. The signals corporal had pursed his lips in disapproval, but had not looked surprised. Nick had a habit of ignoring the correct procedures.

'Sir?'

'Endex, bring them in – over.'

'Wilco. Permission to close down?'

'Roger. Close down now. I'll meet you on the road.'

Nick turned back to Worembrand. 'Do you know what I could really do without?'

Worembrand said, 'No, sir,' and waited for Nick to tell him about pasty-faced base rats who infest the rear areas of the army. But at that moment Nick's personal radio buzzed, and Collins told him a priority signal had arrived via courier from the NATO communications satellite in geosynchronous orbit over Scandinavia.

'OK, Mason, get me back to the Land-Rover.' Nick swung himself on to the Snow Leopard, which jerked forward suddenly, then spun ninety degrees in a spray of snow and blast of black smoke from its exhaust.

Sergeant Worembrand wondered if perhaps they might remember him, and stop, but they didn't. The Snow Leopard bucked and roared its way up the valley side, a mechanical rodeo horse with Nick clinging to its back.

On the distant tree-line he could see the other Snow Leopards slowly moving along the ridge track, each pulling a dozen men on skis. He was on his own, and it was half a mile from the track to the road and a further mile back to base.

'Stupid fucker,' he said, not referring to himself.

The signal had been brought five kilometres from the receiving station by a courier from Norwegian Army Brigade North, who was busy turning his BMW wide-wheel motorbike with as much roaring from its exhaust as he could manage. The signal was a stapled flimsy with OC R MERC KIRKENES printed on it. Nick opened it and read:

From: Cdr AMF(L)
To: OC B Coy 1 R MERC
          1. B Coy 1 R MERC is to prepare to
             move with all vehs.
          2. Coy to remain at 12hrs notice to move.
          3. Orders by Liaison Officer, Brigade
             North, time and location to follow.

A signal which, as Nick always kept 'B' Company twelve hours' notice to move, seemed entirely pointless.

Sergeant Malcolm Worembrand clambered up to the ridge track just as the last Snow Leopard crunched its way homewards. He waved frantically to the driver, then to the man in the turret, then to the line of skiers behind. They all waved politely back. He watched the narrow red slit of the convoy lights disappear into the gloom. He walked. As darkness fell he stumbled into snowbanks. In the distance, over the plateau, he could see the lights of the Norwegian refugee station; further away was an occasional belch of yellow flame from the Nikel smelting chimneys. Ahead were the lights of Kirkenes. He finally reached the Hotel Vang, a gaunt weatherboard building that was the billet of 'B' Company. As he turned into the gates and crossed the square (in summer the hotel residents' car park) he passed a soldier drearily engaged in painting the snow with a white aerosol, and was momentarily cheered by the misfortunes of somebody worse off than himself. He went up to the first floor, pulling off his camouflage outers, in search of tea and toast. It had been a long and nasty day.

Two men were standing by the window looking out. They were staring down at the soldier in the snow.

'You reckon he'll go to Colly?' said Staff-Sergeant Beckwith of the REME detachment, and Sergeant-Major Robson said: 'They'll lock him away so deep the crows won't shit on him.'

So the poor bugger outside was going to the glasshouse, thought Worembrand comfortably. He was still wearing three layers of clothes, including a Norwegian army shirt with zip-up neck, khaki pullover, and white fleecy arctic socks. He was starting to thaw out, to warm up even. He ordered tea and toast and strawberry jam from the orderly, opened a beer, and hunted round for a newspaper. The mess subscribed to the *Daily Telegraph* and the *Sun*. He was not seeking the *Telegraph*. It was his ambition to be the next Beverley Goodway, world-famous photographer of beautiful girls, and he was assembling a portfolio to send to the *Sun*'s editor, the celebrated Stuart Higgins. He did not enjoy photographing oversnow vehicles in the freezing cold with keen-arsed Ruperts bawling at him every time he nipped into the warm to thaw out his fingers.

He said: 'Has anybody seen the *Sun*? I've spent all afternoon trying to take photos with keen-arsed Ruperts fucking me about.'

'If you're talking about Captain Chard, you can keep your trap shut,' said Robson coldly.

Worembrand settled on the chintz-covered sofa with Britain's favourite newspaper. 'Ask Dad if he remembers Luscious Linda Lusardi!' he quoted, 'One of Beverley's all-time greats. And she is, too. Just look at them. Bloody hell—' He looked up in wary alarm as the door crashed open and Sergeant Doran appeared.

Doran was six foot four in his socks and intensely physical. He smiled at the photographer.

'That wasn't you, back there, waving, Mal, was it?'

'You know it was fucking me.'

'I thought it was a fuckin' troll. My driver said "That's Sar'nt Worembrand" and I said it never is, it's a fuckin' troll.'

Worembrand bared his teeth in a grin. His dislike for the beefy sergeant was intense.

'A fuckin' troll!'

Doran was advancing on him, still crowing about trolls.

Worembrand buried his head in Linda Lusardi's bosom, an ostrich burying its head in sand. Doran was the sort of mindless oaf who was likely to punch him playfully, or demand a game of arm-wrestling.

'Now, don't bugger about . . .' he began, as Doran grabbed him in a headlock and started to haul him across the room.

Worembrand yelled. He had not been held in a headlock

since he was at school, where he had been held in headlocks quite a lot. Doran was asking him where his sense of humour was. He kicked out in rage, and Doran released him.

'Well, you've got your colour back now, Mal,' he said.

Worembrand swore foully but impotently, and retired to his armchair, thinking not for the first time how vital it was that he should get out of the army, graduate to the world of the grown-ups, build a new life amongst the page three lovelies.

The door opened. A soldier said that Staff Beckwith was wanted by the OC.

'All I can tell you,' said the adjutant's voice from two hundred miles away in southern Norway, 'is that the Old Man was summoned to brigade at eleven, and we haven't seen or heard from him since.'

'That might not be anything to do with me,' said Nick. 'My signal's from ACE Mobile Force HQ.'

'I don't see what else it can be about. Perhaps you're coming down to the Baltic. There's nothing going on up there, is there?'

'The Kirkenes ski championships in April. A Halloween dance next week at the nurses' hostel.'

'You don't want to miss that.'

'Not really.'

'Of course, the signal could have been sent to the wrong outfit,' said the adjutant, displaying what he regarded as entirely justified national prejudice. Two years previously, on Exercise Welcome, a French brigade commander had withdrawn a battalion of Green Jackets in mistake for Green Howards, and allowed two German armoured divisions to overrun NATO's entire northern flank.

'I shouldn't think so,' said Nick. 'It says I'm to liaise with Norwegian Brigade North.'

'"Curiouser and curiouser said Alice."'

Staff-Sergeant Beckwith's head appeared round the door. Nick waved him in and pointed to a chair.

'I'm going to assume it's a move south, and start the ball rolling. Ring me if you find anything out, will you?'

'You could try the Wives' Club back at Rheindahlen. They know everything before we do.'

'Cheers, Simon.'

Nick put the phone down. 'OK, what's the damage?'

'It's totalled.'

Nick closed his eyes.

'He did a good job, sir,' said Staff Beckwith. 'You've got to give him that.'

'Collins!'

Collins's head came round the door.

'Sir?'

'Get the sar'nt-major and Sar'nt Doran. I want to see Sykes now.'

Private Graham 'Syco' Sykes was no longer painting snow. From being deep-frozen in the square, he was on rapid defrost in Dixieland, the cook sergeant's washing-up area, scrubbing baked-bean sludge from an aluminium pan. Wire wool penetrated his fingers, pricking them until the blood came. He scrubbed stoically on.

By him, sitting on the cookhouse work surface, swinging his boots, was Lance-Corporal Leech. Leech had generously abandoned his duty as telephone orderly to comfort his friend in his hour of need.

'Where d'you reckon they'll hold the court martial?' he asked, chattily.

'There won't be a court martial.'

'It's what they reckon,' said Leech.

'Piss off.'

They were mates from way back. They had been pupils together at the Edward Elgar Comprehensive, Bridgnorth, and joined the army together in June 1992. They had been through the depot, two tours of Northern Ireland, Kurdistan in '95, and Hong Kong in '96. They went on leave together, and Leech was Sykes's best man when he married Karen Kennedy, a barmaid, in Belfast in 1994.

The army had tried to keep them apart, on the principle that a bow and arrow are only dangerous when put together. The army had failed.

Karen Sykes, née Kennedy, had tried to keep them apart on the principle that two men getting drunk every leave is one man too many. Karen had failed.

Syco and Leechie were a team. Together they had seen the world, from the exotic jungles of Malaysia to the frozen beauty of Lapland. At night they shivered in their dossbags and dreamed of The Kiwi pub at Bulford, and the knocking shop on the Devizes Road where Syco lost his Access card and they had to leave their watches as security.

A cook poked his head round the door waving a piece of card and said: 'Fried haddock, stewed beef, dumplings, plum pie or trifle. *Menu du jour*. Haven't you finished them dixies yet?'

Syco carried on scrubbing, his thin face pale and unhappy.

'What made you do it then, Syco?' asked Leech gently.

Syco stopped scrubbing. He dug into his pocket and produced a tightly folded letter. Leech took it without a word.

He had seen 'Dear John' letters before. Tight tiny words of reproach and self-justification on Woolworths lined notepads, hastily scrawled on pastel notelets with Snoopy or Peanuts in the corner – they were always the same: *'This is probably the most difficult letter I've ever had to write . . .'*

The lads usually stuck them up on the company noticeboard so their mates could have a laugh.

But not Syco. Not this time.

'Your Karen?'

Syco nodded.

'Bloody hell . . .'

The door to the canteen crashed open. 'Right, Sykes,' yelled Lance-Corporal Holmes, otherwise known as 'the Shaved Rottweiler', one of four regimental police attached to 'B' company, striding into the kitchen, his uniform smooth and immaculate. 'The OC wants a word in your shell-like.What d'you think you're doing here, then?' he said to Leech, who said quietly: 'Minding my own business.'

'You stop this bugger working, and you're in deep shit.'

Holmes turned to Sykes, who was patting his hands on a teacloth, leaving little dots of blood. 'Put it in the bin, you filthy bugger, and get a move on,' he snapped.

'Left-right-left-right-left-right!' Sergeant-Major Robson's voice boomed as it beasted Private Sykes at an impossible pace up the corridor into the room, bringing him to a halt with a crash of boots.

Nick looked up.

'Are you 2754925 Private Sykes, G?'

As if either of them didn't know it.

'You are charged with Conduct Prejudicial to Good Order and Military Discipline, contrary to Section 69 of the Army Act of 1955, in that you, at Kirkenes on 23 October, did make unauthorised use of a military vehicle . . .'

Section 69: the catch-all charge, while the battalion in Narvik worked out all the sins that could be laid at Sykes's door.

'Sergeant Doran.'

'Sir, on the night of 23 October I was acting as duty officer at the "B" Company location, Kirkenes. At midnight Private Grey came to inform me that his vehicle keys were missing from his bunk. On searching the vehicle park I discovered that Private Grey's vehicle was also missing. I immediately took the duty vehicle and, in company with Staff-Sergeant Beckwith, I drove down the Kirkenes road. A mile down that road we came across the SL vehicle crashed into the bank. Private Sykes was seated in the middle of the road in a dazed condition. His eyes were glazed, his speech was slurred, and in my opinion he was drunk . . .'

'All right, Sykes, have you anything to say for yourself?'

Sykes was pale, his skin grey, his right arm trembled slightly, the bruise on his forehead was a livid purple.

'No, sir.'

Nick looked at him for a few moments.

'What does the MO say?'

'Says I'm lucky to be alive, sir.'

'If I were you, I'd get a second opinion on that.'

'Sir,' said Sykes.

Nick sighed and looked again at the charge sheet.

He hated sending his men back to Narvik, to the 'monkeys' of the Royal Military Police, beyond his protection.

Sykes said hopefully: 'I'll take your award on this one, sir.'

'My award? Fourteen days' pay? For God's sake.'

'Sorry, sir.'

'I'm remanding you for CO's. No doubt he'll send you for court martial. You'll remain under open arrest until transport can be arranged to send you back to the battalion.' He nodded to Sergeant Doran.

'Prisoner and escort . . . right turn. By the front, quick march!'

Sergeant-Major Robson remained.

'All right, what's it all about?' said Nick.

'Whisper is he was going abbo.'

'What the hell for?'

'Wife fooling around at home.'

'Poor sod.'

Robson nodded sadly. 'Believe it or not, he was a good lad till he married her.'

Robbo's world was full of good young lads ruined by bad marriages.

'Well, keep an eye on him, Sar'nt-Major,' said Nick. 'We don't want him trying it again.'

There was a knock on the door and Lieutenant Jamie Pendred came in. 'Another signal. A Norgie courier just brought it up from Brigade.'

The signal read:

From:	Cdr AMF(L)
To:	OC B Coy 1 R MERC

       1. B Coy 1 R MERC is to prepare to move to aid children's hospital Lake Imandra nr Mončegorsk.

       2. Op will involve delivery of med supplies + 3 x Luftwaffe med pers.

       3. Orders by Liaison Officer HQ Bde North 250800

       4. No move before 260600 Alpha.

Nick said: 'Relief mission to Lake Imandra, near Mončegorsk. Where the hell's Mončegorsk? Find it for me, will you, Jamie?'

Jamie and Robbo turned to the map on the wall. Nick started scribbling the timings into his notebook.

'Doesn't sound Norwegian or Finnish. It must be up towards the border,' said Jamie.

'No, it isn't,' said Robbo. 'Bloody hell.'

Nick looked up. 'Found it?'

'My God,' said Jamie, 'they're sending us into Russia.'

FIVE

Munich, Saturday, 24 October

Lawrence, her American lover for four years, had said, 'It's about Ingrid,' and Brigite had said, 'What about her?' and he had leaned forward and said, 'Look, honey, I don't know any nice or painless way of saying this,' and Brigite had picked up the coffee cafetiere and thrown it at him, and Lawrence's mouth had gaped open in shock, principally because very hot coffee was streaming down his shirtfront, but also because they were sitting in the lounge of the Leopoldstrasse Holiday Inn, Munich, where discreet music played and imitation birdsong was piped through the greenery.

'Jesus,' he croaked, his desire to scream and his instinct to whisper producing a near fatal paralysis of his larynx. He dabbed hopelessly at the coffee with his well-manicured, automobile-executive hands, and tried to tell the hotel staff it had been an accident, but by this time Brigite was walking along Leopoldstrasse in the cold November afternoon, tears streaming down her face.

Half an hour later, and Lawrence was still in the hotel, sitting by the Egyptian-style swimming-pool while he waited

41

for a clean shirt, when the police arrived.

Brigite was wanted urgently by Luftwaffe Field Hospital Headquarters, Hanover. A woman friend had told the authorities that she was in Munich, and the name of the man she was with.

'I don't know where she is,' said Lawrence, 'and I don't care where she is, and if I never see her again, I'll be a sincerely grateful man. OK?'

A girl on reception said Brigite had left the hotel and turned right past the bierkeller. Two hours later a police crew pulled off autobahn patrol and given her description: age twenty-six, five foot six, slim build, short brown hair, wearing jeans and English waterproof dark green jacket – found her sitting on a bench in a children's playpark.

'We've orders to take you to the airport,' they said. 'You're booked on every flight to Hamburg for the next twelve hours.'

At the Holiday Inn, Lawrence was putting on a clean shirt when she walked through the bedroom door.

He backed into the bathroom, his trousers in his hands. She threw her clothes into her case in silence. A policeman stood in the doorway. Lawrence said: 'I didn't want it to be this way. You can see that. Come on, chérie. We can still be friends.'

Brigite finished packing her case. She had come for a romantic two days in Bavaria. A cheap out-of-season weekend, she told herself now, with a cheap out-of-season lover.

Lawrence said: 'Ingrid and me – we don't either of us want to lose you. We can still play squash together. *Partir c'est mourir, un peu*, as the French say.'

Brigite picked up a heavy glass ashtray from beside the bed. Lawrence smiled and gave a little laugh, a man who would never learn, and put his hands out in a gesture of friendship. She threw the ashtray, he ducked with a muffled curse. The bathroom mirror smashed behind him, he slipped and fell heavily. He howled as several shards of glass embedded themselves in his buttocks.

It took Brigite half an hour to get the shards out, using the hotel first-aid kit and a pair of eyebrow tweezers. Lawrence lay face down on the pale lemon sheets, blood trickling down on to Kleenex tissues. The police and hotel management shouted, Lawrence howled, but she never said a word.

Then the police took her to the central police station and started to work out the charges. It was four hours later, after several calls from the Luftwaffe Field Hospital HQ, Hanover, and one from the Luftwaffe Rapid Reaction Force HQ, Berlin, before she was finally sitting in the Lufthansa Regular Customer Lounge at Munich; just her and a Hamburg businessman who watched television and laughed at an American sitcom and crunched his way through half a kilo of complimentary pistachio nuts and drank five complimentary bottles of strong beer.

'When in Bavaria . . .' he said, offering her a bottle. She shook her head. It was eleven o'clock at night and she was dog-tired.

Twenty minutes later the last Lufthansa flight to Hamburg was cancelled because of engine trouble. The businessman swore angrily. 'It's cancelled because you haven't enough passengers. You don't care a shit about passengers, only about your balance sheet. What about me, eh? What about this young lady?'

He didn't have to worry about the young lady, they said. A Luftwaffe jet was coming to pick her up.

The commandant said: 'I've got no interest in your private life, but you are a doctor, for God's sake.'

She meant a doctor in the Luftwaffe.

'A reservist,' said Brigite. 'My private life is my concern.'

'It's 02.00 hours on a Sunday morning, and a lot of people, including me, have spent the best part of the night sorting out your private life.'

Brigite said nothing. The commandant didn't look like a bad sort; just a middle-aged woman who needed her sleep.

'I understand you and this man were practically engaged,' she went on, 'so I don't want to sound unsympathetic. I've got daughters of my own. My eldest is nineteen and she spent two months decorating her boyfriend's flat with him and sewing curtain linings, and now he's thrown her over for a seventeen-year-old music student in Hamburg.'

'All men are bastards,' said Brigite. 'It's the only fixed point of truth in the universe.'

'You could be right. You probably are. It's no reason to go pouring boiling coffee over the buggers and sticking

44

bits of glass up their bottoms. Even my daughter knew better than that.'

'She'll grow wiser as she grows older,' said Brigite. 'We don't always realise what we want at that age. But I don't see the point in talking about it.'

The commandant was looking at her file. 'I see your father was a Berliner,' she said, as if that accounted for a lot. 'You've been selected for a mission – with the English. Don't ask me why. Perhaps the computer has heard how much you like foreign lovers.'

Heavy humour, but commendable at two o'clock in the morning. She passed a file across the desk.

'You've an hour to read this and ask any questions.'

'What is the mission?'

'Norway. You're going to Narvik, and then joining the English at a place called Kirkenes.'

An hour before dawn, she was driven to the Luftwaffe base north of Hanover. The sentry on the gate seemed to be the only soul alive, but sodium lights burned on every corner as they drove between endless hangars and acres of deserted concrete.

Finally they turned a corner, and there was a Wessex Cobra jet, its navigation lights throwing green psychedelic circles across the rain-wet runway. Orderlies from Hanover Field Supply were loading medical stores into the machine's belly.

The two nurses who were to accompany Brigite stood shivering in the cold, their hands deep in the pockets of their grey and red anoraks.

One was young, blonde, her freckled face flushed with excitement despite the ungodly hour. The other was older, a woman with a Dresden accent, who said her name was Erike Schmidt.

After a few minutes, a ground crew orderly suggested they wait in the mechanics' room until the pilot was ready, so they trooped inside and he gave them coffee, and the young blonde nurse, Anneliese Bausch from Hamburg, said, 'What wouldn't I give for a hotdog or a bowl of soup!' and the man went away and returned with a plate of small Danish chocolate cakes in gold wrappers.

'I can't eat those! What about my figure?' said Anneliese, and the orderly patted his Bremerhaven beergut and said what about his.

Outside it had started to sleet, droplets of slush pattering against the window. The orderly wandered off. Brigite sat next to the warm radiator and looked out across the concrete hard-standing and the sixteen-seater executive jet to the distant perimeter fence. She half listened to Anneliese quizzing Erike, who had been in the East German army medical corps and spoke perfect Russian.

'That's why *you're* here, then,' said Anneliese. 'I was told it was because I went on a four-week all-weather survival course in Scotland.'

'I spent six months at the hospital at Mončegorsk,' said Erike.

'You've been there!' exclaimed Anneliese. 'You've actually been there!'

Erike nodded nervously, as if she had made a confession that would cost her dear. Brigite thought she looked ill, but that could be the effect of being transported from one side of Germany to the other at ten minutes' notice.

At 05.20 the pilot came and told them their flight path would take them west of Kiel and up the east coast of Denmark, crossing the Kattegat to Göteborg in southern Sweden, and again up the coast to Oslo. 'Our ETA at Narvik is 11.00 but I don't mind telling you I'm worried about the weather up there. OK?'

Again, Brigite thought Erike looked anything but OK.

'Right,' said the pilot. 'The sooner we're on our way, the better.'

Ten minutes later, and they were airborne, heading north, the lights of Kiel merging with the dawn.

They slept, and when they woke, the navigator, a boy of about twenty, gave them coffee and Luftwaffe transport division 'Good Morning' breakfasts in plastic bags – sliced sausage and gherkins, caramel wafer bars, rolls of stale bread and foil-wrapped butter pats. The three women were the only passengers.

'We normally have Bundeswehr generals to entertain,' said the boy.

'You're not doing much to entertain me,' said Anneliese. 'What do you do for the generals?'

'OK,' said Brigite, 'so let's get to know each other. Erike, it says here you've been working for a freelance nursing agency in Dresden and Warsaw. How did you find your way to Mončegorsk?'

Erike had responded to an advert for Russian-speaking nurses, EC nationals, on a three-month tour of duty. That had been in May. She had returned to Dresden in August.

She was worried and anxious; nervous when Brigite asked her about the hospital, though there was more colour in her cheeks now. She had gulped down the coffee gratefully, but hardly touched her 'Good Morning' breakfast.

'They explained to you what we have to do?' asked Brigite, and Erike nodded vigorously.

'Well, have you any questions?'

Erike looked worried at not having any questions. She said: 'How long will we stay at Mončegorsk?'

'Just a couple of days – and then we come back out with the convoy. None of us will be left in Karelia. If there are any really sick children, we bring them out of the military zone to a helicopter pick-up point.'

Erike nodded vigorously again. Brigite saw from her file that she was thirty-six. She seemed older.

'Get your head down,' she advised. 'Catch up on as much sleep as you can.'

Erike went back to her window seat, where she stared out at the brilliant sunshine and hazy blue sky.

Anneliese had a hundred questions. How many children were at the hospital? How many nurses and doctors?

There were ninety children when Erike was there, all suffering from food-related allergies. Most of them were Russian from the Murmansk oblast, the remainder Lapps from the Kola reindeer farms. Four doctors, a dozen EC nurses, Russian medical staff on call from the hospital in Mončegorsk.

'The situation over there is not good,' said Anneliese.

'They're living on food aid and pig potatoes. What if we get attacked?'

'We've got UN and EC flags and sixty soldiers to protect us,' said Brigite.

'Yeah, but who protects us from the soldiers?'

'I protect you from the soldiers,' said Brigite. 'And if necessary I protect the soldiers from you.'

'Cold and sexless Englishmen, right?'

'They're cold at the moment. Have you got a boyfriend?'

'Wolfgang. We've been going out for three years, would you believe it, and we're getting married next May.'

'Lucky old you,' said Brigite, who had had twenty-two meaningful emotional relationships since she was fourteen. ('I can't believe it myself,' she had told her friend Ingrid, but it was less than one every six months, for Christ's sake. Ingrid, of all people, needn't have made it sound like she was a whore.)

The plane dropped into black, dirty cloud. 'We're coming in to land at Narvik. Please fasten your seat belts,' said the navigator.

'You can help me if you like,' Anneliese told him. 'Just like you help all those Bundeswehr generals.'

The plane dropped like a stone, the jet engines screaming as they sucked for air, then gave a sickening thud as it hit a rising air current and bounced forwards again, buffeted from side to side in the turbulence. The navigator held on to the back of Anneliese's seat. She put her arms out and grabbed hold of his leg. The lights flickered and went out, but, before they did, two images imprinted themselves on

Brigite's mind: Lawrence's face, sixteen hours ago, when the coffee splatted like brown blood across his chest; and Erike now, sitting by the window, her body rigid with fear, her mouth open wide in a soundless scream.

They were the last flight into Narvik that day – or for forty-eight hours to come. Had they been a civilian flight, they would have been diverted to Stockholm. A force-eight gale was sweeping down from the Arctic, coating Finnmark in a fresh blanket of white.

SIX

Kirkenes, northern Norway, 26 October

'B' COY 1 R MERC
ORBAT

Coy HQ
OC Major Chard
CSM WO11 Robson
C/Sgt Taylor (OC Rear Party)
Radio Operator – Pte Collins
Driver – Pte Best
Co-driver – Pte Grey

Signal detachment	*REME detachment*
Cpl Willis (i/c)	Sgt Beckwith (i/c)
L/Cpl Kelly	Cpl Bateman
Pte Fowler	Cpl Denis

4 Platoon	*5 Platoon*
OC 2Lt Pendred	OC Sgt Doran
Pl/Sgt Cpl Hoddinot	Pl/Sgt Cpl Finch

'That looks fine, Sar'nt-Major,' said Nick, blowing

warmth back into his hands. He had just returned from a three-hour intelligence briefing at Brigade North.

'Chopper's left Narvik, sir,' said Private Collins, poking his head round the office door.

'OK, let's get a move on. Snow Leopards. Two each for the platoons, and one for the anti-tanks.'

'We're taking Milan?' said Jamie, surprised.

'Yes, we're taking Milan.'

'It adds to the fuel, sir,' said Staff Beckwith, going over his figures with a pencil.

'Well I'm not going without Milan, or Starstreak. There are several thousand armoured vehicles in Karelia – battle tanks, self-propelled artillery, and aircraft – and God alone knows who's in charge of them all.'

'Oh, good,' said Jamie, cheering up. 'I'd like to see Milan fired for real.'

'Right,' said Nick, 'let's get one thing clear. We have strict orders to avoid confrontation. You shoot anybody, and you might as well not come back.'

'We'll need more than two vehicles a platoon, sir,' said Robbo. 'Twenty men each, plus kit.'

'We'll have flank patrols out. I also want to throw a permanent screen in front. We'll be travelling across the tundra, so for most of the time the roads will be non-existent, and according to Norgie Intelligence there are gangs of soldiers roaming all over the place. OK, let's get on.

'My command vehicle, an ambulance vehicle for the German medics, one for rations, one for the medical supplies – there's your lads and the recovery vehicle, Sar'nt Beckwith, and we've got three reservists arriving.'

'Reservists? Where from?' asked Jamie.

'UK. They're specialists in LodeStar,' said Robbo.

'It's the first I've heard of it.'

'Can we just get on with this, instead of yattering questions like a bunch of schoolgirls?' said Nick. 'We've got to get through intell, met reports, movement orders, admin, orders, and we haven't even started. OK, Staff, how many vehicles for fuel?'

'Depends how much you want in reserve, sir.'

'There's no possibility of an air drop. Assume twelve days travelling.'

'Four vehicles, in that case.'

'That many?'

'And every other vehicle loaded with jerrycans.'

It was always the same problem: how to move fast and light when you had to take a supply train with you.

'OK. The medical supplies will have to be split between the platoons.'

'Sir, what about injuries,' said Jamie determinedly, 'if the vehicles are full of supplies . . .?'

'Tell your lads they are strictly forbidden to break their legs in the first two days. Tell them we'll have space for them when we've dumped some fuel cans.'

'Hang about, sir,' said Colour-Sergeant Taylor, 'you wouldn't do that to me. I've signed for those cans. And these reservists, are they on our ration strength?'

'I neither know nor care, Colour.'

'I haven't seen any paperwork, sir.'

'Well, they'll need feeding, and I doubt if they'll bring

a rucksack full of Mars bars.'

There were a few laughs. The atmosphere lightened.

'OK, anything else before we move on to the movement orders?'

They worked through the logistics of transporting sixty men and a medical team a hundred kilometres and back through hostile winter terrain.

Seven hundred individual compo ration packs – the men would be sick of them, and craving fresh food after two days – tents, sleeping bags, cooking stoves and cooking fuel, skis, spades, first aid, rifles and ammunition.

'This is the rear party, sir.' Robbo passed Nick a piece of paper. 'There's Colour-Sergeant Taylor, three sick, lame and lazy, and I suppose Sykes is stopping?'

Nick hesitated, but there was no point in delaying the inevitable. 'Yes. He goes back to the battalion on the first transport.'

Robbo nodded. 'And I've assumed you didn't want Sar'nt Worembrand?'

Nobody entering the small bedroom at the top of the Hotel Vang would have realised that Malcolm Worembrand was happy.

The casual visitor would have seen a plump middle-aged man snuggled in an armchair, fully clothed and wrapped in a duvet; would have noticed the expression on his face, and would have left at once, so as not to intrude upon private grief.

And yet Sergeant Worembrand was very happy.

'B' Company was going to Russia, but he was not. The lists had been posted, and his name was nowhere to be seen.

Once again he had been forgotten about. In nearly twenty years in the army, he had brought being forgotten about to a fine art. He had learned, long ago, what a sweet life was to be had in the byways and backwaters of a large organisation; and few organisations were as large and well provided with such byways and backwaters as Her Majesty's Forces.

Worembrand was not a vindictive man. He did not, even to himself, express the hope that Nick's invasion of Mother Russia would end like all previous invasions. But if it did, then Worembrand was ready to shake his head over the folly of hotheaded young officers and the endemic insanity of the Brigade staff.

What mattered was that soon he would be home. Rheindahlen! With his cosy little office, his warm darkroom, Werner's café and the Cherry-Ripe Club . . .

It was three-thirty, time for tea and toast, but he decided against going down to the mess – keep a low profile, let them forget you exist – and instead turned his television on to satellite news, and dozed through the Baltic crisis.

'Yeltsin's Commonwealth is long dead, and few doubt that the Russian Federation itself is now collapsing,' said the commentator. Worembrand yawned and bit into a Crunchie bar.

Ten minutes later they were showing Visnews footage of starving refugees being tended by the Turkish army (personally he'd rather be left to die), when suddenly an image came into his head, so terrible it made his heart lurch.

It was the image of tearful, half-starved, sickly children being rescued by British squaddies after a desperate and courageous mercy dash across frozen wolf-infested tundra.

The photo opportunity of the year! Scooped by some poxy agency snapper from Murmansk, with Reuters syndication worldwide (not that the Yanks would take it), photo by Ivan the Sodding Terrible. Ivan the Sodding Terrible at Kensington Palace to receive the grateful thanks of the Princess of Wales. ('Anything I can do for you?' 'Well, seeing how you ask, a quick snap of you by the roses, ma'am.') And that wasn't entirely fanciful, given that she was Colonel-in-Chief of the Royal Mercians, and always took an interest in what they were up to.

For some moments he sat frozen in his armchair, torn by terrible indecision. Eight days of hell in the snow (the Ruperts said six, but he knew better), and God alone knew what horrors were waiting along the way.

But *then* a lifetime among the page three lovelies.

There was much to do. Should he approach Chard? What if the bastard said no? He needed to ring his friend Werner – but he'd left his contact book in the sergeants' office.

Destiny had called Malcolm Worembrand, and she had not called in vain. Shrugging off the duvet, he leapt into his carpet slippers, darted through the doorway and scurried down the corridor. It was the fastest he had moved all week.

* * *

'It's that bugger Ray. That bugger who sold her the fitted kitchen while we were off in Kurdistan.'

'It doesn't say anything here about another bloke.'

'I might be thick, but I'm not that fucking thick,' said Syco. 'I know our Karen. There's only two reasons she'd leave me: one, because she was sick of me; or, two, because of another bloke. She can't be sick of me, because I'm not there. It's only when I'm there she gets sick of me . . .'

'I had noticed that . . .'

'So if she's left me now, it's for another bloke, and it's nobody her family knows, because her Dad'd thump her halfway to Liverpool, so that leaves Ray . . .'

'I just don't see that, Syco . . .'

'I tell you, it's fucking Ray. Why did she buy a fucking ten-thousand-quid kitchen if she didn't fancy the bastard?'

'All right, keep your voice down, for Christ's sake . . .'

Leech had filled their mugs with bright orange-coloured tea. Now he stirred a dessert-spoonful of sugar into each.

The canteen was nearly full. Outside, the darkness was falling. Most of the men in the room had been on skiing exercise for six hours, or working on the Snow Leopards. Tea came with bread and butter and jam, and at five o'clock there would be a roast or stew or casserole ('chicken Marengo', 'boeuf en croûte', said the hopeful chefs) with chips and roast potatoes, and a pudding sticky with jam and sugar, and custard or cream from huge five-litre jugs.

On active service in the Arctic, British Army dietary

experts urged an intake of 5,000 calories a day. Anxious to please, the men added Kit Kats and several pints of beer.

They were sitting in a corner. Lance-Corporal Holmes, the Shaved Rottweiler, walked past and gave them a sour look.

'What will you do about Holmes?' said Leech.

'He's going to Russia,' Sykes said quietly, 'you're going to Russia, every bugger's going to Russia except me and Colour-Sergeant Taylor.'

'That doesn't mean they won't have somebody sticking to you like shit to a blanket.'

'I can get away . . .'

'But how far away?'

'Bergen to Newcastle, Newcastle to Belfast. And don't ask how will I get to Bergen. That lot with the candles, they'll get me to Bergen once the road's open.'

Leech looked at Sykes, quietly amazed.

'The Peace Dividend? Why should they help you?'

'They're always trying to get blokes to desert from the army.'

'But you're not deserting, Syco. You're going abbo to beat up your Karen's boyfriend . . .'

'Shut it, for Christ's sake,' hissed Sykes.

They drank their tea.

'I suppose you don't want me to tell you she's not worth it?'

Sykes said nothing.

'Listen. Wait till the court martial. Get a bleeding barrister. I'll slip you a hundred for a down-payment. Ask Captain Chard to be your Prisoner's Friend; he'll speak up for you. Tell them about Karen, about the letter . . .'

'I'm not going to tell them I was going abbo! What's the fucking point in getting charged for going abbo?'

'All right, all right!' Leech looking anxiously round the canteen.

Nobody was taking any notice. Holmes was on his way out of the room.

'Listen. You weren't going abbo. You were going to phone home from Kirkenes because the phone here wasn't working, and you'd just got the letter, and you were drunk and distressed.'

'I was, too.'

'Yes, well, that's all blood under the bridges,' said Leech awkwardly. 'Get yourself a good defence, and you might not get sent to Colly . . .'

'I'm not going to be sent to Colly,' said Sykes quietly. 'I'm going to Belfast to sort that bugger out.'

Leech sighed.

Sykes said: 'Come on, Leechie. You'd do the same.'

'They'll catch up with you, Syco. They'll catch up with you in the end. They always catch up . . .'

Lance-Corporal Holmes's voice boomed across the canteen: 'OK, Sykes, on your feet.'

He was heading towards them through the rows of tables, and he was smiling, which was not good. It took someone else's misfortune to make Holmes smile like that.

'Come and get your kit packed.'

'What the hell for? I'm not going anywhere.'

'Oh yes you are. You're going to Narvik.'

What Staff Beckwith had once called the ugliest smile in NATO spread itself across what was universally acclaimed the ugliest face in Europe.

'They've sent a helicopter to fetch you.'

SEVEN

The noise was deafening, the air was dank, there was nothing to sit on except canvas stools lashed to the interior supports, there was no lavatory – the men piss into bottles, said the Luftwaffe sergeant, taking no responsibility for passengers who travelled without the proper personal equipment – and there were no 'Good Morning' breakfast bags.

'I'm going to complain to the holiday company. It was never like this in the brochure!' Anneliese shouted in Brigite's ear.

Twin rotors of high-tensile steel pounded above their heads. There was the high-pitched hum of infra-red suppressors that would dissipate engine exhaust heat should anybody try to fire a missile at them from the barren Troms below.

Brigite smiled, and Anneliese turned and shouted in Erike's ear, making the same joke, presumably. Erike looked puzzled.

They had spent twenty-four hours in Narvik before the wind dropped, on call at one hour's notice, twice being taken out to the airport. The army had billeted them in a tourist hotel, empty and overheated; the three of them sitting in a vast gloomy lounge reading old magazines.

'I am ready to testify that Erike is not the world's greatest conversationalist,' Anneliese had whispered during the evening, after attempting a discussion on home furnishings and true romance.

Anneliese and Wolfgang had a flat in Hamburg. Wolfgang's parents were loaded. Anneliese liked to talk about it, and who, thought Brigite, would not?

She looked out of the window. They had left the long shadows of the mountains behind, and were flying over the high plateau of the Finnmark. Barren, snow-covered, a sombre grey in the afternoon light, a few stunted trees. No sign of life, or of the four million reindeer that eked out a miserable existence in this part of Lapland, bitten by mosquitoes in summer and frozen in winter.

The sergeant was crouching before her, handing her a paper cup of coffee. She took it gratefully. He put both hands up in front of her and opened all his fingers, and shouted, 'Ten minutes, OK?'

The helicopter began to circle. She could see the coastline, black cliffs along a fjord. Below, now, a town of wooden houses; a road running out along a causeway to an island; a ship with lights moving into the harbour; a tall chimney on a hill, belching grey smoke; stains, the colour of ochre, on the snow.

The sergeant was speaking to Anneliese, who turned and shouted to Brigite: 'Oh my God, they want to chuck us out.'

62

The sergeant said: 'We might be able to get down; we might not. We won't take you back to Narvik if we don't have to. At least we can get rid of this stuff.'

The pallets of medical supplies were in the centre of the cabin, covered in protective foam and waterproofing.

A red light flashed over the pilot's cabin, and a klaxon screamed. Erike slammed her hands over her ears.

'Just an automatic warning device, so we won't crash. Don't worry. Look, we may get low enough to hover for a few seconds. We may even be able to land. Either way, this is what you do . . .'

'It's no use,' shouted Brigite.

She could hardly hear him. Erike still held her hands over her ears. The sergeant swore soundlessly, and went back to his seat by the pilot. A moment later he returned with a Siemens internal comms unit, and passed earphones to them. Anneliese tapped Erike's shoulder, then helped her put the tiny circle of foam against her ear.

'Right, OK, you can hear me now?'

They nodded. His voice was clear and close and calm.

'The helipad's been cleared, but the wind's gusting, and the only place that's sheltered is covered in two feet of fresh snow. When you jump out, you lie flat, understand? You do not try to stand up under any circumstances, because if we come down on the snow we will sink into it, and if you are standing up at the time the rotor arms will . . .'

The sergeant drew a hand across his neck.

'You all understand?'

They understood.

63

'Personally,' he went on, 'I prefer to holiday in Crete.'

'That's my joke,' shouted Anneliese.

'What?' said the sergeant.

Anneliese said: 'Forget it.'

The helicopter swept low over the helipad with its huge yellow H and curved left towards a wood. Through the window they could see flurries of snow swept up by gusts of wind, then falling again. Beyond the wood was a group of vehicles, their headlights on, their emergency lights flashing, and a landing area marked out by naphtha flares.

'OK, get ready,' said the sergeant, pulling the restraining cords off the medical pallets.

They stood up. Brigite helped him heave the pallets to the door, and he said, 'Thank you, ma'am.'

At a signal from the pilot, he slid back the door, and they were engulfed by wind and swirling flakes of snow. Nothing could be seen outside but the blizzard whipped up by the rotors. The sergeant heaved the medical pallets over the door ledge, the helicopter rocking like a ship at sea. For a moment the pallets were poised on the thick rubber door seals, then they were gone. The sergeant grabbed Anneliese and helped her to the door. She looked down, hesitated for a moment, then jumped, her arms outstretched.

Erike was next. At the last moment she tried to turn, but the sergeant's hand was in the middle of her back, and out she went.

'Goodbye, and thank you,' shouted Brigite, and the sergeant nodded.

She landed on one knee and pain shot up her leg, then

she tumbled forward, spreadeagled, her face pressed into the burning snow, in her ears the sound of an English voice shouting.

'Come back you bastards!'

'Welcome to Kirkenes,' said a voice that contained more than a hint of amusement. 'I think you can probably get up now, if you want to.'

'Well, of course I want to,' said Brigite, gritting her teeth with pain. 'I just don't want my head sliced off, OK?'

She looked up. The helicopter was fifty feet overhead, its landing lights flashing, the flight sergeant waving as he closed the door. Brigite felt a sudden moment of homesickness for Narvik and the tourist hotel, and the overheated, silent, womb-like lounge where she could think about Lawrence and Ingrid, hold herself tight, and nurse her sad, sad wounds.

'If you'll excuse me for just a moment . . .' The man, an officer Brigite realised by instinct, not by the standard-issue clothes he was wearing, smiled and turned away. Three soldiers were looking up at the circling helicopter; a fourth stood with a suitcase in one hand and a kitbag at his feet, snow settling on his small moustache, staring ahead at nothing in particular.

The officer said: 'Try signalling. Tell him we've got a passenger for Narvik.'

'I've told him that, sir.'

'Tell him it's a four-star general dying of pneumonia.'

'I've already told him it's a four-star general's tart with big tits.'

'Fucking Germans.'

'Hang about.'

They turned and grinned uneasily at Brigite, who gave them a stony look. Anneliese and Erike were brushing snow from their anoraks. Anneliese waved at the helicopter pilot with both arms.

'All right, corporal, we did our best. Get him back to base.'

'All right, Sykes. You heard.' The soldier with the suitcase lifted his kitbag and turned towards one of the Land-Rovers. The officer returned to Brigite.

'Major Sendlinger?'

'Yes,' said Brigite.

'I'm Nicholas Chard. If it's all right with you, we'll get back to the mess and talk. No point in freezing our backsides off out here.'

He meant no point freezing their balls off, of course, but somebody must have told him women didn't have any. And he didn't really mean 'if it's all right with you'. What the hell else was she supposed to suggest – an ice hockey match?

'That would be great,' she said.

EIGHT

Kirkenes, northern Norway, 26 October

They sat in the mess, and a soldier said he'd bring them some tea.

Nick said, 'I hope your leg is all right?' and Brigite said, 'It's OK. I jarred it a little. I've taken a couple of paracetamol.'

'And your rooms are all right?'

'Yes, thank you,' they said politely.

Nick wondered where Jamie had got to. Jamie had been told to be here and socialise, an activity he was good at, leaving Nick to get on with some work.

'The first leg should be easy,' he said. 'It's down through Pasvik National Park. I was down there pike-fishing six weeks ago. It's very beautiful. At least it was in the autumn.'

The three women looked at him silently.

He said: 'Not that we'll have much time for admiring the scenery. Our ETA at Mončegorsk, by the way, is noon on Saturday.'

'They have a food problem?' said Erike, the first words she had spoken since he picked them up out of the snow.

'Yes,' said Nick. 'So I understand.'

'According to Nurse Lewandowska, the free market closed a month ago. When I was there in the summer we were buying food in exchange for drugs. Nobody wanted money. You can't eat money. It was terrible.' She turned to Anneliese, seeking support, and Anneliese nodded in sympathy.

'But now with the free market collapsed, I don't know what they are doing. Perhaps the commune is helping . . .' She stopped. 'I'm sorry.'

'No. You tell us,' said Anneliese.

'I think we can say that every day counts,' said Brigite. A soldier came in with tea.

Nick said: 'By the way, just a formality, but Nurse Bausch and Nurse Schmidt will have officer status while you're at Kirkenes.'

'Why?' said Anneliese, startled. 'What do you want us to do?'

'It's just so that you can eat here in the mess. Save you from pigging it with the likes of Whitby. That right, Whitby?'

'That's it, sir,' said the soldier.

'Oh, I see,' said Anneliese. 'Spoilsport.'

Jamie came in then, and Nick called to him in relief: 'Jamie, come and say hello. This is Lieutenant James Pendred, whose sole object in life is to attend to your every need.'

'Hi, Jamie,' said Anneliese.

The soldier said: 'Do you want any biscuits, sir?'

'Yes,' said Nick. 'Nice ones.'

'And some toast for me,' said Jamie, sitting next to

Anneliese. 'Why don't you have some toast?'

'Can I have some toast?'

'Whitby!'

'Sir.'

The soldier went away. There was a pause.

'I don't know if anybody's seen the twenty-four-hour sitrep?' said Nick.

They looked at him expectantly. He tried to remember what was in it.

'Well, Third Shock Army is still approaching the Latvian border but nobody expects it to take offensive action before the oil-shale barter conference. That's not until the seventh of December, so we should be back safe and sound by then.'

There was another pause.

'The thought of a Baltic war is just horrendous,' said Brigite.

Nick said: 'I wouldn't worry too much. American intelligence says the situation is stabilised.'

'God help us when the Americans say that,' said Jamie.

Anneliese laughed.

'Anyway, what do they mean by stabilised?' said Brigite. 'Do they mean stabilised at five hundred deaths a week – or a thousand?'

Nick wanted to get on with his rosters, he had a thousand and one things to check, he had an RV that could only take place at dusk when even the Russian MX14 spy satellites over Scandinavia were reduced to below ten per cent efficiency. He would not want to sit in the mess making polite conversation even if he did have a talent to amuse, which he was quite aware he did not.

'Well, if you'll excuse me, there's a hell of a lot to do. I'll see you at the general briefing, and then I expect there'll be a truck going down to Kirkenes for an hour if you want to taste the dubious delights of the town. But I'd like everybody back by 22.00.'

'Can I speak to you for a moment?' said Brigite.

'Yes, of course,' said Nick. 'Come down to the office.'

'What delights?' asked Anneliese, when they had gone.

'There's a disco,' said Jamie.

'Yeah?'

'But that's for Other Ranks, so we can't go there.'

'Why not?'

'Because we're British Army officers.'

'I've only been one for five minutes, and I'm not enjoying it, so I think I'll resign.'

'Sorry, you can't do that,' said Jamie.

'So where do officers go?' said Anneliese.

'Usually the lounge bar of the Arctic Ocean Hotel. We share it with the mining engineers and the chaps from the fish factory.'

'Great,' said Anneliese. 'I definitely resign.'

'Captain Chard is nice, isn't he?' said Erike.

'Our Nicholas? I should say so,' said Jamie. 'Ah, toast and strawberry jam. It is the strawberry, Whitby?'

'Yes, sir,' said the soldier gloomily.

Jamie and Anneliese ate toast. 'Come on, Erike,' said Anneliese. 'You didn't eat any breakfast, and there wasn't any lunch.'

Erike smiled but shook her head.

* * *

'I haven't anything on any of you,' said Nick. 'As far as I'm concerned, you're the medical team and I'm the bus-driver ferrying you about.'

'Can I call Hanover?'

Nick nodded.

'She's old for a job like this, and she's under stress,' said Brigite, dialling. 'I don't know – it's probably just my being foolish.'

'Better safe . . .'

'Than sorry, yes.'

She spoke rapid German. Collins appeared in the doorway.

'16.00, sir,' he said.

Nick said: 'I'll be a few minutes.'

Brigite said: 'Psychiatric files are in Berlin. They'll call me back.'

'Perhaps she's just a bit tired.'

'Perhaps she is. Look, you don't have to sit here trying to appear concerned and sympathetic. I realise a German nurse suffering from stress is the last thing you need right now.'

She wandered round the office. On one wall was a colour print of the regiment's stand at the Siege of Savannah: Ensign Piper stuffing the colours under his tunic ready for his legendary escape, a handful of exhausted men with bayonets facing outwards, French guards and fiendishly grinning Americans closing in.

'The Bloodybacks' Stand,' Brigite read aloud, faintly mocking.

71

Nick looked at her, irritated.

'It was quite heroic, actually. They held the position for six hours against incredible odds. It saved Savannah.'

'And saving Savannah saved the war?'

'No, but bravery like that is still worth remembering.'

'Why Bloodybacks?'

'In the eighteenth century the regiment had a reputation for hard drinking, and consequently the men got flogged rather often.'

'Barbaric, eh?'

'Oh, I don't know,' said Nick, remembering Sykes and the wrecked Snow Leopard.

He stood up and looked out of the window. Under floodlights, in the vehicle park, the REME soldiers were running their final checks. Brigite went to stand next to him.

'Vickers Snow Leopards,' said Nick. 'We're the first unit in NATO to get them.'

'They're British?' said Brigite.

'Mercedes engines,' said Nick.

'Right.'

She sounded relieved.

Collins again poked his head round the door.

'OK, I'm coming,' said Nick. 'Look, Brigite, do stay here till the call comes through. Make yourself at home and I'll see you at the briefing. Bye.'

'Bye, Nicholas.'

She turned off the fluorescent light and sat at the desk. A lamp threw a pool of green light. Her knee was still aching.

Half her wardrobe and personal effects were in Lawrence's flat. Perhaps he was making Ingrid pack them into a suitcase.

On the desk was a small piece of card, and written on it: *'Remember that you are an Englishman and have consequently won first prize in the lottery of life.'*

Dear God . . .

The phone rang. Berlin was not happy to fax a copy of Nurse Schmidt's medical file on open line to a non-Luftwaffe number.

Brigite said: 'Can somebody just read out the last psychiatric assessment.'

Nurse Schmidt had been examined forty-eight hours previously at Dresden. She had been given a clean bill of health. Her stress levels were just where they should have been.

Collins brought the Land-Rover to a halt and turned off the engine and the lights. They sat in the darkness, looking out over the ink-black waters of the fjord.

'Madonna or Mozart, sir?'

Collins had respect for the older generation.

Nick said: 'Madonna.'

The sound system in the Company HQ Land-Rover was Collins's pride and joy: its construction the main fruits of a six-week signal cadre with the Second Battalion at Rheindahlen.

'How shall I love you,' sang the husky voice, 'when I'm old and past my prime? How shall I love you, when my heartbeat marks the time, passing time, so much time?'

'When?' said Collins. 'Did she say *when*?'

'Be quiet, philistine.'

As Nick's eyes grew accustomed to the dark, the bay was lit by a faint luminance: the lights of Kirkenes bouncing off the low cloudbase; the lights of Prestoya visible across the water.

A headland shielded the bay from Kirkenes itself. When the quay had been built in 1941, there had been no hospital at Prestoya, no prying eyes to worry about.

This was the U-boat harbour, isolated, remote, protected by nature and machine-gun posts from the RAF hurricane squadron at Murmansk. This was where the killer submarines of the north had taken their rest, deep under the shadow of the cliffs, their crews smoking their ration of five cigarettes a day and listening to Radio Eismeersender.

'Underneath the lamplight, by the barracks gate,' said Nick.

'Is that Madonna, too?' asked Collins.

Nick said: 'One of her greatest hits. Do you know what Churchill said?' Collins did not. Nick said: '"U-boats are dastardly villains that sink our ships, while submarines are the noble and gallant craft that sink theirs."'

'Very good, sir,' said Collins, wondering how they had got from Madonna to Churchill.

Nick looked over the bay.

'16.30, sir,' said Collins.

Gently, from the quiet luminescent waves, there rose a black shape, smooth and round, white water rushing from its fin.

Collins turned off the sound system.

A green light flashed twice. Nick said: 'Respond.'

Collins flashed the lights of the Land-Rover. Within moments a launch was dimly seen heading towards the shore.

The submarine was a Trident, its body as long as the pitch at Wembley, as tall, out of the water, as a three-storey house, as big as ten U-boats.

The launch was fast approaching the quay. Nick zipped up his parka and prepared to meet it.

NINE

The three men quickly unloaded their gear from the rubber launch, which slipped away into the darkness. Then they loaded it into the back of the Land-Rover. From out in the bay there came a gurgling sound and a fleeting patch of white water, as the submarine slid beneath the surface. The men piled into the back of the vehicle.

'OK, let's go,' said a voice.

Collins looked at Nick, who nodded.

He recognised one of the men: George Munro, a former lieutenant from the Royal Mercians' Second Battalion. Five years ago, as subalterns, they had been in the same syndicate at the Royal School of Infantry at Warminster. On the last night of the course, celebrating in the pub at Heytesbury, Munro had confided to Nick that he had applied for SAS selection.

'You haven't, have you?' Nick had said, always an infantry man, scornful of spooks and staff officers; himself destined to command a company in action since the day he was born. 'Don't they make you swim through a trough of pig shit or something?'

'"The Sickener,"' said Munro. 'Leopard-crawl through

77

a trench of sheeps' innards and afterbirth.'

'Typical of the army,' Nick had said, 'to encourage its best and brightest young officers to die of septicaemia.'

Munro had looked him over and said: 'Death is just nature's way of telling you you've failed selection.'

Nick later heard that Munro had gone to Hereford and, to the relief of his brother officers, had not returned.

'Nick.'

'George.'

'Small world.'

'Small army.'

'Leaner and fitter.'

They laughed briefly. The old ones were the best ones.

Munro leaned over from the back of the Land-Rover and shook his hand, then indicated his companions. 'Sergeant Noon and Corporal Fuller. May I say how delighted we are to be joining your little expedition.'

'Delighted to have you,' said Nick, trying, because Collins was all ears, to sound convincing.

Collins, Noon and Fuller went into the hotel. Munro moved into the front seat next to Nick. With the engine turned off, the cold began to creep in, a drop of temperature palpable from one second to the next.

Nick said: 'You appreciate that my primary and overriding task is to take a medical team and supplies to a hospital. I don't want any trouble.'

Munro said, in a relaxed voice: 'We won't be any trouble. Royal Mercian insignia, no badges of rank. Nothing to say we're not reservists under your command.'

'Except that you're not under my command.'

Munro nodded in the darkness. They agreed on that.

'Come on, Nick. We just want a look-round over there. After all we haven't been on the ground in Russia since . . .'

'1944. Yes, I know. That was what the brigadier said, and I sympathise, but my mission comes first.'

'You might be glad of us. There's a lot of angry little insurgents running about Karelia. Over a million – a *million* – sidearms have gone missing from the Federal Army in the last two years alone.'

'I've got orders to avoid confrontation.'

'It's easy to spout that sort of shit in Narvik.'

Nick felt a moment of comradeship. 'That's true.'

'It's good to see you again, Nick. Good to be working with a bloke I can rely on.'

'You're not working with me. You're cadging a lift. And I think I've enough problems without having three Secret Squirrels in tow.'

'Come on, Nick. You won't know we're there. Anyway, it's been decided. Yours not to reason why, and all that.'

'Yes,' said Nick, opening the Land-Rover door, 'I seem to remember it was the Russians that time as well.'

There was an atmosphere of restrained ebullience in the dining-room. Whatever was to come, it had to be a change of routine, a change from endless maintenance and field exercises. As usual, the REME detachment sat in a group: Staff Beckwith, Corporals Bateman and Denis. A few glances were thrown at Munro and his men, who insinuated themselves into a corner and started reading back copies of *The Soldier*. Colour-Sergeant Taylor had sent for a twenty-four pack of beer, and cans were passed along. Twenty men were due at the briefing: NCOs, signallers and drivers. Jamie and Nick stood by the woodburner stove, warming their backsides.

'What's he doing here?' Nick was looking with disfavour at Sergeant Worembrand.

'Signal from Army PR, Hanover. They want some pictures of us at the hospital. I think the lads would like it, but you can always say there isn't room.'

'No. Let him come if he wants to.'

'Mariana says I'm taking her to the Halloween disco,' said Jamie. 'What a life.'

Mariana was a Swedish nurse working at the hospital on Prestoya.

'Mariana is going to be severely disappointed,' said Nick. 'Unless she's coming with us to Russia, and you've tickets for a dance in Mončegorsk town hall.'

In the doorway stood the German medics. Everybody had heard about them; few had seen them.

'Good evening, girls,' said Staff Beckwith in a deep hearty voice. 'Evening, girls,' heartily chorused the soldiers.

'Hi, everybody,' said Anneliese.

Nick said, 'I'd like to formally welcome Nurse Bausch, Nurse Schmidt and Dr Sendlinger. Now if everybody's here, I'd like to get started.

'One: the route. Corporal Willis has prepared the map you see behind me. Please will everyone, and particularly the drivers' – there was a ripple of laughter – 'study it carefully. As you see, we will not be crossing the Federation border at Skafferhullet, but going down through Pasvik on the first day and crossing at Nyrud. We join the Winter Route near Verchnetulomskij – and don't ask me to say that again, for Christ's sake – and we'll join the M18 about 15k north of Mončegorsk. We don't expect to travel on the road all the time. Yes, Foster?'

'What about the Russians, sir?' Foster was an ambitious Lance-Corporal in 4 Platoon. 'I mean, are they expecting us?'

'This is authorised by Moscow. By the very top.'

'I hope somebody's told the *pekhota* that,' said a voice from the back.

'The nearest infantry is a motor rifle battalion south of Kirovsk and pulling back to Arkhangelsk. It's abandoned its BMPs to conserve fuel for its Brone transporters, so it can't move off the roads even if it wants to. The border patrols aren't going to bother us apart from trying to scrounge fuel and fags. We do not, under any circumstances, get ourselves tangled up with deserters.'

They went through the route in detail, the signal codes, the recognition procedures.

'Right. You know what you have to do. We leave at 08.00, and we can expect to be back in six days. Now I'll hand over to Major Sendlinger.'

Brigite looked startled.

'Come on, Major,' said Staff Beckwith heartily.

'I don't know how much you know about the hospital. It was one of eight, I think, eight or nine set up by the European Community. The Mončegorsk hospital is very small, dedicated to treating children from Karelia. It specialises in food allergies, some of them caused by the long-term effects of radiation. Even after all this time, people are still suffering from the effects of Chernobyl. It had a devastating effect on the reindeer herds. Caesium entered their food chain, and a lot of Lapp children in the Lovozero area have been raised on reindeer meat . . .'

She spoke for a further five minutes. Everybody listened with rapt attention. A lady Luftwaffe officer in jeans and a tight Icelandic sweater was a rare treat in the Frozen North.

TEN

Jamie Pendred had finalised his admin orders, checked his platoon tents, checked that rifles were cleaned and oiled, skis waxed, route maps printed and distributed to drivers, flanking patrols rostered, and recognition signals passed down the line. He had then checked his platoon vehicles and was wearily finishing a final kit inspection when Collins found him and said: 'Major Chard's compliments, and he wants to see you *now*.'

'Did he say what for?' he asked, as they clattered down the stairs.

Collins said: 'Nothing to me, sir, but he looked bloody furious.'

Jamie hurried through the signallers' room and into the office. Nick was studying the route map for the first day.

'I suppose you think everything's now been done in a proper manner in accordance with the training you received at Sandhurst and during your six months with the battalion?'

'Well, no,' said Jamie. Field officers were always sodding awful to subalterns, of course, by a law of nature.

Nick looked up and smiled. 'Well, I do. Let's go for a beer.'

They collected CSM Robson and went to the Arctic Ocean Hotel, and took Collins in with them, because Nick would only stay in town for thirty minutes, and there wouldn't be time for him to go anywhere else.

'Well, sir,' said Robbo, raising his glass. 'The best of luck.'

'Bread,' said Jamie. 'Oh God, I was going to send some blokes down for fresh fruit and bread.'

'It's been done,' said Robbo.

'We got the UN flag off the Norgies?' asked Nick.

'Relax,' said Robbo. 'It's all under control.'

'Hello, Jamie.'

'Hello, Mariana,' said Jamie, to a small, solemn, dark-haired girl with very large breasts. 'How nice to see you.'

'Is it true? You are really going over there to save those kids in the hospital?'

'Through fire and pestilence,' said Jamie. 'The white doves of Norway, Mariana, the army of peace; that is how we have always looked on ourselves.'

'My God, what a lie . . .'

Mariana belonged to the Peace Dividend. They serenaded NATO bases, singing nostalgia songs like 'Give Peace A Chance'.

'You would keep telling us to go.' Jamie shook his head reproachfully. 'It was very painful.'

'Well, Collins,' said Mariana, ignoring him, 'plenty of girls for you now. This is the first time I knew the German airforce sent the British soldiers some tarts in a heli-copter.'

'You shouldn't say tarts,' said Jamie. 'It's not polite for

a post-feminist Swedish peacenik. It's an expression used by the vulgar soldiery who know no better.'

'Yes, well. I'm talking to Collins – aren't I, Collins?'

'That's right, ma'am.'

'So, Collins, what does the Queen say about these tarts being choppered in?'

'Couldn't tell you, ma'am.'

'Collins, why do you call me ma'am every time you speak to me?'

'He does it because you're an officer's tart,' said Jamie. 'If you were a soldier's tart, he'd call you luv. Now, tell me about this dance again.'

Nick and Robbo turned away, leaned on the bar, and drank their beer.

'You know, you forget how bloody wonderful the army can be,' Nick said. 'One day intense boredom, the next they send you with an armed convoy of sixty men into Russia.'

'They don't send just anybody,' said Robbo.

Robbo was proud of Nick Chard: they went back a long way. In Kurdistan, when Nick was first made platoon commander, Robbo had been his sergeant, and had looked after him and kept him out of trouble, because, unlike half the gentlemen coming out of the Rupert Factory, Nick always wanted to learn, always wanted to be a soldier.

Four years later, the situation was reversed when Nick was Company second-in-command and Robbo was struggling with the unfamiliar stress of being colour-sergeant. Nick had covered for him more than once in those anxious days in Belfast, when the ultimate goal,

Company sergeant-major, had seemed for Robbo a distant and fast-fading dream.

A group of NCOs had come into the bar, with Worembrand tagging along behind them.

'I'll be back in a minute,' said Mariana. 'That's the man I want to see.'

'Sar'nt Worembrand?'

'Yeah, Max. He's a portrait photographer in civilian life. He wants me for his collection called "Girl Child of the North".'

'He wants locking up,' said Jamie.

Elsewhere in the Atlantic Ocean Hotel, Leech was naked and sweating, his white flesh damp on the wooden slats, looking gloomily down at his incipient beergut. Opposite, two fat matrons of Kirkenes, blubbery as whales, were also steaming gently.

Leech was supposed to be scouring the town for bread and fruit. Instead he was in this dim, aromatic warmth, huge bosoms beaded with moisture wherever his eyes rested. Sex in the warm was what Leech liked. In the far north 'high risk sex' had acquired a new meaning since a 2 Platoon signaller, shagging a Norwegian tart up a back alley in Voss, leaned his bare backside on a metal dustbin lid and stuck to it like superglue, as flesh *will* stick to metal at minus-40. Leech shuddered. A hospital job and a skin graft, and the corporal mincing round barracks like a fairy for the next six months.

Syco was coming to Russia.

Leech had engineered it. A word with Colour-Sergeant

Taylor after a driver in 1 Platoon had gone sick, and Syco was back on the strength. Not that it had been easy. 'Sykes? He's the worst bloody driver in NATO,' the CSM had exploded. 'Only when he's pissed, sir,' Leech had argued persuasively. 'He's brilliant when he's kept off the pop.'

'B' Company was short of drivers. Sykes, at this moment, was frantically putting his kit together.

The sauna door opened, and three figures slipped in.

'A sauna sweats out the poisons and impurities from the skin,' said a Scottish voice.

'Believe it if you like,' said Brigite, 'but I'm a doctor and I know better.'

'You're supposed to sit on your towel,' said Munro. 'That's what the notice says. To stop perspiration going on the wood. The Norwegians are very particular about hygiene.'

'If I sit on my towel, what will I put round my body?' said Anneliese, now revealed, despite her towel, as the most beautiful thing Leech had seen since he left his 1997 *Sun* calendar in Narvik.

'You don't need anything round your body. It's medically inadvisable to have any restraint on your body in a sauna. I'm surprised that a nurse does not know that.'

Anneliese laughed but kept her towel tucked firmly in place. Brigite spread her towel on the wooden slats of the highest shelf, climbed up, and lay on her back. She held up the leg she had injured, and massaged the knee gently in the heat. Munro sat on his towel and looked at Leech with a cold eye.

Leech smiled uneasily. This was one of the reservists, so they said – Wolverhampton postmen, ex-Second Battalion, out on a jolly. Leech, and every other soldier in 'B' Company, knew better. These were not reservists but Secret Squirrels. SAS. Lean, mean killers, one and all.

'Leechie,' said Munro.

Jesus, the bugger even knew his name, Leech panicked.

'Sir?'

'Briget,' said Munro.

'What?' said Brigite, lying looking up at the pine-slatted roof.

'Why has this man got his name and yours emblazoned across his biceps?'

'He has too,' Anneliese said. 'And we've only been here seven hours.'

'Girl in Hong Kong, sir,' said Leech. 'Long time ago now. Indiscretions of youth.' Why was he saying 'sir'? The bugger was never an officer, that he'd been told.

'Well, if you'll excuse me.' He got up and left, careful not to look at Brigite, who was a major, for God's sake, even if it was only in the German army.

Transport back to the Hotel Vang was at 21.00. It was snowing again and he plodded down the road with his head deep in his parka hood, but looked up as a convoy of trucks came slowly down from the Pečenga Highway. Norwegian Army trucks, full of refugees. In the harbour was a ship, its lights ablaze: one of the Hurtigruten fleet that plied the Norwegian coast and offered tourists a passage on 'The Most Beautiful Voyage in the World'.

Soldiers were helping refugees up the gangplanks: women laden with bags, men carrying small children. The camp at Pasvik, capable of holding five thousand people and opened only a month ago, must already be full to overflowing.

The Bedford transporter pulled up outside the Northern Lights disco bar, and soldiers started to pile into the back. Anybody late in barracks tonight faced an automatic seven days' staff parade when they returned from Russia – turning out with the guard twice during the day and again at 22.00 hours in full inspection kit, the most loathed minor punishment in the army.

Leech hurried to get a place amid the warm fug of bodies.

ELEVEN

Headquarters, ACE Mobile Force Northern Europe, Kolsaas, near Oslo, 26 October

It was midnight and Operation Terrier was meeting in the Secure Room.

On a screen, grainy black-and-white images clarified into a coastline, a river estuary, and zoomed in to pan across a series of harbours.

Biggin said: 'Those are the submarines . . . Charlie class, Oscar class, a clutch of the old Victor class at the bottom left . . . a bloody great Typhoon over there . . . and here are the carriers. That's the *Kiev*, and there's the last capital ship to join the fleet: the *Nicholas*.'

He paused, then said: 'Navy Int say there's no doubt about it: winter manoeuvres were scheduled to begin two days ago. Moscow daren't admit it, but the fleet's refusing to go to sea.'

'Odessa,' said Generalleutnant Hoepner. '1905.'

'The remake of the movie,' said Biggin.

Brigadier Grenfell, who looked tired and irritable, said: 'I appreciate the significance, but we are concerned with Terrier and the Royal Mercians won't go anywhere near Murmansk.'

'No,' said Biggin, 'but Norgie Intelligence say the Reds are organising into disciplined formations. ScanSat shows them moving south towards Pulozero. They could also threaten Verchnetulomskij – directly in the Royal Mercians' path.'

'Oh Christ,' said Grenfell. 'We'll have to send them south on the Winter Route, and that will add forty k. Get G2 working on it. Get them out of bed.'

Griffiths-Jones said: 'Yes, sir.'

Biggin pressed a pad. The lights came up.

Generalleutnant Hoepner lit a cheroot. 'Already a delay. When do they cross the border?'

'Tomorrow morning 11.00 hours at Nyrud,' said Grenfell.

Hoepner sat deep in thought. Then he said:

'I have been told by Norwood that we must have Terrier in place in six days.'

There was silence in the room.

'Well? Can we do it?'

He looked round the table.

Grenfell said: 'The column should get to Mončegorsk in three days. After that it's up to the SAS.'

'Don't worry about us,' said Biggin. 'Just get us to Lake Imandra.'

Hoepner nodded, then said crisply: 'All right. Charles, you and Peter had better move up to Narvik. Keep in touch. Goodnight, gentlemen.' He stood up, nodded and left.

Biggin and Grenfell got up to follow him. Griffiths-Jones picked up the phone to wake Intelligence and set them working on a new route.

'I wonder,' he said, while he waited for an answer, 'if we shouldn't have put Nick Chard in the picture.'

Biggin turned back, startled. 'Why? He's taking a medical team to a hospital. He's not part of Terrier. He has no role to play.'

'He's got to get our people to Mončegorsk.'

'The less he knows about Terrier the better,' said Grenfell. 'It will just add to his problems.'

'I expect you're right, sir,' said Griffiths-Jones.

Grenfell gave him a hard stare. This was one G2 getting too big for his boots. Of course, he was right.

PART TWO
THE TAIGA

We are the pilgrims, master; we shall go
Always a little further: it may be
Beyond that last blue mountain barr'd with snow
Across that angry or that glimmering sea.

James Elroy Flecker – as inscribed
on 22 SAS regimental clock, Hereford

When next, my friends, you two intend
To sally forth for fun,
Get Deadeye Dick a sugar stick
And buy yourself a bun.

'Eskimo Nell' – as recounted by
Lance-Corporal Leech

ONE

Nyrud, northern Norway, 27 October

For once the met men had got it right. Conditions were
almost white-out as the Snow Leopards moved through the
birch trees, past the Norwegian Brigade North reception
centre, into the no-man's-land of the frontier.

The vehicles halted. They were on a ditch at the edge of
the wood: a primitive tank trap according to Nick's
operational intelligence briefing, first dug by Jodl's
Mountain Corps XIX rearguard in 1944.

Men emerged, fitted their skis, slung their rifles. Patrols
would work out on either flank, keeping in sight of the
convoy, in constant touch by radio.

Nick skied forward, and the flank patrols followed, into
the ditch and up the other side. Collins came behind him, a
radio strapped to his back. Skiing into the driving snow,
they mounted a small rise.

Ahead, where the snow was already swallowing the two
flank patrols, lay Russia.

In August, he had attended a forward strategy seminar for
NATO Northern Command officers.

It had been called, starkly, 'Collapse'.

An academic from Cambridge had said: 'Look for an overall weariness. An exhaustion. Don't look for food riots, but for famine without food riots. Look for a localised reversion to primitive organisation of society. Bartering. Foreigners murdered even though they may have lived in a locality for decades. Look for disease. At the moment we are watching the progress of a viral illness that is killing old people and children in eastern Siberia.'

In September the viral epidemic had spread (ominously in the late summer, when people should have been best able to fight infection) from the gold-mining settlements round Artyk and Ust Nera in eastern Siberia, across the Urals, and into the north-west.

It had been followed by storms and freezing cold: the worst October in living memory.

In the end, collapse in Karelia had come as softly as the first snows of winter.

The last man of Jamie's flank patrol disappeared into the wall of white. The Royal Mercians were operational on Russian territory for the first time since the Crimea; since Sevastopol and Inkerman.

'Well, Collins,' said Nick, impressed by the solemnity of the moment.

'Sir?' said Collins, deep inside his camouflage whites, not sharing his OC's sense of history.

Nick smiled wryly. He took the radio handset and said: 'All stations. This is Zero. Move now. Out.'

The Snow Leopards moved forward.

They were the most advanced all-weather all-terrain

vehicles in NATO, their pale-cream Arctic paintwork and black camouflage markings distinguishing them from the Sand Leopards used in the Middle East, their air-filters and overpressure systems allowing them to operate in Nuclear, Biological and Chemical Warfare situations, their armoured glacis giving protection against small-arms fire and shell fragments, their 670mm-wide snow tracks dealing effortlessly with the broken ground.

Nick's command vehicle led the way, Robbo next to the driver, the EC and UN flags flying for anybody who could see. Then came the rest of the column: the Luftwaffe team in the ambulance, the rations vehicle, four fuel vehicles festooned with jerrycans, behind them the vehicle carrying Milan, and behind that the REME wrecker, its crane sheathed in canvas and secured with chains. Staff Beckwith was in the turret, defying the weather to give Nick an 'eyes right' and salute as he passed; and Nick grinned and returned the salute, his spirits lifting suddenly. The hours of planning and checking, and ACE Mobile Force briefings and Norwegian Brigade North briefings, were over.

He dropped his hand as the final Snow Leopard reared up out of the ditch and the fishlike eyes of Sergeant Noon peered out.

The SAS man seemed bored, as if he was accustomed to more interesting jobs.

Now the first vehicle passed the frontier sign: battered metal peppered by hunters' shotgun pellets, a memory of times long past:

Norsk-sovjetisk grenseomrade.
Det er bl a ikke tillatt
Norwegian-Soviet border area.

It is prohibited:
To cross the border
To make contact across the border
To photograph Soviet territory
For foreigners to fish or to have boats in border
    rivers and lakes.

Another hundred metres and they drove through a line of ghostly concrete posts, ten feet high, trailing frozen tentacles of ancient barbed wire. The first frontier line had been manned to keep Westerners out; this line had been built to keep Soviet citizens in.

The Zapoljarnyj road was hidden deep under fifteen feet of snow. Without stopping, the column turned and headed towards the National Winter Route, ten kilometres to the south.

The Winter Route was the all-weather highway from Pečenga to Murmansk and the interior. It was the lifeline for the town of Nikel with its twenty thousand inhabitants.

'Sir!'

Robbo was standing in the turret of the stationary command vehicle when Nick skied up from the rear of the column.

'According to LodeStar, this is it, sir,' Robbo said. 'According to LodeStar, we're standing on it.'

Nick looked round. The highway should have been cleared by snowploughs. It should have been busy with traffic. Satellite pictures taken only six days ago had shown at least one lane open for over sixty per cent of its distance.

They were in a wasteland of snow and scrub. In every direction the wind blew across empty tundra: a plain to the east, low, broken hills and a distant pine forest to the south.

Nick said: 'Either LodeStar's up the creek, or we've got no road to follow.'

Jamie and his flank patrol appeared over a small rise and skied rapidly down to the column, swerving to a halt in a spray of snow. They were eighteen- and nineteen-year-olds having a hell of a good time.

'There's a depression up ahead, and a line of poles sticking out of the snow,' said Jamie. 'We're on the road, all right. Forbes thought he saw a Little Chef, but it turned out to be a mirage.'

'I could smell it, sir,' protested a soldier. 'Cheeseburger and French fries.'

Nick looked at his watch. It was just after 11.00. 'All right, let's get a forward patrol organised, and then let's keep moving.'

The flank patrols moved off. NCOs went back to their vehicles. Nick sent six men ahead of the convoy. They would guide the column along the line of the road, using satellite navigation.

At noon they were zigzagging up a long slope, through

101

huge boulders, when with a screech of metal on metal the leading fuel vehicle lurched over, one set of manganese steel tracks clawing the snow, the other slicing the cab of a Russian truck, suddenly revealed like a rock at low tide.

They dug down to check that nobody was inside. Brigite walked up the column and stood by to give aid.

The cab was empty. Brigite said perhaps the driver had climbed into the back of the truck. Nick said: 'If he did he climbed into his own coffin.' Brigite looked at him, furious, and Robbo said: 'We don't think anything's moved on this road for three days, ma'am.'

'A man could live for three days if he had food and water and some form of insulation.'

'Staff Beckwith!' Nick shouted down the column.

Staff Beckwith brought a portable acetylene torch and cut a metre-square hole in the top of the truck, and they waited for half a second for the metal to cool, then Nick shone a torch down into the interior.

'Empty,' he said. Brigite took the torch and also looked down.

'There's a pile of skins in the corner . . .'

'Nobody could survive under those for three days at minus-40, and I don't want to waste another hour just to look at a dead Russian.' Nick's tone was pleasant but decisive. 'All right, Sar'nt-Major, let's get moving. And let's keep moving, if we can.'

'He'd have abandoned that truck with an entire family alive in it just to save ten minutes,' said Brigite in rapid German. 'I'd forgotten how stupid army officers are.'

'Erike thinks he's rather nice,' said Anneliese. 'Don't you, Erike?'

Erike smiled unhappily.

'He's arrogant,' said Brigite, 'and self-satisfied.'

'He's a right Rupert,' said Worembrand. 'Do you know why I call him a Rupert?'

Brigite and Anneliese looked at him, startled.

'You speak German?' said Anneliese, foolishly, since he had just done so.

Worembrand had chosen the ambulance in the early hours of dawn. It was no more comfortable than a regular Snow Leopard, but it did have red crosses painted on its side and behind its turret, and Worembrand believed there were still people in the world who would hesitate to shoot up a Red Cross vehicle – despite much evidence to the contrary. Its medical gear included four electrically-heated thermal sleeping bags, and it had been in Worembrand's mind that he might spend the journey inside one of them. Brigite, when the suggestion was made, had said 'No' very curtly. Foiled, he had built himself a nest among his camera bags, and had dozed under his duvet for most of the morning, waking only when Anneliese passed him mugs of hot chocolate.

'I speak the odd word,' said Worembrand. In fact he spoke German like a native, the best years of his ungilded youth having been spent in Berlin and Rheindahlen. Speaking German comforted and cheered him, recalling nights on the Bacardi-and-Coke with Werner in the back room of the Cherry-Ripe Club.

'OK,' said Anneliese, 'why do you call him a Rupert?'

'Because he's from the Rupert Factory,' said Worembrand cleverly.

The hours passed. The flank patrols and the forward patrol changed. Snakpaks were opened and eaten on the move.

At 15.00 there was a ten-minute break. The men drank from their flasks, and some lit cigarettes. Those who had been on flank patrol leaned, exhausted, against the vehicles. Dusk was falling.

'OK, how far can we get?' said Nick wearily. He had spent most of the day skiing up and down the convoy.

'There's a tourist resthouse at Kirjan, sir,' said Robbo. 'It's mentioned in route information.'

'Dear God, no,' said Jamie. 'I've read about those places. Terrible beer and no hot water.'

'Who's been letting you drink beer?' said Nick. 'I promised your mother you'd be given nothing but Orangina. OK, Kirjan it is. Let's get moving.'

'At least we won't have to get the tents up,' said Robbo. 'Faster start in the morning, too.'

There were six cabins nestling in pine trees, grouped round a picnic area. A notice in English said: '*A gift from the People of the Ukraine.*' Anneliese climbed stiffly out of the back of the ambulance and went into the first cabin. She dumped her sleeping bag on the floor and looked round.

There was a hole in the roof where the stove had been ripped out. Two iron bedsteads were screwed to the wall. The wall by the door was scrawled with graffiti: '*Why does*

Tarzan live in Russia? Because he's king of the Apes.'
Sinclair Macdonald, Selkirk. *'World's northernmost
pisshouse.'* Johnny R, St Louis.

Jean François from Annecy had slept here . . . Svenja
from Copenhagen . . . Maria from Milano . . . Belinda and
Diane from Exeter.

A notice behind the door was printed in Russian, German
and English over a sketch of reindeer, wolverines and
eagles.

'Welcome to Northern Karelia designated National
Park, sponsored by the Swedish Forestry department.
Home of reindeer and ancient boreal forests, of tundra
and marshes, of monche-tundra mountain of pre-
Cambrian origin. Unspoilt home of many interesting
wildlife. Always use mosquito cream during summer
months.'

Soldiers came in with polystyrene sleeping mats and
sleeping bags. One set up a portable stove. 'REME and
signals. You in here with us, ma'am?'

'That's right,' said Anneliese. 'All three of us.'

Corporal Willis was inspecting the hole in the roof.
'Dear, oh dear, a two-star hotel and I can see both of them
through the ceiling. Spew dinner, unless you want to keep
to separate rations?'

All-in-stew dinner, he explained, was when they put
everything left over from their twenty-four-hour ration
packs into a dixie, heated it up and ladled it out.

'That's fine, isn't it, Erike?' said Anneliese. Erike had

followed her in, and was struggling to unroll her new Norwegian Army sleeping bag. She looked severely unhappy.

'Last hotel I stayed at in Voss, the landlady came and banged on my door at midnight,' said Willis, bending over the stove. '"Have you got a woman in there with you?" she shouted. "No," I said, so she opened the door and threw one in.'

'I'm sorry, I don't know what you're talking about!' said Erike, her voice suddenly high and irate.

Willis looked up, surprised.

'It's a joke,' said Anneliese. 'Are you all right, Erike?'

Erike said, 'Yes, I'm sorry,' and lay back on her sleeping bag, her face turned to the wall.

Two soldiers plugged the hole in the roof, and pinned sheeting over the doorway to form a double wall against draughts and stop the warm air being sucked out. Soon the temperature began to rise. The young soldier tending the stove, who said his name was Mark, brewed a rich-smelling meaty drink and served it out in polystyrene cups.

'Wonderful,' said Anneliese.

'Oxo,' said Mark. 'Haven't you had Oxo before?'

Soldiers began to strip off their combat jackets and boots. One snagged his pullover and said 'Oh fuck' and a lance-corporal said 'Language'.

Anneliese said: 'Look, don't worry about us, OK? Just pretend we're not here.'

Erike lay with her back to the room, her face in shadow. She said she was resting; she would be all right in a bit. Anneliese saw beads of sweat on her forehead.

Anneliese said: 'Erike, are you sure you're OK?'

Eike nodded, her legs drawn up, her hands between her knees.

Sergeant Doran had taken out a clearance patrol one kilometre in each direction, and found nothing. The country around them was made up of low glacier-scoured hills covered in scrubby trees. The nearest settlement was three kilometres away, the nearest town, Prirečnyj, twelve kilometres to the east.

Stags tonight would be for thirty minutes: the man on sentry duty taking over from the man on tent stag for a further thirty minutes. Only six sentries would be out: enough to guard the perimeter. Everyone else could sleep.

The met report was for a clear day tomorrow. Thank God for that, thought Nick. According to the map they would pass through open country in the morning, and would be able to dispense with flank patrols.

'We're going off-road, out on the tundra,' he said, pulling off his boots. 'Bugger the designated route. I'm not fartarsing around Karelia till Christmas.'

'Dinner, sir,' said Holmes, the regimental Rottweiler, doubling as cook for HQ Company. On the plate was rehydrated ration-pack beef curry and rice, and chicken-à-la-crême mushed up into a stiff little pile, and by it a sliced tomato.

'A tomato,' said Nick. 'Look at this, Sar'nt-Major.'

'Bloody hell,' said Robbo, impressed.

'I rescued it from 1 Platoon,' said Holmes. 'They were trying to nab all the fresh stuff, but I nabbed it back.'

'Luxury.' Nick leaned back, forking food into his mouth, and wriggling his toes. 'What a life.'

They had been lucky to find the huts still standing. Civilisation. A home from home; a Vang – as Jamie put it when he came in for the 'O' group briefing – from Vang.

Later Nick went in search of Brigite. He found her in the cabin allocated to the SAS team, sitting on the floor with a pack of tarot cards, telling Munro's fortune. The hut was otherwise empty, Sergeant Noon and Corporal Fuller presumably about their nefarious business.

'Isn't that The Hanged Man,' Munro was saying. 'Does that mean I'm going to die?'

'It doesn't necessarily refer to you,' said Brigite, 'and it does not necessarily mean death.'

'I expect it does, though,' said Munro, 'for somebody.'

'I'm only a novice,' said Brigite. 'I only bought these last week. I'm still using the instructions.'

Nick said: 'Can I have a few words, Major?'

Munro stood up and said he had better go and check his vehicle.

'Take care,' said Brigite. 'Come back and I'll finish you later.'

Munro smiled, and said what a good idea, then stretched and said to Nick, 'Sentries Out? Good Old Heavy Infantry!' and went.

'A bit of a joker that one,' said Brigite in a friendly voice. 'Doesn't go round saying "yes, sir" and "no, sir" every three seconds.'

'I didn't think anybody did,' said Nick.

'You ought to listen.'

Nick sat down on the floor. 'I don't mean to neglect you. I appreciate that this is really a joint-services operation. I'm sorry if I seem to keep cutting you out.'

'No problem. You just get us to the hospital. Until then we'll keep out of your way.'

'You should have been invited to the "O" group. I thought Collins had asked you.'

'Well, yeah, I think he did, but he didn't say what it was, and it sounded like some kind of weird blood-transfusion party, so I thought I might give it a miss . . .'

'Orders group,' said Nick, not laughing. 'They have them in the Bundeswehr.'

'Ah. Right. I'm an officer, so I go to the "O" group.'

'Suit yourself, but at least you'd know the progress we were making and any change in our plans.'

'Yes, OK. Thanks, Nicholas.'

'How's Nurse Schmidt?'

Brigite hesitated.

'Your driver says she hardly spoke a word all day.'

'She says she is all right. A Luftwaffe medical found her A1 only four days ago. Apart from holding her down and forcibly examining her, there is nothing more I can do.'

'She could have developed flu or something.'

'If she has, we've plenty of vaccine.'

Nick stood up. 'Perhaps you'd like to tell my fortune?'

Brigite looked up at him and said: 'You will become a colonel and marry a nice English girl and have nice English children and a nice English dog and play golf and die a very old man.'

Nick nodded. With luck and a following wind, she was probably right.

The Snow Leopards were dispersed among the trees. Munro was leaning against the SAS vehicle, smoking.

'It's not my business,' said Nick, 'but none of them have security clearance that I know of, and if I were you, I'd consider it my job to keep a very low profile.'

Munro said: 'You take things too seriously. You ought to relax – have a laugh.'

'Bollocks,' said Nick, who was not going to be found humourless by a cold Scotch bastard like Munro, a man who had admitted, at Warminster, that he found his fun killing grey squirrels at forty yards with a Spetznaz knife. 'I don't know what you're doing here, of course – "Just having a look-round", OK – but if Fuller and Noon are out looking at things now, I hope you've told the sentries.'

'Fuller and Noon are having their dinner,' said Munro. 'Brigite's a fascinating girl, don't you think?'

'A reservist who hates the army.'

'A girl of sound judgement.'

'In particular she hates officers.'

'Not all of them.'

'She doesn't know you're an officer, though, does she?'

Munro laughed in the darkness, threw down his cigarette, and went back to the SAS cabin.

Anneliese was in her sleeping bag, her back propped against her Bergen, her blonde hair reflecting the glow of her laptop word-processor. Next to her, Erike was snoring gently, knocked out by three anti-flu tablets. Soldiers were asleep all around, apart from the young soldier called Mark, who was on tent stag, tending the stove. He had earlier told her how his father had been in the Royal Mercians in Aden, his grandfather with the Gloucesters in Korea, and his great-grandfather with the Cheshire Regiment at Gallipoli.

Now he brewed himself hot chocolate, and held up his mug to see if she wanted some.

She smiled and shook her head, and he grinned awkwardly.

Hi, Wolfgang (she wrote) well here I am, 20k inside Russia and talk about cold! It's like living inside your freezer compartment (the temperature is actually lower than the freezer!). The cold's like something alive. When somebody opens the door – every hour the sentry goes out; we're being very military about this although we've travelled a whole day and haven't seen more than four vehicles – anyway the cold is so solid you can see it. Want to know what cold looks like? It's pale and wraith-like, with tendrils that sneak round the curtain.

You should see what we're all wearing. First of all bra and pants (me, that is, not the soldiers, although I haven't actually checked, at least not all sixty of them, ho ho) and then long thermal trousers the Brits call 'long johns' and amazing thick white fleecy socks. On top of that there's a 'Norgie shirt' which is a soft Norwegian Army shirt that zips up the neck, and a Norgie Army pullover.

After that we really start to put clothes on – jumpers and woollies and scarves and combat trousers and jackets, and, on top of those, 'camouflage whites' so the enemy won't spot us and shoot us down like dogs, etc, etc.

You'd have laughed earlier. The soldiers in our hut (we're in a hut tonight – real luxury) all took their combat jackets and cam whites and stuff off and sat there in their Norgies. They were all incredibly sweaty and I thought they wanted to wash. 'Don't worry about us,' I insisted – I wasn't going out in the cold just to preserve their soldierly modesty – 'I'm a nurse. There's nothing under that lot that can surprise me. Just get them off and wash, OK?' They looked horrified. It turned out that they had no intention of washing. Once those long johns go on, they stay on. A boy called Mark (my favourite, a pet) said they stink like polecats after a few days, but as they all stink, they don't notice.

What should I do? Wash and douse myself in perfume or stink like the rest of them? Erike shows no sign of doing anything except sleep. She's older than us, and I think she's ill, and Brigite tried to examine her tonight, but she wouldn't let her. She just said she had a headache from the diesel fumes in the vehicle.

Brigite is terrific. She's a reservist, but also a

pacifist and a member of the Peace Dividend. How
mixed up can you get? When she was nineteen she
joined the Luftwaffe because she wanted to be a
doctor and see the world – didn't we all? What
have I ever seen? Wolfgang Wittich and the
Hamburg to Hanover autobahn! Anyway, she
couldn't stand being bossed about and left, *loathes*
officers, is a clairvoyant, and has just split up with
her boyfriend (or lover as she calls him) and says
all men are bastards, which hasn't stopped her
getting chummy with a tough-guy bloke who's
some sort of technical expert in satellite
communications. She's with him now, talking
zodiac signs and human relationships. I'm faxing
this, by the way, via army commsat unless they
want to vet it first, in which case I'm not sending it
at all, and you'll read it when I get back.

PS. They're vetting personal mail. You'd think
there was a war on.

Leech was shattered. Leech wanted a piss. Syco had droned
on till midnight about reconciliation with Karen one minute
and going abbo to Turkestan the next. Before that he had
tried to phone Karen to tell her she was a fucking slut, but
Signals were only accepting emergency faxes. During the
day, driving his vehicle through the endless unchanging
snow, Syco's feverish brain had conjured up a new
nightmare: Ray from Belfast Co-op fitted kitchens
department (now newly promoted, Syco imagined, to Co-
op soft furnishings) spending his way through the pay

Syco has been handing over to Karen by direct debit: a river of peach-coloured curtains and beige fitted carpets and apricot satin settee covers, while secretly retaining (this the final horror) his sales manager commission on every purchase.

Now Syco snored while Leech, exhausted by a day skiing up and down on his NATO planks, desperately wanted to sleep but could not, because he needed to piss, and he could not piss without unzipping his cosy warm green maggot and venturing out into the icy Arctic night.

It was another half hour before he finally zipped back his dossbag and heaved himself out and lumbered to the door, where a pair of massive 'moonboots' stood on duty. He staggered into them, then crept out and scurried round the side of the hut to escape the wind, fumbling at the same time with the buttons of his fleecy long johns.

'Bugger me,' he muttered in greeting to the sentry. But the sentry was at that moment reaching for his personal radio, his eyes fixed beyond the huts, through the fir trees, to where a line of skiers was faintly outlined against the luminous northern sky.

TWO

West Karelia, 28 October

'Hello, Two, this is Two-One. Fetch Sunray. Over.'

Collins acknowledged the message then stood in the command vehicle's turret to look back down the column. The Snow Leopards were moving in single file, in white hazy sunshine, along a broad valley. Towards the rear he could see the German nurse, Anneliese, standing in the turret of the ambulance, viewing the country through a pair of borrowed binoculars.

Nick was riding on the second vehicle, chatting to the co-driver. He had travelled this way for most of the morning: climbing from one vehicle to another whenever the column halted.

'Sir! Sir! Mr Pendred, sir!' Collins shouted, pointing at his headphones.

The second Snow Leopard slowed, and Nick jumped down and ran forward along the hard-packed snow trail laid by the command vehicle. He swung himself up, clinging to the cab roof with one hand, and took the handset from Collins.

'Hello Two-One, this is Two. Sunray speaking. Over.'

Jamie's voice was muffled by his throat mike.

115

'I can see people on the far side of the valley about a mile due north. There's five of them, civilians, including a child of about twelve or thirteen. They look as if they're in trouble.'

'What kind of trouble?' Nick was leaning into the cab, looking at the map spread in Collins's lap.

'They're on foot, struggling in deep snow.'

The MoD four-miles-to-the-inch map, prepared for RAF low-level bomber crews, showed a small settlement two miles to the north-west of Jamie's position.

He pressed the handset.

'We have to push on. We're behind as it is. They're probably from the farm at 386-297.'

'They're not heading that way. They look as if they're lost.'

Nick looked up to the heights to the right of the column. There was no sign of Jamie's flank patrol – they must have dropped over the skyline. There were probably a couple of false ridges.

'All right. I'm on my way up.'

Ten minutes later he stood on the ridge, scanning the next valley. How much military history, he wondered, had consisted of small groups of men standing on hills looking through binos and wondering what the hell they were looking at?

The civilians were floundering along the side of a slope, moving through about four feet of soft snow without skis or snowshoes. The man in the lead was trying to beat a pathway, the women clinging to branches of stunted birch trees. They were heading towards empty taiga. It was fifty kilometres to the Norwegian border.

They would never make it.

'I don't see how we can just leave them,' said Jamie, lowering the binos.

'No,' said Nick. They could not just leave them, even though Karelia was heaving with human misery and desperation, and his orders were to avoid civilian involvement of any kind, and the column was already half a day behind schedule.

He thought quickly. He had ridden up to the ridge on 4 Platoon's Snow Leopard. He could leave it here with Jamie and ski back down to the column.

'Right, this is what you do,' he said, stuffing his binoculars and map inside his jacket. 'Take this vehicle. Go down and see what their problem is. You'll have to make it clear to them that we haven't time to mess around. If they want, you can run them up to the farm at 386-297, but after that it's somebody else's problem. I'll halt the column on high ground at the head of the valley.'

He watched as Jamie's patrol piled their skis into the back of the Snow Leopard and clambered aboard. 'See you in a bit, sir,' said one. 'Don't let them eat all our dinner, sir,' said another. They were laughing and joking. Slogging across miles of empty taiga had lost its appeal; it was much more fun to swoop about in a Snow Leopard rescuing grateful civilians.

He turned back to look down on the convoy. Robbo had halted on the crest of a small hill, and had put sentries out. From the ridge the column looked like a collection of shiny toy vehicles, tiny ants moving around them very slowly. From a less childlike point of view they looked extremely vulnerable to mortar attack, he thought, his smile fading . . .

He had doubled the sentries during the previous night, and at dawn moved cautiously out from the resthouse to inspect the tracks left by the line of skiers.

Munro had examined them. 'Racing ski on the inner side, telemark on the outer. Could have been about their own business. On the other hand we can't expect them not to take an interest.'

Nick had said, 'Expect *who* not to take an interest?' and Munro had replied, 'No idea, *old boy*,' in the exaggerated English accent that was his idea of wit.

Nick raised his binoculars and scanned the horizon carefully in every direction. To the south, where the hills dropped away to the river Lotta, was the second flank patrol, grouped on a minor summit, taking a rest. He looked east: at the head of the valley the ground opened out. When they reached that point, he would be able to pull the flank patrols in and move forward at speed.

The land was empty of either civilians or ski patrols.

He skied back down to the column. People were eating or were stretched out on the roofs or bonnets of the vehicles. He skied back to the SAS vehicle. Munro was seated on a pack, drinking from a flask of tea. He passed Nick a cup.

'Well?'

'Just some civilians.' Nick swallowed a mouthful of warm sweet tea gratefully. 'If it happens again, I might need one of your chaps to translate.'

Munro said: 'If it happens again, I hope we'll just pass on by.'

'Sorry, I'm not going to leave people to die in the snow,' said Nick. 'Thanks for the tea.'

By the time he reached the command vehicle, Jamie was back on the radio.

'The girl speaks some English. She says they're from a settlement about 15k from here. They were heading for Nyrud but their truck ran out of fuel.'

'Well they won't make it on foot. Do they want to go to the nearest farm?'

There was a pause. Nick looked at the sky. Another hour and it would be dusk. Brigite came and stood by him. She looked at him as if faintly embarrassed.

'Yes?'

She sighed and opened her mouth to speak just as Jamie came back on.

'They're not too happy about it. They're terrified of army deserters. They had trouble at home just before they left.'

'Well it's all that's on offer. They either go to the farm or stay where they are. We have to get moving.'

There was another pause. Brigite said: 'You know you were worried about Erike?' Nick nodded. 'Well you were right. We've got a big problem.'

Nick looked at her. What, he wondered, constituted a big problem on Brigite's scale of difficult situations.

119

'An hour ago she started vomiting and . . .'

'Hang on.'

Jamie was back on the line. The Russians would go to the farm.

'OK, take them within walking distance of the place, and then kick them out. Don't go up there yourself. *Don't* get involved. Dump them and get straight back here. Do you understand, Two-One? Over.'

'Two-One. Wilco. Out,' said Jamie cheerfully.

Nick turned to Brigite. 'Go on.'

'She has admitted to suffering pains in the upper abdomen, with loss of appetite and dizziness for the last week. She has been taking anti-flu vaccine – 229, the strong stuff – to suppress the symptoms. The pains have now intensified and moved to the lower right side of the abdomen. There is also fever as well as vomiting. In other words we have the classic symptoms of acute appendicitis.'

'And it's taken you two days to spot it?' said Nick, opening a raisin-and-date energy bar.

'I beg your pardon?' said Brigite.

'OK, let's go and look at her, shall we?'

The farm stood on a small plateau; rocks and stunted trees behind it on one side, on the other, buried now under snowdrifts, was the road to Prirečnyj.

The Snow Leopard had approached from below, along a small gully, following the course of a frozen stream. Then it had crept up cautiously, still hidden but with the farm just visible to Jamie standing in the turret.

He swept from left to right with his binoculars, taking

his time, moving from background to foreground, just as he had been taught.

Three wooden buildings, badly in need of paint, grouped round a courtyard. Windows broken except for the second floor of the central building – presumably the living quarters placed, as usual, over the top of a ground-level cattle barn.

There was a path trodden through the snow from the central building to the barn on the right. A bright metal chimney pipe ran up the end gable of the central building. Jamie looked for smoke, but none was visible.

There was no sign of movement. No sign of life.

Jamie leaned down into the turret and said: 'All right, back off.'

The driver released the brake and the Snow Leopard slid quietly, almost noiselessly, back down the slope. After twenty metres it stopped in the cover of some bushes, and two soldiers instantly took up sentry positions. Jamie walked round the back. Inside, wedged in amongst his lads, warmer now and slumping in a coma of exhaustion, sat the five Russians.

They were a family – mum and dad in their forties, a son in his early twenties, a young daughter, and an older woman, presumably a grandmother. They wore grubby fur coats and had bundles – God only knew what was in them – and a cardboard suitcase that looked as if it might fall apart at any moment.

Jamie spoke to the girl. She had been learning English at school. She knew about England: at least she knew about Sherlock Holmes and about businessmen in bowler hats. She had a thin, angular face with deep, expressive eyes. From a distance, as the Snow Leopard ploughed across the valley towards the watching group, she had looked about twelve; close up she seemed fifteen or sixteen. This was not a good time to grow up in Russia.

'The farm is up by the stream,' said Jamie, in a cheerful and confident voice. 'Two hundred metres. Everything looks OK.' He gave a thumbs-up sign and smiled encouragingly. 'You get out now. All right?'

The girl spoke quickly to her parents, then said:

'Please, we stay with you?'

'No. It's impossible. I told you before. I told you before you got in the wagon.'

The girl nodded, and spoke again to her parents, then said:

'You have space in here. Please?'

The mother was gesturing with her hands to show that they took up little space. The men were looking at him coldly, as if calculating his weakness.

'You cannot stay with us,' said Jamie crisply. 'You have got to get out. Now. OK?'

The mother started to speak again, appealing to Jamie, her hands outspread.

The girl said: 'We are very afraid. Very afraid.'

'Well, I'm sorry, but I'm sure you'll be all right,' said Jamie, who was not sure at all.

There was a crackle from the radio in the cab, and the driver leaned out. 'It's the OC, sir. He wants to know what's happening.'

'Tell him we're approaching the farm now – oh God, just fob him off!'

He heard the driver pass an unimaginative 'Wait. Out' over the radio.

'Want us to chuck them out, sir?' asked Corporal Hoddinot, quietly.

Jamie looked at the girl, and she met his gaze. Russians learned to speak with their eyes, he had been told, because as babies they were swaddled tightly and could not move their limbs. This girl was desperately tired, frightened, almost certainly hungry – at least he could give them food!

'Corporal.'

'Sir?' said Hoddinot.

'How many ration packs have we got?'

'None, sir, but what we've got with us for ourselves.'

'Get as much together as you can – chocolate bars, that sort of thing. I'm taking Childs and Sykes to check out the farm.'

They climbed up by the frozen stream. Jamie was not sure why he had chosen Sykes, miserable, brain-dead, walrus-faced and gloomy, except that he knew Sykes was due for a court martial and needed to do something to redeem himself.

Nick would be on the radio any minute now, wanting a sitrep. Jamie grinned faintly. What the hell! Officers were supposed to use initiative. Having picked up the Russians, they had some sort of responsibility to leave them in a place of safety.

'Looks quiet enough, sir,' said Childs.

Jamie again scanned the farm, and for a moment hesitated. He was twenty, nearly twenty-one. Rugby School, Sandhurst, then straight into the Royal Mercians. 'Just an innocent child,' Nick and Robbo used to sigh sorrowfully when they were out on the pop, and Jamie, after a couple of pints, asked for a Perrier water.

He would get a hell of a bollocking from Nick, but at least he would have left the Russians safe inside a building. It was bloody pointless starting a job and not finishing it. What if it had been his own mother and father, and his teenage sister Henrietta, floundering through the snow with army rebels on their heels?

It was difficult, though, to imagine this happening in Dorset.

'All right, spread out.'

To reach the farm buildings they had to cross forty metres of virgin snow on an upwards incline, and there was no cover. They were halfway, labouring up the slope on the edge of their skis, when there was a sound up ahead – and in the nearest barn a shutter opened slowly, like a sleepy eye.

Nick was bending over Erike, shocked by her grey, muddy face, her anxious eyes.

'Are you in pain?' he asked.

'Well, of course she's in pain,' Brigite said, making no attempt to conceal her irritation.

Erike nodded. She was in pain.

'Then why the hell,' said Nick, turning, 'don't you give her something?'

'She has acute appendicitis. What do you suggest, an aspirin?'

Outside, standing in the snow, Anneliese and Sergeant

Worembrand exchanged glances.

'She's already stuffed herself full of painkillers,' murmured Anneliese. 'Anyway it's not Brigite's fault. How were we supposed to know?'

'They'll have to lift her out,' said Worembrand. 'Casevac. Big silver bird from the skies. You mark my words.' He shivered, frozen to his fatty marrow despite the sky-blue and magenta skiing parka he wore over his regulation jacket, and the tartan scarf tucked round his neck. 'Some things are so obvious, I don't know why people don't just get on with it. But it's all jaw-jaw with some people, have you noticed?'

'Hey, you can take my picture while we're waiting,' suggested Anneliese. 'Now the sun's shining. A picture of me in Russia to send to my boyfriend.'

Worembrand looked at her, blonde hair and blue eyes and cute little nose and a healthy blush in her cheek, and imagined her posed on a Snow Leopard turret, bare-bosomed at twenty below freezing, her nipples standing out like organ stops.

If Kelvin MacKenzie didn't go for that, then Worembrand was a Dutchman – which he most certainly wasn't.

'Has anybody ever told you you could get your picture in the papers?' he asked.

Nick emerged and said, 'What the fuck do you think you look like? I don't want to see that scarf again. You look like bloody Rupert Bear,' and strode back to the command vehicle. Both Worembrand and Anneliese stared after him indignantly.

'She's got appendicitis,' he said curtly to Robbo, and reached for the radio. 'Hello, Two-One, this is Two. Sunray speaking. Fetch your Sunray to this set now. And if you tell me to "wait out" I'm going to come down there and kick your arse . . .'

Then he heard the shots, over the ridge to the north.

Two shots from a high-velocity automatic rifle.

Everyone with the convoy froze, heads turned towards the sound of the gunfire.

Sound travels clearly over snow, as it does over still water. The gunfire sounded as though it came from half a mile away, although Nick would later be able to state, in his official report, that the farm was three and a half miles distant.

Over the radio the voice of Corporal Hoddinot said: 'Two, this is Two-One. Contact. Wait out.'

Contact!

The word was echoed by radio operators all down the line. Robbo was already scrambling from the cab as Nick said: 'I'm taking 5 Platoon. Get them bombed up.'

'Five Platoon! Sar'nt Doran!' yelled Robbo, running back down the column. Soldiers tumbled from the vehicles, throwing kit and baggage out into the snow. Corporals started kicking open ammunition boxes and passed rounds to riflemen and linked belts to machine-gunners. In under a minute 5 Platoon's lead vehicle was forcing its way off the beaten snow, its engine growling, soldiers running to jump into the back.

Nick was still by the command vehicle, the headset clamped to his ears, his fists slowly pounding the side of the cab. *Don't badger the commander on the ground* he had been taught. OK, but who was the commander on the ground? It seemed to be Corporal Hoddinot, so what the hell had happened to Jamie?

Two more Snow Leopards spun slowly round to face the hills to the north, machine-gunners sliding their weapons into place in the turrets, soldiers clambering into the back, their rifles unslung and at the ready. Brigite ran up, holding a medical pack. She pointed to one of the manoeuvring vehicles. Nick nodded, and she climbed in.

Over the radio Nick heard another burst of firing. Had Hoddinot left the link open and abandoned the vehicle? Christ, what was happening!

'Two-One,' he said crisply, 'this is Two. Sunray speaking.'

The third Snow Leopard was ready. Sergeant Doran, in the cab, was giving Nick the thumbs-up.

'OK, let's go,' said Nick, climbing into the command vehicle and slamming the cab door. With a roar they jerked round and then plunged forward, crashing through the drifts of snow.

At the first ear-splitting crack, Jamie had thrown himself down, his face in the snow, burrowing with gloved hands to make a shallow scrape, his skis hanging loose and his rifle God only knew where. How much snow stopped a high-velocity bullet?

God, he'd been told often enough. Think, think!

Another crack, and the furious angry buzzing of a bullet ripped along the snow, tumbling off course unpredictably, as they always did.

He managed to free his skis, rolling on his back, and then over on to his stomach again, pressing his body into the snow, trying to scrape snow piles in front and around him, like a child with a sandcastle.

This was not how he had imagined his first action. In his dreams he had been storming ahead of his platoon to win an impregnable, vital position; there had been cheers from his lads, good-humoured mockery in the mess, a Military Cross, a photograph outside Buck House with his parents and Henrietta, his arm in a sling from a very minor wound.

His hands scraped desperately at the snow as another shot cracked out over his head.

A cry from over on his left. That was Childs.

'Sir? I think I'm hit.'

Jamie said: 'Where are you hit?'

'My leg. I can feel it wet underneath. It's blood.' Across to his left, Childs's hand appeared for an instant, the blood on it already congealing.

'Syco, you all right?'

'I'm all right,' came Syco's voice, seemingly from underground. Jamie started to tunnel slowly towards Childs, pushing the snow into a ridge and then wriggling along behind it. He was breathing heavily, gasping at the muscular effort of heaving his body through the snow. Childs lay on his back, his gloves discarded, fumbling with a field dressing. Jamie took it from him, rolled him over, and with his clasp knife started to cut away the clothing round the wound.

Another shot.

Jamie ducked and lay flat on the snow, paralysed. He had time to think now, time to remember what a high-velocity round could do to the human body. He had seen the photos: slab shots from Northern Ireland morgues. A neat little hole in front, and a hole at the back big enough to put your fist in.

'Sir?'

Jamie slowly forced his head up from the snow, and started to cut again at Childs's clothes: the plastic outers, the combat trousers, the blood-drenched wool beneath. He found the entry hole in Childs's thigh. There was no exit wound – the bullet was still in there. It must have ricocheted through the snow and been almost spent when it hit.

Placing the pad on the wound, he guided Childs's hand to the spot to hold it in place, then wound the bandage round it. Then he took hold of Childs's rifle, poked it through the snow towards the farm, flicked the safety to 'automatic' and squeezed the trigger, firing off a whole magazine, his head buried in the snow, neither looking nor caring where the bullets went.

Hoddinot was from Leominster, a calm man of farming stock, hard to ruffle or excite, and he was speaking slowly and steadily.

'Contact grid 386-296. Riflemen and automatic weapons. Four or five, maybe more. They're in the farm buildings. They're engaging my Sunray, and two men and have them pinned down. Am observing. Over.'

'Roger. Out,' said Nick.

What the hell was Jamie doing at the farm with two men! Thank Christ, Hoddinot had the sense not to go charging in. Nick switched to intercom, 'Get me their platoon frequency,' then went back to the map, struggling to read it as the command vehicle pounded through the snow.

There were two approaches: from the south, which was where Jamie was pinned down; or from the north, the Prirečnyj road. It would mean a detour. He remembered a line from a lecture years ago, in his first weeks at Sandhurst: *'In tactics the longest way round is often the quickest way there.'*

'Got them, sir,' Corporal Willis's voice cracked over the intercom. He had switched the frequency.

Nick said: 'Hello, Two-One. This is Two. Sunray speaking. Over.'

No answer. Then Jamie's voice: 'Nick?'

Nick abandoned radio procedure.

'Jamie, we're on our way. How many are they?'

'I don't know. I'd guess ten, maybe more. One light machine-gun. The rest semi-automatic.'

'OK. Now, listen. I'll need you to keep them occupied. Five minutes from now, open up with everything you've got. I'm telling Hoddinot to do the same.'

'Roger. But for Christ's sake . . .'

There was silence.

'Jamie! Two-One, this is Two. Acknowledge. Over.'

Silence. Nick flicked to intercom and yelled, 'Keep trying,' then grabbed the map.

* * *

Now he was breaking every rule in the book. No flank guards, no secure start-line, just a map recce and radio briefing.

He led the way in the command vehicle, working his way round a hill spur, keeping to low land on a route that kept him out of sight of the farm but dangerously exposed him to ambush from the higher ground. (They all knew the drill if ambushed – they'd practised it often enough. Go straight for the enemy, firing with everything you've got. Virtual suicide, but better than waiting to be picked off.)

His chosen assault position was a slight depression north of the Prirečnyj road, on the opposite side of the farm to where Jamie's group was pinned down. Eight minutes after first contact he reached the position, and LodeStar confirmed it. The driver slewed the command vehicle to a halt as Nick stood in the turret, pointing with both arms in the direction of assault. The other vehicles deployed on either side of him.

They would burst over the crest in line; there would be fifty metres of open ground sloping to the east, then they would be in among the farm buildings.

He flicked to intercom. 'Anything?'

'Nothing, sir,' said Corporal Willis.

Nick flicked back to Jamie's frequency.

'Two-One, this is Two. Acknowledge.'

Nothing. But from over the crest came the sound of rapid gunfire that, with luck, would have covered the sound of their approach.

He jumped down from the turret and sprinted up the slope, crouching as he neared the top, throwing himself on

131

his belly in the snow. Sergeant Doran followed him. Behind them, men were spilling out of the back of vehicles, strapping on skis, shaking out into formation, readying weapons.

The farm lay across the road, only the upper storey of its buildings visible.

Doran turned and waved for the section corporals to join them.

When they arrived Nick said: 'We're going straight in. One Section clears the building to the left, Two Section the building on the right. Three Section and Company HQ will go firm at the farm entrance, and push on when the flanks are clear. I'll be in the centre; take your pace and direction from me. Questions?'

There were no questions. Nick clicked his safety-catch to automatic.

'Let's get on with it.'

They went in behind a wall of fire: four machine-guns hammering out a thousand rounds a minute; a line of riflemen pumping bullets through every window and doorway; the farm swept by a blizzard of tracer that smacked into woodwork, ripped through thatch, and ricocheted high into the air. Men tore across the open land. Nick saw a flash of khaki in a gap through the buildings. Twenty metres to go. Ahead, to his left, three men from One Section reached their target building and threw themselves against it. He led his men into the yard, swerving in surprise as he came across a huge tracked military vehicle. He reached the central building, flattened himself against the wall, and glanced back at the ground they had crossed. Not a man was down.

Now only the Snow Leopards were in the open, wheeling slowly, gleaming black-and-cream killers hosing the farm with their turret guns.

Above him a shutter opened and was smashed back against the wall by the force of fire directed at it. Beside him Lance-Corporal Kelly, a Company HQ signaller, pulled a grenade from his ammo pouch and started to edge along the wall towards the opening. His arm was half raised, fingers on the pin, when a blue and white striped shirt was dangled over the window-sill, and a voice from within shouted loudly, incomprehensibly, but with obvious anger and indignation.

'Cease firing,' said Nick.

'Ready! Move! Clear!'

The shouts echoed round the stillness of the yard as soldiers covered each other through the barns and outhouses. It was all done with practised ease. How many barns in south Armagh had they been through, Nick wondered; how many backstreets in Belfast?

He felt lightheaded with relief.

He had thought there were a dozen men in the farm, at most, and guessed they would be frightened conscripts on the run.

Before him twenty-two men were lying in the snow, face down, hands behind their heads, loaded rifles pointing at their backs; and they were not conscripts but Russian naval infantry, members of the 'Black Berets', armed to

133

the teeth with AKM assault rifles, Dragunov sniper rifles, four RPK machine-guns, while each of their two BTR-70PB amphibious assault vehicles was equipped with a 7.62mm anti-tank gun.

'Bloody hell, sir,' said Sergeant Doran, looking at the BTR assault vehicles and the pile of weapons, 'Father Christmas came early for these lads. Good job they were all pissed.'

Nick looked at the machine-guns, then at the anti-tank guns, thinking what would have happened had the Russians used them against Jamie's Snow Leopard, or against his own vehicles.

Jamie was alive. His personal radio had been smashed by a bullet while he was still speaking to Nick.

He and Childs had been discovered in their snow-hole by Hoddinot and the flank patrol, their ammo exhausted, their heads down. Sykes had taken longer to find. He had practically buried himself.

Now Jamie was sitting hunched in the back of a Snow Leopard, watching Brigite dress Childs's wounded leg, trying to look useful. He looked up warily as Nick approached.

Nick spoke to Brigite: 'How is he, then?'

'I'll take the bullet out later. He'll be OK.'

Nick wondered if she was saying it for Childs's benefit, then thought not. If Childs was dying, Major Sendlinger would no doubt tell him so in the same brisk tone.

'Well, Childs, how do you feel?' said Nick, knowing it was a stupid question, but knowing it had to be asked.

'Hurts like fuck, sir,' said Childs, then added: 'Sorry, ma'am.'

'Don't say sorry to me,' said Brigite, turning to Nick. 'The Russians – how long do you plan to keep them lying in the snow? If it's part of the masterplan to give them frostbite, fine, but I've enough problems myself at the moment . . .'

'They'll be moved inside as soon as all the other buildings are clear,' said Nick. 'Just as soon as I've got somebody free to look after them.'

Jamie was looking up at him blankly. Nick looked at him for a moment, then said: 'I'd like a word.'

He moved away. Jamie got out of the vehicle and followed him.

'Of all the stupid fuckers,' said Nick quietly, 'in the stupid fucking army . . .'

Jamie was pale and still.

'OK, get those men inside. Get Sar'nt Doran and One Section to help you.'

'Yes, of course.'

Jamie tried to run, but stumbled. His sweat must have frozen inside his clothes. He had been coming to the end of a two-hour flank patrol when he first spotted the Russian family. By now he must be exhausted.

Well, there you go, that's life in the army, thought Nick. Tough shit.

Brigite said: 'I need to talk to you about Erike.'

He stayed with her while she finished with Childs. The rest of the convoy was moving slowly up past the frozen stream towards the farm, the SAS vehicle in the lead, Munro standing in the turret looking at the BTR-70PB amphibious vehicles with bulging eyes. He jumped down and walked over to them.

'Dear God, how did they get those here? Whose are they?'

'Russian marines,' said Nick.

'You didn't tangle with them, did you?'

'They tangled with us. Two dead.' He turned to Brigite. 'If you want to have another look at Erike, then we can talk.'

She nodded and moved away. Munro was staring at the corner of the farmyard, where men were rolling two bodies on to a canvas tarpaulin.

'No casualties on our side,' said Nick. 'Oh – except for a soldier who caught a spent bullet in his leg, and Jamie who bruised his wrist.'

Munro said: 'If this is what you're like on a Save the Children jaunt, what are you like when you turn nasty?'

'I'd be grateful if you would talk to the prisoners. I assume interrogation's in your line.'

'We don't say interrogation,' said Munro. 'We say aggressive military interviewing.'

'Either way, I'd like to know what conditions are like between here and Verchnetulomskij. And I'd like to know why they fired on my men.'

He walked out into the middle of the yard. Staff Beckwith was forming the Snow Leopards into a vehicle park of two orderly lines. The ambulance took its place on the end of one. As Staff Beckwith passed his finger across his throat, the drivers cut their engines, one by one.

Silence reclaimed the farmyard.

Brigite had gone to the ambulance and opened the rear door, and was now leaning in to talk to Anneliese. As Nick walked over to join her, he saw Anneliese's pale, anxious face, and a solemn Sergeant Worembrand, who had taken off his sky-blue and magenta parka, and placed it over the prone figure of Erike.

Brigite turned and said briskly:

'I need four men and a stretcher, and I need them quickly.'

THREE

When she had left the GDR army nursing corps, she was
out of work for one year and eight months, and was living
alone in Dresden, thirty-six years old, divorced, with a
teenage son in Berlin ('a wide boy' she said, half sad, half
apologetic), and she had no real friends, though she did
have a small black-and-white cat called Carl ('That's
nice,' said Anneliese, wondering who was looking after
Carl now) and one or two acquaintances she liked to meet
for coffee and *Kuchen* in the afternoons.

Then she saw the job in Mončegorsk advertised by the
St Petersburg EC Commission, and she applied and secured
a three-month contract (what happened to Carl then?
wondered Anneliese, but said nothing) and she was quite
cheerful for a while, even when the contract was over and
she was out of work again in Dresden. The world will
always need nurses, she told herself; but she knew, really,
that the world did not need ex-GDR medical corps nurses
who had trained at the KGB Second Directorate hospital
at Minsk.

'Did you really?' asked Anneliese, startled. 'The KGB?'
She had been sponsored! It was quite an honour at the

139

time. She and another nurse, her friend Caroline (now married to a farmer at Wernigerode in the Harz Mountains) had both been sponsored, just like the KGB sponsored the Moscow Dynamos football team. 'We're the Dresden Dynamos,' Caroline had joked.

There had been nothing sinister!

KGB Second Directorate operatives and their wives and children got bronchial flu and suffered from hernias and developed cancer in the same proportion to the rest of the human race; wasn't anybody supposed to treat them?

Was Erike to suffer because she cared for sick men and women without questioning their politics?

'I haven't really thought about it,' said Anneliese truthfully, 'but no, of course you shouldn't suffer.'

'No,' said Erike.

But she believed her name was now on a Stasi file deep in the Normanstrasse complex in Berlin, and that that was why the only nursing job she could get was occasional, low-paid temporary work at a private Warsaw clinic – and she found Poland a terrible place.

'Please try to relax,' said Anneliese, holding her hot, puffy hand. 'Everything's going to be all right.'

She had been lying in bed in her flat in Dresden on that previous Saturday afternoon, with a dull aching pain in her stomach, wondering if she had the energy to get up and go to her doctor (she had joined the AOK health scheme, and managed to keep up the payments), when the police came and said the Luftwaffe had a special job for her.

'Oh, Erike,' said Anneliese, meaning: why had she not told the Luftwaffe she was ill; why had she lied?

A tear formed in the corner of Erike's eye. Her world was not the sort of world a girl like Anneliese could know about: the poverty-stricken wards of eastern Europe, where patients had to supply their own bandages and bedsheets, and penicillin was rationed, and the food abysmal, and non-surgical equipment dirty, and hot water a luxury.

Nobody had ever equipped Erike for life by providing a rich boyfriend, or training in the Luftwaffe Field Hospital, Hanover. Nobody had ever offered her a six-week all-weather survival course with the Royal Marines in Scotland.

She gripped Anneliese's hand, and moaned softly, despite herself.

In the next room, where a hoarfrost of cabin sweat covered the walls, and metal brackets in the timber structure were bright orange with rust, Brigite said to Nick: 'We can't leave her here. It's out of the question.'

'In that case you'll have to operate,' said Nick, who had spoken at length to ACE Mobile Force HQ.

'Let me explain. The appendix could burst at any moment. The risk of peritonitis is acute. I have no proper surgical experience. The equipment here is a battlefield surgical kit, which means a knife, a large selection of clamps, and a pair of forceps, and I have no anaesthetist or skilled assistance.'

'Can't you treat it with antibiotics?'

'We are way, way beyond treating this with antibiotics. There's no choice here. She's got to be lifted out by helicopter.'

A soldier brought in a pressure lamp to replace the

battery light. Weird shadows were thrown against the walls. The smudges under Brigite's eyes were like bruises.

'Christ,' said Nick wearily, 'what a shambles.'

'I'd rather not go into that now, interesting though your views on my powers of observation might be. Just get me a helicopter, or Erike is very likely to die.'

Anneliese sat by Erike, still holding her hand. There was a smell of cow dung and rotting linoleum. Two stoves burned, but it was still well below freezing. It was five minutes to midnight.

Brigite went quietly to Erike's side, knelt down, and said gently: 'How are you feeling? All right?'

Erike nodded and smiled.

'If the pain gets impossible say so – but I'm frightened of giving you too many drugs, just in case . . .'

In case she had to operate.

Erike's system was already coping with a frightening amount of anti-flu vaccine. She had been methodically dosing herself to suppress the symptoms of her illness.

Why had nobody seen her do it?

Because nobody had cared about Erike, even though she looked sick and hardly spoke. Because Brigite herself had been obsessed with her own personal problems.

'I felt her abdomen a moment ago,' said Anneliese quietly, looking at Brigite with serious eyes.

Brigite took her hand from its glove and slipped it under the covers. They had sliced open two army sleeping bags to make a warm double duvet; the ambulance's heated thermal bag had been too restricting. Erike's abdomen was distended and hot. She groaned and moved as Brigite lightly touched her.

Anneliese said: 'Can I go for a little while? I ought to look at Childs.'

Brigite nodded. When Anneliese had gone she held Erike's hand. Nine hours to dawn, but if she got through the night, a helicopter could get her into a Norwegian hospital inside thirty minutes.

It was the only sane thing to do.

Men were sleeping everywhere, two-thirds of the company resting, the other third on sentry duty surrounding the farm and positioned on the high ground to the north-east. In a corner of the main living-room, which was empty of furniture, the Russian marines having burned it all, Jamie's refugee family was asleep, well stuffed – as Staff Beckwith put it – on army rations, and now tucked up in the unbelievable luxury of army sleeping bags.

Childs was lying on his back, snoring. Anneliese felt his forehead, which was cool. His eyes opened, but then closed without sign of recognition. She decided to let him sleep, and went quietly through into the next room.

In the corner, Jamie was sitting upright in his dossbag, hugging his knees, his face lit by the flickering yellow-blue flame of a stove.

'Well, hi,' she said quietly, picking her way through the sleeping bodies.

'Hello,' said Jamie, not taking his eyes off the flame. A boy, she thought, going through the worst night of his life.

143

She sat beside him, on the end of his dossbag, and warmed her hands.

'You waiting to go on stag?'

He shook his head.

She fumbled in her pocket and said, casually, 'I can't sleep. I'm going to take a pill. Do you want one?'

'No thanks.'

'Just a mild tranquilliser. You're bound to be a bit stressed. It's not every day you're shot at.'

'It's all part of the job.'

They both knew that for Jamie it had never happened before.

'Does anybody know why they opened fire?'

Jamie's face tensed.

'Sorry. I don't suppose it matters.'

After a moment Jamie said: 'They thought we were Russian special forces rounding up deserters.'

Beside him was a mug of tea. He picked it up and raised it to his lips, then, remembering his manners, offered it to her.

'Thanks.'

His hand was shaking slightly. She pretended not to notice. The tea was cold and unbearably sweet. How could the English drink this stuff?

'That's great,' she said, handing him the cup. 'Well, anyway, I heard people say you were very brave going up like that.'

'*Stupid*. I think you'll find stupid's the word you're looking for.'

'I don't think so.' She took two pills out and passed him

one, placing it on his sleeping bag. 'I've broken them out of the packet now. You might change your mind.'

He nodded and managed a smile. 'I might. Thanks.'

'Hey, cheer up.'

She leaned over and kissed him on his cheek.

'What was that for?'

'I don't know.'

She didn't either. She stood up, confused.

'Bye.'

'I'm starting to feel better. Another one like that might help.'

'Bye, Jamie.'

On her way, she passed over Worembrand, whose body was curved banana-like round the room's black cast-iron stove, his tartan scarf snug round his neck. For someone who dozed all through the day, he had a remarkable ability to sleep through the night.

'How's Childs?'

Nick was standing in the doorway.

'He's OK. He's fine. He's a calm sort of guy.'

She left. Nick crossed to the stove. He took two paper cups from the box marked '*Choc 200 units*' and poured water into them, then crouched down next to Jamie, passing him a cup.

'This is what you call service,' said Jamie bravely.

'Sorry I'm not a beautiful blonde blue-eyed nurse.'

'She's an enemy agent. She tried to give me a knock-out pill.'

'That's how they get their way with young soldiers.'

Jamie smiled tensely.

Nick said: 'You were a bloody fool, but in the end you did well. You kept your head and you looked after Childs.'

Jamie looked up sharply.

'Just put it behind you. Learn from your mistakes.'

'It's no good. I was terrified. Childs was the one who stayed calm . . .'

'Childs has been there before. He was in Northern Ireland with Wallace, when Wallace was hit in the chest. He spent three months in Kurdistan last winter. God only knows how many dead bodies he saw out there. As far as I'm concerned, it's over; it's in the past. OK?'

Jamie nodded. 'Thanks.'

'How's your wrist?'

'Just bruised. It'll be all right.'

'I tried to get you the radio as a memento, but Corporal Willis wouldn't let me have it. "It's an accountable item, sir," he said, "even if it is fucked."'

Jamie smiled. 'I'll nick it when he's not looking.'

Nick said: 'Why don't you take the pill, get some sleep?'

'I'm going round the sentries at 02.00.'

'I'll go instead.'

'No.'

'All right, I'll go with you.'

A signaller appeared in the doorway, holding a folded yellow flimsy.

'Sir? Answer to that signal you sent half an hour ago.'

Nick found Collins and shook him awake. 'I want to use

146

the high-frequency set, and I want you on it.'

Collins muttered, 'Yes, sir,' and instantly slipped out of his dossbag and into his jacket and moonboots. He followed Nick out of the farm and across the yard to the command vehicle.

Sudden duty at any hour of the day or night was the downside to the privilege of being OC's signaller in Company HQ, a job generally regarded as dead cushy, tucked up all day long in the Snow Leopard's steamy fug or in the outer office at base, while other blokes were being beasted up and down hills by screaming NCOs. 'How's the OC's bum chum?' was the occasional sneer, but Collins had never been bothered. He was eighteen when he was chosen for a cadre run by signal platoon; selected for having above-average intelligence, a sense of responsibility and steadiness.

Two soldiers were on radio stag: Private Fowler on the high-frequency set, and Corporal Willis on the inter-company radio. A green light glowed on the maps pinned to the walls and on the fax machine, illuminating the notice: WARNING THIS MEANS IS NOT SECURE.

The high-frequency system operating via satellite allowed normal telephone conversation, automatically scrambled, moving its waveband every 1.3 seconds. It had a high-security rating.

Nick sent Private Fowler back into the farm, and Collins sat at the set, whistling gently through his teeth as he punched in the codes.

The fax machine started up: medical notes for Brigite, somebody at ACE HQ thinking of everything.

'Anything you might hear,' Nick said to Corporal Willis, 'is for your ears only.'

'Right, sir,' said Willis.

'Narvik, sir.' Collins passed the phone to Nick.

'Bloody hell,' said a voice half jocular, half irate, 'what time do you call this?'

'OC Matchmaker for duty officer ACE Command,' said Nick curtly.

'Sorry, sir,' said the voice, suddenly keen and alert.

Presumably he had been expecting a call from one of his chums, a gossip to while away the dead hours of the night. These days, ACE Mobile Force Narvik was a sleepy backwater. All the glamour was down in the Baltic with the units watching Third Shock Army on the Latvian border.

Nick could see Brigite crossing the yard from the farm building.

'Duty officer,' said a voice. 'Hello, Matchmaker.'

'I received a signal five minutes ago. I want to talk about it.'

'The officer who sent it has gone to bed. You want me to wake him?'

'Yes,' said Nick with some satisfaction. In Narvik's overheated, highly-polished HQ quarters a lieutenant-colonel (with any luck) would soon be hopping out of bed and hurrying down the corridor, trying to collect his wits.

Brigite opened the door and climbed in next to Collins.

Nick said: 'There's a fax for you.'

She reached over and took the sheets that were still feeding themselves out of the machine.

'Hello, Matchmaker.' The voice was curt.

'Narvik, reference your message of 00.30.'

'Yes.'

'Leaving the casualty here is not an option. The best option is a helicopter evacuation at dawn. We are preparing a landing pad now. The only other option is an emergency operation. We do not have facilities. I strongly request a helicopter casevac for Nurse Schmidt.'

'Met forecast makes a heli-lift impossible, as you've already been told, Matchmaker . . .'

'Bullshit. I've got the met forecast. I've seen it on CNN television, for Christ's sake. I need a helicopter. If you have to get Russian permission, get Russian permission, but *do* something because we are not prepared to attempt a serious operation under primitive conditions because of idle sods who won't get their fucking finger out.'

There was a pause, then the voice in Narvik spoke slowly, as if deliberately trying to sober Nick by implying a controlled rage.

'Your orders were clear. Your objective is the hospital at Mončegorsk, and you are already a full day behind schedule. We have no authorisation to send a military helicopter over the Murmansk Oblast Military District.'

'Get authorisation. Work at it. Get a civvy chopper,' said Nick. 'Get a Russian chopper, if you like, but get one here at first light tomorrow.'

'Standby for call from NATO Northern Command Chief of Staff in approximately three minutes.'

The line went dead.

'Wow,' said Brigite quietly.

Outside, a group of white figures drifted in from the dark, returning from sentry positions.

'Two-Two alpha in position,' said a voice through the inter-company radio. 'Roger, Two-Two alpha,' said Willis, studiously pretending not to have heard Nick's conversation.

Brigite's fingers idly rested on the stereo pad, and Madonna's voice suddenly filled the vehicle, singing 'Like a Virgin'.

'Oh God, I'm sorry,' said Brigite.

Nick pressed the pad and there was silence.

'Didn't quite catch that, Two,' said a facetious voice on the inter-company radio. 'Am I being crooned?'

'Don't worry, Two-Two alpha,' said Willis in a bored voice.

Nick remembered, for no reason, that one of Jamie's refugees, the girl, had been wearing a *Madonna in Moscow* badge.

'Chief of Staff,' pondered Brigite. 'I think you're in trouble.'

'I don't give a shit,' said Nick, who at this particular moment didn't.

There was a tap on the window. It was Munro. Willis opened the door and he squeezed in next to Brigite.

'We're trying to raise a chopper,' said Nick.

'How about shoving your earphones on for a minute, lads?' asked Munro with a foxy grin. After a quick look at Nick, Willis and Collins put earphones on, and bent over their radio sets.

Munro said quietly: 'They're not going to send a chopper. It's not going to happen. You can scream and you can shout, but you're just wasting time.'

'I'd rather you didn't tell my blokes what to do,' said Nick. 'It was your idea to ponce around incognito, but let's try and keep to it now it's established, shall we?'

'We have to move at daybreak.'

'Wake me before you go. I'd hate not to say goodbye.'

'The convoy has to move, Nick.'

'The convoy moves when I say it moves.'

'I've been talking to my people . . .'

'Well, that was bloody stupid for a start. If traffic's being monitored, they're going to wonder why a hospital resupply mission needs two high-frequency sets in operation.'

'We're behind schedule. You're wasting time, and time is the one thing we haven't got.'

Nick leaned past him and opened the door. 'I'll talk to you later. Now bugger off.'

Brigite was looking from one to the other.

'I don't understand this. Have you got some sort of a message?' she asked Munro.

Munro gave her an irate look and left. Willis slammed the door closed. A voice spoke on the high-frequency speaker.

'Hello, Matchmaker.'

'Narvik, sir,' said Collins, passing the phone.

The duty officer said, 'Brigadier Grenfell,' announcing the Chief of Staff, C-in-C NATO Forces Northern Europe, in a voice that silently included the query: will this do for you?

'Nick?' said Grenfell.

'Sir.'

Nick spoke, his eyes on Brigite who stared out of the cab, her face strained.

Grenfell listened in silence. When Nick had finished he said: 'I won't quarrel with your assessment. But you know that we cannot send helicopters into Karelia. If we had been able to do so, there would have been no reason to send you. This situation will not change in the next thirty-six hours. You can either detach two vehicles to return Miss Schmidt to Norway, or you can leave her in the farm with whatever medical support she needs, and we will send a medical team overland from Finland via Nyrud, starting at dawn.'

'She'll probably be dead when you get here,' said Nick. 'Dr Sendlinger believes her condition critical. Do you want to talk to her?'

'No. I'm sorry. You must do the best you can. And you *must* get moving. You are now twenty-four hours behind schedule.'

'If she dies because you failed to send a helicopter 50k, at a time when NATO planes are virtually operating a non-stop airlift into Petersburg, it will be for you to explain.'

'Your comment is noted. Anything else?'

'No,' said Nick.

Grenfell, when touring army units, had a reputation for descending on private soldiers and asking keenly, 'Enough bogs, are there?' thereby showing himself in touch with the needs of the common soldier, even if he himself carried a fieldmarshal's lavatory roll in his knapsack. Nick half expected the question now, but Grenfell simply said: 'Good luck.'

They had moved outside, away from Collins and Willis. Below, over the frozen stream, on the water meadow where cows grazed in the short summer months, two Snow Leopards were slowly marking out an emergency helicopter landing pad: a huge figure H illuminated by the light of naphtha flares, bordered by stones heaved out of the frozen stream.

In two years, a new family would move into the farm and find the same stones lying on the green pasture when the snows melted; and they would wonder what ancient symbolism these might represent.

Munro was watching the men working with the Snow Leopards. 'They're wasting their time,' he said. 'You should call them in.'

'I just have,' said Nick. 'Let's tidy a few things up.' He turned to Brigite. 'Major Munro has a job to do that is quite separate from ours.'

'*Major*,' said Brigite, 'did you say *Major*?'

'Don't worry about it,' said Munro. 'Let's just get on with this, shall we?'

'You said you were an ordinary soldier. You said you were a satellite communication expert. What the fuck's going on?'

'Major Munro,' said Nick, 'represents a special unit.'

'What special unit?'

'Anything you like,' said Munro, exasperated. 'GSG 9, *Fernspähkompanie . . .*'

'GSG 9 is police antiterrorism . . .'

'That's it: police antiterrorist,' said Munro. 'You're with us at last. I'm antiterrorist, there's no chopper coming, and God knows what you're doing telling all this to a bloody foreign reservist, Nick . . .'

'Now, hang on a minute,' began Brigite.

'And what, in your view, George, are foreign reservists for?' asked Nick. 'Screwing?'

'Now excuse me,' said Brigite. 'Excuse me for just one mo-ment . . .'

'No time,' said Munro, 'we've got no time. If you're going to operate on Nurse Schmidt, my sergeant will help you. Sergeant Noon has trained in a Herefordshire hospital. He is particularly good with small children, or so he tells me.'

Brigite chose the scullery, a small room with an ancient stone sink and only one door which was now swathed in blankets to keep in the warmth. REME rigged two lighting systems, one operating on battery, the other from a Snow Leopard parked outside the window.

'What can I do?' asked Nick, helplessly.

'Go away,' said Brigite. 'Please, I'm not being rude, but just go away.'

Sergeant Noon helped Anneliese to prepare the operating table. She found him polite, efficient and reassuring. 'Bit of a bugger this,' he said once, and, 'Still, all in a day's work,' at another point.

'We've decided we might as well operate,' Brigite told Erike, who had been carried through from the bedroom so slowly and so carefully that she seemed unaware that she had been moved. 'It's simple and straightforward, and we'll have you tucked up in a Norwegian hospital before you know it.'

Erike was already drifting into a coma. Brigite gave her 0.5g of D-Pentzadryn and felt her tense, rigid muscles relax. At the same time, her facial muscles slackened and a dreamy look fell like a curtain over her eyes.

No more worries for a little while, thought Anneliese; no more cares.

'There's folk pay a lot of money to be where she is now,' said Sergeant Noon. D-Pentzadryn was the happy drug: the latest discovery on the Zurich drug scene.

'Right, let's get on with it,' said Brigite. 'I'm afraid she'll have a scar on her tummy after this. I've no laser. I'm not one of these shit-clever surgeons who can work through a three-centimetre cut.' Her voice shook slightly.

'Hey, come on,' said Anneliese and, on an impulse, put her arms round Brigite and gave her a hug.

On her other side Sergeant Noon said again that it was a bit of a bugger, in a husky voice, looking at her sidelong, perhaps hoping that hugs all round were an accepted ritual in German operating theatres.

Anneliese folded back the white cotton sheet. Revealed under the blue-white halogen light, Erike's stomach was distended, tight as a drum. From outside came the steady purr of the Snow Leopard's engine. Brigite referred again to the surgical notes faxed from Narvik, then gently started to outline the incision mark in blue pencil.

* * *

Out on the hill, as Nick and Jamie were inspecting the sentry lines, they came across a fox trap, a black wooden box standing stark in the moonlight, baited with bits of dead bird, the remains of a crow with the breasts cut out.

Crow pie was bitter and unpleasant to taste, Nick had always been told in his youth on the Welsh Marches, not worth bothering about; although sometimes it would be cooked by an obliging pub landlady after a crow shoot, just the tenderest bits of breast with a large amount of diced fat bacon and chunks of pheasant or pigeon.

He had a sudden memory of a Sunday lunchtime in a pub near Leintwardine, with the old crowd he had gone round with as a teenager – solicitors' daughters from Ludlow, young farmers driving old MGB sportscars . . . drinking pints of Bass after a morning shooting crows in Hasslett Woods.

That had been the day he drove Emma home, and her parents were out for the afternoon, and Emma had turned the central heating up to full, and they had gone to bed for the first time: him, Emma, and three hot-water bottles, she being obsessed by the cold.

'All right, Leech?' said Jamie, as they came upon a squat white snowman in the lee of a rock, only the eyes visible between his khaki headover and the low peak of his quilted hat.

'Sir,' said Leech.

'No more ghostly skiers?'

'Not yet, sir.'

'Drop of something in your coffee?' said Nick – and Leech, with speed, produced a lurid plastic thermos and unscrewed the top. Nick poured in about two fingers of whisky.

From here they could see a distant flicker of light: Prirečnyj, perhaps, or an outlying farm settlement. Presumably the Niva River Hydro-Electric plant was still functioning, even if the oil-fired stations were closed. He looked east towards Mončegorsk, but the land was dark.

'Your chum Sykes enjoy the excitement?' Jamie was asking, his voice unnaturally casual. Nick felt a mixture of sympathy and annoyance. Jamie was trying to find out what the soldiers thought of him: whether their confidence in him was now as low as his confidence in himself.

'Not much bothers Sykes, sir,' said Leech unhelpfully, giving nothing away.

By the time of the main assault, Sykes had burrowed down through five feet of snow; another ten minutes, according to platoon wags, and he would have been through the permafrost and halfway to Australia.

Nick warned Leech there might be foxes about, told him about the trap. 'Early winter – this is the time of the runners: young foxes out on their own.'

'Oh yes, sir?' said Leech, a Wolverhampton man who cared nothing for wildlife.

They turned back towards the farm.

'I was looking in one of the barns,' said Jamie. 'There's a box with crow feathers in it and a pair of gloves. I wondered what it was for.'

'To use when they're baiting the trap, so they won't leave any human scent,' said Nick, still thinking about his Shropshire days.

He had gone out with Emma for six years, all through university, all through Sandhurst and his first two years in Germany. Then she had written a little note inside his birthday card, a variation of the '*I think this is the hardest letter I have ever had to write . . .*'

Not that she didn't love him, but waiting six years for a chap was enough, really, flesh being flesh and blood being blood, and Emma not getting any younger. (In fact she was twenty-two he recalled.)

He had last seen her at the Green Dragon in Shrewsbury, about nine months ago: he dropping in for a solitary beer; she emerging from a hunt ball in the Conference Suite, running across the courtyard in the rain, bursting into the lobby in a fetching low-cut dress, a raindrop coursing down her cleavage, a thin little bastard of a Ludlow estate agent in a Burton's dinner-jacket oiling his way after her with a Kleenex.

'Nick, oh my God,' she had said, startled, wide-eyed, a hand over her bosom, and then had kissed him on both cheeks, a depressing embrace at the best of times . . .

They clambered down the rocks, back to the farm. 'I'm not trying to excuse myself, but there is something else to bear in mind, I suppose,' said Jamie, who had his own preoccupations. 'If I hadn't tried to check the farm, the Russian family we rescued would have been dead now. There was no way those soldiers would have taken them in.'

He was probably right. God only knew what had happened to the original owners of the farm. Questioned by Munro and Fuller, the marines claimed they had found the place deserted, but it hardly seemed likely, not with a dozen cows busy munching silage in the byre.

They reached the bottom of the path and crossed the yard. Robbo was standing outside the farmhouse door.

'Bad news about the nurse,' he said. 'I thought I'd warn you.'

FOUR

Near Prirečnyj, 29 October

Nobody could be blamed: not even Narvik. A helicopter at dawn would almost certainly have been too late. A helicopter the previous afternoon, when she first started to vomit, could perhaps have taken her to a Norwegian hospital in time; but at that moment Jamie had been under fire, and all the column's attention had been on his rescue.

Erike herself could be blamed, of course.

A Luftwaffe personnel officer staring at a computer screen must have hesitated originally over her name, looked at her qualifications, her experience at Mončegorsk, her almost perfect Russian, her repeated applications for the Luftwaffe, and decided to give her a chance.

Erike was the one who had muffed it.

Nick said to Collins, 'Get me Narvik,' and used a pencil torch to study the map on the wall of the command vehicle, while he waited.

'Narvik, sir,' said Collins.

'This is OC Matchmaker, I want to talk to the Chief of Staff.'

'You want him now?' said the duty officer carefully. It

was just after four-thirty in the morning.

'I want him now.'

'Hold on, Matchmaker.'

Nick wondered briefly why HQ NATO Northern Command had moved from Kolsaas to ACE HQ at Narvik. No matter: it meant he could rouse senior staff officers from their pits.

In the green glow from the machines, Collins sat immobile. Another signaller had taken over from Willis on the inter-company radio. Outside, a face appeared at the rear window. The signaller pushed open the door and Anneliese climbed in.

'A fax,' she said. 'It's official and it's urgent.'

The signaller hesitated.

'The major will have to look at it,' he said. Anneliese nodded. The signaller passed Nick the sheet of paper. The high-frequency set hissed.

'Duty officer to Matchmaker; he's just coming.'

'Thank you, Narvik,' said Collins.

Nick glanced at the fax, then passed it to the signaller. 'He must think a lot of you,' he said, 'to go to Dresden for a cat.'

'Perhaps I'm testing him,' said Anneliese. She smiled, sadly, and left.

'Hello, Matchmaker.'

The Chief of Staff did not like being roused from his bed, first at one am, when he had only just entered it, and then again at three am as he was in his deep and properly restful sleep.

'I thought you'd like to know,' said Nick, 'that

Nurse Erike Schmidt died at 02.40.'

There was a slight pause.

'Thank you for telling me. I'm sorry.'

'She started to recover consciousness during the operation. Dr Sendlinger was forced to inject a further dose of D-Pentzadryn, and her heart simply stopped beating. We had no life-support system. There was nothing that could be done.'

Another pause, then: 'I've no doubt Dr Sendlinger did everything she could.'

'You will inform the Luftwaffe.' It was not a request. There was a pause.

'Of course.'

'We are leaving here at dawn. We will drop the refugee family at the next settlement.'

'And the naval infantry?'

'We can chuck them out or leave them here. You've seen the report. They've got no officers or NCOs.'

'Suit yourself.'

'We'll leave them. Somebody has to look after the cows. We will be in Mončegorsk tomorrow as per schedule.'

'That's not possible. We are now estimating your arrival as noon Sunday.'

'Tomorrow,' said Nick, 'a bottle of malt says tomorrow as per schedule.'

There was another pause.

'Glenmorangie?' said Brigadier Grenfell.

'If you like,' said Nick.

FIVE

Nick was looking out over the ice, a lake the size of an English county, indistinguishable from the land except that it was as flat as a billiard table and marginally colder.

It was beautiful, clean, and empty. A white and crystal wilderness that merged on the northern horizon into a sky that still, two hours after dawn, held a moon and stars.

There was not a sound. Small scattered puffs of vapour from the column behind him, cold air transformed by human breath, drifted silently over his head.

The swamp lakes of Verchnetulomskoje. The vastness of Russia.

Swinging round his binoculars he found the nearest point of the opposite shore, two kilometres away: a low swell of land dotted with dwarf larch trees and stunted firs.

Amongst the trees, digging into defensive positions now, would be Jamie's clearance patrol.

Halfway across the ice was a solitary figure, a small black shape in the early sunlight, tiny in the huge expanse of white, bending over – like an Eskimo fishing through an icehole.

This was Staff Beckwith, testing the ice's thickness with an auger.

'You can't do it. You won't be able to do it for another month.'

Munro had come down the slope behind him, moving silently over the snow, startling Nick – although by now Nick was used to the silent movement of the SAS.

Munro sounded resigned, but his voice held an underlying urgency, a tension. His face had always been lean and alert, the taut, healthy face of a man who exercised regularly and strictly controlled his intake of food and alcohol. Now it seemed as if an invisible hand had stretched the skin tight over the fleshless bones. Nick was reminded of a corporal in the Second Battalion who had developed a passion for long-distance running, and had worked and starved his body until he looked like a walking skeleton, his head cropped, his eyes sunken, his face permanently set in a forced, obsessive smile; his entire existence devoted to gaining the Combined Services running championship. He had finally collapsed during the Berlin marathon, Nick remembered, and been found unfit for service.

'It will save us the best part of a day,' said Nick. 'It's you I'm thinking about.'

'We're wasting time.'

'Well, we'll know soon enough.'

He turned and went back to the command vehicle, leaving Munro to stare out over the lake. Behind the command vehicle the rest of the column stretched back up the slope, like trucks waiting for a ferry.

Collins sat in the warm fug, the engine running to power the heater, playing a hand-held computer game, listening to Radio St Petersburg play a record about *Ded Moroz*, the Russian Santa Claus, sung by sugary-squeaky children's voices.

'And it's not even November,' said Collins. 'It gets worse every year, doesn't it, sir?'

Nick pulled out the maps, looking at them again, trying to find another answer.

North was Verchnetulomskij, a town in chaos, full of conscript sailors deserted from the Northern Surface Fleet. South, along the lake, lay their prescribed route, through open taiga, avoiding towns and villages.

Crossing the lake would shorten their journey by twenty kilometres. 'Lake crossings at Verchnetulomskoje are usually possible from the first week in December' said Nick's intelligence summary. They were a month too soon.

Through the windscreen he could see Sergeant Noon and Corporal Fuller joining Munro at the lake's edge. Perhaps they were planning to take a pulk and cross the lake on foot, leave the column, go about their business.

It would be one problem less if they did.

Staff Beckwith was skiing slowly back across the ice, but even through binoculars Nick could not tell anything from his expression. His face looked grave, as it always did when he was working. If he had not been a Methodist, he would have made a good poker player.

Nick opened a folder and took out two sheets of paper

faxed to him, during the night, from Bundeswehr archives in Berlin.

> We have started pig rearing! And vegetable growing! Yes, even inside the Arctic this is possible. We have found a way to make greenhouse glass out of parchment paper soaked in codliver oil. We do very well for rations – pork and sauerkraut on Monday, rice soup with beef today, and we get five cigarettes a day per man and chocolate once a week. Even our skis are the best Norwegian type, with Kandahar bindings. So don't worry, eh? We are at a new station – I can't tell you where, but I'm picking up Radio Eismeersender again, if you want to ask for a record for me – and I'm away from those swamps now. We surprised the Russians by crossing a frozen lake – the entire company with heavy vehicles and guns. The Finns are good soldiers and know all the tricks, so it is as well they are on our side in this little show.

Nick stopped reading. The Bundeswehr archivist had done a good job. And, yes, if the soldier writing home had been part of Sixth Mountain Division, which pulled back to Pečenga in the first week of November 1943 (which he was), then the lake they crossed must have been Verchnetulomskoje; and early winter 1943 had not been exceptionally cold in west Karelia, certainly no colder than this year . . .

But he could not be sure of the exact point at which they crossed.

And he could not know how lucky they might have been.

'What weight was a Second World War German oversnow troop-carrier?' he said abruptly.

'What type?' asked Collins evasively.

'Fuck knows,' said Nick, opening the cab door.

'I know those shits in Narvik get on your wick,' said Munro, 'but don't do it. It's not the prescribed route. We'll have Russkies swarming round. You'll lose your vehicles.'

'Not more than a couple,' said Nick. 'And if it's worth sacrificing a woman's life to get to Mončegorsk on time, George, it's worth a couple of vehicles.'

'Stupid,' said Munro, and then, as an afterthought, 'and sanctimonious.'

'Well, Staff?' said Nick, ignoring him.

Staff Beckwith came sliding the last few metres to the bank, bending down to release his skis. Sergeant Noon reached out a hand and tugged him up.

'Ten inches, sir,' he said. 'But I don't know about currents. The ice may be thinner in places. It depends if there's free-flowing water down there.'

Robbo had joined them on the bank. 'You look puffed, Dave,' he said. 'You ought to have got your skates on.'

Munro was doing a sum on a calculator. It was a complex equation involving vehicular weight, ice thickness and air temperature, that would give a reading in square centimetres of pressure.

'Nowhere near. You need 136 and this comes out at . . .'

'125,' said Nick, who had been doing similar sums in the cab for the last hour. 'Staff Beckwith!'

'Sir!'

'Mark out the route. Sar'nt-Major!'

'Sir!'

'Bring forward one of the fuel vehicles. I want everything unloaded – *everything*. I want that vehicle stripped down, and then I want REME to strip it down again, and I want it all done at the double.'

'Sir!'

First out were the jerrycans, spare track, shovels, haversacks and ammunition boxes, machine-gun, LodeStar equipment and vehicle spares. Then integrated lights units were lifted out, and doors and passenger seats were stripped.

Then, with Nick travelling on top of the cab, Staff Beckwith slowly edged the vehicle out on to the ice.

Future vehicles would have only a driver, and would consequently be lighter by twelve stone; a safety factor, said Nick, providing a rational explanation for his determination to cross with the first vehicle.

Fifty metres to either side of them, parties of skiers trailed safety ropes.

'If it's got to go, let it go here,' Nick said to himself; in his head a vision of the evening of Austerlitz, with the Russian army fleeing across the Pratzen Lakes, redhot cannonballs breaking the ice, men and horses drowning in the freezing waters.

On the bank behind them, Brigite had come down from

the ambulance, a medical case in her hand, a soldier behind her carrying silverfoil insulation blankets.

They were a few metres from the shore. He called back, hardly needing to raise his voice. 'If we go in the water, how long have we got?'

'Ten, fifteen seconds,' said Brigite softly, her voice floating clearly over the ice. 'If the shock doesn't stop your heart beating instantly.'

'I just wondered,' said Nick.

He squirmed round on his stomach, looking down at the crystal snow surface in front of the vehicle, waiting for the first tell-tale creaking, the sudden crack as the chasm opened. Snow crunched gently. Its engine barely purring, the Snow Leopard crept over the surface of the lake.

Staff Beckwith called up: 'Halfway, sir.'

'Already? I don't believe it,' said Nick casually.

Suddenly, in a rush – although Staff Beckwith later swore he had maintained a steady speed – they were approaching the opposite bank, and Beckwith was changing gear as the tracks bit into thick snow.

Soldiers cheered; not only on the far bank, but above them in the larch trees – where men of Jamie's standing patrol must have been watching with interest when they ought, thought Nick, to have kept their eyes glued to the surrounding hills.

'What did I tell you, sir?' said Staff Beckwith. 'Piece of piss!'

Nick skied back across the lake. Brigite was still by the shore, watching, an unusually reflective look on her face.

171

'I think we'll be at Mončegorsk tomorrow, after all,' said Nick, pleased, climbing up the bank.

She smiled wearily. 'You've done very well.'

'How are you feeling?'

'All right.'

She turned away, scrambling back up the slope, back towards the medics' vehicle. He followed her.

'You're not blaming yourself about Erike?'

'No. There was nothing I could have done. I'm not a sentimental sort.'

'No,' Nicholas agreed.

She looked at him suspiciously, then said: 'Nicholas, tell me, do you always carry a prayerbook, I mean, is it *usual*?'

'Yes. Soldiers are people, they're not animals.'

They had buried Erike in a temporary grave – to await eventual return to Germany – on the hill above the farm, near to where the Russian naval infantry were quietly burying their own dead.

Five Platoon had been in attendance, as smart as they could manage in their camouflage whites; the body was stitched in a black tarpaulin. Two pressure lamps hissed. Nick had thought of Corunna and the Peninsular War, and another, earlier burial attended by the Royal Mercians.

> We buried him darkly at dead of night,
> The sods with our bayonets turning
> By the struggling moonbeam's misty light
> *And the lanthorn dimly burning.*

Nick read a shortened burial service.

'I know that my redeemer liveth, and that he shall stand at the latter day upon the earth. And though after my skin worms shall destroy this body . . .'

For worms read wolverines, thought Nick, as they piled stones over the snow grave.

Poor Erike, thought Anneliese, to die in the Arctic, with twenty soldiers officially summoned to mourn her passing, and be buried according to the rites of the Church of England – the most interesting thing, probably, that had ever happened to her.

Sergeant Worembrand was a worried man.

Tent stores and personal kit had been ground-loaded in taped-off areas, ready to be hauled over the ice to identical areas on the other side. Each vehicle was positioned to pass from its unloading bay to the lakeside, then cross the ice, then line up in the same order on the far bank, ready to be reloaded. From a distance it appeared as if the column was being looted; in fact it was a well-ordered exercise, the jumble of equipment already forming itself into sixteen orderly piles of kit.

But not Worembrand's kit.

While he had been tracking down coffee and shortbread fingers, his kit had been extracted and placed neatly to one side. He had promptly slung his camera cases back into the ambulance, but his personal goods remained: his aluminium cases, his Lufthansa travelbag, his dossbag, his duvet.

He looked round. Two soldiers passed, pulling a half-empty pulk.

'Right, you two,' he shouted with authority, 'over here!'

The soldiers stopped and looked at him. All three of them were aware that, although Worembrand held a sergeant's rank and wore a sergeant's stripes, he had never actually commanded anything. His rank was a recognition of his presumed skill as a photographer, not his qualities as a leader of men.

'Am I speaking Chinese?' Worembrand roared, recollecting a favourite phrase of barracks-square sergeants at Rheindahlen. 'Get this kit on that pulk.'

'Sorry, Sar'nt,' said the older of the two men, not looking noticeably sorry. 'We've Three Section's cooker and some jerrycans to go on here.'

'Never mind that,' said Worembrand, dismissing Three Section's cooker with a wave of his hand. 'You can come back for that. Just get this kit on.'

'Sar'nt Doran said we had to take the stove,' said the older man stubbornly. 'You have a word with Sar'nt Doran.'

'Sorry, Sar'nt,' said the other.

They skied off. Worembrand cursed under his breath. That was the trouble round here: everybody belonged to somebody else. It was useless asking Doran to help him. Doran wouldn't piss in Worembrand's ear if his brain was on fire.

'Sar'nt Worembrand!'

It was Staff Beckwith, walking up the line of vehicles, swinging Worembrand's camera cases, which were by no means light, round in the air. Oh dear God, thought Worembrand wearily, yearning, not for the first time, for his barstool next to the radiator in the Cherry-Ripe Club; a couple of large Bacardi and Cokes before a roast beef lunch in the sergeants' mess.

'These are yours, I believe.'

'Just my camera kit, Dave,' said Worembrand. 'It's vital for it to be protected from the snow, and it hardly weighs a feather.'

'See this?' said Beckwith, his hand groping in a camera case and pulling out a lens filter.

'I'd rather you didn't muck it about, to be honest, Dave . . .'

'This, Mal,' said Beckwith with emphasis, 'could be the straw that broke the camel's back. This small piece of equipment could be the difference between a safe crossing and a watery grave for some poor sod.'

He dropped the camera bags at Worembrand's feet and strode off.

Worembrand looked at his pile of gear, helplessly, then sighed and started slinging bags over his shoulders.

'You OK, Max, or do you want some help?'

It was Anneliese, she of the cornflower blue eyes and the champagne-coloured hair, the stunning good nature.

'Come on, let me help you.'

'What about *your* kit?' asked Worembrand.

'It's going on one of the pulks.'

That figured, he thought, but not bitterly; he knew the world, he knew the score. Had he been Miss Worembrand, nineteen years old with long legs and big breasts, there would have been a dozen slavering soldiers begging to look after his duvet and nightie.

'I offered to help the lads pull the pulk, but the sergeant wouldn't let me. You're all such gentlemen.'

'I should hope so,' said Worembrand, who had never been and never claimed to be a gentleman.

'Perhaps you could take that one, by your feet, and this one too.' A bag slid from his shoulder and thumped heavily into the snow.

'Golly gosh,' said Anneliese, a phrase picked up, bizarrely, from the Royal Marines, lifting the case with an effort. 'It's heavy enough.'

They toiled down through the thick snow on the lake's edge, and out on to the ice. After ten minutes a group of soldiers passed them, going the other way, larking about, leaping on and off a pulk that two of them were dragging, shouting to Anneliese, offering her a sledge ride. Worembrand eyed them sourly, then trudged on. Anneliese stopped for a rest.

'Max! Wait! I'm tired.'

He turned and trudged back a couple of metres, then thought better of it and dumped his bags down on the ice where he was. She joined him. Despite the cold, two thick trickles of sweat ran down either side of his face. She wondered why he wore so much clothing. Other people removed or added layers according to circumstances. Worembrand just added. Once he put something on, it stayed on.

'Max, can I ask you a question?' she said. 'Why did you join the army?'

He looked at her, puzzled.

'What do you mean?'

'It's just that you don't seem to enjoy the army very much.'

'This isn't the army!' he cried, bitterly, with a sweep of his hand dismissing everything from one horizon to the other. 'This lot . . . they're in the bloody Stone Age. Do you know what they were doing when I came from Germany?'

She shook her head, startled by his vehemence.

'Forming a committee to celebrate Inkerman! Sitting in the mess, planning a party!'

'What's Inkerman?'

'It's some battle, isn't it, hundreds of years ago: an almighty bloody cock-up like all the others. And they're going to celebrate it. We're on the verge of the twenty-first century, and they're celebrating Inkerman as if it was yesterday. They don't know, they don't *realise*, that the British Empire is dead and gone.'

As if Inkerman Day were a personal affront, Worembrand took up his bags and set off again towards the far shore. Anneliese took up her cases wearily, and followed him.

He was a funny sort of soldier, she decided; and if she was carrying the lightest of his bags, he must be stronger than he looked.

Fifteen vehicles and all the equipment were across; the rear party of three machine-gun groups were retreating down to the lake's edge.

The last Snow Leopard was poised on the bank, Syco in the driving seat, Leech reluctantly preparing to abandon the warm cab and ski across the lake behind him.

Leech, by tradition, always managed to be the fourth

man when there were only three shovels. It had been no surprise to Syco when he had turned up that morning as co-driver.

Now they could see the Snow Leopards on the far shore, lined up and loading up. As soon as the last vehicle reached the bank, Robbo would be after them: 'Come on, come on. You're keeping everybody waiting!' It was always the same in the army: rush to wait, and wait to rush.

'Here we go, I suppose,' Leech said, reluctant to move, dozy after three hours of warmth. 'I still reckon you made a big mistake.'

'Yeah, all right,' said Syco.

It was Leech's contention that when the nasties opened fire at the farm he, Sykes, ought to have dashed heroically forward, rifle firing from the hip, grenades lobbing in all directions, the West Mercian battlecry 'Inkerman!' on his lips.

'Now, I never said all that,' Leech reproved. 'I merely said you should have worked your way forward, done yourself a bit of good.'

'Worked my way forward?' exclaimed Syco. 'It was like fucking World War Three.'

'A bunch of jackers,' said Leech. 'They threw their handbags in as soon as 5 Platoon arrived. No, it was your big chance. You could have had the lot of them lined up against a wall and been standing there with a fag in your mouth when the OC turned up. Nobody would have mentioned courts martial then, would they? It would have been regimental honours and tea with the colonel's wife and your ugly mug in the bulletin. The trouble is you don't have the energy, Syco. You're too fucking lazy.'

Syco didn't reply. For Leech to preach on laziness was beyond everything. But, on the other hand, who better?

'Here we go, then. See you.'

Leech climbed out of the cab, where he had been slouched on the floor felting, and slammed the door.

The cab echoed oddly, stripped of half its equipment and seating. Outside, Lance-Corporal Holmes, in charge of the rear-bank party, motioned him forward down the slope.

Holmes eyed him coldly as he went past, a Rottweiler with one ambition: to get Sykes into clink; to get Sykes into Colly.

But he was not going to Colly – at least not until he had been back to Belfast and dealt with Ray from the Co-op. After that he didn't really care. They could do what they liked to him after that, he told himself, a look of set determination on his thin face, his thoughts a thousand miles away.

Clang!

The lead skier hit the back of the vehicle, to tell him they were ready. Syco edged his Snow Leopard down on to the ice, following in the tracks of vehicles that had gone before.

There was no warning. One moment he was moving slowly, peacefully, forward over a huge emptiness, in his imagination arguing with Karen over the fitted bedroom suite, forcing her to send it all back: he grim and dignified, she tearful and sorry. The next moment, there was a loud groan as a pressure ridge fell away, and the grinding of disintegrating ice, and the Snow Leopard was pitching slowly forward into blackness.

The slight buoyancy of the ice on which the vehicle rested gave him perhaps two seconds, by which time his door was open and he was out, and clutching wildly for the safety rope stretched across the top of the cab, his feet and legs suddenly seared with pain as the water closed over them.

The vehicle slid forward. His mittened hands found the rope, then lost it, then found it again as the vehicle fell from under him, and now he was in the water up to his chest, with one hand clutching the rope and his other hand scrabbling at the foot-thick ice plate, trying to gain a hold, his hands losing all feeling, all purchase power, his body slowly slipping back into the black water, then suddenly jerking upwards as a hand grabbed his combat jacket and another his hair and a voice shouted in his ear:

'No yer fucking don't!'

His eyes were blind with ice, the water in his clothes was freezing and cracking, his body, tugged by the rescue rope, was skimming and tumbling over the surface of the ice, his face was bloodied and stung with flying snow . . . until he came to rest at the feet of the rescue party, and lay there before them like a sightless, freshly-clubbed seal.

Lance-Corporal Holmes came staggering behind him, his lungs rasping for breath, his face triumphant. 'You're not going that way, you bastard! You're mine! I've signed for yer!'

* * *

He remembered nothing of being stripped naked and wrapped in thermal blankets, or carried on a pulk to the medics' Snow Leopard. But he remembered the horrendous, unbelievable pain as feeling returned to his fingers and toes, Brigite and Anneliese rubbing and rubbing them, the throbbing and burning as if his fingers were being held over invisible flames, the blisters that formed on his finger ends during the following days.

And he remembered Leech sitting by him while he was swearing in agony, and saying:

'I left a packet of fags on the dashboard. I don't suppose you managed to . . .'

SIX

Night on the taiga, 29-30 October

At dusk they reached a plateau, over nine hundred metres above sea-level. When they had crossed it, and the ground was starting to fall away, Nick said on the intercom, 'All stations Two. Make camp.'

The Snow Leopards formed up in three lines. Sections of men moved out to form a defensive perimeter, a triangle with machine-guns at each point, so that attackers from any direction would be caught in an overlapping, interlocking arc of fire.

'I expected we'd be in a circle, like a wagon train,' said Anneliese, who'd been riding in the command vehicle for the last hour, giving Nick a lesson in elementary Russian.

'The principle's the same,' said Nick.

Except that instead of the rolling prairie and coyotes, and beans and coffee, there was snow, wolverines and twenty-four-hour ration packs.

The Yanks always did better, he thought. American arctic forces ration packs had self-heating hamburgers complete with onions, dessert out of a tube, and their oversnow vehicles had little microwave ovens.

He stood in the turret.

They were on high ground on the western edge of the broad Murmansk valley. He looked to the east, down over a vast darkness. On the far horizon was a necklace of lights: Pulozero and Olenogorsk, and the occasional flash of yellow that indicated vehicles on the M18 motorway to Murmansk.

The M18 was his boundary, his stopline. In his orders it was codenamed *Puma*. His most imperative instruction was not to cross it under any circumstances. Curious, he raised his night binoculars to the far distance, beyond the motorway, to the forbidden lands.

There were tiny pinpricks of light on Mount Kirovsk.

He brought his binoculars back to the line of the motorway, trying to follow it to the south. After a moment he found a small glow of reflected light in the sky.

Mončegorsk.

He felt weary but contented. Crossing the Verchnetulomskoje isthmus had shortened their journey by a day. They were in sight of their objective.

He jumped down and walked towards the ambulance.

Men were pulling tent pulks down from the storage racks, shaking ice from their stiff folds. Corporals were marking out sites, standing where the tent pole would go, and holding a ski-stick out at arm's length, another man holding the other end and tramping round in a circle. Other men started to dig out the circle with shovels, digging out the snow until they were waist deep, and the dug snow formed a wall around them.

The tents would be half buried, protected from the wind, more snow piled round the edges to keep in the heat, a white camouflage net thrown over the top and stretched to make an irregular shape that would confuse prying satellite cameras, and would be effective, to a limited degree, against the heat-seeking sensors on helicopters and spy-planes.

While this was going on, the cooks were lighting their stoves in the open, ready to be carried inside as soon as the tent pole went up. Plastic bags were being filled with snow for water.

A regulation thirty metres from the camp, latrines were being dug.

'OK, miss,' said the boy Mark, and Anneliese, who had waited huddled in her anorak, scrabbled gratefully on all fours into HQ Company tent, and screamed as she fell straight into a deep hole dug just inside the flap.

'I told you we'd catch one.'

'That's never a rabbit.'

'That's never a rabbit? What the fuck is it, then, if it's not a rabbit?'

'Bastards!' she yelled.

'There you are. Rabbits can't talk.'

'Siberian rabbits can. Pop her in the pot, cookie.'

'You schoolboys – *bloody* schoolboys,' she spluttered.

'It's the cold-hole, miss,' said the boy Mark, who was trying to get in behind her. 'It's for the cold air to sink into. You didn't think we dug it for a laugh, did you, miss?'

She did. She had witnessed Royal Mercian sense of humour at Kirjan, when the soldier next to her had suddenly shaken his mate awake and asked, urgently: 'Do you want to buy a battleship?' Ten minutes later, when the first man was sound asleep, his mate had woken him in return to ask, equally urgently: 'What colour?'

She shook snow off her polystyrene roll before it could melt and turn to water.

'Spew dinner?' said the cook, collecting together the remains of the day's ration packs. 'Shove it all in, shall I?'

Why not, thought Anneliese, fed up. It all tasted the same anyway. Horrible.

The tent began to warm. Nick came in – and Brigite.

'How is he then, ma'am?' asked Leech.

'He'll live,' said Brigite. Sykes had been half immersed for about nine seconds, his main complaint was a bruised shoulder and ice-burn on his hands. Tonight he was sleeping in the back of the command vehicle, which was kept heated for the men on radio stag.

'He's not requiring constant nursing care, then, is he?' Leech persisted.

'No,' said Brigite, surprised.

'He's all right. He's fine. You heard the doctor,' said Robbo, aware of the widespread belief amongst the men that Sykes's furthermost extremities – his fingers, toes, and genitals – needed to be rubbed vigorously every fifteen minutes by Nurse Bausch to stop gangrene setting in.

They ate their dinner – chicken and rice and minced lamb macaroni, but nobody would have recognised it as such. The food was warm when it left the dixie, cool when it first reached the lips, the last spoonfuls congealed and stiff and cold. Men ate like dogs, gulping it down, finishing in seconds.

It was still only four o'clock, Anneliese saw in dismay.

They would be like this until seven o'clock the next morning, apart from visiting the latrine, not something she could anticipate with pleasure, out in the freezing cold, keeping a watchful eye out for stray Russians and Royal Mercians.

'You girls OK to take a turn on tent stag?' asked Nick.

Anneliese noted with interest that Brigite, whose eyes would previously have narrowed at the word 'girls', nodded politely and said, 'Yes, of course.'

They had both slept for several hours during the afternoon. Anneliese was wide awake.

'Shall we play "I Spy"?' she said. She had played 'I Spy' with the Royal Marines in Scotland.

They played 'I Spy'; at least she did, and Nick and Robbo and, without enthusiasm, Brigite. There were not many things available to be spied.

'I spy with my little eye, something beginning with D.'

'Dossbag,' said Robbo.

The soldiers huddled down and dozed.

'Leech,' said Robbo. 'Play "I Spy".'

'Me, play "I Spy"?' said Leech.

'Come on, come on,' said Robbo menacingly.

'I spy with my little eye,' said Leech, 'something beginning with FS.'

'FS. FS?' puzzled Robbo.

'Fucking snow,' said Leech, when they had all failed to guess.

'Right, Bunnies!' said Nick decisively. 'Everybody sit up. Come on, come on, you lazy lot!'

Soldiers groaned and sat up, their backs resting against

their Bergens. Their hands went up to their ears, and their fingers started to waggle.

'For the benefit of non-Royal Mercians amongst us, you start by waggling your Bunny ears. I will be General Bunny to start. When I take down my hands, I will point at one of you. The person I point at will continue to waggle his ears, and the person on his right will waggle his left ear and the person on his left will waggle his right ear, but nobody else will waggle any ears at all. Major Sendlinger will be Chief Sneak.'

'I will not!'

'Yes, you will. Anybody caught waggling when they ought not to be waggling, or not waggling when they should be waggling, will drink a cup of very hot tea. So if you don't want to be climbing out of your dossbag to relieve yourself all night, you *stay alert*.'

The tent-group cook grinned, and started melting more snow on the stove.

Outside, the sentries changed; the camp settled to its routine. Men hung their wet gaiters on cords, and placed their boots in the bottom of their sleeping bags so they would not be frozen solid in the morning. In the cold-hole was stored the snow bag for drinking water, and the gash bag for rubbish. Some soldiers chatted about past exercises, some read magazines, most just got their heads down.

At 04.00, when the hourly stag changed, Nick was woken up and went out to look round the sentries.

As he walked, the snow disturbed by making camp had

already formed into solid shapes, hard and crunchy. There were no stars visible. Climbing a mound of snow he saw that the lights to the east had disappeared. A low but penetrating wind from the Barents Sea had collected a rolling, thin fog as it crossed the tundra, tendrils of white drifting through the tents and vehicles.

The 'reservists' had elected to live in a separate tent, and were not part of the camp routine. Nick decided to see if Munro was on tent stag; to talk, if possible, about the SAS plans for the following day, when the column reached Mončegorsk.

He unlaced the outer flap and pulled open the Velcro inner flap. The tent was empty and dark. His torch showed three dossbags carefully laid out, three Bergens neat and undisturbed, an unlit stove with a dixie of water on it.

He left the tent and found the nearest sentry.

'Seen anything of the reservists?'

'They've not been out while I've been here, sir.'

'Did the man before you report them leaving camp?'

'No, sir,' said the sentry, an eighteen-year-old called Gates from 5 Platoon. He looked startled and defensive. Falling asleep on stag was serious: a court-martial offence that in theory still carried the death penalty.

Nick said, 'All right, don't worry about it,' and went to the SAS Snow Leopard. It was locked. He thought for a moment, then went to the command vehicle. Two men were on duty in the dim, green light, and Sykes was lying on his back in a deep sleep, his walrus moustache just visible over the edge of his thermal blanket.

'We've been waiting for the blonde to come and see to

him, sir,' said the soldier on inter-company radio, 'but she hasn't been yet.'

Nick said: 'Anything to report?'

The man shook his head. 'No, sir, nothing.'

Kelly, the signaller manning the high-frequency set, said: 'Do you think somebody should go and tell her he's waiting for his rub down?'

'No, I don't,' said Nick.

'We thought of peeking under his blanket, sir,' said the first soldier. 'See if it had dropped off.'

'You do,' said Nick, 'and I'll throw you in a lake.'

Nick left them and went on his rounds. The sentries were strung out in a circle three hundred metres from the camp. It took him over an hour to visit each man, exchange a few words, offer a mouthful of whisky-laced tea.

When he got back, he went again to the SAS tent, opened the flap and looked in.

Noon was tending the stove, Munro and Fuller were taking their boots off.

'Where the hell have you been?'

'Hello, Nick.'

'Did you have the password?'

Munro looked tired and strained. 'Why should we need the password?'

'You went out through the sentries, and then back. For Christ's sake, you could have been shot.'

'Nick, if we can't get through your sentries, we deserve to be shot.' He spoke quietly, leaning back against his Bergen.

'Beef drink, sir?' said Noon. Nick shook his head.

Munro said: 'If you want to know, we were taking a look at your skiers.'

Nick stared.

'We had a look at them last night, as well. At least me and Fuller did, didn't we, Toby?'

'Sir.'

'Being as Sar'nt Noon was otherwise engaged.'

Nick entered the tent, zipped up the flap, and sat down.

Munro said: 'For Christ's sake don't get worked up. There was nothing I could tell you. They're nothing to do with you. They're just keeping a watchful eye.'

'Go on.'

'There's thirty of them. Part of a reconnaissance company – but not Spetznaz. Trained to work behind enemy lines, but only a divisional operations area. They've got two MT-LB reconnaissance patrol vehicles 5k north.'

'Whose reconnaissance company are they?'

'How the hell should I—'

'Don't,' said Nick, 'start that again.'

'I promise you, they will not interfere with you. They are not interested in you – Jesus, they watched while you smashed up those marines, and didn't bat an eyelid.'

'Why didn't we see them?' said Nick, more concerned than he was indicating.

'Nick, this is their territory, their home ground. You could drive within five metres of their *dnovka* – their foxholes – and you wouldn't even see them.'

'Have they seen you?'

'No.'

'Shit clever, eh?'

'I hope so,' said Munro with feeling. 'We're leaving you tomorrow night, and if they do see us, we are dead.'

'Beef drink or coffee for you, Toby?' said Noon.

'Coffee, please, Terence,' said Fuller.

'I have to warn you,' said Brigite, spreading the cards on her sleeping bag, 'that I'm only a beginner. What is your sun sign?'

'Libra,' said Nick.

He had found her on tent stag, sitting by the quietly hissing stove. Everyone else in Company HQ was asleep. Robbo snored gently, Collins lay on his back, Anneliese lay next to the boy Mark, her face, framed by her blonde hair, only inches from his. They looked like young lovers.

'It's so peaceful,' Brigite said. 'I wouldn't have thought a tent in the snow could be such a comfortable place.'

Nick was still gagging at the smell of unwashed human bodies, stale breath, and warm wet wool. In a moment, he knew, he would cease to notice any smell at all.

She was right: it was peaceful. He had always liked tent stag, from when he had been a subaltern. It was a time of solitude, rare in the army: a chance to read and reflect.

Brigite spread the cards, then said quietly:

'So Munro is SAS?'

'I wouldn't like to say what he is,' said Nick.

'How much do you know about his mission?'

She emphasised the word 'mission' with faint irony.

'As much as a soldier in the line ever knows. Bugger all.'

'What made you join the army, Nicholas?'

'It's hard to say. I suppose the truth is I never thought to do anything else.'

'You are from an army family?'

'Not particularly. I had a great-great-grandfather in the Twelfth Foot. We're no connection at all to the famous Chard.'

'Is there a famous Chard?'

'Rorke's Drift. South Wales Borderers. Defended a cattle station with a company of men after Isandhlwana. A handful of blokes against a Zulu army.'

'The English won?'

'The Zulus were so impressed by their bravery that they retired and let them live.'

'I was right the first time,' said Brigite, sighing gently. 'You're an elitist, imperialist, arrogant bastard.'

'Oh, I don't know.'

'"To be an Englishman is to have won first prize in the lottery of life" – Ensign Piper saving the flag at Sevastopol . . .'

'Savannah – fighting the Yanks that time, not the Russkies . . .'

'And you're proud of it all! Everything you believe in reinforces your conviction that you are better than anybody else.'

'Bunnies?' said Nick, after a moment.

'Bunnies. Bunnies, *yes*. Bunnies!' she hissed. 'Because you are thinking all the time how jolly English and superior you are, and how puzzled the foreigners must be.'

'Is that what the cards say?'

'No, it's what I say.'

'Munro's worse than I am.'

'No he isn't. Munro's a simple, straightforward shit. Believe me, I've known a lot of them. I said goodbye to one only last Saturday.'

She collected up the cards.

'I'm too tired for fortune reading. I'm sorry. Anyway, I only bought the book a week ago.'

Nick said: 'But I want to know about this English wife and the dogs.'

She looked at him, then smiled slightly.

'In Mončegorsk, OK? I'll read your fortune in Mončegorsk.'

'You're on.'

Nick slipped gratefully into his dossbag, turned his face away from the lamp, and huddled down into the warmth.

'Actually,' said Brigite quietly, 'I think you're a very good soldier.'

'Thanks.'

'Perhaps better,' she added after a moment, 'than Munro.'

He had told the sentries to be extra alert. The skiers might not intend any harm to the column, but if they came inside the perimeter tonight, they would face the combined fire power of three 5.56mm light machine-guns.

Elitist, imperialist, arrogant machine-guns, even.

In a moment he was asleep.

SEVEN

Anneliese breathed in the sharp morning air, unbelievably delicious after the noisome vapours circulating inside the tent. The sun was rising, throwing a rose-red tint over the fields of virgin snow. She spoke to Sergeant Worembrand, who had been relieving himself behind the ski-rack.

'Today my first reindeer! Yes?'

'Once you've seen one,' said Worembrand, who had never seen a reindeer in his life, 'you've seen them all.'

Reveille had been at dawn. In each tent the last stag of the night had been done by the cook, so that each man was awakened with a hot drink and a plate of tepid grey porridge.

Now tents were coming down, sleeping mats were being rolled, dossbags stuffed into their waterproof cases. Weapons stored on a rack outside the tent during the night, so that they would not suffer from a temperature change, were being inspected by section corporals.

From a mound of snow, Nick and Robbo examined the ground to the east. For the most part smooth, with occasional rocks and areas of exposed shale, it sloped gradually down to a huge plain: the monche-tundra, dotted with farms and

195

clusters of buildings. Some would be *kolkhozi*: collective farms that encompassed four or five villages, organisations that had survived the end of communism and had, in most cases, benefited.

Binoculars revealed signs of movement on one or two of the farms, vehicles crawling along tracks of hard-packed snow.

'You don't suppose they've any fresh veg, do you, sir?'

After two or three days on concentrated ration packs, every soldier craved fresh fruit and greens: apples, cabbage, crunchy salad.

'Shout out if you see a sign,' said Nick, not entirely joking. Dairying and market gardening, under glass, were mixed with reindeer management in the south of the Murmansk Oblast. 'How long before we're down on the level?'

'An hour I should think, sir. Maybe longer. Depends how soft and deep some of that snow is.'

'Well, we've plenty of time.'

'Have you told Narvik about the vehicle yesterday?'

'Yes,' said Nick.

He had enjoyed telling Narvik that a million pounds' worth of Anglo-German high technology was lying on the bottom of the Verchnetulomskoje swamp lakes.

'Lost?' the duty officer had said. 'Completely totalled?'

'I did better than Jodl,' said Nick. 'Jodl lost six vehicles, two of them tanks.'

'Tanks? What tanks?' said the duty officer, startled, ready to panic. 'Who did you say's got tanks?'

That was the trouble with today's army: semi-literate. No knowledge of history further back than the Beatles.

'Come on then, Sar'nt-Major. Let's not hang about!'

Anneliese was eating a tub of appleflakes with boiling water poured on them when Jamie skied up to her, his flank patrol behind him.

'I had Sar'nt Worembrand watched all night,' he said, 'waiting for him to slip into a foreign tongue.'

'You can joke,' said Anneliese, 'but that man is no soldier.'

'I agree,' said Jamie. 'I can't understand why none of us realised it before.'

She had confided her concern over Worembrand: his unsoldierly behaviour, his habit of eating Crunchie bars although nobody ever saw where they came from – the way he managed to be sitting staring moochily out at the snow one minute, and the next minute biting into a chocolate bar conjured up from nowhere.

Jamie's view was that Worembrand was Federation KGB, probably Second Directorate, Espionage, trained in sleight-of-hand trickery, supremely well disguised as a middle-aged, balding British NCO photographer.

'Idiot!' said Anneliese.

She held up a spoonful of appleflakes. He leaned forward on his ski-poles and ate them.

'I'd have gone to Dresden for a cat,' he said, 'if you'd asked me.'

'How do you know about that?'

'I was looking through the log.'

'Well, you shouldn't have been.'

'Duty. I was checking on Worembrand.'

'Why should I want you to go to Dresden anyway? You're not my boyfriend, and it's not your cat.'

'That's very unkind.'

'So? Go away.'

'And there was me feeling sorry,' said Jamie earnestly, 'about his reply.'

Anneliese's mouth fell open. 'His reply? What reply?'

'Still, it was the strain of being parted, and I dare say she's beautiful. Has he known her for very long?'

'We've been parted for only six days, Jamie, and you're not making me laugh.'

'If you're ready, sir,' said Corporal Hoddinot, 'only the OC's giving us funny looks again.'

Jamie said: 'See you later. And don't worry. These things always turn out for the best in the end.'

He skied off, snaking through the vehicles and groups of men, his patrol behind him. A moment later they were pounding, in an energetic crab-like motion, up a nearby slope; then taking position on the nearest high ground, waiting for the column to move.

She smiled, threw her appleflakes tub into a gash bag being trailed round by a disconsolate young soldier, and climbed into the back of the ambulance.

Worembrand's camera cases were already in place. Anneliese set about building her personal nest, near the rear, so that she could look out of the open tailgate. Brigite would travel opposite her. Sergeant Worembrand, on past experience, preferred the gloom of the interior.

As she settled herself, her eyes fell on Worembrand's bags. If the cases she had carried yesterday were the lightest, how much must the heaviest weigh?

On impulse she reached over and lifted one. It hardly weighed anything at all. In fact it felt empty.

'Well!'

She peered quickly out of the back of the vehicle. Corporals were screaming and yelling and running about, their legs moving but their bodies curiously rigid in the way of NCOs, shouting in loud voices that the column would move off in twenty seconds.

Worembrand was talking to one of the sergeants, hunched up in his parka, tartan scarf round his neck.

Hastily she flicked back the metal catches and opened the case. Looking up at her was a large brown teddy bear.

Her first thought was that the bear must be a Rupert, something to do, perhaps, with Worembrand's frequent references to Ruperts and the Rupert Factory (which she now knew to be the Royal Military Academy, Sandhurst). Then she wondered if the bear might be the regimental mascot, a remembrance of some terrible encounter with bears in the wastes of Afghanistan. But this explanation seemed unlikely; the bear was wearing lederhosen and had a Norwegian flag on his chest.

Worembrand's morning farts, a succession of tremulous squeaks, alerted her to his approach along the side of the vehicle. Acting on the advice of an old Rheindahlen chum, an old lag from the British Frontier Service, he was dosing himself on a kaolin and morphine-based patent medicine,

199

designed to ensure constipation for the length of the operation and so save him from exposing his nether regions to the biting polar winds.

She stuffed the teddy back in the case and tried to close the lid, but the metal catches were stiff and she only just managed to click them closed before Worembrand climbed in and started fussily arranging his duvet.

'Our ETA's 14.00. That should be all right. There's still a bit of light at 14.00. What's the matter?'

'Nothing,' she said, thinking *no*, it could not be possible. Worembrand was surely not carrying round a childhood toy: a furry friend he could not leave behind?

The column was ready to move: the sentries bringing in their machine-guns; the corporals touring the site to check that no equipment remained, that no refuse had been left, that the latrines were shovelled over with snow.

'All right, everybody,' said Nick through the intercom. 'Once we get moving I want to keep moving. We should be down on the level in approximately one hour. As I said last night, we will then be on open tundra interspersed with farm settlements. Depending on the ground and the condition of the snow, I want to bring in the ski patrols and push a vehicle out on each flank.'

They started to snake their way down to the plain. After ten minutes Jamie and his patrol came sweeping down behind the ambulance, whooping like Red Indians, crossing and disappearing in a mist of sun-red snow crystals. Then a few moments later, they were back, skidding on their skies, throwing snow into the open back of the vehicle.

'Stupid buggers,' said Worembrand, shaking himself like a spaniel, but Anneliese leaned out and laughed, looking from side to side, wondering where the skiers had gone to. Just as she was giving up hope, they appeared again over a hillock, flying in the air and landing in a flurry of snow.

'Bloody hooligans,' said Worembrand.

'You ought to be used to soldiers,' said Brigite. 'You've been one long enough.'

Worembrand did not like Brigite. She was a nasty piece of work. He felt sorry for the poor sod she married; assuming that she would marry. Far more likely she would end up a bitter, disappointed old maid. Worembrand's view of sex and society was untroubled by progressive schools of thought.

'You'd think they'd have a bit more respect,' he said, 'seeing as your friend is only just dead.' He had been about to say hardly cold in her grave, but Erike had been cold in her grave within two seconds of entering it.

'Oh, Max!' said Anneliese. 'That's not fair.'

'It's modern life,' said Worembrand. 'I'll grant you that.'

Then the intercom clicked on, and Nick's voice said acidly: 'Two to Two-One. This is Sunray. Please keep your station; look out from the convoy, not in at it; and stop behaving like lovesick third-formers.'

Jamie grimaced at Anneliese, held both his arms in the air in a gesture of resignation, and led his men away – Anneliese leaning out to wave at him.

'Have you heard lately,' said Worembrand, 'from your young man in Hamburg?'

'Well that's it,' said Leech, puffing his cigarette, the air in the cab thick with smoke. 'It was your last chance and you blew it.'

'What did you want me to do – drown?'

'It would have got you off the court martial, and Karen would have cried a bit.'

'Piss off.'

Leech was driving, Syco slumped beside him, nursing his bandaged fingers.

'Maybe if you'd injured yourself just a little bit more; given the OC a chance to plead compassionate grounds.'

'Had my leg amputated, that sort of thing?'

Leech nodded: yes, that sort of thing. He took a long drag on his cigarette.

'I can't see what chance you've got now. We'll be there by dinner time, and this time tomorrow we'll be starting back.'

'You will. I won't.'

'Syco, nobody but nobody goes AWOL in fucking Siberia.'

'We're not in Siberia.'

His watch, he reasoned, would buy him a train ticket to St Petersburg. He could scrounge enough pounds and Deutschmarks from his mates to get himself on a flight to Belfast; he could even use his credit card. He would be in the Shankill Road before anyone traced him to Petersburg even.

'AWOL on active service. They'll hang you.'

'We're not at war!'

'What were you digging to Australia for, then? What were them things flying over your head, paper darts?'

Syco did not reply. Leech glanced at him, noting his thin, unhappy face.

'Relax,' he said. 'You'll be all right. You've been under fire. Your balls have been quick-frozen like garden peas. The OC'll make a lot out of that, you see.'

'Helicopter at four o'clock, helicopter on the skyline at four o'clock . . .'

'Scatter! Scatter!'

As the intercom screamed, Leech wrenched round the wheel and gunned the accelerator, sending the Snow Leopard swerving to the left. Syco had jumped up and was hauling back the turret cover, mindless of his damaged fingers, reaching for the GPMG as the gunship passed overhead, its belly filling the sky, coming in so low that, looking up through the turret, they could read the yellow lettering on the under-nose sensors and low light-level target detectors.

It had come at speed from a spur of land to the west, and behind it came two more gunships that hovered in formation over the rocks.

'Halt at 500-metre intervals. Man machine-guns. Do not fire unless they do,' snapped Nick on the intercom. 'Repeat, do not fire unless they do. Get me Narvik.'

'No go, sir,' said Lance-Corporal Kelly.

The HF was being jammed. It did not have to be deliberate; the mass of electronics hovering over the column would disrupt any radio equipment.

'Mi-28 Hind, sir,' said Collins. 'With the AT-6 anti-tanks. You can see them on the stub pylons.'

Nick could see them. He could not take his eyes off them; eight anti-tank missiles on rails, while his Starstreak anti-aircraft missiles were packed in a Snow Leopard that at this moment was trying to crawl under an overhanging rock like a land crab.

The gunship was turning now and sweeping back, moving gently over the scattered column.

'Christ, look at that bastard,' said Collins.

The gunner was clearly visible in the forward turret, wearing a black face-visor and command helmet, so that as his head moved, so did the direction of the eight-barrelled 12.7mm rapid-fire nose-gun.

He would not be needed: except to pick off personnel trying to flee through the snow.

The first anti-tank missile would destroy a Snow Leopard; it would consume it in a ball of flame. It was just possible that the combined fire of fifteen machine-guns might bring the gunship down, despite its forged titanium hub and high-tensile steel rotors and light-armour cladding, but how long before the other gunships, at a safe distance, loosed their anti-tanks: twenty-four missiles to account for fifteen Royal Mercian vehicles?

It would be a wipe-out; they would be destroyed in seconds.

'Shit!'

In sudden fury Nick remembered his briefing at Brigade North: 'Everything west of the M18 motorway has been pulled back to Arkhangelsk. You'll have to watch for deserters but that's all.' *Nobody said anything about deserters flying formation in the world's most advanced gunships!*

The Mi-28 was holding station over them.

'Sunray to all stations,' said Nick, trying to sound calm, his mind filled with a vision of burning horror, of vehicles trying to escape and being picked off one by one, of his men being gunned down in the snow. 'If they open up, move and keep moving. Do not wait to offer support.'

'Gunner's pointing to his headphones, sir,' said Collins.

'They've got our frequency, sir,' said Corporal Willis. A loud angry voice filled the cab.

Who was their best Russian speaker? It was pointless trying to involve Munro and his men. Nick opened the cab door and looked back. The ambulance was three hundred metres away, facing back the way they had come. It had slewed round, trying to scatter to the left, only to come up against a massive snowdrift. Nick recognised Hendry, a boy soldier from the Second Battalion who had only joined the company a fortnight ago, manning the machine-gun, a terrified look on his face.

'Sunray to ambulance. Miss Sendlinger, will you or Miss Bausch please come to the command vehicle. We need an interpreter.'

'That's you,' said Brigite.

'Oh dear God,' said Anneliese, ashen-faced. Erike had been the Russian speaker: colloquial, almost perfect, with a Minsk accent she claimed to be quite superior and respected.

'Walk steadily,' said Worembrand. 'Whatever you do, don't run.' He was warily taking photographs from behind the cover of his baggage and his duvet. People with cameras, he knew, were the first to be picked off by snipers.

Anneliese jumped out. The shriek of the gunship's twin turboshafts filled the air. She looked round for Jamie, who had been on a neighbouring ridge only seconds before. Jamie and his patrol had disappeared, their white camouflage sinking into the rocks and snow.

She ran down to the command vehicle, and was pulled into the back.

Willis was on the HF set repeating: 'Hello, Narvik, Matchmaker to Narvik. Gunships overhead, threatening convoy. Hello, Narvik. Matchmaker to Narvik . . .'

Nick said: 'Tell me what they're saying.'

The Russian was speaking rapidly and menacingly. Anneliese's brain would not work. She had never spoken – only rarely heard – Russian outside the classroom.

'Well?'

'Disobey.'

'What?'

'Disobey . . . unauthorised . . . I don't know. I can't hear.'

'Just relax, love,' said Robbo. 'See if they mention chocolate. It's usually chocolate, in my experience.'

Robbo had returned only three months ago from Kurdistan.

'Talk to them,' said Nick. 'Ask them if they speak English or German.'

Anneliese nodded. 'OK. I'm sorry, but you see it was

206

Erike who was the language expert . . .'

'Never mind,' said Nick. 'Just do the best you can.'

She pressed the handset and spoke. Did anyone speak English, German, or, she added on her own initiative, French.

'*Niet niet,*' said the voice, angry, annoyed.

'*Niet,*' said Robbo.

'At least we're in contact,' said Nick.

The Russian was speaking again, his voice almost drowned by the scream of the rotors.

'Can I ask him to move away from us?' she asked Nick, but he shook his head violently. She realised that he would not want to pinpoint the command vehicle, although they had clearly seen her run to the head of the column.

A moment later the gunship moved position of its own accord, traversing the slope, inspecting the vehicles pinned down beneath it.

The Russian voice was clearer and slower.

'They say,' said Anneliese, 'that we have left the prescribed route, and are disobeying the terms of the agreement.'

'Say we are here to save the lives of Russian children. Say we have kept to the agreement,' said Nick, thinking of the naval infantry at the farm, the two Russian dead. 'Willis, get me Munro.'

'They say,' said Anneliese, 'that we are failing to display our correct flags.'

Nick stared at her.

'What?'

'They say the mission should have flags on all vehicles.

We are exposing ourselves recklessly, stupidly . . . I don't know exactly . . . to danger by failing to abide by this agreement.'

'Mr Munro on personal radio, sir,' said Willis.

Munro was on his handset. The SAS must have managed to leave their vehicle, to have tunnelled away through the snow. It would probably suit his plans if the rest of the column was annihilated.

'Tell them,' he said to Anneliese, 'we only have two United Nations flags and one EC flag, but will display Union flags on all other vehicles.'

Anneliese slowly began translating. 'Union flag? I don't understand "Union". What do you mean?'

'British. English.'

'OK.' Now she was becoming more fluent, her brain unfreezing. When she had finished there was silence.

Nick said: 'Anneliese, tell them if there is any danger, Major Chard, officer commanding, strongly requests a helicopter escort to Mončegorsk.'

Again there was no answer. A moment later the gunships moved away, wheeling gently in formation, heading over the plain to the east, until they were specks in the haze over Mount Kirovsk – and were gone.

The flank patrols rose slowly out of the snow. The column reformed.

'Narvik, sir,' said Willis.

'Give them our position,' said Nick. 'Say our ETA is still as per original schedule. Sar'nt-Major, break the flags out.'

* * *

Now the column sped across the open plain, snow spray rising in a cloud behind, reflecting all the colours of the rainbow. One last settlement lay ahead: a farming township a kilometre from the north-south Murmansk railroad.

'Straight through,' said Nick into his intercom.

'Yeah?' said Jamie.

'Why not,' said Nick. 'Tell the lads to wave, and the gunners to keep a low profile.'

The township was the centre of a collective: twenty or so farm units, a shack used as a cinema and ballet school, a modest cluster of grain silos.

They passed the first weatherboard farms, then an ugly concrete and glass building that must once have been the local communist headquarters. Faces peered from windows. A group of children appeared in a doorway.

The children saw the flags and waved. Anneliese, leaning out of the back of the medics' Snow Leopard, waved vigorously back.

'Why haven't we any German flags?' she shouted to Hendry, the young gunner. 'Bloody Brits!'

She reached down and grabbed Worembrand's Lufthansa travel-bag and waved it, shouting, 'Hello, how are you?' and was astonished when a dozen Crunchie bars flew out in a glinting arc and landed behind them on the snow. Worembrand's arm reached out and grabbed the bag back.

'Chocolate! Chocolate! *Shokolats!*' she shouted. Children were cautiously approaching the gold-foil bars as the school was lost to view.

In the central square two army vehicles were parked,

aged BRDM lightweight transports, men in navy blue and khaki sitting on them.

Nick stood in the turret and gave a crisp salute. Soldiers gaped; two of them saluted in return.

Then the township was behind them. Ten minutes later they reached the motorway, six lanes wide, but reduced to two lanes of sporadic traffic. They turned south, not trying to join the trucks on the road, but bowling along the hard-packed snow beside it, on the stretch of land between the motorway and the Murmansk railway.

The Sixth Mountain Division's objective for four long years, thought Nick; the vital link that had carried south the guns and tanks and munitions delivered round North Cape by the Arctic convoys.

They reached the outer northern suburbs of Mončegorsk and skirted them, proceeding in a wide circle through the snow fields until they hit the shores of Lake Imandra. In the command vehicle a corporal was making intelligence notes on the number and type of vehicles they had seen, the extent to which normal life seemed to be functioning.

They turned along the lakeside towards Sopcha, the village where the EC hospital had been built.

Erike had said: 'It's in pine trees, on the shore. You can wave to trains on the other bank of the lake. There's fishing in the summer, even swimming. Pollution is not too bad at all. We had barbecues in August. A band called the "New Yorkers" from Mončegorsk came to play for the children's dance.'

Erike had spent a golden summer there; she had had a wonderful time.

The LodeStar computer told them they had arrived. A wide track opened on their left, leading into the trees. Nick stood in the turret and signalled to the vehicles behind. The column turned. After a few moments through the dark pines, the hospital appeared before them.

It was built in local style: a two-storey wooden building surrounded by log cabins. Erike had lived in one of these, Anneliese remembered, a cabin at the water's edge, sharing with two other nurses.

The command vehicle pulled up in front of the main entrance, the other vehicles forming up round it, men of the clearance patrol jumping down before the vehicles had come to a standstill, then fanning out into the woods.

Worembrand was hastily sorting his cameras. 'Hold this,' he said to Brigite, handing her a camera loaded with black-and-white film, at the same time slinging a colour camera round his neck.

'That bag; the aluminium.'

'Aren't you giving them Crunchie bars, Max?' said Anneliese.

'No,' said Worembrand, in his voice a new note of authority. 'Listen carefully. What I want is for you both to wait here, I want the lads first, and then I'll call you. Oi, where are you going?'

Brigite had climbed out of the back of the vehicle and already disappeared.

'Bloody marvellous. I say one thing, she does the other,'

said Worembrand, hastily gathering his cameras. 'Now, where's that fucking Rupert?'

'It's in here,' said Anneliese, opening the metal case and reaching for the bear.

'Not that fucking Rupert,' said Worembrand, jumping with surprising agility out of the vehicle and hurrying towards Nick, who was standing with Brigite at the hospital's entrance.

'We can stage the pictures with the girls and the toddlers later, sir, but I'd like a shot of you and the chief doctor when he comes out: a shake of the hands à la "Dr Livingstone I presume" and a bit of shoulder slapping, if you're so inclined.'

Nick ignored him.

The snow round the front of the building was disturbed, covered in footprints, but the door was locked and there were no lights shining.

'I suppose this actually was a hospital?' Nick said to Brigite. 'You don't think they invented the entire thing, do you?'

Two days ago 'they' would have been the Russians. Now 'they' referred to Narvik. Nick Chard's view of life was changing.

PART THREE
NOVYJ YENA

Ah, if soon I might behold her,
Rest my eyes on my beloved!
Kulnasatj, my little reindeer,
Can you not now see her eyes?

           Lapland love song

Two things greater than all things are,
The first is Love, and the second War.

           Kipling

ONE

*Princess of Wales Hospital, Lake Imandra, Mončegorsk,
30 October*

Nick took off a mitten and gingerly touched one of the
radiators. It was tacky with cold; another hour and flesh
would stick to it like superglue. On the radiator's valve
was the name of a Ruhr manufacturer. In the kitchen they
had found French cooking utensils. The beds and furniture
were Swedish pine, the colour-coordinated carpets and
curtains were from Finland. The Princess of Wales Hospital
for Children was equipped with the best the European
Community could provide.

Britain, he noted, had made a special contribution: a
framed photograph of the Princess of Wales herself, with
William and Harry, watching the Badminton horse trials,
eating a picnic. Now hoarfrost was spreading across the
glass, the building's sweat transmuted into visible form as
the temperature fell; the faces of the princes were already a
white blur.

'They ran out of oil yesterday afternoon. They had six
portable electric radiators, enough only to keep a single
ward above freezing . . .'

Brigite was reading from a sheet of paper. Her face was

illuminated by an oil lamp that hissed quietly, a comforting noise in the deep silence of the hospital.

'There were also problems with the power supply – it sometimes goes off during the evening, when demand is at its highest. They were terrified a blizzard would cut them off . . . The local hospital refused to take responsibility. It is full of flu victims.'

A few hours ago this had been a safe haven, full of warmth, and light, full of bustle and noise. Now it was empty. Filled with a sense of desolation. Children's pictures were stuck to the walls: Mickey Mouse, a fairy-tale castle, pirates on an island, a witch on a broomstick in a snowy sky . . . an imaginary trip to Euro-Disney by the sick children of Karelia.

'Well, go on,' said Nick.

'Give me a moment, please Nicholas. I was not selected for this mission because I spoke Polish.'

He looked out of the triple-glazed window. It had been designed to keep the warmth in. It would, with equal efficiency, retain the cold. Another twelve hours and the Princess of Wales hospital would be an ice-house.

Brigite said: 'They tried to phone Petersburg, to the European Commission, but the lines south are not operating. It says here, by the way, that they have been deliberately cut – and the satellite phone in Mončegorsk has been seized by *zampolits*, GlavPU officers.' She spelt the letters out. 'I don't know what that means.'

'Political directorate. Red army units used to have politicos, *zampolits*, shadowing the fighting men. In the late eighties they turned into welfare officers sorting out soldiers' housing problems. Their main role was to invent stories about new apartment blocks being built.'

'So why should they seize a satellite comms centre?'

'Why should they even exist? The last organised army units are supposed to have been pulled back to Arkhangelsk.'

He could see Jamie dispersing the vehicles, spreading them out through the pines. Beyond the trees and the cabins was Lake Imandra, a vast sheet of ice. Jamie was selecting a site for a machine-gun post. A reconnaissance company attacking on skis could be amongst them, silently, in seconds.

Brigite said excited: 'Here we are. This is it! Yesterday an opportunity came to send the children from the south to St Petersburg by truck. The two doctors went with them. The remainder of the children and two nurses have gone to Novyj Yena – to a school.'

'A school? You've got that wrong.'

'I have *not* got that wrong. School, *skelva*, OK? The Director said he would give them emergency shelter until they found a hospital that could accept them . . .'

The door opened. It was Munro. He closed the door quietly behind him. Brigite carried on reading.

'They don't know if the hospital at Novyj Yena will take them in. They have no specialist drugs left. They have no anti-flu vaccine. They have run out of frozen goat's milk and compound foods, and several children with Crohn's disease are now suffering bloody diarrhoea. They have only bread and pig potatoes to eat. Children who cannot tolerate gluten are starving in the sight of food.

They have no raw liver for the boy Misha Andreyovich. They hope to get reindeer liver at Novyj Yena. It is his only hope.'

Nick pulled his map from inside his pocket. 'OK. We'll move at first light. I think it's about 20k north . . .'

'I just wonder,' interrupted Munro, 'if we can talk about that? Before you do anything rash?'

They walked by the lake. Behind them, on the hospital roof, two soldiers hacked ice off the satellite dish, while Staff Beckwith watched them fretfully and urged them to work faster. *Madonna in Moscow* was scheduled live on St Petersburg TV at 21.00.

Munro said: 'Stay two days, Nick: forty-eight hours. Get the heating on, have a sauna, give the lads a can of lager. We all know you've a couple of packs tucked away.'

'I'm moving tomorrow.'

'Two days, Nick, and I'll be clear.'

'Tomorrow at dawn,' said Nick, 'we leave for Novyj Yena.'

Munro shook his head. 'No way are you going to Novyj Yena. Just listen a moment. Listen to reason. You've done your job. You've brought drugs and medical help to Mončegorsk . . .'

Nick said: 'My job was to deliver supplies to children, not to an empty building. I've got compound foods, drugs, a hundred pounds of raw liver for a six-year-old boy who will die if we don't get it to him.'

'I hear what you're saying. I understand what you're saying.'

'I don't care whether you understand or not.'

'OK, Nick,' Munro said, 'have it your own way. Speak to Narvik, tell them what you want to do, tell them how you feel.'

Nick stopped. A watery moon shone over the sheet ice.

'I'm not going to speak to Narvik.'

Munro's head jerked round.

'Not going to speak to Narvik?' He stared at Nick, incredulous. 'Have you gone crazy?'

'I'm not really sure I trust Narvik. They don't tell me the things I need to know. They don't tell me about roads that are closed, or GlavPU officers operating in Mončegorsk. They don't tell me about organised reconnaissance patrols shadowing us, they don't tell me about helicopter gunships that know our radio frequency. All they do tell me is that your activities are none of my business and that they can't casevac a member of my unit who's dying. Well, I was sent on a mission and I'm fucking well going to finish it.'

'Oh Christ. You still haven't got it, have you? You're not the mission. I'm the mission! *I'm* the reason you are here. I'm the *only* reason you're here . . .'

'Bugger off, George.'

'Call Narvik! Get them now!'

'Excuse me, sir.'

It was Robbo, approaching through the pines, his voice matter-of-fact, discreet.

'Clearance patrol's back. Nothing about. Thought you'd like to know, sir.'

'We're staying for one night, Sar'nt-Major,' said Nick.

'Right, sir.'

'Organise stags with Mr Pendred. We move at dawn.'

'Sir.'

Nick walked towards the command vehicle. Munro followed him.

'Nick?'

Nick said: 'If you can tell me something about why you're here, about why I should abandon the children, perhaps let them die, for the sake of an extra twenty kilometres up the motorway, I'll listen.'

'I can't,' said Munro. 'There isn't a need to know. There's only a need for you to cooperate.'

Nick opened the back of the command vehicle. Collins was on duty on the high-frequency radio.

'Collins?'

'Sir.'

'Thank God,' said Munro. 'If you're in any doubt, Nick, talk to Generalleutnant Hoepner. You don't have to take any shit from Grenfell – not on this one.'

'Turn the set off. Go and watch the concert.'

Collins looked confused for a moment, then pressed two switches. The lights died. On the company intercom a signaller looked hopeful that he might be allowed to go and watch the concert as well.

'Sorry, Kelly,' said Nick.

'Sir,' said Lance-Corporal Kelly, philosophically.

Nick said: 'I don't want the HF set used again without my express order. I'll tell Corporal Willis myself. You tell the next man on the inter-company radio.'

'Sir,' said Kelly. He would watch the concert on the six-inch monitor; the command vehicle had its own satellite dish. But it wouldn't be the same.

Nick walked away from the vehicle. Munro followed him. They stood in the darkness.

'I think,' said Munro, 'I ought to put you under arrest.'

'Try it,' said Nick.

After a moment Collins was seen walking towards the hospital entrance, almost colliding with Staff Beckwith, who ran out and shouted up at the roof: 'I'll give you five minutes, just five minutes, to fix that cable.'

'You realise they'll hang you for this?'

'Court martial for obeying orders?'

'Don't be naive.'

'No,' said Nick.

'If my job turns pear-shaped because of you,' said Munro, 'a court martial will be the least of your worries.'

He turned abruptly and walked away.

Nick was back in the administrator's office with Brigite.

'The Mount of Luna,' she said, holding his palm, tracing a line with her forefinger. 'The realm of dreams, fantasy, and imagination. Very strong. Unusual for a soldier, I think.'

'Oh, I wouldn't say that. Lovelace, Sidney – it used to be quite a tradition.'

'Now, this is the heart line, which tells us about your emotional and sexual nature: your love life. Oh dear.'

She looked up.

'What?'

'Poor Nicholas. What was her name?'

'Emma,' said Nick.

'And where is Emma now?'

In the Feathers at Ludlow, probably, he thought; some ghastly overweight estate agent's son feeding her scrambled eggs on brioche, salmon with wild mushrooms, steamed double-chocolate pudding. Emma could be amiable and loving when fed.

'England,' he said. 'Shropshire.'

'She did not want to be a soldier's wife – to follow the colours, as you say?'

'I can't see her, somehow, in Russia,' said Nick, thinking of the rose-brick Georgian house with the central heating turned up high, and the three hot-water bottles, and Emma's 'It's so co-o-old' as she sat on her bed with the teddy bears, one of them rather like Sergeant Worembrand's teddy bear and called, for some reason, Mycroft.

'Turn Mycroft's face to the wall. We don't want Mycroft to be shocked,' she had commanded, a sudden shiver in her voice; though whether from the supposed cold, or because his hand was sliding up her indubitably warm thigh, it had been hard to tell.

Emma. A memory of warmth past.

'Bastard.'

Fuller was in the doorway.

'You're a load of shit,' said Fuller. 'You know you're a load of shit?'

Brigite dropped Nick's hand. Nick stared across the desk, shocked more than he would have believed possible.

Dark, thickset, Fuller had been the quiet one. Nick was

not even sure of his rank. Had Munro said he was a corporal? Nick could not recall having heard him speak, other than when he responded to Noon's query, 'Beef drink for you, Toby?' in the SAS tent. Now his body was tensed, he rocked very slightly, very menacingly, on the balls of his feet. His eyes were cold, venomous with intense anger.

'Get up,' said Fuller.

Nick had fifty men within call. But if he shouted for help, it would be horrendous for morale. It would end up with Fuller under close arrest – there would be no other option.

Fuller shouted: 'GET UP YOU BASTARD!'

Brigite said: 'Go away! Get out!'

Fuller was moving slowly forward. He was a trained killer. He could break Nick's arm, or his neck, in seconds. He said, almost pleading with Nick, 'What are you playing at, eh? What are you fucking playing at?'

Nick stood up.

'Toby?'

Sergeant Noon was in the doorway. Fuller ignored him.

'Feeling a little bit sulky, are you,' he said, 'because you weren't kept in the picture? Jacko's dead, but you weren't kept in the picture.'

'Come on, Toby.'

'We're supposed to be on the same side. We're supposed to be part of the same army!'

'The boss wants you, Toby. In the vehicle.'

Fuller said: 'I wanted him to know.'

'Well, now he does. Go on, then.'

Fuller said: 'Load of shit.'

'In the vehicle. Now!' said Noon, and this time his voice made Fuller blink.

He opened his mouth to say something, thought better of it, turned and left.

There was a moment of silence, then Noon said casually, 'Sorry about that,' and made to follow him.

Nick said: 'Sergeant?'

Noon turned.

'There's three of you, but your regiment normally operates in groups of four.'

Noon nodded.

'Jacko?'

'Didn't quite beat the clock, sir.' Noon stood for a moment, then said: 'Ten days ago.'

He turned and followed Fuller.

'Oh my God,' said Brigite, 'what was all that about?'

There was a sudden loud cheer from the reception hall, a thump of music. REME and Signals between them had fixed the satellite receiver. Madonna, live from the Kremlin, was beaming across Karelia.

It was first light. Drivers were revving engines, stores were being packed into pulks. Nick was gulping down a mug of tea by the command vehicle when Robbo came up.

'It's Munro and his men, sir.'

'What about them?'

'They've gone, sir. During the night.'

The SAS Snow Leopard was empty and cold. The sentries had seen nothing. The area round the vehicles was covered in footprints and ski tracks. It was impossible to identify those of Munro and his men.

'If they've gone out on patrol, they've taken hell of a lot of kit,' said Robbo.

'No,' said Nick, 'they've not gone on patrol.'

He looked at the hillside that rose behind the wood, away from the lake, just visible in the cold mists of dawn. They would, he guessed, make for high ground: every soldier's instinct.

They would be up there, somewhere, watching.

He suddenly felt uncomfortably exposed.

'All right, Sar'nt-Major. Allocate a driver for this vehicle. Mount up! Let's get going!'

TWO

Lake Imandra, Mončegorsk, 31 October

The binoculars swept the column from front to rear, and followed it until the lights of the last Snow Leopard passed out of sight.

It had taken them six hours to cover a thousand metres. Manpacking 150 pounds of kit, they had climbed through the pines and the birch trees, first using the ski-tracks of the Royal Mercians' clearance patrol, then using branches to cross the eggshell crust of virgin snow. They had moved as delicately as ballerinas in the frozen darkness of the night.

Sergeant Noon's binoculars watched the last Snow Leopard disappear – then returned to scan the lake and the woodlands.

Behind him, Munro and Fuller were completing construction of a cave, a refuge burrowed in a bank of snow, deep in the wooded slope; a *dnovka*, the Spetznaz called it.

The snow extracted from the bank was scattered, swept with branches in the way they had learned on the Brecon Beacons, on Pen-y-fan and the stark, barren summit of the Skirrid.

In different circumstances they would have surrounded the *dnovka* with a thin, almost invisible wire attached to a small charge that would explode if the wire was disturbed. Here, the chance of silver fox or wolverine setting off the alarm was too great.

An hour passed.

'Sir . . .' said Sergeant Noon quietly.

Munro crept forward to join him, taking the binoculars.

White-clad skiers were emerging from the forest by the hospital, tentative at first, in twos and threes, cautiously sweeping past the entrance.

Then the main body, closing in on all sides.

Two hours later the MT-LB armoured personnel carriers arrived, and the skiers piled into them. When the vehicles had gone, Munro, who was on watch, followed their lights, noting the point where they skirted south of the town of Monĉegorsk, two kilo-metres away, and crossed the empty, frozen marshlands until they reached the Murmansk railway line and the M18 that ran, north to south, down the far side of the lake.

Over the railway and road they were lost from sight, but Munro noted their route: the way they chose to approach Mount Kirovsk. It was the path the SAS themselves would have to tread.

They were in the *dnovka* now, its entrance reduced to a small observation window camouflaged by branches.

An average person, an average soldier, could pass

within inches of the cave without suspecting that it was there.

A Spetznaz or Reconnaissance Company soldier would be a different matter. But the Spets and the Recce troops, they hoped, were still watching the column.

The binoculars were cleaned, carefully dried, packed in dessicant, placed in Munro's Bergen between a slim HF transmitter unit and three pairs of dry socks.

The cave was three metres high, and ten metres deep. There was just room for the three of them, their dossbags and Bergens. The walls sparkled: they had each spent several hours rubbing the snow with their spoons, polishing the surface so that the walls and roof would reflect back the heat. On a shelf at the back, a small stove burned. The choice in a *dnovka*, they had been told by humorous instructors on *Sickener 2* at Hereford, was generally between death by asphyxiation or death by cold.

For good or ill, this would be their home for the next forty-eight hours. They would eat here, they would sleep here; when they wanted to shit, they would shit into sealable plastic bags.

Fuller was sleeping, fitfully: exhausted, as they all were, by the efforts of the night.

Noon was preparing food. He had the reputation of being a bit of a gourmet, a man with a delicate appetite, a fussy eater. When water on the stove became warm – they could wait all night for it to boil – he sprinkled into it grey unappetising granules of ration-pack beefstew, then he crumbled tack biscuits in as a thickener, then he reached into the inner recesses of his Bergen and pulled out a

Mexican-bottled brew, his special contribution to the feast: a fearsome Tabasco and chilli sauce.

'Toby?' he said, and Fuller's eyes opened.

'Smells good,' he said.

'Sir?'

Munro took the food.

Spoons raced between plate and mouth. In seconds the meal was over.

'It's always the same,' said Sergeant Noon. 'You spend hours cooking it . . .'

Munro opened his Bergen, took out the transmitter, opened the slender plastic cover and pressed a pad. The keyboard shone faintly luminous.

He started to mentally compose the message he would send.

It should have been routine, the wording agreed days before, as HMS *Revenge* sped west along the Murman coast, after their abortive attempt to penetrate inland from Umba on the White Sea.

Now everything had changed. He spent the best part of an hour working at the small screen, cramming as much as he could into the fewest words. He did not notice as Noon crawled in between him and Fuller, and dropped into a cold, troubled sleep.

Finally, it was done.

He pressed a pad – the message was scrambled.

He pressed another and the message was passed. A burst transmission, so fast as to baffle the most sophisticated monitoring device, the most alert operator scanning routine traffic; so fast that even if, in a blink of an eye, it was noticed, there would be no time to lock on and locate the sender.

From the desolate woodland slope of Lake Imandra the signal passed in a split second through the ionosphere, into a comms satellite over Cape North, and instantly down to an aerial farm near Narvik. In moments it was being unscrambled, spewing out of the printer, its first words MOST SECRET.

By that time, slumped over his transmitter, cold and shivering despite his dossbag, Munro was asleep.

THREE

ACE Reaction Force Headquarters, 1 November

Lieutenant-Colonel John Fielding, Commanding Officer, First Battalion Royal Regiment, knew in his bones that bad news lay ahead.

He knew it from the way he had been summoned from Battalion HQ in Bergen: the terse priority signal, the lack of an accompanying telephone call of explanation.

He knew it from the attitude of the driver who met him at Evenes airport in the grey, wet afternoon, and the respectful, distant manner of the duty officer who greeted him at NATO Forces Northern Europe's temporary headquarters in Narvik.

Corporal and subaltern, they knew what was going on. They knew which senior officer was the favourite, heading towards a pat on the head and a juicy bone; which poor sod was heading for the doghouse.

His fears were confirmed when he entered the Secure Room. Two men sat at the table. One was a stranger, the other Grenfell, who said: 'It's your man Chard.'

So Chard was 'his' man, rather than 'our' man. Already the Chief of Staff was washing his hands of future embarrassment: Grenfell was a thruster on the fast track to high command. Two more minutes and he would deny even having been told that First Battalion Royal Mercians were in Norway, let alone part of NATO Northern Command.

'Come and sit down. This is John Biggin, 22 SAS.'

Biggin was in his late thirties. Lean, intelligent-looking. Old enough to be clever, young enough to be arrogant, thought Fielding. He was wearing a Daks jacket and eating a pizza out of a cardboard box.

'Sorry about this. Up before dawn. All the RAF could manage was a packet of biscuits.'

'Mr Biggin,' said Grenfell, 'has flown over from Norwood. He represents the Joint Intelligence Committee.'

Fielding's father had been a major in a commando unit in the Second World War. Out of harmless affectation, Fielding himself still referred to spooks as belonging to a 'secret show'.

Biggin belonged to MI6 at Cabinet Level. Operations Division, presumably, as he was SAS. The most secret show of all.

'Nick Chard,' Biggin said, 'is causing us some problems. We need to know more about him.'

'What's happened?'

'"B" Company are safe and well,' said Grenfell, and added acidly, 'as far as we know.'

'So what's the problem?'

Grenfell hesitated, choosing his words. 'As you know, Chard has taken "B" Company and the Luftwaffe team to the Princess of Wales Hospital at Mončegorsk.'

'I recommended him for the job,' said Fielding. 'I was the one who made him up to OC "B" Company in the first place.'

'We're not requiring you to commit hara-kiri,' said Grenfell. 'We didn't ask you here so that you could fall on your sword. You can do that later, when there's more time.'

'He is an outstanding officer,' said Fielding. 'I'd like it put on record.'

'Without authority,' Grenfell continued. 'Without requesting authority even, he has left the hospital at Mončegorsk and proceeded north towards Murmansk.'

'Why?' Fielding asked, startled.

'Presumably because the hospital has been partially evacuated to another location. We can't ask him,' said Grenfell, 'because he has switched his HF radio off. And don't say it might be broken, because the SAS team who were accompanying the column say it isn't.'

'And what SAS team is this?'

'They were using "B"Company as cover.'

'For an operation?'

'The most important operation since the Gulf,' said Biggin.

'Did anybody tell Nick what was going on?'

'Of course not,' said Grenfell, failing to mask his irritation. 'The SAS mission has nothing to do with him.'

'Did anybody think to tell me? It's my battalion, for Christ's sake.'

'The SAS mission is quite separate from the relief mission.'

'They were,' said Biggin, 'what you might call travellers on the same road.'

'Well then, what are you complaining about? You gave Nick Chard a job to do. You told him it was humanitarian and not military. You sent him and a company of my men 150k into Russia to do it. You didn't choose to tell him about this other operation. What do you expect?'

'I expect him to obey orders. Can we all stop being indignant and obtuse?' said Grenfell. 'Chard knew we were about to order him out of Karelia. He decided he wanted to stay there. So he turned his radio off.'

'Simple and effective,' said Biggin, reading from a yellow file, 'just like it was in south Armagh in '94.'

Fielding had thought that might be coming.

'There's no evidence that he crossed the border.'

Grenfell said: 'There's two men sitting in the Maze now who'd tell you they were three miles inside County Monaghan when 2 Platoon yanked them out. And you were his company commander at the time, John. You know his radio wasn't on the blink when he went over.'

'A maverick,' said Biggin. 'He's a maverick. Let's go back to the beginning.'

He opened up another yellow file.

'Shrewsbury School, then Teddy Hall on a bursary. Upper Second in English, special subject the sixteenth- and seventeenth-century minor poets: Sir Philip Sydney, Waller, Suckling, Lovelace. Dear me, he did an option on Lovelace – that tells us a lot.'

'It tells me a lot about army graduate recruitment policy,' said Grenfell.

'"Tell me not sweet, I am unkind,"' said Biggin, '"That from the nunnery, of thy chaste breast and quiet mind/To war and arms I fly." I expect he's trotted that out to a few tarts in his time.'

Grenfell said: 'He might be a poet, but he was bloody rude when he woke me up to tell me that German nurse had snuffed it.'

The heavy door whispered open. Generalleutnant Hoepner came in. The three men at the table stood up, Biggin pushing his half-eaten pizza to one side.

'Sit down, please. Sorry I couldn't be with you before. The Latvian border.'

'They haven't crossed?' said Biggin.

'No, but they're making noises. Probably because the conference opens tomorrow. I might want to move your battalion across at any time, John.'

'We're ready, sir,' said Fielding.

He liked Hoepner. He remembered when he had come to Bulford to inspect the regiment. It had been a bitter cold day in January. Hoepner had stepped out of his chopper, breathed deeply, grinned and said: 'What my father used to call "Stalingrad weather".'

'We're just looking through Major Chard's file, sir,' said Biggin.

'Carry on.'

'Not married. Platoon commander's course at the Royal School of Infantry. Passed staff college examinations at first attempt, June 1994, JDSC course in '95, picked up for staff college last year but turned it down. Why was that?'

'He didn't want to go.'

Grenfell said: 'Didn't *want* to?'

'He's a regimental man. Didn't want to end up in a headquarters with a lot of shits and thrusters.'

'His words?' asked Hoepner.

'No,' said Fielding, 'mine.'

'I see,' said Grenfell.

Fielding already had his thatched cottage between Andover and Marlborough, his colonel's pension, the boys safely through school. There was nothing they could do to him.

'A romantic and a maverick,' said Biggin, closing the file. 'On the loose in Karelia.'

Hoepner said: 'Is there anything we can do to get him out?'

There was a moment's silence.

'No,' said Grenfell.

'What will he do, John?' Hoepner turned to Fielding. 'He has written instructions, a stop line he is forbidden to cross. Will he disobey those orders?'

'He's a good soldier,' said Fielding. 'An intelligent soldier. He's trained to think. To use his initiative. You've sent him to find a hospital, and he'll find it, and if he's turned off his HF set, he'll keep it turned off until he's got where he wants and done what he was sent to do. I'm sorry if that buggers up your secret show.'

Biggin shook his head. 'I don't really think it will affect

our "show". It might even provide a diversion.'

The atmosphere had changed, become awkward, embarrassed.

Fielding felt suddenly uneasy. 'In that case, there's no problem . . .'

Hoepner said: 'It's "B" Company we're worried about. You need to be warned. That's why you're here. If Chard takes them east of the Murmansk rail line, and is spotted, the column will be destroyed.'

FOUR

Novyj Yena, 1 November

They were directed to Novyj Yena's Culture Heritage
estate, where sulphur-stained tower blocks had names like
Pushkin and Turgenev, Solzhenitsyn and Dostoevsky.

They moved slowly between the dreary buildings. At a
pedestrianised junction they crept round a massive iron
sculpture of a matchstick man and a movie camera, erected
in 1987, according to the British Gas Tourist Guide to
Karelia, to show the achievements of Soviet cinema.

Everywhere the snow was crusted with dirt: mustard-
brown sulphur stains, black stains from the exhaust fumes
of low-grade fuel.

They saw few people, but there was a sense of order: the
town was still functioning. A party of women, *babushkas*,
were clearing snow with twig brooms.

They asked the way to High School 46 (Novyj Yena)
Murmansk Oblast, and were given directions: it was on the
far side of the estate, next to the Murmansk railway line.

The column approached down an avenue of apartment
blocks. At the far end stood a single-storey concrete
building. They could see teachers at blackboards, children
in rows.

In one of the classsrooms a boy turned to look, vacantly, out of the window, bored perhaps with the lesson, waiting for the bell to go home. His mouth fell suddenly open. Fifteen cream-and-black Snow Leopards, flags flying from each aerial, a soldier standing in each turret, were suddenly illuminated by the classroom lights as they fanned out into a line, machine-guns pointing forward through the windows.

From the dark shadow of the ambulance, Sergeant Worembrand appeared, running towards the school entrance, his body festooned with cameras, clutching a large teddy bear.

Now it was nearly midnight.

Outside a shimmer of polar light rippled across the mists of polluted air, over the dreary apartment blocks, in through the windows.

It showed soldiers lying asleep, their dossbags and Bergens laid out between the desks.

Above them, on the wall, it showed a huge slogan, the letters now menacing and black – though when seen in daylight they were a vivid red.

What did the slogan say, Nick wondered, leaning back against a warm radiator, drowsy but sleepless. 'Big Brother is watching you' – 'Don't forget your dinner money' – 'Grade 12 *will* win the house cup!'

He smiled gently.

They had found the children, the children that were left, the remnants of the Princess of Wales Children's Hospital at Mončegorsk: eighteen of them, with two Polish nurses, camping in a makeshift dormitory.

* * *

The door from the corridor opened. Anneliese slipped into the classroom. He watched her find her way delicately through the ranks of sleeping soldiers to where her dossbag had been laid out. She collected it up in her arms and staggered back out through the door. Evidently she and Brigite were going to sleep with the children.

Earlier he had watched her restart a course of four-hourly meals of raw liver to six-year-old Misha, who had been discovered on his last legs, his skin bluey-white. He ate the bloody, defrosted but ice-cold offal with obedient resignation, blood trickling from the corner of his mouth, while other children watched and sympathised.

Jamie had been visibly affected: moved as much, perhaps, by the tears in Anneliese's cornflower-coloured eyes as by the woes of the boy Misha.

'My God,' he said to Nick, as they left the dormitory, 'she's lovely. She really is lovely.'

Jamie by this stage had drunk several glasses of *zubrjovka*, vodka flavoured with buffalo grass, pressed upon him by the Director of the school.

'Don't you think she's the most beautiful girl you've ever seen?' he demanded.

Nick, who also had consumed several glasses of *zubrjovka*, had thought yes, Anneliese did have a look of Emma. It was the blonde hair and the tits.

He wondered why he was thinking about Emma again.

Because she had unexpectedly sent him a birthday card? Because it stopped him thinking of anything else?

243

* * *

The door opened. It was Robbo, back from checking the sentries round the vehicles. He saw that Nick was awake, and crossed the floor delicately, wearing army boots that had appeared, miraculously highly polished, within an hour of the column's arrival.

'Got a minute, sir?'

Nick looked round. Most soldiers were asleep, but one or two were lying awake, their eyes open in the semi-darkness, thinking perhaps of family, children, girlfriends.

Nick motioned towards the door. Robbo turned back towards it. Nick left the comfort of the radiator and followed him out into the corridor.

'You've done it again, haven't you?' said Robbo quietly.

'Done it again?'

'MacDermot and Young? Armagh? We switched the radio off then, as I recall.'

'I don't remember that, Sar'nt-Major.'

'I bloody do, sir,' said Robbo. 'And so does MacDermot. He's still in the high-security wing.'

'Ah, well,' said Nick, 'we might not win them all, but we've won the occasional victory.'

He stopped at a classroom and looked inside. His torch showed a room empty except for four ancient ultraviolet lamps.

'In winter they give all the children treatment with sunlamps,' he said. 'Stand them in a circle, a dozen at a time. Have you seen the school museum?'

Robbo shook his head.

Nick moved down the corridor and opened another door.

'It's going to mean a slapped wrist,' said Robbo, not a man who believed in overstatement. 'Turning the radio off. Not reporting to Narvik. Not mentioning to anybody where we were going.'

'Don't worry about it,' said Nick. 'It's not your responsibility.'

The room contained memorabilia of Second World War battles on the Karelian front. A metal air-raid shelter sign was fixed to the wall; posters urged renewed effort in the fight against the Nazis. There were ration-books on display, call-up papers, copies of the newspaper of Frolov's 14th Soviet army.

'Look at this,' said Nick. 'A British sailor's cap.'

In the torch light they could just make out the lettering: HMS EDINBURGH. 'There were eight hundred survivors,' said Nick. 'We couldn't get them home by sea. Had to send them south in small groups. They had a terrible time. Some of them didn't get home for a year.'

There was a menu from a war canteen in Murmansk. 'Fish gruel, black bread, pineneedle tea,' said Nick. 'The school Director said it was a better diet than most Karelians are getting now.'

'It's not just me. It's the signallers, sir,' said Robbo unhappily.

'Tell them I don't want to use the HF set because those helicopter gunships had our frequency. Anything else?'

'If you're planning a bit more of a mystery tour, sir, Staff Beckwith wants to talk about fuel and rations.'

Nick shook his head.

'We're heading back to Kirkenes as soon as Major Sendlinger has sorted things out. Tomorrow's unlikely, but probably the day after.'

They left the museum. As they reached the classroom, Robbo said: 'Perhaps you ought to have a word with Lieutenant Pendred, sir. He's out with the sentries now. I know they've been asking the odd question.'

Nick was tired, longing to sink down into his dossbag, zip it up, and blank out the world.

'All right, Sar'nt-Major.'

He waited for Jamie to return.

Jamie said: 'My God, what was that stuff we had to drink? I've been poisoned.'

Nick said: 'I came up here from Lake Imandra without orders. You're not involved. You assumed I'd spoken to Narvik.'

Jamie said: 'It was a joint decision. We'll sink or swim together.'

'I don't make joint decisions with subalterns. I don't mind being crucified for disobeying orders. I'm not going to be done for incompetence.'

Jamie grinned.

'OK.'

He crawled into his dossbag. 'I wonder,' he said, 'if I can fix myself up with a shower tomorrow.'

'A shower? What the hell for?'

'It's restricting me, smelling like a polecat. It's undermining my self-confidence.'

'She smells like a polecat too. You only don't notice

246

because we all smell like polecats.'

'But she's going to the Director's house, tomorrow, for a bath. If I'd thought, I could have brought some Chanel to give her: a bottle of perfumed unguent to gently soap her skin.'

'Go to sleep, Jamie, for God's sake.'

Jamie did.

Nick still lay awake. He wanted to sleep, but sleep would not come. He had no illusions: during seven years in the army he had bent the rules and broken the rules, but when he took on the Chief of Staff to NATO's Northern Commander, he had gone, he thought, a brigadier too far.

He smiled faintly. What, he wondered, would they do to him?

FIVE

Novyj Yena, 2 November

'OK, is there anybody from Whitchurch? Anybody from Whitchurch or Market Drayton or Nantwich?' Worembrand's voice boomed crisply round the schoolroom. 'Come on, lads, if there's one thing gets my goat, it's a shrinking violet.'

'How about Bolton, Mal?' said Staff Beckwith.

'Bolton? What do they read in Bolton?'

'*Bolton Evening News*, Mal! Where've you been?'

'Wherever I've been, Dave,' said Worembrand with obvious sincerity, 'thank Christ it's not been Bolton. All right, in ten minutes, outside the front by the fir tree, and thanks for doing your duty. Now come on, Whitchurch or Market Drayton – don't be shy.'

As he harangued, Worembrand stood under the slogan that Nick now knew to read:

'Our schools should give young people the basics of knowledge and ability to work out for themselves a communist point of view.'

'Lenin,' said the Director of High School 46, standing

249

with Nick at the back of the classroom. 'We were going to paint over it, but we had no paint.' He laughed. 'We have been looking for the paint since 1992!'

Soldiers were cleaning their rifles, greasing their canvas boot muffs, playing cards, or chatting. Some were still sleeping, even though it was the middle of the morning.

'That's the thing about being on exercise in Norway,' a soldier had confided to Nick on his first tour. 'Plenty of doss.'

'I am sorry we could not find you somewhere better,' said the Director.

'It's a lot better than we've been used to,' said Nick.

'You would like to talk in my office?'

They passed a soldier smoking. The Director shot him a quick look, then moved on. Nick leaned down and said quietly: 'Lend us a fag then, Cryer.'

Cryer made him take the packet. Nick slipped it into his pocket.

They sat down.

'You would like some vodka?'

Nick said no, the sun was not yet over the yardarm, and then explained what the saying meant. He proffered the cigarettes. The Director shook his head violently, but Nick waggled the packet, and the Director took a cigarette, and Nick dropped the packet on the desk. The Director smiled slightly. They would both pretend the cigarettes were not there.

He was in his early thirties; a Petersburg man. Five years ago, he told Nick, the school had abolished compulsory civil defence, and introduced English lessons for all grades. He had come north from the big city to be head of the new English department.

A woman popped her head round the door. She was thin, in her twenties, angry-looking. There was an exchange in rapid Russian. The woman sounded exasperated.

'I want coffee,' said the Director, 'she wants books. Her husband's brother is living in Uzbekistan, so why can't she get coffee, I want to know. She says she will get the coffee once I get the books. But how do I get the books?'

The woman spoke again. She poked Nick on the shoulder to emphasise a point.

'Books,' said the Director, resigned. 'She says next time you come, bring us books. She is teaching Turgenev's *Fathers and Sons*, but has only one copy among forty students.'

'I'll remember,' said Nick. 'Thirty-nine copies. I've made a mental note.' The woman went.

'No coffee,' said the Director. 'No anything.'

He spoke jokingly, and laughed, but in his eyes – those deep, expressive Russian eyes – Nick saw fear and desperation.

He told Nick about his wife and three children. He had come to Karelia when he was first married. It was double pay inside the Arctic Circle, and there was a rumour in Petersburg that they had special rations in the north: vitamin pills and chocolate and codliver oil. Anyway, there was all that fish from Murmansk, all that reindeer meat; everybody knew people in the country were stuffing themselves on food while the cities starved.

He lit another cigarette.

'Thank God,' he said, 'you've come to take the sick ones off our hands. Thank God we don't have to worry about them any more.'

'We came to bring medical supplies. Drugs.'

The Director nodded.

'Will you take them to Norway?' he said. 'Or to England?'

Out in the corridor Nick called a soldier. 'Whitby!'

'Sir!'

My compliments to Major Sendlinger. I'd like to see her as soon as she's free. I'll be in the billet.'

'Sir.'

'Oh, and Whitby, when you've done that, get a dozen coffee-paks and give them to the Director with my kind regards.'

'Director, sir?'

'The headmaster.'

'The nurses want to go as soon as they can,' said Brigite. 'They've heard there's a train to Petersburg tomorrow, and they want to be on it.'

'How can they go? Who will look after the children?'

'They wanted to take the children with them, but nobody wants the children to go to Petersburg. What would happen to them? Who would look after them? Their parents are in Murmansk and Lovozero. One of them comes from Gremicha, another from Ponoj. They've never been further than Lake Imandra in their lives. What would they do in Kandalakša or Petersburg?'

'So can they be sent back to their homes? We can give them drugs they need, the food compounds, enough to tide them through the next three months.'

'Can we take them to their homes?'

'Us?' said Nick, startled. Take the convoy across the Kola peninsula all the way to the White Sea? He shuddered, mentally, just thinking about it. 'Christ, no.'

'So who can take them?'

'How the hell would I know that!'

Nobody could take them. That was the truth. There was a vestige of organised life along the Murmansk-Kandalaksa corridor, the motorway and rail line. Away from it there was chaos.

'Let's think this through outside,' said Nick irritably. 'I need some fresh air.'

'The nurses think we're a miracle,' said Brigite as they left the building, 'sent from heaven. All they want to do is bolt off back to Poland. You can see their point of view. They came on a three-month contract that expired a month ago. Nobody said anything about being caught up in a civil war, without food or medicines.'

'I wondered why they were slobbering all over me,' said Nick. 'Well, if they want, they can come back to Norway with us. There's plenty of room. But what the hell do we do about the children?'

By the entrance they found Worembrand holding a small fur-cocooned child by the hand, at the same time posing Staff Beckwith against a bedraggled fir tree planted

253

for ornamental purposes, perhaps, when the school was first opened.

Worembrand argued, Staff Beckwith appeared outraged. Eventually he lifted the small furry bundle in one arm, and accepted Worembrand's teddy bear in the other.

'Push his hood back . . . that's better . . . right, smile then, Dave. Oi, love, give him the flag then, will you?'

One of the Polish nurses, a huge smile on her face, ran forward with a small Union flag.

'That's it . . . that's right.' Worembrand half crouched, like a bent old man, peering upwards through his camera lens, and crept towards them.

The small child smiled and waved the Union Jack. Staff Beckwith smiled and waved the teddy bear.

'Don't do that,' barked Worembrand. 'I didn't say to do that. I want to keep it tight, for God's sake.'

Nick said: 'Bolton Soldier In Child Mercy Rescue Bid. Staff-Sergeant Dave Beckwith who hails from Bolton, Lancashire, took part in a mercy dash through the snows of arctic Russia . . .'

Brigite said: 'So, you're a journalist as well.'

'I did battalion PR in Berlin, just before we pulled out. I had an English degree, so I got lumbered. I was the chap who could read and write.'

The beauty of Worembrand's picture set-up, he knew, was that the caption would not have to be rewritten. Sometimes it would be 'Shrewsbury Soldier In Child Mercy Bid' or 'Wolverhampton Soldier In Child Mercy Bid', but basically it would stay the same, and photographers liked that, not being totally at ease with words.

Worembrand gave them a suspicious look as they walked past.

'Well done, Sar'nt,' said Nick, feeling that he had done little, so far, to boost the portly snapper's self-esteem. 'Army PR will be proud of you.'

Worembrand gave a sickly smile. The pictures would not go out through army PR, not if he had anything to do with it. Worembrand had travelled through storm and torrent; he had risked an icy grave in a foreign land. These snaps would go out via a little agency in Fleet Street; they were over and above the call of duty.

'Can I put the little lad down now, Mal?' asked Staff Beckwith.

'No. Now smile, smile, smile . . . oh Jesus, look love, can you ask the little mite to put his arms back round the nice soldier's neck. I never said anything about him stopping doing it. Come on now, we don't all want to freeze to death . . .'

They walked down the avenue. A man came out of an apartment block and said something in Russian. He was middle-aged, his face thin, etched with deep lines. Brigite replied. The man nodded, courteously, bowed to them both, and walked away.

'He says they will always be grateful. They will always remember what you have done for the sick children.'

'That's nice,' said Nick heavily. They walked for a few minutes until they reached the pedestrian square with the iron statue of the film-maker. Flat-roofed shops were empty and closed. There was nobody about.

Beyond the estate the land fell away. They could see down over the chemical works to the centre of the town. Smoke drifted from a low factory chimney. A pall of pollution hung over the scene; the snow was a dirty yellow.

'At least the factory is still operating,' said Nick.

A Snow Leopard came up the hill towards them, returning from the observation post set up by Nick to watch the approach roads, counting the flow of traffic on the Murmansk Highway.

'Well,' said Nick, signalling for the vehicle to stop, 'we'd better decide what to do. Let's assume we stay here for another day. Can we talk to the hospital, explain that we have the drugs and special food compounds, get a ward set aside, buy extra food supplies on the black market if we have to?'

He had twenty thousand US dollars and two hundred gold sovereigns, kept in a strongbox bolted to the floor of the command vehicle.

'We can try,' said Brigite, 'but I don't think we'll find a black market. According to the Poles, the profiteers have been killed by soldiers from the interior.'

The hospital was full to overflowing. 'It is impossible. They will be better off in Norway, in America,' said a weary doctor. 'Have you any penicillin you can let us have?'

'A little. Most of our drugs are designed to treat allergic asthma, rhinitis, conjunctivitis.'

'Antihistamines?' asked the doctor. 'Oral steroids?'

'Yes.'

'Anything you can spare. I'll write a paper on all this. I'll be published in the West when this is over.'

'I'll send what I can.'

They drove back to High School 46.

'How come they don't mind sick kids going to America, but don't want them to go to Petersburg?' said Nick.

'They're not starving in America,' said Brigite.

'No.'

They drove in silence. Then Nick said: 'The Director wants to get them off his hands, but the school's the best place for them. We can buy extra fuel for the boilers. I can send a couple of Snow Leopards and commandeer extra coke if I have to . . .'

'It's not the answer. There are no facilities, no medical equipment, no beds or proper blankets. The school is almost collapsing under its own problems. There is nowhere for Anneliese and myself to stay.'

'You? You can't stay. The local doctors can take over administering the drugs, surely?'

'Nick, there's an epidemic raging! You saw what it was like in the hospital.'

'In that case,' said Nick, after a moment, 'it's Petersburg. Will you go with them?'

'Of course.'

'So they'll have you and Anneliese and the two Polish nurses to look after them. The European Commission will take charge, once you're there. We'll send a signal, OK?'

Brigite nodded.

'Let's find out about this train.'

'Nicholas . . .'

'What?'

Brigite turned and looked at him. 'We thought Misha was going to die at four o'clock yesterday afternoon. There are at least four other kids who were seriously ill because their drugs had been unavailable. The teenage girl, Irana, had not eaten for five days. She was starving to death, but every time she tried to eat bread, her throat swelled and she choked. I know you're worried about the army, I know you're in big trouble, but you did the right thing. You'll always know you did the right thing.'

At the school the Director wanted him to give a talk to the twelfth grade on the English political system. Anneliese had been to the Director's flat, and now her blonde hair was shining, her face rosy pink.

Jamie was horrified. 'I daren't go near her,' he said. 'She'll think I smell.'

Worembrand was taking 'art' photographs: little children on their own in the playground, or by the school gate, or in an empty road, staring unsmiling at the camera, ordered to look hungry and lost and very sad. They were for his exhibition: 'Children of Karelia'.

According to the television news, the train was leaving Murmansk at midnight, under the auspices of the Red Cross. It was due in Novyj Yena at noon the next day.

The Director and Brigite went to the office of the sub-oblast and phoned the Red Cross in St Petersburg, asking them to reserve space on the train for the sick children.

In the afternoon Nick spoke to the twelfth grade, with the Director and Anneliese as interpreters. He declined to talk about political systems, and spoke instead about English 'poets for freedom'. He told them that stone walls did not a prison make, nor iron bars a cage. 'If I have freedom in my love,' he said:

> 'And in my soul am free.
> Angels alone, that soar above,
> Enjoy such liberty.'

A student asked: 'That is beautiful. Is the writer in detention? Can we write to urge his release?'

Afterwards Anneliese said: 'Why is Jamie avoiding me? What have I done?'

Robbo caught up with Nick and said: 'You don't think we ought to call Narvik now, sir?'

'No,' said Nick, 'not until we've put the children on the train.'

He had not yet refused to obey a direct order. He would like to avoid the ultimate military crime.

Later, just before dark, the observation post reported three helicopter gunships down the valley, crossing in formation, making towards the high ground between the valley and the Verchnetulomskoje swamp lakes; the place where the column would have been, had it been heading back to Norway.

SIX

Mount Kirovsk, 3 November

Fourteen kilometres to go, perhaps fifteen. They were circling from the north, climbing to the high ground where they could look down on the huge expanse of Lake Umbozero, with Mount Kirovsk, its summit in yellow mist, now to the south-west.

This time they were being cunning. They were not trying to creep up the frozen river Umba (SAS instructors recced the Umba back in 1991, supposedly enjoying a salmon-fishing trip. They might have fooled the salmon; they didn't fool the KGB, watching helplessly but shooting plenty of video).

This time Munro and his team were coming in from the Kola, the frozen wastelands, the last place on God's earth.

Which was, perhaps, why the Spetznaz had not seen them.

For the Spetznaz were out and about on Mount Kirovsk, combing the slopes and gullies in brigade strength, four hundred men in three battalions, which meant they should have seen every fox and wolverine that moved as they swept through the valleys, their skis pulled by MT-LB oversnow personnel carriers, old but reliable, their flank patrols fanned out a thousand metres on either side.

Sergeant Noon touched Munro's arm. He pointed to the frozen scree to the south. A flank patrol was working its way up the valley side. It would pass perhaps fifty metres below their position.

The sky was a dirty yellow, as it had been since yesterday, but the wind had died and visibility was good. Munro indicated with a jerk of his head that they should move back from the ledge.

They lay in their *dnovka*, their dossbags jammed against each other. They did not dare to light a stove. For food they put chocolate bars against their bodies, under their armpits and between their legs; it took an hour for a chocolate bar to unfreeze sufficiently to be eaten. They sucked cautiously at balls of snow, careful not to swallow liquid before it had been warmed in the mouth. A man's extremities can withstand thirty degrees of cold, but if his core temperature drops by one degree he is dead.

The nearest independent Spetznaz units were supposedly based at Pečory in the Leningrad MD. They weren't supposed to be within a thousand miles of Mount Kirovsk. But this was the SAS team's second day pinned down by Spetznaz patrols.

A Spetznaz soldier can hit a stationary target at 1,600 feet with a rifle, at 130 feet with a machine-gun, and 100 feet with a pistol.

But we can do better than that, right?

Right!

A Spetznaz soldier can use an anti-tank grenade launcher accurately at 1,300 feet and throw a hand-grenade accurately from 100 feet, either standing still or running.

But we can do better than that!

Right!

Munro lay and shivered ('Shivering is a good thing,' said the SAS instructors. 'It generates body heat, it proves you are alive.') remembering the lecture on Spetznaz techniques in the pub near Llanfihagel, at the end of *Sickener 2*. He remembered the sudden release of tension as the beer was gulped and the alcohol hit the senses, the warmth of the pub fire, the handfuls of crisps crammed into their mouths, the euphoria of knowing that they had pulled through, that they were not being RTUd, were not heading for the lonely wait for the Cathedrals Express on platform four at Hereford station.

We can do better than any bugger!

Yeah!

Toby had duffed up a youth-hosteller in the car park. The man had passed a comment about Toby's smell – Toby had spent two days and nights on the Skirrid since crawling through the honeytrench of sheep's afterbirth – but Toby didn't take offence at that.

What had annoyed Toby was the youth-hosteller reading the *Guardian* right next to where Toby was putting back the pints of Bass, right where Toby could see it.

'Toby? You OK?'

Fuller had stopped shivering. Noon, lying in the middle,

had noticed the sudden stillness.

'Toby?'

Munro said: 'Get in with him, Terence.'

They stayed in the *dnovka* until dusk, Noon in Fuller's dossbag, holding him in his arms, warming him with a faint glow of bodyheat.

At 16.00, the communications satellite was in position over Bear Island, and Munro sent a burst transmission to Narvik, reporting the presence of elite special service troops, questioning whether they were attached to 101 Independent Rocket Regiment or if they were playing a game of their own.

Something for Biggin to fret about.

He crawled to the tiny opening of the *dnovka*. The valley looked empty, although he knew that it was not.

They had forty-eight hours to their deadline, and at least ten kilometres to go.

He was not seriously worried.

Spetznaz patrols were in their path, but were not aware of their existence. They would travel at night. They would kill, if they had to, without hesitation.

Who can beat shit out of Spetznaz?

We can!

SEVEN

Novyj Yena, 4 November

The time had come. Syco was going AWOL. He was going to slip aboard the Red Cross train to Petersburg.

'In uniform?' asked Leech, startled.

'Keep your voice down!'

Lance-Corporal Holmes was prowling the vehicle park, his suspicious small eyes seeking out anything in which a regimental policeman might take an interest. It was 09.00: First Parade Service. Around them, Snow Leopards were parked in a three-sided hollow square with their bonnets yawning and a driver's head thrust, like a lion-tamer in a circus, under each one.

Sykes unscrewed the dipstick and wiped it with a cloth. The special low-temperature oil – normal vehicle oil would have frozen solid inside the engine – fell away in golden globules.

'I'll buy some old clothes.'

'You'll have to kill somebody first,' said Leech. 'They don't throw old clothes away here.'

'I'll barter. I've got seven days' worth of ration packs. This lot'll eat anything.'

It was true, thought Leech. They'd eat Sykes if

he put jam on his overalls.

'Don't do it. Try and forget you ever had the idea.'

Syco said reproachfully: 'I told you, Leechie. I told you in Norway.'

'Yes,' said Leech, resigned. The idea was in Syco's brain now. Few ideas entered Syco's brain, Leech had noticed; but when one did, it stayed there.

It probably liked the solitude.

'Sykes!'

Staff Beckwith's voice boomed across the park.

Leech said: 'But even if you get to Petersburg . . .'

'They'll take plastic at the airport. Or there's a train from Petersburg to France . . .'

'Through the Baltic, Syco. Through Third Shock Army. There's a war starting down there, Syco. You've seen the telly.'

'Petersburg to Calais. I'll hire one of them mopeds they run through the old Channel Tunnel workings.'

'Sykes! Get your body over here!'

'Staff!'

Syco lolloped off, still clutching an oily component.

Sykes was going AWOL. It was going to happen. Leech hadn't seen his mate this happy since Grey sneezed into Lance-Corporal Holmes's porridge and Holmes didn't notice.

The train was now due at noon. There were two hours to wait. Nick and Brigite sat in the Director's office. The Director himself was in the town, attending a meeting of the sub-oblast council, putting in his weekly bid for food and fuel. He had not tried to hide his relief that Nick was taking the sick children away.

'It's getting worse,' he said, 'much worse. Put them on the train, my friend, and scoot.'

'We'll be all right,' said Nick.

'Scoot! As quickly as you can. I don't want to see you any more. Send the copies of Turgenev. Send us the novels of Dickens and Wodehouse. OK, I've got to go. Goodbye, my friend.'

'Will you be all right?'

'Listen, this community will protect the schoolchildren. I will get food and coal while there is food and coal in Karelia.'

He gave Nick a bottle of vodka. Nick gave him twenty ration packs and ten Crunchie bars. The chocolate had come from Anneliese, who had said: 'It's a present from Max to the kids of High School 46. He is too shy to offer it himself.'

'Max? Who the hell's Max?'

'Malcolm, you know? Max is his professional name.'

'I thought his profession was being a soldier.'

'Don't be a stick-in-the-mud,' Anneliese had said.

The sick children had been told that they were going to another hospital, a place like the Princess of Wales, but in the south. Most of them nodded, mutely accepting the situation. 'The only wise course,' said Brigite, 'for a child in Russia.' Some cried.

They wanted to go home, said Anneliese, her blue eyes swimming, her arms holding tightly the boy Misha. These days he was usually in her arms; his eleven-year-old sister

Kaka, who had been left at the hospital to keep him company, trailing behind.

Nick watched Misha eat his liver and said: 'Good boy.' Misha always ate everything up when Nick was there. Anneliese dabbed the blood from his chin.

'There's a brave little soldier.'

'Always eat up your liver,' said Nick, 'and one day we'll enlist you in the regiment.'

Brigite looked out of the office window and said: 'I'd be happier if you took Misha back to Norway with you.'

'What?'

'His sister could look after him.'

'We're an army unit. There's a civil war breaking out.'

'His food has to be kept frozen. How can that be done inside a train?'

'You'll be in Petersburg in twenty-four hours.'

'Come on, Nicholas. It could take a week. And what makes you think there are supplies of raw liver instantly available when we get there?'

'There's a European Commission employing two hundred people in Petersburg. They can start earning their money.'

'I think they do already, actually. But it's a boy's life we're talking about here. You're talking about what might be, what should be. We're sixteen children and four medics on a refugee train.'

He joined her at the window.

'If things look bad, I'll send half a dozen men with you.'

'Have you spoken to Narvik?'

'The moment you're on the train.'

'And what will they say if you tell them that, apart from everything else, six British soldiers are on their way to Petersburg and will have to be flown home at the taxpayers' expense?'

'They'll congratulate me on using my initiative, substantiate my Majority, commission a portrait of me to hang in the mess, and beg me to go to staff college so that they can promote me to lieutenant-colonel.'

'Bad as that, eh?'

It had got warmer and snow was falling, fat flakes coating the vehicles and the bedraggled line of firs running down to the motorway. In the yard, soldiers had set up a ski-jump and were launching themselves off it with cries of 'Banzai!'. Collins – who had spent the last week snug in a Snow Leopard's cab, and had now been forced out into the cold by Sergeant Doran – was slithering down the slope. With a monstrous yell he crashed down on to his back.

He had been 'got', he would now be claiming, by a snow snake. All soldiers were lectured on snow snakes when they first toured Norway: warned against the smooth-white reptiles that moved like lightning and wrapped themselves round the skis of unwary skiers, bringing them tumbling to the ground. Most snow snakes, the familiarisation officer would explain, were in the pay of the KGB. Anyone who captured one and brought it in for interrogation would get a fortnight's leave in UK.

The other piece of advice Nick remembered from the familiarisation lecture was: 'Watch your language. They don't all speak English, but they all know what "fuck" means.'

Army life. Army humour.

'So,' said Brigite, 'what do you really think they will do to you?'

'They could court-martial me if they were determined. But that would mean going public, and they wouldn't want that. They could wait a year or two and then cashier me – find a reason; it's not too hard. If they really try to garotte me, I might appeal to Diana.'

Brigite looked at him, inquiringly.

'The Princess of Wales,' said Nick. 'She's awfully nice. She asks our subalterns to drinks at Kensington Palace every year.'

'What on earth has the Princess of Wales to do with your regiment?'

'Colonel-in-Chief. We had to fight like hell to get her, most line regiments have to make do with the Grand Duchess of Schleswig-Holstein or the King of Belgium.'

'You know, occasionally, Nicholas, just for odd moments, I've been managing to forget how arrogant and chauvinistic you are.'

Brigite, thought Nick, was an example of somebody with no sense of humour. Few Germans did have, of course.

A primitive howl rent the air. Looking down they saw Jamie emerging from the school. As they watched, he ran at great speed across the yard, his legs thrusting high into the air as if he was running on red-hot coals. He was stark naked. The soldiers at the ski-run cheered. Jamie dived into a snowdrift. He rolled over then jumped up again. He rubbed snow behind his ears and neck and howled. He rubbed snow under his arms and howled. He fled back towards the school, still howling.

'He was saying,' said Nick, 'how much he wanted a bath.'

The office door opened. It was Anneliese. Her face was bright pink.

'Can anybody tell me why Jamie is doing that?'

'I think he's developed an interest in personal hygiene,' said Nick. 'Funny, really. He's never bothered about it before.'

There was a new howl: a shriek of outrage. They looked out. Jamie was pounding on the school door. Two corporals were peering out of a window, grinning.

'Let me in! Let me in, you bastards!'

Nick came out of the station and over to the command vehicle. He opened the rear door and got in. Brigite was sitting on the strong box, next to Collins, who was manning the inter-company radio.

'The platform's crowded. You can't move an inch. There must be two hundred refugees waiting for that train. Anneliese and Jamie are trying to find out what's happening. You'd better tell your Polish nurses to prepare to move fast.'

Brigite nodded, and left.

Nick said to Collins: 'Get me the sergeant-major.'

'Sir.'

Collins also left.

Nick pulled out the MoD map of Novyj Yena. He was studying it under the green map-light when Robbo climbed into the back of the vehicle.

Nick said: 'Major Sendlinger is having a word with the Polish nurses. The train is going to be very overcrowded. It's supposed to be Red Cross organised but I think it will be chaotic. I want a vehicle posted at 334-569, that's 2k north, overlooking the railway line. The moment the train appears I want to know about it. That's when we move into the station. Get a dozen men to stand by. No guns, no aggravation, no tempers lost. We'll take the UN flag with us.'

'What if the train's packed?'

'We clear a space.'

Jamie pulled Anneliese through the crowds, shouting, 'Excuse me, excuse me, madam. Excuse me, sir,' holding tight to her hand. The station master's office, when they found it, was locked. They fought their way into the booking hall, Jamie holding firmly on to her hand just in case she thought he might want to let go. The hall was dirty, draughty, and surprisingly large. The station, Jamie had discovered, was a sort of Karelian Crewe, a junction of three branch lines from the mining region round Mount Kirovsk, the nickel factories along the Yena, and the sawmills and berry farms along the main valley.

The wooden-shuttered ticket counter was closed. On the stained pink-distempered walls were large photos of grinning girls in beehive hairdos. Jamie stared at them in astonishment.

'Stop ogling the bints,' said Anneliese, another phrase picked up from her time with the Royal Marines.

Families sat on the frozen concrete floor, huddled groups of brown and black fur. Whenever the door opened the wind flowed in, almost liquid, cold as ice.

Anneliese spoke to a woman, asked if she knew when the train would arrive. The woman spoke volubly. She waved an arm to indicate the groups around her, the crowds on the platform. Anneliese made sympathetic noises.

'Well?' said Jamie.

'She doesn't know,' said Anneliese. 'These are mostly miners and their families. They say they only came here to work. They saw something about the Red Cross train on television. They want to put eight hundred kilometres between them and what's coming south from Murmansk.'

'What's coming south? What does that mean? King Kong, men from Mars?'

Anneliese spoke to the woman again.

'The war,' she said. 'The war is almost here.'

Nick and Brigite stood at the head of the column. Behind them the station was silhouetted against the western sky: a dusky pink edifice with a dome and a rocket-like spire. Nick looked north over the dreary concrete buildings. There the sky was an oily yellow, a colour he had not seen before. It presaged a change in the weather.

'It'll be dark soon.'

'Yes,' said Brigite shortly. She was huddled in army camouflage whites, deep in her own thoughts.

Nick looked down the column. The vehicles had been

standing in line, their engines running to supply heat, for four hours. Two sentries passed to and fro, their rifles cradled in their arms. Sometimes they stopped and exchanged a few words; sometimes they danced from foot to foot like footballers warming up, or kicked the ground to warm their toes.

Civilians, trudging past, their clothes grubby and almost invariably the wrong size, regarded them with little curiosity. Armed men had ceased to be a novelty in Karelia.

Nick said: 'Do you know what Lenin said about the Germans and railway stations?'

'Yes,' said Brigite wearily. 'He said the Germans couldn't storm a railway station unless they all had platform tickets.'

'I think I'll see if the kids are all right,' said Nick.

'You do that,' said Brigite.

Nick walked down the line. He was worried about what would happen to Brigite and Anneliese and the children on the train. He was even more worried about detaching armed men to protect them.

If there was real trouble, half a dozen men would be helpless. It was a basic military maxim: in any given situation there will be good reasons to send in an armed force, and good reasons not to; there will never be good reasons to send in an inadequate force.

He looked into the back of the command vehicle. Collins and Willis were watching CNN news. On the tiny screen was a map of the Baltic. NATO forces had moved into Latvia. A politician was demanding to know why the West was still sending food relief to Russia when Third Shock

Army was threatening a small and defenceless independent state. On screen was film of Russian T-82A tanks lumbering through trees.

'It's different from the T-82,' said Collins interestedly, 'in having a second cupola above the loader.'

'That right?' said Willis, bored.

Nick walked down the column.

In the back of the REME Wrecker, sitting on toolboxes, half a dozen children were being entertained by Staff Beckwith, while one of the Polish nurses did her best to interpret for him.

'You've never heard of Lancashire?' said Staff Beckwith. 'You've never heard of Bolton, Lancs?'

Heads were shaken. They knew they had a lot to catch up on, a lot to learn about the West.

'There's a seaside resort called Blackpool,' Staff Beckwith was reciting, as Nick walked away, 'that's noted for Fresh Air and Fun. And Mr and Mrs Ramsbottom, went there with young Albert their son . . .'

In the cab of the ambulance, Sergeant Worembrand was asleep, his duvet wrapped tightly round his body, his tartan scarf snug under his chin. Nick looked in through the windscreen and shook his head incredulously. A sentry, Corporal Hoddinot, grinned as he walked past.

Nick had a sudden thought. Could he send Sergeant Worembrand on the train with the medics' party?

He was not a Royal Mercian; he was not a fighting soldier; but he was, in a manner of speaking, a man. His only purpose on the mission was to photograph the children for Army PR. How could he do that if he wasn't with them?

He looked at Worembrand: middle-aged, thin-faced but stout of frame, wisps of sandy hair on his balding pate, his lips puckered, smiling occasionally in his sleep, dreaming presumably of Rheindahlen and the Cherry-Ripe Club he was said to have shares in.

Would 'Max' be any use on a crowded refugee train, if it came to standing up to gangsters trying to grab food supplies?

He'd bloody have to be.

Nick opened the cab door. As the cold air gusted under his duvet, Worembrand awoke with a peevish cry. Nick said: 'Come outside, Sar'nt, I'd like a word.'

When Worembrand was on the pavement, Nick said: 'The situation in Latvia's looking serious. Have you been watching the news?' Worembrand shook his head, too confused to speak.

'We could see NATO troops in border clashes before long. God knows what the Russkies are playing at – presumably they're trying to divert attention from their domestic problems – but it's a bloody dangerous game . . .'

Nick spoke briskly. Worembrand's mind, foggy from his dreams, tried to focus on what he was saying. As far as he could gather, Chard, who had not spoken more than three words to him since their arrival at Lake Imandra – the three words had been 'Don't *slouch*, Sergeant' yesterday morning, when he was halfway through his porridge – had dragged him out into the cold so that he could discuss with him the convoluted politics of northern Europe.

Chard, then, had gone mad.

'In theory a NATO soldier in uniform would be at considerable risk in Petersburg, if a land war broke out, but I don't see any danger in your case. You are part of an international rescue mission agreed by Moscow. You will be transported forward under the auspices of the European Commission . . .'

Light dawned.

'You will be in Petersburg in twenty-four hours. I want the party to have a man attached to it. When it comes to women in authority, and sexist attitudes, the Russians are still in the Middle Ages . . .'

It was the old story. The story of his life. A fucking Rupert was intent on fucking him about. An officer was intent, yet again, on sending a Worembrand into the jaws of hell.

Lance-Corporal Holmes, a fit, outdoor type of man, restless when cooped up, was also walking up and down the column. He passed a Snow Leopard and saw Leech sitting in the co-driver's seat, smoking a cigarette. Holmes passed on, then stopped and retraced his steps. He peered into the cab. Leech appeared not to have noticed him; he was looking dreamily out through the windscreen. Holmes tapped on the side window, sufficiently cautious of Leech's temper not to open the door and disturb the warm fug inside. Leech turned his head, a look of polite enquiry on his face.

'Where,' said Holmes loudly, pointing at the empty driver's seat, 'is he?'

'Gone for a crap,' mouthed Leech.

Holmes's eyes narrowed. He looked across to the station, then back at Leech. Leech looked out at him calmly.

'Go and get him,' said Holmes loudly. 'Tell him to get back here.'

'Fuck off,' mouthed Leech.

Holmes gave him a look of deep malevolence. Next time Leech was reduced to the rank of private soldier, an occasion that could not be that far distant, Holmes would have some scores to settle.

He walked slowly across the road and into the station entrance.

The lavatory was a long, dim, foul-smelling chamber, its tiles encrusted with grime, lit by a single dirty electric light.

It had wooden cubicles down one side, and each cubicle had a door that started at knee height, so that underneath could be seen a row of bent knees, and trousers crumpled over ankles.

Most of the cubicles were occupied. An ancient *babushka* walked laboriously down the row, poking under each cubicle with a stick, pushing the turds down into holes in the ground.

Holmes's nose twitched like a terrier's, his mind flooded with warm, nostalgic memories of Kurdistan and the outside lavs of Londonderry.

He looked around, seeking out Sykes.

A man called out excitedly from within a cubicle, and the *babushka* grumbled and thrust a handful of newspaper over the top of the partition.

Holmes walked slowly along the row, his head lowered and cocked to one side. His eyes were searching for camouflage whites, for army boots and toe muffs, for a sight of Syco's trousers.

He reached the woman and she spoke sharply, pointing to an empty cubicle.

'What's that, sweetheart?'

She tried to push him into the cubicle. He resisted. She started to shout. He retreated in reasonably good order. She followed him to the door, wailing in outrage, accusing him of God only knew what perversion.

He picked his way, with dignity, through the refugees, and made his way to the station exit.

Syco, shivering with cold and excitement, collapsed into the driver's seat and slammed the door.

'Well?' asked Leech.

'Got them in the hotel. Fifty Deutschmarks and the ration packs.'

From under his camouflage whites he pulled a black coat and a greasy grey fur hat.

'Jesus, there can't be a rat left in Russia,' marvelled Leech, holding the hat up between his finger and thumb.

'OK, so it's not a fashion statement,' said Syco, stuffing packets of cigarettes into the coat pockets. 'But when they start moving the kids into the station, I'm off.'

'Holmes is after you.'

'So what? He'll have enough to think about once that train comes in.'

'There's nothing I can say, is there?'

'No, so don't waste your breath.'

'I'll do my best for you, Syco. I'll go and see Karen. I'll write to you in Siberia, that's assuming they don't shoot you for spying . . .'

'Leechie, you know what they say about a friend in need: a friend in need is a bloody nuisance.'

'You'll never know how good a friend I've tried to be – watch out, he's coming back. Well, hide it then, hide it!'

They stuffed the coat and hat between their feet as Holmes emerged from the station, his eyes seeking Leech's vehicle.

He saw them both sitting in the cab. He stared hard. Then he wandered off, over the road, peering into the dark foyer of the Arctica Hotel, drawn by some psychic instinct to Sykes's last port of call.

'Syco?'

'What?' said Syco, irritated, tense.

'When you get to Belfast, give that bugger a real pasting, eh?'

Syco lit a cigarette. He smiled.

'It'll be on the news,' said Syco, 'you see. They'll have it on the news.'

Now the light was going, and the sky to the north was a deep ochre. And the wind was rising.

In the station hall nothing had changed. The station office and ticket counter were closed; the groups of refugees were still huddled on the frozen concrete, though now they had stopped talking.

'Anybody know when the train will arrive?' Jamie asked loudly and cheerily.

'*Kugda poyezd?*' translated Anneliese, but nobody responded. Anneliese turned to go but Jamie pulled her back.

He said: 'I've been thinking. We won't have much chance to say goodbye once the train comes in.'

'It doesn't take long to say goodbye.'

'Will I see you again?'

'I expect so. Perhaps. Why?'

'Because I'd like to,' said Jamie.

'Well . . . we'll all meet up for a reunion.'

'I don't mean that. Look, you must care for me a little bit. I don't see how it's possible for me to care for you so much without you caring for me a little bit.'

She blushed and looked down at her feet.

'I've got Wolfgang, Jamie. You know that.'

'Things change.'

She shook her head.

'I'd go to Dresden for a cat for you,' he said, trying to joke.

She stared down, apparently lost in thought.

'Anneliese?' he said gently.

'It's stupid.'

'Don't you love me a little bit?'

'Maybe. But that's because of the sort of person I am, and the sort of person you are. It doesn't mean I'm not going to marry Wolfgang.'

'Yes, it does.'

'No, Jamie.' She looked up. 'No.'

He put his arms round her and pulled her to him. They were still – because of their several layers of clothing – some distance apart. They swayed, snowman and snowgirl in a clinch.

'Jamie . . .'

'I love you an awful lot.'

'Oh, Jamie . . .'

She rested her head on his shoulder, possibly so that she would not have to look him in the eye, aiming for a degree of physical and spiritual warmth without too much commitment.

Jamie held her. Several Russians watched. A dull surprise that two foreigners should come all the way to Novyj Yena to embrace was the most evident expression on their faces.

'I love you, Anneliese,' he repeated, more confidently now, suspecting, as had so many before him, that this was a winning approach.

'It doesn't change anything,' said Anneliese, 'but . . .'

She kissed him. Frozen lips on frozen lips, an exchange of army-issue lip salve.

She pulled back and giggled nervously.

Jamie put a mittened hand round her neck, pulled her head towards him, and kissed her again.

'Sir!'

It was Collins, shouting down the column.

'Two-Two on the radio. Train's coming, sir.'

'Sar'nt-Major!' shouted Nick, but Robbo was already

calling the section corporals to get their men ready.

'This is the time to say goodbye,' said Brigite, as he ran up to the command vehicle. 'Goodbye and thank you.'

'Just get your kids on the train,' said Nick with a brief grin.

Jamie was running out of the station with Anneliese. Nick wondered why on earth they had to hold hands all the time.

'Lieutenant Pendred!' he shouted. 'Get the medical supplies on the platform.'

Robbo led the way, holding the United Nations flag. He forced a way on to the platform, six men from 1 Platoon opening a passage behind him. 'Make way, please, if you don't mind,' he bellowed in his best parade ground voice. ''Scuse me, excuse me, love . . .'

The crowd opened. Behind came the sixteen children, some walking, some carried by soldiers, Misha carried by Anneliese who was saying: 'Did you think I'd deserted you, darling?'

Now there was a buzz of excitement along the platform. Misha's sister, eleven-year-old Kaka, held out her hand to Nick. He shook it.

She said: 'Thank you. Thank you.'

'Take care,' said Nick, blinking.

'If anybody pinches anything from my camera cases,' said Worembrand, pressed into Nick's back by the crush, 'it'll be a matter for the provost marshal's department, I give fair warning.'

'Cheer up, Max,' said Anneliese. 'We started together, and we carry on together, yes?'

'I don't carry on with anybody,' said Worembrand grumpily.

Brigite forced her way back to Nick.

'I'll speak on your behalf anywhere, any time.'

'Thanks. Good luck.'

She kissed him on the cheek.

'See you, soldier.'

'See you,' said Nick.

Jamie said to Anneliese: 'Hey.'

She turned. He pushed Misha's head to one side and kissed her. They were still kissing when the train came into the station, and when it went out again. It was a steam engine, blowing up clouds of thick black smoke; the Murmansk line had been electrified for over fifteen years but now the power supply was dead.

The carriages flashed past, huge red crosses painted on their sides, faces jammed against the windows. Further down the platform somebody tried, and failed, to grab hold of a doorhandle and pull themselves aboard. They fell back into the crowd with a scream of pain.

Collins pushed his way forward through the crush, fighting his way to Nick.

'Two-Two on the line, sir. There's half an army coming down the road from Murmansk. He says they'll be on him in another minute. What should he do?'

EIGHT

'Motorised infantry, brigade strength,' said Nick quietly. 'No tanks, but about twenty BTR-80 armoured personnel carriers. A dozen BRDMs.'

'BRD whats?' said Jamie.

'Armoured reconnaissance vehicles, for Christ's sake.'

'Sorry.'

Jamie was trying to make notes. His pen was frozen. He forced his pencil to make a faint smudge in his notebook.

They were crouched on a small rocky outcrop on the hillside. The column was behind them, nose to tail in a wooded gully. They had crossed the M18 moments before troop-carriers had poured down it from the north. Nick had followed his instincts and taken to the high ground.

Below them lines of armoured vehicles were dispersing in the streets. Armed men, some in uniform, some in civilian dress, some in a mixture of both, were occupying buildings. There was a cordon round the railway station. A makeshift dressing station was being set up in the town hall. Wounded were being carried inside.

'Any idea who they might be?' asked Jamie.

'No.'

Narvik had told him that organised Federation units had been withdrawn south to Arkhangelsk. Narvik had told him to expect a few scattered groups of deserters, friendly if anything, blokes who would swap their machine-guns for a twenty-four-hour ration pack and a packet of fags.

In the SAS, he remembered, the Intelligence Corps was known as the Green Slime.

Jamie said: 'Our friends are back.'

The three gunships were approaching in formation, coming back from the high land on the western side of the valley, from the plateau where the column had camped the night after it crossed the Verchnetulomskoje swamp lakes.

Mi-28s. Something else he had not been told about.

He looked back over his shoulder. The column was deep in the stunted birches. The light was fading. The Snow Leopards' black-and-cream markings were superb camouflage, providing the gunships did not target this stretch of ground with their Bloodspot heat-seeking thermal imagers.

'Wait till the choppers have passed, then disperse the vehicles among the trees.'

'Set up camp?'

'No. They'll want to piquet this high ground, once they've sorted themselves out in the town. We have to be ready to bug out.'

'Which way?'

'East.'

'Christ, Nick . . .' Jamie looked at him, worried. 'We're already 5k east of our stop line.'

'East, and then round in a semicircle, to bring us back to the valley further south. I want to cross at dawn, before that lot down there are moving.'

'Hang on . . .'

The gunships had wheeled south of Novyj Yena, ignoring the troops occupying it. Now they were altering course again, this time aiming straight for the hillside: the wood with the column hidden inside it.

'They've seen us.'

'No. Keep still.'

The helicopters had seemed to float lazily across the valley. Now they were rising up the hillside with speed. Nick saw the rocket pods, the red wink of low light-level television and ground sensors that gave the Mi-28 its adverse-weather and night capability. Then he buried his head under the hood of his camouflage whites, his body hugging the snow.

They passed overhead, their turboshafts screaming as they clawed for extra height. Nick counted to twenty. Then he cautiously raised his head and twisted round to see where they had gone.

They were heading east towards Mount Kirovsk.

'Same as last time,' said Jamie. 'I reckon there's a military base over there. You sure there was nothing in the intell briefing?'

'Certain. OK, get on with it. I want the column at five minutes' notice to move. They can run engines to keep the heaters going, ten minutes each at half-hour intervals, two vehicles at a time. Get Beckwith to organise it, and get sentries out.'

'What time are we moving?'

'Assume 02.00. That's if we're left in peace that long.'

Jamie went back into the gully. Below, in Novyj Yena, ribbons of light suddenly appeared as the electricity came on. Nick heard shouting, a muffled cheer. He wondered how they would cope at High School 46. 'We Russians will always look after the children,' the Director had said. 'We are a sentimental nation.' Would they still study Turgenev in the middle of a civil war? Probably.

During the coup against Gorbachev, the literature teacher had manned the barricades in Moscow. 'It was like childhood, terrible and exciting,' she told Nick dramatically. 'I went back to my school and told my class that our country had become like Latin America.'

When the column left, she had given him a flower, a red carnation, and he marvelled at its delicacy, and at the sort of country he was in – at a nation that could starve but still grow hot-house flowers.

Brigite crawled out on to the rock and lay beside him. He passed his binoculars.

She said: 'We've split the children between four of the vehicles. It's very cramped, but the best we can do. They're OK for the moment. Some of the soldiers have given them packs of cards. The Polish nurses are miserable; one of them's been crying.'

'Oh dear,' said Nick.

'Yes, oh dear,' said Brigite. She studied the scene below, then said: 'You don't think we ought to talk to whoever is down there? Ask for safe passage? We're on a humanitarian mission. They can have no quarrel with the

European Commission or the United Nations.'

'They will be desperate for fuel and food. We have both. We also have NATO's most advanced oversnow vehicle, and we have Milan 5 and Starstreak.'

She said, after a moment, 'We don't have much food. Not now.'

'No.'

'Or fuel.'

'No.'

'But we certainly have Milan and Starstreak.'

'And I'll use them if those bastards try anything.'

She smiled faintly. 'And I thought I was the one who had no faith in human nature. So? What happens?'

'We move in the night, and find a way across the valley at dawn tomorrow,' said Nick lightly.

It sounded easy. But the valley was as wide as the Rhône valley, and when he looked from the hills above Novyj Yena to the plateau over Verchnetulomskoje, it was like looking from the Auvergne to the Alps.

'By tomorrow night we'll be back on our authorised route. Three days and we'll be back over the border at Nyrud. Four days and I'll buy you a drink in the Arctic Ocean Hotel.'

'And the children?'

'They come with us to Norway.'

'They do?'

'Why not? When they sack me, I can start an orphanage.'

Night was falling swiftly. They crawled back from the rock, and into the birch trees. Jamie was briefing Sergeant

Doran and three men who were loaded up with packs and night-surveillance equipment. He was issuing orders calmly and with confidence. He had, thought Nick, matured a lot in the last week.

'OK, take up position at the edge of the wood. Expect to be there for a couple of hours. Let us know the moment anything comes out of town in our direction.'

Doran nodded. Bowed under the weight of kit, he and his men filed into the night.

Brigite said: 'Nicholas, call Narvik.'

Jamie, in the near darkness, was looking at Nick, waiting for his answer.

Nick said: 'Our equipment doesn't allow us to send burst transmission. It would give our position away if anyone was monitoring our frequencies.'

'We're a humanitarian rescue mission. We have sixteen sick children.'

'You look after the children, Brigite. I'll look after the column.'

Brigite turned away.

It was midnight.

Syco and Leech were trudging through the wood, returning from sentry duty.

'I shouldn't be out in this,' said Syco. 'I've had frostbite. I could sue that bastard, sending me out in this.'

That bastard was Jamie. Syco, normally tolerant of young officers – he didn't bother them and they didn't bother him – was not happy.

'I could be in Petersburg, sinking in a warm bath in the

Posthouse. I've got a voucher from the Posthouse Gateshead for a free bottle of house red, redeemable worldwide. I could be eating steak and chips.'

Syco stopped to urinate, groaning as he exposed the most valued of his frostbitten extremities. Leech kicked idly at a tree.

'Stay lucky, Syco. You could be in front of a firing squad or chained to the strong box in the back of Chard's vehicle. Holmes nearly found you out down there.'

'Holmes,' said Syco, 'couldn't find his own arse with both hands.'

He buttoned up several layers of legwear. They proceeded through the silent birch trees.

'Who's that?' a voice called softly.

The command vehicle loomed up before them.

'Leech and Sykes, sir – just come off stag.'

Nick and Jamie were looking at a map spread on the bonnet, reading it by the filtered green light of Nick's torch.

'Right, lads,' said Jamie, 'get yourselves inside. Get warmed up.'

'Sir.'

Leech and Syco passed on. After a moment Leech said: 'The most dangerous combination in the world.'

'What?'

'Two officers and a map.'

They reached their Snow Leopard. They opened the cab door. Syco's night-torch revealed Lance-Corporal Holmes. He was sitting clutching Syco's Russian overcoat. In his lap, his banana-like fingers crumpled the soiled fur hat.

He smiled.

'When I saw you at the station, Sykes, wearing this coat, I thought perhaps I was seeing things. But it *was* you, and I've got the evidence. You're going on a charge.'

He climbed out of the cab.

Leech said: 'He was in the cab with me all the time.'

'He was going fucking abbo – abbo while on active service. Jesus, you get shot for that.'

'He was with me in the cab, every minute, except for when he went to the bog . . .'

'He was never near that bog,' said Holmes, moving away.

'And when he bought them presents.'

Holmes stopped. He turned.

'Leech,' he said, 'you'll kill me. I'll die laughing.'

'Presents,' said Leech, 'for the wife.'

'Presents for the wife?'

'He bought them off a bloke. There's half a dozen lads'll swear to it.'

Holmes looked at the greasy hat, the threadbare, smelly coat. 'These the sort of presents you give your missus, Sykes?'

Syco did not speak.

'No wonder she's fucked off with a kitchen salesman.'

Leech grabbed Syco and pulled him to the ground, muffling Sykes's cry: 'I'll have you!'

'It'd take ten of you,' Holmes said judiciously, stating a fact. He had dropped the coat and hat on the snow.

From the darkness Jamie's voice called out, 'Shut up over there!'

Silence fell. Syco stood up. He said in a flat voice: 'How does he know about Karen?'

Leech said: 'Everybody does, mate. Just get in the cab, eh?'

Holmes said nothing. He stood, feet planted apart, head lowered slightly, perhaps hoping that Syco would have another go.

Syco got into the cab.

Leech said quietly: 'What's Syco ever done to you?'

'What's he done to me?'

'Yes.'

'He's under fucking arrest.'

'That's not what I asked, is it?'

For a moment Holmes seemed genuinely baffled.

'He's done nothing to me.'

'Get off his back then, eh?'

Holmes said: 'It's nothing personal.'

He turned and disappeared into the night.

It was probably true, thought Leech. Holmes was a fair man. Black, White, Irish, Scots, Liverpudlians, Cockney sparrows – Holmes did not discriminate. Holmes hated everyone.

It was almost 01.00. Nick was on the rocky outcrop, looking down at the town, looking down along the valley. Robbo and Staff Beckwith were with him.

Below, the electricity had gone off, but a few oil lights burned. Beyond Novyj Yena the valley was in darkness.

'I reckon we've food for four days,' said Nick. 'You agree?'

Robbo said: 'We gave twenty packs to the school, and we've got the two nurses now, remember . . .'

Nick was not likely to forget. He felt a personal loss when every ration pack was torn open, when every unnecessary mouth (Polish nurses were unnecessary mouths, he should have left them at the station) opened to be fed.

Robbo went on: 'The children are eating some of our stuff. The lads are handing over their appleflakes and chocolate.'

It was fair enough. The lads might soon be guzzling little Misha's liver; they had sixty pounds of it, and it would do very well fried up with some non-existent onions.

'Fuel?'

Staff Beckwith said: 'Perhaps five days' travelling, sir, depending on the terrain. We can't afford to run the engines just for heat.'

'We won't need to, once we're moving. What about naphtha for stoves?'

'Plenty.'

'The RAF might be able to manage a supply drop,' said Robbo innocently, 'if they knew we had a problem.'

'No chance,' said Nick, 'but don't worry, Sar'nt-Major. I'm going to call Narvik.'

The HF set gibbered contentedly to itself, its red lights flashing. Corporal Willis said: 'Nice to have it back on, sir.'

Nick gave him a cold look.

A voice said: 'Narvik.'

'OC Matchmaker. I want to talk to the Chief of Staff.'

'Hold on.'

'No,' said Nick, 'I'll open comms again in two minutes. Out.'

He flicked a switch to break the link.

He waited. There had been no hesitation about waking the brigadier this time. He imagined Grenfell tumbling out of bed, pulling on his trousers, scurrying down the corridor. Perhaps he should have given him three minutes. Too late now.

Willis was pretending to read his sci-fi book: *Olga, Ice Queen of Galaxy Nine*.

Two minutes passed.

'All right, Willis.'

Willis called up Narvik. Grenfell's voice was as cold as Olga the Ice Queen.

'Matchmaker Sunray,' said Grenfell. 'Where have you been?'

'Hostile gunships appear to be looking for us. Have not been able to use the HF set without betraying our position.'

Willis raised his eyes briefly from his book. He had been with Nick in South Armagh, the last time he turned off radios and went where he ought not to have gone. Mad bugger!

'Where are you now?'

'We're 2k east of Puma.'

Puma was codeword for the stop-line: the line he was not, under any circumstances, supposed to cross.

'Repeat that.'

Nick did, wearily.

Why was he over his stop-line? Because a motorised

infantry brigade had forced him over, because he had been in the wrong place to start with, because he had taken 'B' Company on an illicit jaunt (picking up a gang of children and two plump Poles) and couldn't get them back.

'Narvik, I need to know about the Mi-28s. I need to know if I can move during the daytime. I'll need a replen of rations before we reach the border.'

'Matchmaker. Move now to a hide location. Adopt full camouflage and deception measures. Go to radio silence and maintain listening watch. On no account break radio silence or move during daytime. Do not move from hide location without specific instructions. Acknowledge.'

'Wilco. Out.'

Nick felt sick. He took off the headset and handed it to Willis.

He clambered out into the night. The cold made him gasp. He felt his way down the side of the vehicle to where a red glow of a cigarette told him that Robbo, Staff Beckwith and Jamie stood waiting.

'Call in the standing patrol,' he said. 'Pass the word down the line. Prepare to move.'

Then he clambered into the cab and slumped into the passenger seat. He closed his eyes for a few moments, letting the peace and solitude flow over him. Then Collins clambered in beside him, and engines started up, and Jamie and his ski patrol passed on their way to find a path along the broad, dark flank of Mount Kirovsk.

And Staff Beckwith's voice came on the company radio saying: 'Ready to move,' and it all began again.

* * *

Grenfell had spoken the way a staff instructor speaks to the rawest and most stupid subaltern. But, try as he might, Nick could not find it in him to worry about Grenfell. There were too many real bogeymen – and too close – for that.

NINE

It was 03.00. Terrier was meeting in the Secure Room. Biggin, Grenfell and Griffiths-Jones were present.

'He's across Puma: 2k east of Novyj Yena,' said Grenfell.

Biggin said: 'What reason does he give?'

'Rabble on the road south from Murmansk. He says he had to move to higher ground.'

'He's got fifteen Snow Leopards. He's got Milan. Why didn't he push his way through?'

'They might be a rabble,' said Grenfell, a line soldier, 'but they're the rabble of a motorised infantry brigade. He's also got a bunch of hospital kids and two Polish nurses, and he's worried about Mi-28s.'

'They've seen him?'

'He thinks they're looking for him. He wants to know who they are and where they come from.'

'Perhaps the time has come to tell him.'

'You're the security expert.'

Griffiths-Jones was marking the column's position on a map.

299

Biggin said: 'You wanted Chard to be briefed. You thought something like this might happen, as I recall.'

'Not really,' said Griffiths-Jones.

'Yes,' said Biggin, 'I remember.'

Grenfell said nothing.

The door opened. Generalleutnant Hoepner came in. 'Well?'

'Over his stop line, and bogged down.'

'Munro?'

'Moving forward as planned. He's come up against some special services patrols: 101 Regiment had a Spetznaz company attached to it, it's probably them.'

Biggin said: 'To be honest, Chard could be a useful diversion.'

Hoepner said: 'No, I don't want that.'

'I just mean it might distract their attention.'

'Tell him to move out now, before dawn.'

'I've got the met report, sir,' said Griffiths-Jones, passing it over. 'Weather's clear for tomorrow, but will deteriorate rapidly tomorrow night. There'll be nothing in the air after that.'

Hoepner looked at the blue flimsy. He said: 'I still want them out. Get them moving.'

Grenfell said: 'I told them to batten down.'

'No. I want them on the other side of the Murmansk valley by noon tomorrow. By nightfall I want some high ground between them and Mount Kirovsk. Tell them to go hell-for-leather and knock out anything that tries to stop them. Tell them to use Milan.'

Grenfell stood up. 'Sir.'

He left the room.

Biggin was reading intelligence reports from Brigade North that had come in during the night. Griffiths-Jones was working on the map, marking out a route on the talc. He coughed as Hoepner lit a cheroot.

'Does it bother you?' asked Hoepner.

'No, sir,' said Griffiths-Jones, thinking, for a fraction of a second, of the impossibility of saying, 'Well, yes, actually.'

Hoepner said: 'I'm having to go to Norwood. Your Chief of Defence Staff wants to know about "B" Company. He wants an assurance that they'll be out of the Kirovsk area within forty-eight hours.'

A phone went. Biggin picked it up.

'Yes?'

Hoepner inhaled on his cigar. He looked at Griffiths-Jones, who was wearing a Norgie sweater over dark green and magenta striped pyjamas.

'Your regimental colours?' Hoepner asked.

'My school,' said Griffiths-Jones.

Hoepner nodded. He had known it would be one or the other.

'A change from regimental duties, Peter.'

'A little bit different, yes.'

'A little bit different,' repeated Hoepner, ironic, faintly amused.

Biggin put the phone down. 'We can't raise Chard. He's being jammed.'

Griffiths-Jones said: 'We gave his frequencies to Moscow. They must have passed them to 101 Regiment.'

'Dear God,' said Hoepner. 'That's all we need.'

TEN

When you look at nature it is rare to see a straight line, an ordered pattern, or a large area of just one colour. Man creates order. Nature is a mess. In camouflage all appearance of order should be avoided. Tents and vehicles and ammo pouches have sharp outlines. Break them up. Use camnets over twigs and saplings at different heights to create uneven shapes.

Jamie had made his notes more than a year ago, in the drowsy heat of a July afternoon lecture at Sandhurst, after a morning that had started with a swim at 06.00 and a ten-mile tramp with a sixty-pound Bergen on his back.

'Remember shadow. A well-cammed vehicle might cast a regular shadow in sunlight. Remember that exhaust fumes stain snow. Cover with fresh snow or spray with white paint. Remember, always, the two keys to successful camouflage. What are the keys to successful camouflage, Mr Pendred?'

'Pardon?'

303

'Deception and discipline,' said a squeaky-arsed Argyll Highlander who knew everything.

'Deception and discipline, Mr Pendred.'

'Sir.'

It was dawn on the broad western slopes of Mount Kirovsk. For two hours Jamie had been busy practising the keys to successful camouflage.

Now he lay on his stomach in the sentry position, looking out from the edge of the wood, listening to the rumble of a solitary Snow Leopard, his eyes intent on the point where two caterpillar tracks disappeared over a rise.

Behind him Nick came out of the hide, stepping cautiously through the pines, and lay beside him.

'It's getting light,' Nick said. 'He should be back by now.'

'I think he's just over the ridge. I hope he is. Sound travels so far over snow.'

When the column had entered the wood, Robbo had taken one vehicle out at the other side to lay a false track, onward through other wooded areas, seeking a civilian road or farm track he could join, or a narrow gully where the tracks might reasonably, without suspicion, disappear. From the air, said the experts, it would appear that a single vehicle had passed through the hide wood without stopping.

Jamie wondered, as he had at Sandhurst, if the enemy might not have experts as well.

* * *

They listened to the steady beat of the Snow Leopard's engine. Jamie's head was filled with the cold, resinous scent of pines.

After a few moments he said: 'Any change with the radios?'

Nick shook his head.

'I don't get it,' said Jamie. 'We're supposed to have the full approval of the Feds. It's Fed kids we're rescuing, for God's sake.'

Nick said: 'We're picnicking our way through a civil war. You've got the circuit laid out?'

'Yep.'

'One track to take in latrines and fuel store?'

'Yep.'

'I do wish you wouldn't say yep.'

'Sorry,' said Jamie, injured.

He had felt quite pleased with himself. He had made sure that routes to latrines, fuel areas and sentry positions ran under the pine trees. He had devised a fiendishly clever track plan – a circuit leading to anywhere that anyone might need to go to. He had told the NCOs to make it clear that any soldier caught taking a short cut would face punitive punishment ('Deception and discipline, Mr Pendred'). He had organised fatigue parties to scatter fresh snow on the tracks at regular intervals, remembering that tracks become polished with frequent use and then shine like gold from the air.

And what he had not remembered, Sergeant Doran had remembered for him.

* * *

Nick said: 'This is bloody stupid. If they get caught in the open, we've all had it.'

'They can't be far now.'

But it was impossible to say how far off the Snow Leopard was.

'It's peculiar doing it for real,' Jamie said. 'Somehow I thought it would be different, but it isn't. It's exactly the same.'

A month ago they had spent three days moving at night in Pasvik National Park, while RAF helicopters of the Rapid Reaction Force tried to find them during the day.

'I think there might be a fractional difference,' said Nick, 'between the attitude of an Mi-28 gunner and the observer in an RAF Sea King.'

'Really? You think the Feds aren't as blind as bats or moronic to the nth degree?'

'No.'

'You don't think they'll drop a note saying "Gotcha, the drinks are on you, and mine's a large gin"?'

'I don't even know if they're Feds.'

'It's beyond me,' said Jamie truthfully. He shivered. 'What we need now,' he said, 'is Mariana.'

Nick said: 'Don't remind me of something I am trying so very hard to forget.'

In Pasvik, whilst they were lying doggo from the RAF, Mariana and a gaggle of nurses had appeared outside their woody hide and skied backwards and forwards over their vehicle tracks. Then Mariana had skied into the hide with a flask of hot chocolate and a packet of smoked salmon sandwiches. Jamie had sworn she was acting on her own initiative, and was only doing it to embarrass him.

To save him further embarrassment, Nick had eaten the sandwiches.

'Thank God!'

First they heard the sound of its engine, then the Snow Leopard came in view, five hundred metres away, carefully driving along tracks it had laid earlier. It entered the cover of the firs. Robbo gave Nick a thumbs-up sign from the cab. It took its designated place on the circuit that ran under the trees. Soldiers appeared to break down the hard edges of the caterpillar tracks and cover the exhaust burn with freshly dug snow.

The engine cut. Silence fell.

'What a night,' said Jamie. 'I'm shattered.'

'Go and get your head down.'

'What about you?'

'Later.'

Jamie left him. He stared out at the landscape. They were higher here. To the east rose the Khibiny Mountains, and to the south Mount Kirovsk. To the north he could see where the swampy taiga turned into the harsh arctic tundra: a place where even the stunted fir trees could not survive.

The light grew stronger. It was calm and still, but the sky was yellow, the colour of pale egg yolk, and there was a yellow mist over the northern horizon, something he had not seen before.

He looked back into the hide. The tents were well dispersed. Strung with camouflage, they looked like weird snow palaces. From the air they ought to be invisible. In these hidden, secret places soldiers would be gulping coffee or crawling, exhausted, into their dossbags. Brigite, Anneliese and the Polish nurses would be feeding and settling the children, then curling up to sleep themselves.

Under a thin protection of gauze and canvas, Matchmaker was going to ground.

He stayed at the edge of the wood. Leech, on sentry duty, stood a few feet away.

'How's Syco after his immersion?' asked Nick quietly.

'Tough as old boots, Syco, sir.' He added, after a few moments: 'Looking forward to his court martial.'

And me to mine, thought Nick.

Half an hour passed before the helicopter appeared. It came from behind Mount Kirovsk, heading towards Novyj Yena. As Nick watched, it crossed the caterpillar track made by the column. It swung round, hovered for a few moments, then started to follow the track back towards them.

'Don't move,' said Nick. 'Just stay still. Sudden movement is what they notice.'

The gunship came overhead, slowly crossing the hide wood, following the twin golden threads onward through the snow, through a further forest plantation, until they joined a track leading east to the mining town of Kukisvumchorr.

Then it wheeled back on to its original course, heading to the valley.

For such small mercies, thought Nick, let us be thankful.

He raised himself stiffly, frozen with cold.

'Tell Sykes we'll make as much as we can out of his sterling act of heroism.'

'His what, sir?'

'The way he diced with death and risked a watery grave just to save the government the price of an oversnow vehicle.'

'It's not how I remember it.'

'Yes, it is,' said Nick, starting to walk back towards the command vehicle.

'Cheers, sir,' said Leech quietly.

In the back of the command vehicle Robbo and Collins were discussing the gunship.

'It's basically just a variation of the old Hind-D,' Collins was saying. 'It's the armour and weaponry that makes it the best attack helicopter in the world.'

'That right?' said Robbo, massaging life back into his legs.

'Amazing,' said Collins, 'truly amazing. I wouldn't have missed this, I can tell you.'

In barracks, soldiers' lockers were usually plastered with photos of topless tarts, the walls over their beds festooned with pairs of girls' knickers, the trophies of war brought back from nights out in Salisbury or Rheindahlen. Collins was different. His locker and wall were festooned with technical drawings of tanks and helicopters and Great Western Railway steam engines.

Robbo said: 'And they still can't make a washing-machine that works.'

'You fooled them, Sar'nt-Major,' said Nick.

'Thank fuck for that, sir.'

Willis, headphones on, was slumped over the HF set.

'What news, Corporal Willis?' said Nick, easing himself into the seat next to him.

Willis jerked his head up. He took off the headphones. The sound of hissing filled the vehicle, a mushy sound with an underlying rhythmic beat.

'Sends you into a coma, sir,' he said.

'You've kept trying the other frequencies?'

'They're all the same.'

'It can't be atmospheric interference?'

'I know jamming when I hear it, sir.'

Willis was an old hand. He had exercised on the inner German border before the Wall came down; the East Germans jamming their frequencies, and 'Magdeburg Annie' playing music through the night to bugger up their comms.

Nick left them to it, went to the HQ Group tent, climbed into his dossbag and fell into an exhausted sleep. Sentries changed. The tents grew warm, or at least less cold. A child cried loudly, an unfamiliar noise that jerked Nick into wakefulness. The child was quickly hushed, and he slept again. Fifteen kilometres away, down in the broad Murmansk valley, south of Novyj Yena, fighting broke out between deserters of the mechanised infantry and MVD troops trying to restore the land-link between Murmansk and the south. A sharp engagement left two acres of glasshouse flattened: a market-garden operation that had taken ten years to establish now destroyed; tender plants and flowers shrivelled and burned by instant frost.

The column heard the echoes of gunfire. The sentries stared out over the empty snow, relaxed but alert for any movement on the smoky-yellow horizon. A fox, now in its silver winter coat, loped across the snow, its nose down, looking neither to left nor right. A black dot appeared in the sky and excited sudden interest from a sentry, but when he realised it was not a gunship his interest disappeared; his eyes fell back to the horizon.

The golden eagle hovered over the scene, then drifted west to survey the farmlands. On this day the war was spreading rapidly, down the Murmansk valley, over the plains, into the starving suburbs of St Petersburg. But on the broad western slopes of Mount Kirovsk there was stillness and peace.

'Malcolm? Mal? Mal?'

It was noon. The camp was stirring. Worembrand was comatose in his green maggot. He had been pondering, in his half-awake state, on whether or not to buy himself further into the Cherry-Ripe Club. Werner was offering him a half share, and he was sorely tempted, but could he trust Werner, that was the question.

'Mal? Come on, Mal.'

It was Staff Beckwith, crouched over him, shaking him roughly.

Worembrand snarled and shut his eyes tightly.

'Wake up, you bugger.'

Worembrand opened one eye.

'The lads,' said Staff Beckwith quietly, 'want to wake

up to a drop of tea with whisky, and there's only the Sar'nt-Major and Sar'nt Doran from the Royal Mercs, so how about you and me helping?'

He didn't need to spell it out. Worembrand had spent a lifetime hovering uneasily round the edges of military life. He had developed an intuition for the ludicrous and incomprehensible: the bizarre or dangerous (usually dangerous) behaviour of men who were resolutely opposed to growing up.

'Don't tell me . . .'

Staff Beckwith nodded and grinned.

'Yes,' he said. 'Inkerman Day.'

'When thousands of poor sods were slaughtered. So the sergeants serve the tea?'

Worembrand sometimes felt he could sob at the hopelessness of it all.

He turned over, huddling deep into his sleeping bag, one hand pulling the hood over his ears.

'Mal? Mal? Oh, come on, Mal . . .'

Misha ate his liver obediently, because Nick was watching him sternly. A Polish nurse said something in delighted tones. Misha's elder sister, Kaka, smiled uncertainly. She was a worried soul, left at the hospital to help look after her sick brother, but uncertain, at the age of eleven, how best to discharge her duties.

'We'll have you in the regiment yet,' said Nick, and the nurse interpreted, and Kaka looked more worried than ever. This was the second time the Angleesky soldier had declared his intention to steal her brother away.

Other children clapped as the last of the liver, chewed with infinite slowness, was gulped down.

'Good boy,' said Brigite.

Nick was learning to tell the children apart, to realise their differences.

Two of them, Nils and Paulus, were slant-eyed Sami – Karelian Lapps who came from a reindeer *sovchos* north of Lovozero – and had never been in a village with more than a hundred people in it before they arrived at Mončegorsk. They had spent their lives camping on the tundra – each child, from the age of ten, caring for three thousand reindeer. Their one ambition was to own a Japanese snowscooter.

Others were city kids: Lara a pert teenager from Murmansk, who had worked as a cleaner at Pizza Hut and spoke the English and Norwegian of the cruise-liner crews. She was allergic to gluten and to tubular vegetables. Bread gave her diarrhoea; potatoes caused her mouth and neck to swell and threatened to choke her.

Three days ago she had been lying on a camp bed, too sick to move, starving to death. Now she enjoyed shocking the Polish nurses by announcing her ambition to be a hard-currency whore in Berlin.

'Diplomats and journalists,' she said. 'No sailors. I'll live on strawberries and melons. I'm strong. I can look after myself.'

Inga, her friend, was a farmer's daughter. 'In our Russian life woman is strong, but ideally she should be weak. The power of woman is in her weakness. She should be pretty and tender. She should be a slave to men.'

The Polish nurse translated – approvingly, Nick thought – into English.

Lara spread her hands to Nick and Brigite. 'I think I am not hearing this,' she said. 'Waddayouguys think?'

'So you were right,' said Brigite, 'we shouldn't have called Narvik. We gave our position away.'

'I had to call Narvik,' said Nick. 'I didn't have a choice.'

'So what happens now?'

They had left the children's tent and were standing by the rear of the command vehicle, looking out through the pines.

Nick said: 'My orders were to go into hiding and sit tight. They were going to come back to me.'

'So we stay here?'

Nick looked out through the pine trees.

'We've got four days' rations. If we stay here another day, we will have lost our ability to make it back to Norway.'

'So?'

'Tonight we go back to the original plan. We sweep eastward reaching the valley 20k south of Novyj Yena at dawn.'

'It will be tough going in the hills.'

'It'd be tougher trying to get across the valley up here, fighting our way through a brigade of mechanised infantry.'

'I understand your reasoning, but you're assuming that once we get across the valley we'll be OK. You are

314

assuming that the eastern side of the valley represents safety, that the hills round Verchnetulomskoje will be as empty as when we came here. But what if they're not?'

ELEVEN

Mount Kirovsk, 4-5 November

When night fell they had crept from the *dnovka* and the cold had gripped them in a fist of ice. They had planned the route carefully, to avoid having to stop and think in the cold, but still they found they had to stop every few yards to check their bearings. Every time they stopped, the ground sucked the warmth from their feet. Every time they stopped, it seemed harder to start again.

After two hours Fuller began to stumble, and every stumble required a vast expense of effort to right himself.

Munro and Noon placed him between them. Then they moved forward, hands on shoulders, like blind men.

They should never have tried a second time. Not so soon. When the captain of the *Revenge* pulled back the curtain of the bunk, where Munro lay in a fog of exhaustion, and said: 'They want you to go in again,' he should have declined – with honour, surely, for they had one man dead.

During the night of 4 November they moved the distance three men of iron will can move in minus-30, roped together on a mountainside, carrying one hundred and twenty pounds on their backs.

Now they were making another *dnovka*.

A metre into the bank of snow, then a chamber four metres long and three metres wide, scoring hardpacked snow with the edge of the shovel and lifting it out in building blocks. Scattering it.

One more day to survive. At dusk they would creep forward, across the ridge; crawling, if they had to, the final kilometre to the target.

Munro had signalled their position to Narvik.

On the bed of the Barents Sea, *Revenge* would be positioned for the countdown. A slim, gleaming missile would already be sliding forward to the launch tubes.

Just another twelve hours to go.

Fuller seemed to have recovered. While Munro and Noon slumped exhausted on their backs, he went to work with ferocious energy, smoothing the walls with his mess tin, hauling the kit inside, cutting a pine branch and sweeping away their tracks.

They lit the stove and heated water. Steam rose in small clouds of ice vapour, which cracked loudly.

'*Shit!*' Noon grinned but his eyes widened in alarm, and he reached to turn out the stove.

'No, we risk it,' said Munro. 'OK, Toby?'

Fuller took no notice. He had not heard the ice vapour cracking.

'Grub, Toby. Grub . . .'

They ate, devouring the high-protein, high-calorie rations, licking at the frozen slabs of mintcake, gulping the sweet, tepid coffee.

'Come on, Toby, get it down . . .'

To be hungry was good. It was good when the body screamed for calories to burn against cold. When a man stopped feeling hungry, he was in danger. In the Arctic, they said, a man would freeze before he starved.

Later, by the paraffin stove's flickering light, Munro and Noon sat pinching at each other's toes. Then they pinched at each other's faces, like apes searching for ticks.

This was the way they always did it; seeking patches of pale waxy skin, the first sign of frostbite; working in pairs, the old buddy-buddy system.

Fuller sat and waited his turn. His buddy was dead, buried in a snow grave ten days ago by the banks of the Umba river, on the other side of this same mountain.

'OK, Toby, let's have you . . .'

Munro went on guard at the *dnovka*'s entrance. The yellow light was back in the sky and there was no wind. The mountainside was empty.

They could all have slept, but Noon, the medic, looked closely at Fuller, then said to Munro: 'Best keep the stove alight.'

So they organised stags and kept the stove alight. It would provide a minimum degree of warmth, and melt snow for hot drinks.

It was a sudden shriek of wind, a slam of air, that woke

Munro and Noon. Their heads jerked up, their eyes swivelling to the tiny entrance of the snowhole, their gloved hands reaching for their weapons. The entrance was filled by a deep yellow light and swirling shards of snow-ice.

Then they saw Fuller. He was crouched over the stove, talking to himself. He had stripped to the waist and his body was mottled blue.

TWELVE

Pine forests near Kukisvumchorr, 5 November: Inkerman Day

'Hello, wind's rising,' said Jamie, looking up from the stove as the tent suddenly shook. He was making coffee. The senior NCOs were playing three-handed whist while Staff Beckwith regaled them with salty northern tales.

'This lass, working for a Bolton businessman, right?'

'Yes, Dave,' said Robbo, dealing.

'A lovely lass, all curvy. Well she drove him insane, till at the end he put it to her: "How about a weekend in London" he said, "all expenses paid" "All right," she said, "but I'll need the afternoon off on Friday.""What for?" he said, and she said: "To buy myself a sexy white silk nightie."'

'Is hearts trumps?' asked Robbo.

'It is,' said Sergeant Doran. 'Somebody hasn't backed up.'

'Dave? You haven't backed up.'

'"Yes, yes! Have the afternoon off!" said our panting businessman. Then, when she'd gone, he thought perhaps he ought to buy himself some sexy white silk pyjamas. He didn't want her to think he wasn't sophisticated, you see.'

321

'Coffee, Staff?'

'Ta, sir,' said Staff Beckwith.

'Ta very much, sir,' said Robbo and Sergeant Doran.

'He went everywhere. And in the end, just as he was giving up hope, he found a pair of beautiful cream-coloured silk pyjamas with a red rose embroidered on the pocket. A red rose, got it?'

Jamie poured hot water over the coffee powder in his flask.

Sergeant Doran said, 'Fancy a drop of something, sir?' and produced a bottle. It was brandy.

'Bloody hell, Sar'nt.'

'Don't look so shocked, sir,' said Doran. 'I've seen that flask tucked in your ammo pouch.'

'Well, to cut a long story short . . .' said Staff Beckwith firmly.

'Back up, Dave,' said Robbo. 'You haven't backed up.'

'They went to London for the weekend, and on the Monday they were back in the office and at dinner time the girl's friends were all round her saying, "What happened? What was it like?" "Lovely," she said. "We went to the theatre and to a beautiful restaurant and stayed in a wonderful hotel." "*No no no*, what was he like in bed?" they asked. "Oh, he was wonderful," she said, "and so he should be. He fucks for Lancashire."'

Robbo said: 'I think I've missed a vital line somewhere.'

Well hi, Wolfgang (wrote Anneliese), well here we are still in Russia and not very comfortable.

I've been with the children for six hours and now I'm off-duty. What a life. How's Erike's cat? We're moving soon, we hope, and should be back in Norway in three days, so can you send a message care of 1 R Merc, Kirkenes, telling me that you and the cat are all right. Have you organised her cat flu jabs?

Do you know what I dreamt about, Wolfgang?

She hesitated, thinking of some of the things she had dreamed about lately.

Then her fingers tapped again.

I dreamt about making cassoulet with roast duck legs. It was Christmas and we'd been shopping in Hamburg and bought a Christmas Lily plant for your mother and a barbary duck and chocolate Stollen for us. We were in our new flat, I could see the French pans gleaming, and I was looking out over the cold city and out to sea, and it was lovely and warm in the kitchen and I was making the cassoulet. I can hardly bear to tell you about that cassoulet. There was runny hot fat from the spiced sausage, and the fat from the duck's legs was running over the beans, and the garlic and tomato and duck fat smell filled the kitchen, and Erike's cat was mewing for a little bit.

Wolfgang, this Christmas it's going to happen! I'm going to make that cassoulet!

I dream about fruit as well. Pears mostly. I

323

dream I'm just biting a fat juicy pear. I long to feel
the juice dribble down my chin. Would you like to
lick it off, Wolfgang?

Anneliese paused, read the last sentence, then pressed
the 'delete' button.

Yesterday, after we left Novjy Yena, we were
moving in convoy up into the hills and I was in the
turret with Misha, looking for reindeer (I've never
seen a reindeer! Seven million reindeer in the Kola
and I haven't seen one! I've told Jamie: no way
does this convoy go back to Norway until I've seen
a reindeer!) when suddenly we were surrounded by
tanks.

Hundreds of them. T-62s and 2S1 Gvozdikas,
according to Jamie. (Have I mentioned Jamie
Pendred before? He's a lieutenant.) Ghost tanks,
rusting away in rows. Max got them to stop the
vehicle so he could take a picture of them with the
column and the kids. An arty job for the
Independent, he said shrewdly. He's a shrewd
cookie, in my view. In my view he's still got some
Mars bars and Snickers bars.

The back of the Snow Leopard opened. Worembrand
stirred under his duvet and snapped like a bad-tempered
dog. Jamie climbed in and quickly slammed the door.

Anneliese said: 'Do you know how long it has taken us
to get this warm?'

'You ought to do press-ups for a bit. Writing home?'

Anneliese pressed 'lover' and 'save' and closed her word-processor and put it in the pocket of her anorak. Jamie sat down beside her, closely. He leaned forward and looked at the top of Worembrand's head, just visible, tiny baby hairs curling up from his balding scalp.

'Why does he always have to be here?' he said in a loud whisper.

The duvet moved slightly.

Anneliese's face screwed up in embarrassment.

Jamie sighed and pulled a flask out of his pocket. 'Coffee and cognac,' he said.

'You know something? You're wonderful.'

'At great cost I procured it,' said Jamie, 'just for you.'

Again the duvet quivered. Disgust, perhaps, rather than a longing for cognac, Worembrand being a Bacardi man.

'So,' said Anneliese, gulping her coffee. 'When do we move again?'

'Dusk. The wind's getting up, and the gunships'll have to bugger off. We've got about three hours to kill. The sergeants are playing whist . . . Sar'nt,' he added loudly, 'wouldn't you like to go and play whist?'

The duvet was motionless. It would take more than whist to entice Worembrand out.

Anneliese dug Jamie in the ribs. He said, 'Ouch,' and they giggled. They drank their coffee. He took her cup and put it down, then leaned over and kissed her.

They kissed for a long time. There was nothing else to do, after all.

Finally Anneliese disengaged and said: 'Jamie, do you know what a *purga* is?'

Jamie said that he didn't.

'Lara – you know, the Murmansk girl who wants to be a tart in Berlin – she was talking to the two Lapp boys, Nils and Paulus. They were looking at the sky and saying that a *purga* was coming.'

'Sounds a bit worrying,' said Jamie absently. His hand was under her camouflage whites now, and lying over her breast, except that it was hard to feel anything remotely relevant through two Norgie sweaters and several sets of thermal underwear.

'Lara says it's something to do with the weather.'

'Ah – right.'

He massaged gently. It wasn't doing a lot for him, if he had to tell the truth, but Anneliese was lying back dreamily, looking into his eyes, and seemed happy enough.

'Do you know what I need?' he whispered after a while.

She nodded.

Jamie turned and looked thoughtfully at the duvet.

It was motionless. Worembrand was playing dead soldiers.

A direct order, perhaps – sending Worembrand out into the icy afternoon? A photographic mission: *'B' Company First Battalion under camouflage in Russia, Inkerman Day 1997*, to hang on the wall of the mess at Bulford.

'Sar'nt Worembrand,' said Jamie smoothly.

His personal radio bleeped.

One of his hands was trapped behind Anneliese's shoulder. The other had found its way under the first dozen layers of her clothing, and could not easily be pulled out.

It was Anneliese who wrenched his radio from his belt and pressed the switch and said, 'Lieutenant Pendred's personal secretary.'

'Tell him we've got visitors,' said Nick.

So Anneliese saw her first reindeer, a massive, many-antlered buck with a bell round his neck that rang softly but with great clarity. And behind the buck came a herd of fifty or more does and young bucks, obediently following through the firs, occasionally stopping to paw for juicy lichens in the tree roots. Scattered clouds of vapour, the animals' hot breath transformed by the cold, rose to be whipped away by the rising wind. As they walked delicately, timidly, through the wood, the huge yellow haze of the sun began to sink behind them, and snow crystals the colour of lemon tinkled on the trees.

'This is so beautiful,' whispered Anneliese, crouched in the turret of the Snow Leopard. 'Oh, Jamie, look . . .'

The buck had halted. It stood staring at a perimeter sentry. The sentry stared back. Behind the buck the herd was suddenly still, frozen, poised for flight.

A whistle sounded. A man's voice called a word of command. A dog ran out from behind the herd. Three men skied forward through the trees.

'Halt!'

The sentry's voice cracked out. A ripple of alarm ran through the deer. The skiers stopped instantly.

'He's frightened them, Jamie. Do something or they'll scatter.'

One of the skiers called a command, quietly but urgently. The dogs circled round behind the herd. Two of the skiers slowly backed away, also moving round behind the animals.

The sentry and the remaining skier stared at each other.

Jamie's personal radio bleeped again.

'Yes?'

'Ah, Miss Bausch's secretary this time. I wonder if she might like to come and interpret for me.'

'They mostly want fuel for their snowscooters. They are trying to get the herd down to shelter, but have no gas.'

'Neither have we.'

'A few litres.'

'No. Tell them we have only diesel fuel, high octane. It would blow their engines to bits.'

'If they try to isolate any of the deer, the rest of the herd will scatter, and without snowscooters they will not get them together again.'

'That's not my problem. Say they can have dollars, Deutschmarks, or pounds sterling.'

'They say Deutschmarks.'

'How much per animal?'

'For a young doe, twelve months, good eating, fifty Deutschmarks.'

'I expect they'd settle for five.'

'Shall I offer five?'

'No, thirty. It's not my money we're spending.'

The Lapp looked surprised but nodded vigorously, when the offer was made.

Nick held out his hand to seal the agreement. The Lapp

looked at it, puzzled. He spoke rapidly.

Anneliese said: 'He says a storm is coming. Not an ordinary storm. It's not easy for me; his Russian is not good. He says they cannot stay any longer, but do we want them to kill the animals.'

'Say yes. They can do it while I get the money. Lance-Corporal Holmes?'

'Sir?'

Holmes, standing stiff and awkward, was the third member of the newly-formed rations commissariat. He had been a regimental butcher before joining the regimental police, and had been on a catering course at Aldershot. 'Failed on cooking, sir,' he had told Nick, 'but got a distinction on me butchery.'

'Four young does – make sure they're tender and plump. I want two of them cooking within the hour.'

'Sir.'

Reindeer steaks sizzled, the smell of roasting meat unbearable, men and children gulping back their saliva as they waited and watched the white fat clarify in the heat and drip, as the cooks turned the steaks in the pan. On the flame next to the steaks, thick, fatty stews of reindeer meat and army-ration rice and tomato ketchup bubbled in pots.

The fat round the eyes was the most highly prized, said Nils and Paulus. The ears, they said, were delicious. The marrow from the leg bones was the greatest delicacy.

Worembrand plodded through the afternoon, from tent group to tent group, taking photographs. This Inkerman Day would go down in regimental history: the day 'B'

Company dined on reindeer and vodka, showing itself nothing if not adaptable.

'I want you to hold your plates up in one hand,' said Worembrand, fiddling with his light meter, 'and your mugs in the other. But only when I say so.'

'Get on with it, then,' said Sergeant Doran. 'We're supposed to be celebrating Inkerman Day, not Christmas Day.'

Worembrand shot him a look of dislike.

'Bit different from our usual Inkerman Day,' said Collins.

'Why? What do you do usually?' asked one of the REME lads.

'We have a buffet lunch at dinner time,' said Collins.

'You don't, do you?' said the REME lad in a voice of amazement.

'You take the piss and you'll get knuckled,' said Sergeant Doran.

'Pâté sandwiches and fried chicken legs,' said Collins, fondly remembering, 'and mushroom and prawn vol-au-vents. And then we have inter-company sports, and the CO's wife presents the boxing cup.'

'All right hold up your sodding plates and cups and smile, everybody,' said Worembrand. 'I'm only taking this picture once.'

Collins said: 'Don't you have any traditions in *your* outfit, Sar'nt?'

'No, they have habits. Don't you, Mal,' said Sergeant Doran, leaning forward and punching Worembrand playfully but painfully on the arm. 'Bad ones.'

'Don't *do* that,' snapped Worembrand, goaded beyond endurance.

'Come on, David fucking Bailey,' said Doran, 'get on with it and be quick. I was only being humorous.'

Nick had sought out Brigite. He had found her in one of the children's tents. 'Lieutenant Pendred and I,' he had said, 'hope that you will join us for dinner in the mess.'

And here they were, the four of them, in the back of the command vehicle, with a little stove, and a pan filled with chunks of tongue and fillet steak browning beautifully in reindeer fat and margarine.

'Bread,' said Brigite. 'I just long for fresh bread. Bread and lettuce and avocado.'

'Waiter!' shouted Jamie.

'Saturday,' said Nick, 'at the Arctic Ocean Hotel at Kirkenes. As much bread and avocado as you can eat.'

Jamie said: 'You really ought to phone and book a table.'

'I would,' said Nick, 'but a rival hotel is jamming the telephone line. That's what's making me so mad. Your glass, Miss Bausch.'

'It's terrible,' Anneliese mourned. 'My first reindeer, and we buy her for the pot.'

'Drink,' said Nick.

'I think we've drunk enough,' said Anneliese. 'We've had Inkerman Day drinks in every tent. What happened on Inkerman Day?'

'Two VCs for the South Shropshire Light Infantry,' said Nick; 'our senior regiment.'

331

'I do believe,' said Jamie intently, 'that the tongue will be ready first. It's cooking faster than the steaks, and is just that bit tenderer.'

They watched and waited, and then they seized little chunks and bit into them quickly before they cooled. The fat froze in a film on their lips.

'My God,' said Jamie, 'this is lovely.'

They ate.

'Chocolate raisin bars for dessert,' said Anneliese. 'I'm thawing four chocolate bars in my bosom.'

She blushed suddenly. Brigite looked at her, and wondered who had put them there.

'A little of the brown fat, Brigite?' offered Jamie, finding a morsel and spearing it.

'Will we really be back in Kirkenes by Saturday?' asked Anneliese.

Nick said: 'Should be. Once we move from here, we don't stop until we've crossed the valley. That should be tomorrow at dusk. Three days on from that, and we ought to be at Nyrud. You could be back in Germany by early next week.

'Or you could stay on with us for a day or two,' said Jamie; 'rest up, see the sights.'

Anneliese said: 'Have you got a girl, Nicholas?'

'No.'

'Jamie has. Jamie has a little fat Swedish girl.'

'Now that is not true, Anneliese. I can't help it if I get followed about and mobbed. It's the price I pay for being a handsome young officer.'

'My man left me for my best friend,' said Brigite.

Everybody paused for a second, and then started to chew again.

'Oh, Brigite, when?' asked Anneliese.

'The day before we came to Kirkenes. The bastard took me all the way to Munich to break the news.'

'Oh, that is so sad.'

'Sorry. I don't know why I told you.'

'It's the vodka,' said Jamie. 'Those Russkies have laced it with a truth drug.'

'My girl went off with a wine merchant's rep,' said Nick. 'We went out together for seven years, and then . . .'

'Oh, Nicholas . . .' said Anneliese. 'There's no loyalty any more. I really hate it.'

'Sometimes,' said Jamie, alarmed, 'these things are for the best. Here, try this. This is a nice bit.'

'No, but it's true.' Anneliese held the proffered piece of tongue and bit into it, and hot juice ran down her fingers. 'People let each other down too much these days.'

Worembrand's face appeared at the rear window.

'Aha! Let the man in,' said Jamie in a relieved voice. 'A photograph! Come on, come on, hurry up. You're letting the cold in. Now, are our glasses charged?'

Nick filled their glasses with vodka. Worembrand pulled bits out of his camera case.

Nick said: 'Mr Vice, the Queen.'

Jamie said: 'Ladies and gentlemen, the Queen.'

Before drinking, Nick said, 'God bless her,' as he always did, on mess nights and at university club dinners and at hunt balls (so often with Emma beside him in a low-cut gown, dutifully passing the port).

'God bless her,' said Anneliese obligingly.

Worembrand snapped.

Nick said: 'Mr Vice, the German Chancellor.'

Jamie said: 'Ladies and gentlemen, the German Chancellor.'

Anneliese said: 'I didn't vote for her, did you?'

'Yes, actually,' said Brigite.

They drank. Worembrand snapped.

Nick said: 'On Inkerman Day it is the privilege of the youngest subaltern to recall the moment when Lady Sale watched the army begin its retreat from Kabul, the South Shropshires mounting the rearguard and holding off with perfect discipline the forces of the enemy. The conduct of the South Shropshires reminded her, she said, of a verse from Thomas Campbell's "Hohenlinden". Mr Vice?'

'I can't remember it! They always write it down!'

'That all right for me, then, is it, sir?' said Worembrand.

'Yes, thank you.'

Worembrand gathered together his bits and pieces.

'You're being looked after, Sar'nt?' asked Nick awkwardly. He had not spoken to Worembrand since they were at Novyj Yena station, and before that at Lake Imandra, when he had said, 'Don't *slouch*, Sergeant.'

'I'm fine, sir.'

'I hope we're making you welcome, making you feel part of the battalion?'

'Don't you worry, sir.'

'You're a part of regimental history now, Max,' said Anneliese.

Worembrand gave a ghastly smile and departed. The

NIGHT OF THE BEAR

last thing on earth he wanted was to be part of Royal
Mercian regimental history. It was a succession of bloody
assaults and bloodier last stands.

They ate their chocolate bars.

Brigite said: 'God, I'll be glad to be home, even if he
has moved that whore into our house.'

She rested her head in her hands.

Outside the wind was stronger, moaning louder.

'Dark in half an hour,' said Jamie.

Nick said:

> 'Few, few shall part where many meet,
> The snow shall be their winding sheet,
> And every turf beneath their feet,
> Shall be a soldier's sepulchre.'

They looked at him. 'The quotation,' he said, 'from
"Hohenlinden".'

'I'll never understand you,' said Brigite.

There was a pause.

'It's a lovely poem,' said Anneliese.

'All right,' said Nick, 'let's get moving. Let's go home.'

PART FOUR

MOUNT KIROVSK

Their shoulders held the sky suspended;
They stood, and earth's foundations stay;
What God abandoned, these defended,
And saved the sum of things for pay.

A.E. Housman

ONE

Slopes of Mount Kirovsk, night of 5 November

'Keep closed up – not more than ten metres behind the vehicle in front. Use convoy lights only, unless I tell you otherwise. Whatever happens, don't break radio silence. If you break down or lose sight of the vehicle in front, press your "send" button once. As soon as I see the light flash, I'll stop the column until you catch up. Understood?'

The drivers were gathered round the bonnet of the command vehicle. The wind was up and it was starting to snow, the first snow to fall since they had left Novyj Yena.

'Co-drivers, keep checking to make sure you haven't lost the vehicle behind you. Staff Beckwith will be bringing up the rear, as usual. Anything you want to add, Staff?'

'No, sir.'

'We've been monitoring the met forecasts. This weather's going to get worse. Tomorrow it'll be bloody awful, but by then we'll be down in the valley, and I intend to keep moving. I know that's hard on the drivers, but the more distance we can put between ourselves and that pig's breakfast in Novyj Yena, the happier we'll all be.'

One or two drivers smiled briefly, most did not. Nick

was not worried. These were West Midlanders, permanently underwhelmed.

There was nothing left to say. He had painstakingly gone over the route, selecting the best type of going for the vehicles. Jamie and Robbo had written out simple route cards for the co-drivers to paste to their dashboards, giving RVs, distances, and grid references at which they would change direction. Each vehicle had LodeStar, giving them an accurate six-figure grid reference.

The wind gusted suddenly, throwing one of the men off balance.

'Bloody hell, drunk again,' said Sergeant Doran.

'All right,' said Nick, 'mount up. Let's go.'

They were moving at night on an un-recced route in mountainous terrain, in minus-30, through thick snow; and the glass was falling.

They bunched and then stretched out like a caterpillar. Vehicles rolled into dips and then laboured up the other side, drivers straining to keep close to the Snow Leopard in front, co-drivers watching for the Snow Leopard behind. Vehicles collided. A dozen times the red light flashed in the command vehicle, and Nick halted the column and stumbled back down the line until he met Staff Beckwith stumbling towards him. Then, assured that the convoy was still together, he clawed his way back to his cab and the column again lurched forward into the night.

They were still climbing, still moving east. Only at the third RV would they turn back to the south-west, down the broad shoulder of Mount Kirovsk towards Lake Imandra and the Murmansk valley, cross the M18, and regain the authorised route back to Norway.

They reached the second RV at midnight, two hours behind schedule but still on course, and still together. Visibility was down to twenty metres. Nick clambered out on to the bonnet and signalled back down the column with his torch. Suddenly a gust of wind hammered into his side, and sent him tumbling off the bonnet into four feet of freshly fallen snow.

Collins left the cab and clawed his way towards him. Nick spat out snow and waved him back. Staff Beckwith and Robbo toiled up the column.

They had been moving for six hours. Nick had planned a half-hour break for the drivers.

'Ten minutes, Sar'nt-Major,' he yelled. 'We're moving in ten minutes.'

Robbo stumbled back down the column, passing the word. In each cab, drivers and co-drivers opened their flasks. Cigarettes glowed. The Brecon Beacons or the Khibiny Mountains, it was all the same to them, thank God, thought Nick.

There was no shelter here from the wind. It came from the Barents Sea, from Siberia, from the Pole, it was funnelled up the Khibiny Mountains, and sent roaring down through the passes. They were high enough to feel its power.

'Might as well use full headlights, sir,' shouted Staff Beckwith as they crouched in the lee of the command vehicle. 'There'll be no bugger out in this.'

Nick nodded. They looked at their maps and, as far as possible, at the lay of the land. They would be going downhill from now on, at first across the broad, open mountainside, then feeling their way down gullies. They parted. Nick worked his way round the front of the vehicle to the passenger door of the cab. Before he heaved it open and sank into the warmth, he pulled his hood aside for a moment and listened. The noise of the engines was lost in the howling of the wind: they would have no cause, tonight, to worry about detection by audio-surveillance posts.

The hatch opened over Leech's head. An icy blast down the back of his neck startled him into wakefulness. Syco was standing next to him, his head invisible, poking out into the night. He instantly grabbed Syco's legs and tugged vigorously. Syco's head reappeared. He closed the hatch.

'I was just seeing what's going on.'

'Seeing what's going on? I thought you were going fucking abbo.'

'In this? What do you think I am, stupid?'

Syco sat. They both lit cigarettes.

'Hang about . . .'

A white, swaying figure had appeared on the vehicle in front.

'Tarzan,' said Leech, 'of the Alps.' The figure crouched, and sprang down on to their bonnet, then clambered up over their windscreen and hauled open their hatch. 'Put your headlights on when we move. All right, lads?' Then it was gone, its feet clumping over the roof and the cab behind, not waiting to find out if they were all right at all.

Leech poured the last of his coffee from his flask.

'I went to a court martial once,' Syco said. 'Hong Kong. When Stokes out of the mortar platoon filled in the bastard who ran the Yellow Goddess Club. The court martial couldn't believe he did it. He had a broken leg at the time.'

'The Chink?'

'No, Stokes. Hammered the poor bugger with his crutches.'

'Happy days,' said Leech.

'It was hot and sweaty,' said Syco; 'one of those sweaty Kowloon days. You remember how sweaty Kowloon was, Leechie?'

Leech remembered for a moment, then said:

'What were you doing at Stokey's court martial?'

'Character witness.'

'Bloody hell.' Leech was impressed. 'Did he get off?'

Syco shook his head.

The lights of the vehicle in front glowed suddenly bright red. Syco flicked a switch, and his headlights came on. The red lights moved slowly away into the snow. Syco let out the clutch.

'I'll bet it's warm in Colly tonight,' he said.

'What you don't understand is that they're not normal. They're not ordinary like you and me, or like anybody else for that matter. They're living in a time-warp. You go into a pub in Basildon, say, or Croydon or somewhere, and start going "Mr Vice, the Queen", and see what reaction you get, not that I know much about pubs in Basildon myself these days. The less I see of UK the better, quite frankly, it's got sod-all to recommend it, but I do know they don't sit in the Man of Essex saying "Mr Vice, the Queen", not without getting duffed up in a back alley. You see they go to public schools when they're little tots: Eton and Harrow for the nobby regiments like the Queers on Horseback – that's the Queen's Own Hussars to you, love – or schools like Marlborough and Shrewsbury if it's a line regiment. Either way, they've got matron to wipe their bottoms, and then they go into the army, where they ponce around in pretty uniforms saying "Mr Vice, the Queen", and they can get to *middle-age* without ever touching real life. If they arse-lick enough to be made colonels and fieldmarshals, they can *go to their grave* without ever finding out what life is about. I know it must seem totally weird to a German lassie, but it's weird to the rest of us, too. And it's not just Chard and Pendred; there's hundreds of them, all identical little Ruperts – hello, we're moving again. "Journey Into Hell"episode four hundred and fucking forty.'

Worembrand stopped. In the dim light he could see that Anneliese was asleep, her blonde, unwashed hair falling over her eyes, the two children she had brought into the Snow Leopard curled up against her.

The vehicle was rolling more gently now, creeping smoothly over the soft new snow. He snuggled deeper into his dossbag, his duvet round his ears.

After a while he slept. But it was not an easy sleep. His repose was disturbed, unusually, by dreams of military glory. He was with the South Shropshires at the Last Stand at Gandamak (there was a vivid print of this on the wall of the sergeants' mess at Rheindahlen), surrounded by growing piles of dead soldiers and Afghan fanatics. He was stumbling through the carnage clutching his camera bags and saying to anybody who would listen, 'I shouldn't be here. I'm supposed to be covering an open day at Osnabrück,' while Chard shouted 'Don't *slouch*, Sergeant' and howling Ghazis clambered over the ramparts of the dead, intent on butchering him with their bloody Khyber knives.

He woke suddenly. The Snow Leopard was stationary, though rocking slightly from side to side. Beside him a little girl was fast asleep, curled towards his duvet like a dormouse, her head on his arm. He gently pushed her away, and she fell back, still sleeping, against Anneliese.

The vehicle lurched again. For a confused moment he thought they must have arrived at their next RV, and Sergeant Doran and his lads were jolting him awake as a merry joke.

Suddenly the rear door flew open – Christ, they were going to drag him out for a snowball fight – and a soldier peered in and shouted, 'OK in here? They've caught up and we're moving again,' and slammed the door closed.

Caught up? Who had caught up? What was going on?

He burrowed deeper into his bag. Whatever was happening out there, he wanted no part of it.

'It's no good, sir!'

Collins braked, pulled on the handbrake and flicked the pre-select to neutral.

'Just keep moving steadily. You're all right,' said Nick.

'I can't see anything!' Collins's left hand was shaking as he moved it up to grip the wheel again. 'I can't do it, sir, I can't drive blind.'

'Just take it steady. You're doing fine.'

Collins's sweatband was drenched; sweat ran down his cheek.

'It's not right, not on a mountain. We could be driving over a cliff . . .'

'Just keep moving, Collins! It's like a bloody billiard table out there. Trust LodeStar. Trust the compass. Trust me.'

Collins nodded. He slowly eased the vehicle back into gear.

'Good lad.'

The engine revved. Collins, his nose up against the screen, crouching over the wheel with his tongue out like a learner driver, edged the vehicle gently forward.

Ahead was a moving wall of whiteness, a solid mass of snowflakes tearing across the screen, glimpsed for a millisecond through the flickering wipers. The ground had vanished, the sky had vanished, Mount Kirovsk had vanished. Nick's eyes ached and smarted. Beside him Collins pressed slightly on the accelerator.

'Good lad. It can't keep this up for ever. We'll be down on the sheltered side of the escarpment soon. Ten minutes to the next RV. It'll be easier after that.'

But he knew that they had not yet reached the difficult part of the journey: the descent into the gullies with their rocky outcrops and cliff faces. A false move then could easily send them plunging thirty or forty metres, the rest of the column following them over the edge like lemmings, Snow Leopard smashing down on Snow Leopard, the survivors crushed as they tried to crawl to safety.

There was no point thinking about it. He pressed the LodeStar pad. There was a delay of three seconds, then the two sets of numbers appeared: green, precise, and comforting.

They reached the third RV. It was four hours to dawn. The most difficult, most treacherous part of the descent lay ahead. Nick considered making camp, waiting for daylight to help guide them down.

No, they had to press on. He imagined the storm dying and the sun rising, and the gunships finding them on the exposed mountainside, a good ten kilometres short of Puma.

He knew now that Mount Kirovsk was the home of some kind of high-security military base. He dared not risk being caught inside it.

Reluctantly, like a miser spending his gold, he agreed to a thirty-minute stop. The men had to eat, hot drinks had to be made, flasks refilled.

Staff Beckwith wanted to put relief drivers into some of the vehicles, some of the lads who had still been taking oversnow driving courses back in Kirkenes.

'No,' said Nick. 'Not for the next section. Wait till we're down in the valley.'

At 04.00 the column moved off. At 04.30 the light on Nick's radio flashed: yet again a co-driver had lost contact with the vehicle behind. Collins stopped and massaged his eyes. Nick clambered over him to get out on the lee-ward side of the vehicle. Even then, as he dropped into the snow, the violence of the wind shocked him. He ploughed down the side of the command vehicle, braced himself, and stepped out into the gap. The wind nearly felled him.

He struggled past the second vehicle, and on past the third, giving Robbo a weary wave, heading for the halfway point where Staff Beckwith would be waiting to meet him.

He reached it.

There was no Staff Beckwith. And no more vehicles.

They were in the back of the command vehicle: Nick, Robbo and Jamie, poring over the maps.

'They must have forked right in that last dip,' said Robbo. 'It's easily done.'

Nick knew it was – if it could happen on Lüneburg Heath on still, starlit summer nights, it could happen here, no trouble.

'We could get them on the radio?' suggested Jamie.

'No.'

'There's nobody can get near us in this.'

'No radios. This could clear any time. I'm going out for them on foot.'

'If you don't mind me saying so, sir,' said Robbo, 'that is just plain bloody stupid.'

'It's a white-out,' said Jamie. 'You wouldn't last five minutes.'

'Look, they'll have stopped as soon as they realised what has happened. They could be less than a hundred metres away, sitting it out, waiting for us to go back and find them.'

'Or they could be ten times that far away, sir, still moving down that side gully,' said Robbo.

'Well, I'm not abandoning them, so let's get on with it.'

'OK,' said Jamie. 'I'll get my flank patrol organised.'

'Not you. You stay here. If anything goes wrong, you wait for the weather to clear, find the rest of the column, and take them home.'

'Are you sure it wouldn't be a good idea for us all to do that?'

Nick ignored him. 'You and me, Sar'nt-Major, and one other man. Any ideas?'

'Sar'nt Doran, for choice . . .'

'No, he stays with Jamie.'

'Lance-Corporal Holmes?'

Nick nodded. Holmes was the man: built like a brick shithouse, anchorman of the battalion tug-o-war team that trounced the Horse Artillery.

They found him. He said he could do with a leg stretch. Ten minutes later the three of them were heading back up the gully. They were roped together, had snowshoes on their feet, and a ski-stick in each hand. They had taken off their cam whites. It was more important for them to see each other than to be camouflaged.

Heads down, they struggled upwards into the wind and driving snow. The caterpillar tracks left by the column were vanishing before their eyes. After five minutes Nick stopped, hauled out his LodeStar receiver, and held it almost up to his nose to take a reading. Then they struggled on: fifty metres, a hundred, two hundred, it was impossible to say. The column's tracks were totally obliterated now. They had abandoned any attempt to follow them. They struggled up into the teeth of the wind through virgin snow.

Nick was soaked with sweat inside his many layers of clothing. The others would experience the same. An hour of this and they would be dead. He imagined Jamie sending out patrols to find them. Christ, why hadn't he given him explicit orders not to . . .

Robbo was tugging on the rope. Nick turned. Robbo was shaking his head, pointing back, down the slope, back towards the column. Nick again pulled out his LodeStar. The others gathered round him, their heads down, forming a rudimentary shelter. The green figures flashed up on the tiny screen. They were close to the false gully.

'That's where they might have gone,' Nick shouted, pointing. They looked helplessly for tracks. Then Robbo staggered over to some rocks, tugging them behind him. In the shelter of the rocks there was the ghost of a depression in the snow, a straight line visible for some five metres. *When you look at nature it is rare to see a straight line. Man creates order. Nature is a mess.*

'Five minutes,' Nick shouted. 'Another five minutes.'

He led them, slithering, down the slope. The wind was at their backs now, making the going easier, except that they would have to clamber up this way again if they failed to find the rest of the column. And God only knew, thought Nick, how they would reverse seven vehicles out of this gully, even if they did find them.

Robbo was tugging again on the rope, but he ignored him, and ploughed on. He was cursing to hell the driver who took the wrong turning – why hadn't he stopped when the lights in front of him disappeared; how fucking clear did an order have to be, for Christ's sake? – when he walked smack into a wall of snow and armoured steel.

TWO

London, 5 November

For Martyn Pine, Operational Systems Engineering Manager at LodeStar International (UK) Ltd, it had been a day of irritations, and it was threatening to get worse.

He had planned to dodge off early at lunchtime, to go to Selfridges' travel shop, and was halfway through the door when a girl in Customer Relations rang to say that LodeStar UK was being publicly criticised at the inquest on six sailors whose trawler had foundered a month ago off Iceland.

'I'm sick and tired,' said Martyn Pine, 'of trawlermen who refuse to pay their subscriptions, then accuse us of trying to make orphans of their children when we cancel their facility.'

'They're not actually blaming anybody,' said the girl. 'They're actually all dead. The coroner is asking did we knowingly disable their equipment in the middle of a force-ten gale?'

'We disabled it automatically when their subscription fell overdue by four weeks,' said Martyn Pine. 'I have no idea what the weather was like at the time.'

'Oh Christ,' said the girl. 'Can you go to the inquest in Grimsby and explain?'

353

'No,' said Martyn Pine, 'because I just do as I am told. It is not an engineering decision, it is a financial decision.'

He put the phone down. It rang again. The little quartz clock on his desk said four minutes to one. The call was from the General Manager's secretary.

'He thinks this might be one for you,' she said.

'Oh, does he,' said Martyn Pine.

'Sorry to bother you. My name's Peter Griffiths-Jones, and I'm speaking from a NATO base in Norway,' the caller said. 'We've some men using LodeStar equipment, and we need to find out where they are.'

'The LodeStar version of NavSat,' said Martyn Pine drearily, as to a child of five, 'is not a communications facility but a navigational aid. Your men can use it to find out where they are, or *you* can use it to find out where *you* are, but there is not a communications link. Such a link can be provided by British Telecom, but we do not have a government licence to run such a network, even if we wanted to.'

'Yes, but if somebody is linking into LodeStar, is it not possible to get a fix on them?'

'No.'

'That is rather disappointing.'

'I'm sorry not to be of help,' said Martyn Pine in a more cheery tone. 'Goodbye.'

'You are absolutely certain that it is actually impossible to home in on a LodeStar user?'

'Listen, you do realise that there are over two hundred thousand users of LodeStar in northern Europe?'

'Not in Karelia.'

'Perhaps not,' said Martyn Pine, who had never heard of Karelia.

Griffiths-Jones said: 'Anyway, don't all users have their own recognition code? Isn't that how you cut the facility if they fail to renew their licence?'

'Yes.'

'So in theory it ought to be possible to detect when an electronic link has been made by a particular user?'

'No.' Martyn Pine was almost enjoying himself. 'Because when an authorised source links into LodeStar, there is no record kept. The call is not logged. It is an open facility – just as a satellite company doesn't know whether you've got your television on or not, even if you do have a licence.'

'A television is a simple receiver of a general signal, surely,' said the caller. 'But with LodeStar the user has to feed a signal into the satellite in order to get specific information back . . .'

'You don't have to tell me how satellite navigation systems work.'

'So it must be possible, in theory, to detect when a LodeStar satellite is being sourced, and from where?'

'Theoretically, well, theoretically . . . where did you say you were speaking from?'

'Norway. Oslo.'

'In that case,' said Martyn Pine, 'you should be talking to LodeStar Scandinavia. I'll put you back to the switchboard, and they will give you the number.'

'You've been very helpful,' said Griffiths-Jones politely.

'It's what we're here for.'

* * *

Martyn Pine went to Selfridges and booked a fortnight's skiing in Megève for himself and his wife Claudile, then he had an open prawn sandwich and a Chelsea bun in the Coffeepot Bistro in St Christopher's Place. What with one thing and another, it was three-fifteen before he returned to the LodeStar International building in Portman Square; but he deserved a few minutes, he told himself, considering how hard he worked.

When he entered his secretary's office she jumped up from her desk, red-faced and agitated.

'Thank God,' she almost wept, 'I told them you'd just gone to the loo and you'd be back in a minute, and that was three-quarters of an hour ago.'

Inside his office were three men, one of them LodeStar International's UK Chairman, a man in his early forties. Martyn Pine assumed they wanted to question him about cutting the signal to the Grimsby trawler. Well, he was in the clear on that one: it was all computer triggered; nothing to do with engineering.

'You've had the army on,' said the Chairman crisply, 'about LodeStar source detection?'

Martyn Pine remembered reading in *LodeStar News* that the Chairman was a major in the Territorial Army.

'I did get a call, yes.'

'If one person, just one person, possesses LodeStar equipment in an area of, say, fifty square miles, and they access LodeStar, is it possible for us to do a back-trace and pinpoint exactly where they are? You can assume that the equipment is in constant use.'

'Theoretically,' said Martyn Pine.

'What do you need, to turn theory into practice?'

The phone rang. To Martyn Pine's surprise, one of the men picked it up.

'Well, I don't know,' said Martyn Pine. 'I'll have to think it through. You're asking the system to facilitate something it was not intended to facilitate. It would mean an adjustment to the satellite receiver systems, and as I tried to explain to the caller this morning, we don't have an international licence for what is in effect a comms link, and it would be asking for trouble to do anything without talking first to Brussels . . .'

The man on the phone said: 'They've cracked it at Cheltenham.'

'What, Dowty plc?' said Martyn Pine, affronted.

'GCHQ. Thank you for your help.'

'If you need Mr Pine to help you further . . .' said the Chairman.

'I think we'll manage now, but thank you anyway.'

The two men shook hands with the Chairman, and with Martyn Pine, and left.

When they had gone, the Chairman said: 'Perhaps you would like to tell me exactly what you believe your function is in this organisation? Think about it. Put something on paper.'

THREE

Slopes of Mount Kirovsk, 6-8 November

The vehicle edged forward, its driver guided by two hooded figures that walked ahead on either side. Nick lay slumped in the co-driver's seat, his eyes closed, listening for the change in engine noise that would come when they reached the head of the side-gully. All he could hear, as the bonnet rose on a huge, moving drift of new snow, was the angry keening of the wind and the feverish whine of the engine as the caterpillar tracks clawed for leverage.

Once they lurched sideways and juddered, as the tracks slithered and the entire vehicle tilted perilously. The driver mouthed an obscenity and jumped up and opened the hatch to peer out at the blackness. Nick did not move. He just braced himself, automatically, in his seat. Let the wagon fall or slide, he would take his chance.

Outside, men leaned on the sides of the vehicle and heaved, and their slight weight tipped the balance, and the vehicle righted itself, skewed in its tracks, then surged forwards, upwards, into the wind. Nick again closed his eyes.

'Sir! Sir!'

Staff Beckwith was hammering on the side window. On

his other side the driver was saying something about him being wanted. Time had passed – God only knew how long. Nick forced his limbs to move. He opened the door and practically fell out of the vehicle, his brain stunned by the ferocity of the wind.

'It's Mr Pendred, sir!' Beckwith was saying, but Nick could make nothing of this, because Jamie was with the main body of the column. He wasn't here with the vehicles that had been lost.

Then Nick saw the light of a shark's-eye torch, and Staff Beckwith was pulling him forward, and there was Jamie – and two soldiers – crouched half buried in drifting snow. They had been stagging on there ever since Nick had left, though with dwindling hope of seeing him again that night. Jamie was smiling. Snow coated his face like shaving foam, icicles fell from his eyebrows, but there was a huge grin on his face.

About two hours before dawn on the morning of the 6th, Jamie would later, laboriously, pen for the regimental magazine 'Bloodybacks', *the column was reunited, much to the relief of the sentries and in particular Pte Forbes whose chilblains were causing him much grief, and L/ Cpl Leech whose cry 'Kurdistan, all is forgiven!' was becoming the 4 Platoon motto. The Company had neither supped nor slept for some fourteen hours and the weather was, unbelievably, still deteriorating. Major Chard ordered the Company to dig in, and in the hours before dawn the column began to form a defensive square . . .*

* * *

'Twelve men from 4 Platoon: Cryer, Hainsworth, Sykes . . .'
Four Platoon was the least exhausted. Nick led them
slowly forward, arms linked, pacing the outline of a wagon-
laager. He dropped off one man to mark each corner, and
one man for every other vehicle, marking out the area of the
camp.

They made themselves a fifty-ton wall of encircling
steel, and they dug out tent spaces. The wind made the
simplest task a slow, laborious struggle. Tent canvas
whipped, ropes sliced the air. Tarpaulins were seized as if
by invisible hands, and flung into the blackness. Tents
rose, swayed, crumpled, then rose again, the vehicles to
which they were being lashed rocking on their springs.
'Hold it, hold it!' screamed the NCOs, and the rows of men
held blindly on to the ropes and canvas. Slowly, one by
one, the tents went up, and snow was piled round them;
and the cooks crawled in with their stoves.

Nick staggered into Jamie, and grabbed him, and then
grabbed Robbo and pulled them against the side of a
vehicle and shouted: 'I want snow piled between the
vehicles. Tarpaulins lashed against the outside to form a
windbreak. Machine-guns at each corner, with tarpaulins
to shield them. Cam nets over the tents.'

Jamie nodded, indicating a thumbs-up with his gloved
hand.

Robbo leaned against the vehicle, his cap-band soaked
with sweat, showing his age. NCOs who could run faster,
climb higher, ski further, slog it out for longer than any
squaddie found, in the end, their limbs moving more
slowly, their heart thumping, their lungs clawing for breath,

a red mist over their eyes, and realised that they were no longer nineteen. They were lucky if the tally for ten thousand pints of ale came gently, discreetly, and not in the guise of some boy soldier offering to carry their bergen.

'Sar'nt-Major? You all right?'

Robbo straightened, blinking.

'Sir.'

'How are the men?'

'Moaning like fuck.'

Nick nodded briefly. That was all right. It was when they stopped moaning that he would worry.

NCOs grabbed exhausted men and formed them into working parties. One hour more of effort and they could all rest, every man with a hot meal and a hot drink . . . that was what the NCOs were supposed to say. But the wind was stronger than ever, howling down through the rocks of the gully, so they said nothing, but pointed to what had to be done, the precautions which any respectable infantry company would take before lying down for a kip in a far and foreign land.

They finished at dawn, a dawn that showed itself only on the hands of Nick's watch, and through a faint lightening of the darkness. But the column was secure. Machine-gun posts were manned, stags organised. Men crawled into tents where dixies of rice and canned meat had been heated. They took off their boots and put them in the bottom of their dossbags. They swallowed the tepid food, gulped warm sugary tea, and slept.

Nick toured the four sentry positions, had a final look

around the laager, then crawled into the HQ tent. Robbo lay by the stove, damp and steaming, his face grey. Nick dragged off his boots, hung up his wet socks and warmed his feet, crying out as the circulation returned to his toes. He put on dry socks and lay down in his dossbag. Jamie would call him in two hours.

Robbo muttered thickly that all weapons and personnel were accounted for. Before he could move on to rations and ammo, they were both asleep.

Nick awoke at midday. Jamie was shaking his arm, offering him a mug of coffee. The wind was muffled, and for a moment he thought the storm was passing, but then he realised that the tent was half buried, cocooned from the elements. A naphtha lamp showed sleeping men all around. Robbo was snoring loudly. Anneliese was crouched over the stove, preparing food.

'Hi,' she said.

'I should have been called earlier,' said Nick, drugged by the depth of his sleep. He crawled out of his dossbag, put his boots on.

Jamie took off his own boots and crawled into Nick's warm bag. 'I've set a working party to shovel snow off the canvas,' he said. He turned over and slept.

Nick remembered that Jamie's dossbag had been given to two girls: Lara, the green-eyed teenager from Murmansk, and her friend Inga. He recalled Anneliese making some tart remark about Jamie perhaps hoping to join them.

Nick went outside. The narrow lane between the windward

line of vehicles and the tents was choked with snow. Jamie's working party was clearing it, although as fast as they scooped the snow away, new snow fell.

'It's like living at the bottom of a bowl of porridge, sir,' a voice yelled. Staff Beckwith was clambering over the bonnet of a Snow Leopard.

Nick opened the door of the cab and signalled Beckwith to join him.

Inside he said: 'How soon can we move after I give the order?'

Beckwith said: 'If we run the engines regularly, keep the tracks free of snow, about an hour.'

'Make it half an hour. The moment the storm starts to ease, I want to move. I want to be over the M18 before helicopters can get in the air.'

'If you ask me,' said Beckwith, 'it's getting worse out there, not better.'

'It's called *purga*,' said Nick. 'A Siberian blizzard that is feared, I am reliably informed, by men and beasts. Assume we're moving at midday.'

He got out of the cab conscious of severe pains in his feet. He walked slowly to the command vehicle and looked in the back. Willis was at the comms console, trying unsuccessfully to coax a picture on the tiny television screen.

'Any chance of a met report?'

Willis said that he had been trying all morning, but the satellite dish iced over the second they scraped it clear, and there was nothing getting through on commercial radio waves. Their own HF frequencies were still being jammed.

Nick went to the ambulance, where Brigite was attending to four exposure cases, and to a soldier who had been severely cut over one eye. The men were bedded down inside heated thermal blankets. Three of them were young, lads of eighteen or nineteen, who grinned awkwardly.

The only old lag to have suffered exposure was Private Grey, the signaller's co-driver, who said: 'Happiness, sir, is to stay here in this blanket for the rest of my life.'

'I can't think why you didn't ask earlier,' said Nick.

He took off his right boot, and his sock, and Brigite sighed and said: 'You're the seventh in the last hour. Give it to me . . .'

She pinched his big toe. They both watched the indentation made by her finger and thumb. The indentation remained.

'Bit like watching paint dry,' said Private Grey chattily.

It was some moments before the flesh returned to its normal shape.

'Stay in the warm, in a vehicle if you can – in the dry.'

'If it was possible,' said Nick, 'to run this show from the cab of a Snow Leopard, with the heater on full blast, I can assure you I would be doing it.'

Brigite reached into her medical bag and pulled out a small plastic box of pills. 'These will help with your circulation. There's nothing else I can do.'

'How are these lads doing?' said Nick, pointing to the casualties under the thermal blankets.

'They can go back to their sections later today.'

The casualties groaned, and said they were really not

feeling very well and were actually quite ill. Nick and Brigite knew that this was true, but that it made no difference. A military forward hospital had to be cleared ruthlessly. It never knew what it might have to cope with next.

At midday Nick and Jamie sat in the command vehicle and peered through the windscreen and flicked a switch, and the heavy-duty wipers sluggishly responded and cleared the clinging snow, but outside was a thick wall of white, and already darkness was falling.

The move was cancelled. The engines were turned off to conserve fuel.

In the evening Brigite came to Nick in the HQ tent, and again inspected his feet.

'I'm not going to keep repeating myself. Either keep them warm and dry, or you risk full-blown frostbite.'

Robbo joined them. They spoke quietly about the rations situation. They still had food for three days, and they had a quantity of reindeer meat.

Robbo said, in a firm, energetic voice: 'We could go down to half rations while we're lying up, sir. We don't need five thousand calories just lying in a dossbag.'

'The men are exhausted,' said Brigite. 'They need every calorie they can get. You look as if you should be in hospital yourself, Sergeant-Major.'

'I'm all right, ma'am. Bloody hell, don't worry about me.'

'Full rations,' said Nick. 'Once we're down in the valley we'll pick up food from somewhere.'

* * *

Late in the evening, after going round the sentries, Nick went to the tent housing the older children, seeking out the two Sami boys, Nils and Paulus. As he crawled past the snow-hole there was a sudden gust of wind, and the tent roof lifted and then slammed down, lamps, knives, and wet clothing swinging from side to side.

'I want to know,' he said slowly, 'when the storm – the *purga* – will be over.'

The plump Polish nurse interpreted. The older boy, Paulus, looked solemnly at Nick and replied briefly. The nurse said: 'He says you don't understand. The *purga* hasn't started yet.'

In the middle of the night, Nick and many others awoke to hear the wind scream with a new intensity. Above them the tent canvas was straining like the sails of a ship, the tent poles creaking like ship's timbers.

Men went out, holding on to each other, to shovel snow from the canvas, but for the most part the wind was too high for the dry, sharp, killing snow to stick.

Nick crawled out with them. He hobbled to Sergeant Doran's tent and organised an emergency section: six men dressed and ready to move instantly.

The wind screamed, the snow piled up into huge, weird drifts, but the column was safe behind its wall of steel, its blanket of white, and more secure than most isolated settlements on the taiga.

He looked in on Brigite, sitting awake with the younger children.

'God help poor sailors,' he shouted, 'on a night like this.'

'Get back into your sleeping bag.'

'If anything happens to the tent, don't try to get out. There are men standing by to help you.'

She nodded.

He crawled back to the HQ tent, back into his dossbag, and lay listening to the wind and thinking of Munro, and Noon, and Fuller. Had they completed their job? Were they somewhere around here in the Khibiny Mountains? He knew enough to know their mission was somewhere across Puma, across his stop-line. Or had they been lifted out? Had they found their way south, perhaps to Petersburg, to a nice warm motel?

'I don't know,' said Staff Beckwith, taking breakfast next morning with his lads in the back of the REME wrecker, 'if you've ever been to Morecambe in February?'

His lads had not.

'Very similar to this,' said Staff Beckwith, 'except they don't call it a *purga* in Morecambe; they call it a stiff breeze. Is this all I get?'

He was looking at a small portion of dark grey porridge, handed to him by Private Doyle. Doyle informed him the column had gone down to half rations.

At midday the wind dropped slightly. Nick hesitated, toyed with the idea of moving. But striking camp would be chaotic: they would have to dig themselves out; they would have only two hours of daylight travelling at best.

He decided to stay, to move later if the storm eased significantly, and to move – whatever happened – the following morning. Engines were started, to warm up the vehicles. Sentries were posted at the top of the gully.

'The question is: why Lara? Of all the kids to choose, why Lara?'

'It was Inga as well. In fact it was Inga more than Lara . . .'

'You don't think there's something Freudian about asking a sixteen-year-old girl who wants to be a tart in Berlin to share your sleeping bag?'

'To share with Inga, not with me.'

'Oh, she'd share it with you, she'd love to share it with you, but perhaps you were planning to share it with both of them.'

'Good God, Inga is a respectable girl. Inga's dad is a Russian Orthodox bishop . . .'

'A pathetic lie. Sorry.'

'Well he's a churchwarden or something. They're very pious; they belong to a sect. She thinks women ought to be slaves to men . . .'

'And you would like that. You would really like that . . .'

Worembrand lay under his duvet, listening to the nuzzling and the sweet talk taking place a few centimetres from his ear. He wished they would go somewhere else. He wondered if there was anywhere else he could go himself. There was nowhere. He had fled from his icy tent filled with farting squaddies. He had crawled gratefully into his old nest in the back of the ambulance, among his bags and his camera cases. He had grabbed his duvet and had found a fucking Rupert fucking under it.

'For Christ's sake . . .' Jamie had said, and Anneliese had said: 'Oh, Max . . .'

He could have wept.

Earlier, at noon (a time when, in his real life, he would be ambling down to the Cherry-Ripe club in the autumnal sunshine for a couple of drinks before ambling back to a plate piled high with roast meat in the sergeants' mess dinner-annex), he had been awakened by Doran shaking his sleeping bag and offering him a cup of water. Doran was washed, shaved, and keen looking.

'Shave,' said Doran. 'In this tent, NCOs set an example.'

Worembrand refused. Doran insisted. Worembrand took the mug, then howled and pulled his hand away, spilling most of the water.

'It's not that hot. It's nearly fucking cold!'

Doran seized Worembrand's hands in his own hairy paws and turned them over. During the night, the nightmare of a night, the worst night of his life, Worembrand had spent two hours shovelling snow. Now his pink palms were puffy and tender.

'Blisters?' gloated Sergeant Doran. 'Oh dear, oh dear.'

He offered a can of shaving foam. The can had a bronzed beach-boy running across it, a surfboard under his arm. Trust Doran, thought Worembrand, fastidious even in the depths of despair, to buy cheap NAAFI shave foam. He himself favoured Givenchy For Men or Chanel, but did not, on this occasion, think it wise to say so. At Lake Imandra he had pointed out to Doran that he, Max, was an artist not an ape; and Doran had gone on about it ever since. To Doran, artist was a term of praise when attached to a drunkard, or of scorn when attached to a puff. Which was Mal, he had wanted to know.

They rustled and squeaked like mice.

'She's sixteen and she's crazy about you, and wants you to make love to her.'

'Do you know what would happen to me if I started messing around with young girls in her Majesty's protection?'

'And what exactly are you doing with me?'

'I know what I'm trying to do.'

'You can't. Not again.'

'Yes.'

'Jamie, no. He'll wake up . . .'

'He won't . . .'

There was silence. Then the dossbag, perhaps a foot from his, began to quiver. Anneliese, or was it Jamie, moaned gently, just like they did on the videos on the big screen at the Cherry-Ripe Club. The duvet, of which he had with difficulty managed to secure a half-share, flapped, letting cold air in. He could have cried with rage and frustration.

What had he done to deserve this? Had he not taken every precaution? Had he not, early in his army career, gone for the softest option he could find, rendering himself useless for all purposes other than taking photographs?

Was he the only person in the column who knew that out there, beyond the walls of the laager, was madness? Rampant, triumphant madness? Men were killing each other – not in films, not in regimental accounts, but killing each other in the sort of way that involved people DYING.

Was he the only one who remembered Munro and the other SAS bastards, and understood the significance of radio-jamming, and gunships? Who knew there would be no voice of a schoolboy rallying the ranks when the cannon ripped through the Snow Leopards' thin armour plating?

Was he really the only one who realised what a fucking disaster the entire rescue mission had been?

Now they were murmuring gently. There was a tiny laugh. Outside, Staff Beckwith was shouting, and then the shout was taken up close by, and somebody was thumping on the side of the vehicle and yelling: 'Stand to! Stand to!'

'Christ . . .'

Jamie squirmed to get out of the bag, Anneliese gave a cry of pain. Worembrand clung to his half of the duvet and closed his eyes.

The sentry was careering down from the ridge. The two sentries posted up the gully were falling back, stumbling in their haste. Sergeant Doran came running along the trench, pulling his camouflage whites over his head, calling to his section, allocating them to positions on the laager wall. Jamie ran to where men were crouched at the north-facing machine-guns, their bodies still, intent and poised.

Round the corner of rock came a Russian armoured carrier, its lights blazing, its tracks throwing up a spume of snow.

FOUR

Mount Kirovsk, 8 November

When he stepped out of the hide the wind sucked the breath from his lungs and threw him to the ground. But he was able to stagger to his knees, then to stand, and to stay upright. The wind had honed the soft flakes into tiny razors, but they no longer penetrated his flesh.

The *purga* was passing.

Like hungry animals scenting the first, tentative changes in the weather, Munro and Noon emerged from their hole in the snow. Like wolverine and wolf and silver fox, they checked cautiously for enemies, for predators.

Then they became predators themselves.

Fuller had died on the second day. For two days before that, his mind had wandered. He had eaten when they gave him food, but without appetite. They had rubbed and pummelled his limbs, but failed to warm his body. He had swallowed snow, perhaps, when they were not looking. Munro, duty bound, had signalled that only an immediate casevac would save Fuller's life, and the signal had bounced down to Bradbury Lines at Hereford, where it was gravely noted, and then passed to Narvik.

Nothing had changed. No casevac was possible. None had been expected.

The cold had crept slowly in, from Fuller's extremities to his heart. And at some point his heart had stopped.

He was the only son of a Rhodesian soldier who had been an NCO in the Rhodesian SAS, the Selous Scouts, long since retired from the struggle against communism in Africa and living, a widower, in England. In Fuller's pocket they found a card with a text: '*Defend us thy humble servants in all assaults of our enemies; that we, surely trusting in thy defence, may not fear the power of any adversaries . . .*'

Like Cromwell before them, Munro and Noon trusted in God and oiled their Armalites.

In the white dawn of the third day they sealed Toby in the white cave of the *dnovka*.

22 SAS travelled light. Munro crouched in the blizzard and punched a code into his hand computer, then carefully, with a low-temperature graphite pen, wrote a set of numbers into his pocketbook.

Fuller's epitaph was a LodeStar reading.

Earlier, in the hour before dawn, they had signalled Narvik. Their food supply was almost exhausted. Munro was now suffering from frostbite on his feet. They would make a final attempt during the course of the day. They were still 13k from the silo. They anticipated that patrols would be out, now that the storm was passing.

Instead of an acknowledgement there had come a LodeStar reading and a brief instruction. Munro had transferred the LodeStar reading to his map.

'What the fuck are they doing *there*!'

His shout had brought a cascade of crystalline flakes, yellow shards of cave sweat, tinkling down from the roof.

They left everything behind, but for food, medicine, their weapons, and the two pieces of equipment contained in sealed polythene tubes, each tube thirty centimetres long. They left behind most of their ammo, because ammo was heavy and they would never win, anyway, in a protracted shoot-out. They left most of their survival kit, their flares, their tent and their sleeping bags.

They had their weapons, but in truth they went naked into the storm.

Munro led the way. North by north-west, two ridges to cross, two shallow valleys. Before they started, he again checked his LodeStar reading provided by Narvik. *How the fuck did they get there? Where the fuck did they think they were going?*

Four kilometres. That was all. The British Army's basic fitness test required a man aged thirty to run two kilometres, wearing boots, in twelve minutes. By that reckoning, thought Munro, savagely, an ops staff officer crouched over his central-heating radiator in the Secure Room at Narvik would expect them to make contact in less than half an hour.

'Perhaps an hour, two hours at most,' said Griffiths-Jones.

'Mid-afternoon at the earliest,' said Biggin, the SAS

man, the experienced operator, looking at the map, at the route drawn by Griffiths-Jones on the talc.

Hoepner asked: 'What happens if Munro manages to make contact?'

Griffiths-Jones said: 'There's a railway tunnel 7k down in the valley, a branch line from Khibiny.'

'Fifty men,' said Hoepner. 'An entire company. And the nurses. And the children. My God.'

Griffiths-Jones was pale, dark smudges under his eyes; he had scarcely slept in three days.

'And we didn't tell them,' said Hoepner. 'They had no idea.'

'They ought to make it to the tunnel, sir,' said Biggin, 'providing Munro and Noon can get to them by 15.00.'

'And if they don't?'

The question was rhetorical. Hoepner stared down at the map. After a moment he nodded.

'OK, gentlemen. Peter, stay with it. John, thank you for your efforts.'

He rose abruptly and left.

Griffiths-Jones said: 'Grenfell's ordered me to stand down *Revenge*.'

Biggin said: 'She can't do the job on her own. No point in her hanging about.'

'I want to leave her in place for twelve hours.'

Biggin looked at him.

Griffiths-Jones said: 'Munro would have made a final attempt today if we hadn't pulled him out.'

'He would have died. Both of them would have died. They would never have made it.'

'He's still in the Mount Kirovsk area.'

'Time's run out. It's too late,' said Biggin harshly.

'I don't think,' said Griffiths-Jones stubbornly, 'we should pull *Revenge* while he's still in there.'

Biggin shrugged and stood up. He was weary, sick at heart.

'Leave her, then. She's only sitting on her arse on the seabed. Grenfell's not going to check. He's busy trying to pretend *Terrier* never existed – or that if it did, he was in Hong Kong at the time.'

Munro had given up trying to see.

When he opened his eyes they watered, and when they watered they froze, and every few seconds he had to scrape away the ice, and this was dangerous. Nature had put salt into tears, into eye lubricant, SAS instructors claimed, to stop them from freezing, but at minus-40 there was not enough salt; and the more tears his eyes produced, the more his eyeballs seized up and refused to move. In the end he let his eyelids freeze over, and trudged blindly forward, keeping the wind at the same angle against his right cheek. Noon was behind him, holding on to his Bergen, and it was only by luck – their first bit of luck, Noon was later to say – that they did not walk, like two blind mice, into the back of the MT-LB personnel carrier parked on the ridge.

Munro had stopped, as he did after every one hundred paces, to take a LodeStar reading. As he and Noon wiped the icefilm from their eyes, the gale of snow parted for a second, and in that second the two men threw themselves face-down into the snow, their Armalite automatics aimed forward, ready to fire.

The curtain of snow fell. For the next half hour the BTR sat with its engine running to provide warmth. Its occupants smoked cigarettes and dozed. There was an officer, the flash of blue on his khaki collar visible for a moment through the driver's window. There were five or six men.

Their vehicle was positioned so that, when the storm passed, they would command a view down a westward-falling slope to the broad Murmansk valley below.

Half an hour went by. A signaller in the rear spoke into his radio, and the officer gave an order. The driver sat upright and took the tillers, ready to move off; and had he done so, the patrol would, in another hour, perhaps, have been sitting over their soup and coffee in the canteen at base.

But the vehicle did not move. Instead the door opened and a soldier jumped out, fumbling with his trousers to relieve himself, then whipping sideways as the bullets tore into his chest. The driver died in the same spray of bullets that killed the officer and the soldiers round him. The signaller died as his hand reached for the send pad of his radio. The rear door crashed open and the last member of the patrol – a boy really, eighteen or nineteen years old at most – fell outwards with a bullet in his body, into the snow. He rolled over and disappeared into the gale.

Munro went after him while Noon checked that every other member of the patrol was killed. Then Noon followed.

The fugitive had no snowshoes, he had no camouflage whites, his hands were bare, and he was leaving a trail of blood. He must have hurt his legs, or the bullet must have severed a vital cord, because he was crawling and slithering through the snow. Munro stopped and wondered if he had the time or energy. Noon came up behind him.

'All dead.'

They both looked at the bloody trail that was being obliterated as they watched.

'Better get him,' said Munro. Noon nodded. They moved forward rapidly but carefully. The trail led behind some rocks. By now, Munro estimated, the boy would be freezing, his limbs would be numb, the shock of the cold would be clawing at his heart. He stopped, and was about to turn back to the vehicle when Noon said: 'There he is.'

Munro looked. The boy had crawled between some boulders and was sitting looking out. He suddenly shouted: a wild hope, perhaps, that Munro and Noon were on his side, that it was all a mistake, that he only had to identify himself and they would help him, or at least leave him alone.

'A conscript,' shouted Noon in Munro's ear, over the howl of the wind.

Noon raised his Armalite 5.56 automatic and at the same time the boy raised his NRS reconnaissance knife, a weapon that also fired a bullet and had range of twenty metres.

Munro shouted a warning, but as he spoke the bullet thudded into his thigh. He fell swinging his Armalite, killing the boy, his vision suddenly blanked out by a fountain of blood, his own blood, spurting into his face. Then Noon was slicing away at the clothes on his leg, and had pulled off his headover and was wrapping it round his thigh, twisting it tight with his commando knife.

'Femoral artery,' shouted Noon.

'Jesus . . .'

Noon heaved him to his feet.

There were five bodies in the vehicle, and two that had fallen out into the snow. Noon helped Munro into the passenger seat at the front. Then he went back out into the snow and searched round for several minutes until he found their bergens. He brought them back and slung them in the vehicle, and slammed the rear door.

In the driver's seat he leaned over Munro, found a vein in his arm and banged in a syrete of quarter-grain morphine. Then he checked their LodeStar reading with the illuminated map, started the engine and pulled away.

After a few moments he pressed a switch, and Munro screamed as a blast of hot air from the heater hit the frozen nerve endings on his leg and frostbitten feet. Noon swore and quickly turned off the heat. The morphine took effect. Munro drifted into unconsciousness.

Fourteen minutes later Noon glanced at the map and saw that, according to LodeStar and Narvik, he and 'B' Company were in the same place. Looking through the driver's slit he saw the sudden movement of a sentry on the ridge of the gully he was descending, and he manoeuvred the vehicle round a shoulder of rock and found a second sentry pressed against the side of the gully, his rifle raised, and before him, half buried in snow, two lines of Snow Leopards.

The reserves from Wolverhampton, two of them at any rate, had rejoined the column.

FIVE

Slopes of Mount Kirovsk, afternoon, 8 November

Brigite released the tourniquet. Blood spurted in time to his pulse, splashing over her smock. Next to her, Anneliese rummaged in the storage bins, breaking out needles and sutures from the sterilised unit.

His eyes were open, fixed on Nick's face. His tongue was feeling slowly over his snow-burned lips. Spots of blood fell on his face, his mouth, in his eyes.

Nick said: 'Can I give him a drink?'

'Please hold the lamp and be quiet.'

Her finger probed deep inside the wound, into the well of blood, forcing the artery against the bone.

Munro's eyes slowly closed.

Blood stopped spurting. She said: 'Haemostat.'

Anneliese passed the clamp. Brigite's hand went back down into the wound. After a moment she said: 'OK. Now I have to stitch it. How many syretes of morphine has he had?'

Anneliese looked at Munro, then said: 'Can somebody go and ask the sergeant?'

Nick started to move.

Munro's eyes opened. He said: 'No. Wait.'

Brigite said: 'I can't give you any painkillers, any form of anaesthetic, until I know.'

Munro said: 'Two syretes.'

'Quarter grain? In an hour? Oh Jesus . . .'

'Nick . . .'

Nick bent over.

Brigite said: 'Anneliese, you'll have to hold the lamp.'

Nick passed her the lamp.

Munro said: 'Orders from Narvik. Ask Noon about Terrier.'

Outside, the wind was less fierce, although the air was still thick with snow. Visibility was about sixty metres. The Company was still stood to: fifty men crouched, facing outwards from the laager, rifles at the ready. Jamie was lying on the cab of a vehicle, peering back up the gully.

Nick said: 'Jamie? Stand down. Send the sentries back up to the ridge.'

Noon was in the back of the command vehicle, inside a sleeping bag, sitting nursing a mug of coffee. Every few seconds he shivered uncontrollably. His hands were purple, splashed with the white, waxy blotches of frostbite.

Collins sat at the radio. He had the SAS pocket burst transmission set in front of him. He looked up, excited, as Nick crawled in. 'Look at this, sir. It's not a tenth the size of our set. We've got a frequency to Hereford that's not being jammed, if you want to talk to them.'

Nick said to Noon: 'Tell me about Terrier.'

Noon said: 'Not with him here.'

'Collins.'

Collins left.

Noon drank, lit a cigarette.

Nick waited.

'101 Rocket Regiment, north-east of Mount Kirovsk. Ten silos and a command bunker dispersed over two square miles. Plans are in the Sony.'

He nodded towards Munro's bergen. Nick reached into it and took out the laptop computer. He also found a two-metre-long, slim package covered in polystyrene foam.

'Careful with that,' said Noon.

Nick handed him the Sony. Noon paused a moment, collecting his thoughts, then punched a code.

Russian military plans scrolled down the screen: Leningrad Military District, Rocket Regiment 101 'Riga', Base 40 'Khibiny/Kirovsk'. Silos, defensive wire, fortified bunkers.

'Do I need to get these printed?'

'I don't know, do I,' said Noon.

'Go on. Terrier.'

'We tried to get in three weeks ago. Four of us. We had a KGB contact but he didn't show. He was supposed to get us in past the guards and the minefield. There's units from the Vilyandi Spetznaz regiment up here now. We waited three days. Then we pulled out. Jacko had caught something, God knows what – something gastric. It must have been incubating beforehand. We had to carry him in the end, pull him on a pulk. He died while we were waiting for the RV at Lesnoy.'

He dragged at his cigarette.

Nick said: 'You came out by submarine? The *Revenge*?'

Noon nodded. He said: 'That lad. He didn't have to do that. I was shooting out of kindness. He had no chance of survival out there. It was a quick bullet or ten minutes of agony. Teach me to do a bugger a kindness.'

His eyes were clouded. Warmth was a form of paralysis, a drug.

Nick said: 'Terrier? What were you supposed to do when you got inside the base?'

'Laser beam on the ventilation shaft. Once that's in place, *Revenge* takes over. A phased missile. Worked well in Iraq. Yanks got the credit, but it was our lads on the ground, blacked up like fuckin Ayrabs, guiding the bombs in. Same bloody story.'

'But why?'

Noon looked at him blankly.

'Why destroy the bunker?'

Noon said: 'Commander of 101. Been a naughty boy.'

The wound was being stitched. Anneliese was fixing a drip to a bracket on the wall; the thin tube snaked down to the vein in Munro's arm. The lamp had also been clipped to the wall. Its light threw sharp, harsh shadows as they began to bandage the wound. Munro lay staring at the roof, semiconscious.

When Nick climbed in, Brigite said: 'It's lucky the artery was in tissue. I've been able to stitch up the whole area. He's lost a lot of blood.'

'Wake him up for me. Give him something.'

'I can't. Not without killing him. He's all right; he's just high on morphine.'

Nick said: 'George?'

Munro's eyes opened.

'Tell me about the commander of 101.'

Anneliese bent down with a mug, 'Glucose,' she said. 'Drink as much as you can.'

He drank. Then he said: 'He's called Kvatov. He's five hundred feet underground in a steel and concrete bunker. He's got ten ICBMs – SS-27 *Satan* – that should have been disarmed in September. He's threatening to nuke Latvia.'

Brigite and Anneliese slowly stopped what they were doing.

In the silence Nick could hear the snow thudding against the thick, armour-plated window.

Brigite and Anneliese were staring intently at Munro.

Nick said: 'Why?'

'What?'

'Why is he . . . threatening Latvia?'

'His daughter was killed in ethnic riots. First he blackmailed Moscow into mobilising Third Shock Army. Now he's threatening to do the job himself.'

Silence. Munro's eyes were starting to close.

Nick said, for want of anything better: 'How did the SAS get involved?'

'KGB's badly infiltrated. Our contact was Fourth Directorate, one of the old *molchi-molchi* guys . . .'

'The what?'

'*Molchi-molchi* – keep your mouth shut, regimental counter-intelligence. Jesus does it matter . . .'

His eyes closed. Anneliese whispered, confused.

'Did he say a nuclear bomb . . .?'

Brigite hushed her.

Nick said:

'George?'

Pause.

'George? What will happen now?'

Munro's eyes opened. His gaze was remote, unseeing.

Nick looked at Brigite. She shrugged. It was the morphine, her expression indicated. Two ampoules, and a day scrunching popeye pills and Betablocks like Smarties.

'George! You said you had new orders for me!'

Munro jerked, a look of alarm on his face.

'Didn't Noon tell you?'

'No . . .'

'Oh Christ . . . there's a rail tunnel. Noon's got the grid. You have to get us all into it by 11.00 tomorrow.'

'Why?'

'Why?'

'Why do we have go into a railway tunnel?'

'Dear God . . .' said Munro, wearily, 'why the fuck do you think?'

Nick's eyes met Brigite's. Her eyes widened: a look of shock.

'I don't believe,' she said, 'that we would do a thing like that . . .'

'George,' said Nick, 'are you saying that we are going to launch a nuclear—'

'Not us! The Russians! They've been told to hold off till tomorrow. Nobody cares about me and Noon, but a company of Royal Mercians, dear Christ . . .'

'It's insane.'

'So's a five megaton ICBM on Latvia. It's the nightmare, Nick. The nightmare. Oh Christ, oh dear God . . .' he gasped with pain. Suddenly he yelled: 'Morphine!'

'Feeling is returning to his leg,' said Brigite.

Anneliese said: 'What shall I give him? What shall I do?'

Brigite turned to her medical kit.

Nick moved carefully, sliding himself towards the rear of the vehicle. He said: 'I'm going to talk to Narvik.'

'Give our position away,' said Munro, sweat pouring down his face, 'and we're dead.'

Outside, the light was starting to go. The MT-LB was coming to a halt next to the REME Wrecker. Staff Beckwith was opening a hatch on the armoured glacis and hauling on his mittens.

'Handles well enough, sir,' he called. 'Lovely wide tracks, very light over snow, but a bit cramped, like all their AFVs. All right for midgets. I reckon they breed midgets in Siberia.'

A couple of mechanics laughed. A tent door opened and a voice called: 'You coming for your dinner, Staff?'

Beckwith and his lads went to their dinner.

Jamie was in the back of the command vehicle, trying to get information out of Noon. He looked embarrassed when Nick came in.

'Just seeing how the sergeant was.'

'Go away, please, Jamie. And you, Collins.'

391

Jamie blushed. He waited until Collins had left, and then followed him.

Nick looked at the HF set. Munro was right. It would be suicidal to open a comms link. 101 Regiment ski patrols had followed them from Nyrud to Verchnetulomskoje. 101 Regiment gunships had tracked them down when the ski patrols lost them. 101 Regiment was jamming their official frequencies. If they were trawling the airwaves, it would take them three seconds to pinpoint a radio signal beaming out of their own backyard.

He asked Noon why they had failed to reach the silo.

'Patrols. We had to watch, work out their routine, their system. See a way through the minefield. Truth is we didn't have a chance. Not in the state we were in. Not in this weather.'

'The storm is passing. Did you spot a way through the minefields?'

Noon looked at him sharply.

'Did you find a way through?'

Noon said, slowly, 'No, but it doesn't matter. Not now. There'll be snowdrifts. Four metres or more deep.'

'So there's only the patrols to worry about?'

Noon nodded.

Nick thought of High School 46. The Director, his wife and three children. The teacher who asked for copies of Turgenev in English. The children who thought Lovelace was a political prisoner and wanted to adopt him and write letters to him.

Noon said: 'I'll need somebody with me. I'll need to start now.'

'You wouldn't make it.'

'No,' said Noon. He closed his eyes.

A nuclear strike on Mount Kirovsk. A clean bomb, one kilaton perhaps. Wind from the north; away from Novyj Yena, a spur of high ground should protect them from the blast. They should be all right at High School 46. Some other high school, number 47 perhaps, or 48, would catch it.

But did the Russians have a one-kilaton 'clean' bomb? And could they aim it accurately if they had? For a generation the Soviets built five-megaton ICBMs because their guidance systems were notoriously inaccurate, and the only way they could be sure of taking out Manchester was to take out Birmingham with it.

It was pointless to speculate. He didn't even know if they would use a land-launched missile or bombers.

He opened the SAS computer and switched it on. He slowly composed a message. Noon sat quietly, sleepily, sprawled on the strong box, his back against the bulkhead. When Nick had finished writing, he realised that he did not know how to send burst transmission. He woke Noon.

Noon told him the sequence. 'I can't get that boy off my mind,' he said. 'He told us he was a conscript. I wasn't really going to shoot him. I only raised my gun because I was turning to go back to the vehicle. He shouldn't have done what he did.'

Nick pressed the send pad. The message shot through the ether, to the satellite, to Hereford; from there, in seconds, to Supreme Allied HQ Norwood, to the SIS Cabinet Committee, to Berlin, to C-in-C NATO Northern Command, Narvik.

Jamie poked his head in. His expression was cold and remote. He said: 'Can I have a couple of seconds at some point? I'm being asked what's happening, and I'm feeling a bit bloody stupid saying I don't know.'

Nick said: 'Come in. Sit down.'

Jamie clambered in, his face clearing. Not a boy to bear a grudge.

Nick had to repeat everything twice, sometimes three times. Jamie had difficulty absorbing what he was saying. He watched Nick's face as if he suspected that he was being tested in some sort of officers' training programme, and would fail miserably unless he spotted the vital bit of story that proved it to be all made up.

A light flashed on the SAS computer. A print-out slowly unwound itself.

From:	Cdr AMF(L)
To:	OC B Coy 1 R MERC
	1. Acknowledged.
	2. Agreed.
	3. H Hour = 1100. No extension.

Brigite said: 'He's unconscious. Two syretes of morphine could have killed him, that and the amphetamines. He's lost a terrible amount of blood and he's got frostbitc in both feet. He's in deep exhaustion. What did you want him for?'

Jamie said, in a tense voice: 'There's this party in Headquarters Tent. He'll be sick as a dog if he wakes up and finds he's missed it.'

Nick said: 'Don't worry, it's all right.'

Brigite gave Jamie a stony look, but he did not notice. His eyes were empty, his thoughts far away.

Thirty-five men were crammed into Headquarters Tent.

He told them about Terrier – that they were fifteen kilometres from Ground Zero, the point immediately below the nuclear airburst. In less than twenty-four hours the gully where they were camped would be snow-less, seared by blast and radiation, the rocks oozing hot metals, the birches crumbled to dust.

He said, crisply and with authority: 'The convoy is going to move at dawn to a railway tunnel. It's about 17k from here. Once in the tunnel, the vehicles will close down and wait until it's all over. The tunnel has been designated by AMF Chief of Staff, Narvik. In due course there will be either an air rescue or the column will be directed to make its way to a contact point . . .'

He did not say 'Make its way through the poisoned fields, the poisoned air, the dead and dying' but a mental picture was in his mind; and, he knew, in the minds of the more imaginative of his listeners.

'You all know the routine. You've done it often enough.'

Many times. On Salisbury Plain, on Lüneburg Heath, in the arid mountains of Kurdistan. Hauling on Noddy suits, parking vehicles behind embankments and under bridges, closing down hatches, waiting for the tactical nuclear strike before continuing their advance on 'Orange Force'.

It was something you did at the end of an exercise, a final embuggerance between you and the barracks, a hot shower and a decent meal.

'The Snow Leopard is specifically designed for this sort of situation. We have crystallite air-filtration systems. We have the most advanced radiation protection in the world. We have the best NCB suits in the world. And we'll be in a tunnel. We will be totally safe. You all saw the video at Bulford.'

The actor's voice-over had said: 'The Snow Leopard is the first oversnow/oversand personnel carrier capable of occupying and holding ground in the aftermath of nuclear attack.' The actor had used the macho voice he had previously employed in a TV cider commercial.

Nick said, finally: 'As you know, our job – the basic job of "B" Company – is to trial these prototypes. Well, now we can trial them for real. Perhaps we'll get a bonus from Vickers.'

There were no laughs. He ought to leave the jokes to Jamie.

'Any questions?'

Corporal Willis said: 'I don't suppose they could have been pulling your plonker, sir?'

Nick shook his head.

Leech said: 'So what's the bad news, sir?'

The men in the tent were the fittest, freshest men in the company. The sick, lame and lazy were in the next tent.

Leech knew – they all knew – that the selection had not been made at random.

Nick said: 'Not everybody is going with the column.'

So that was it.

They stared at him, neither friendly nor unfriendly; certainly not surprised.

'101 Regiment's warheads are dispersed in silos all round Mount Kirovsk. None of them is near the command bunker. None of them can be fired if the command bunker is knocked out. There's a British submarine, HMS *Revenge*, at the bottom of the Barents Sea, waiting for a signal to launch a conventional missile that will destroy the bunker. We have the equipment to help guide the missile in. Sergeant Noon knows how to position it, how to use it. We have the element of surprise. I propose to lead a party drawn from the men in this tent.

'If we succeed, there will be no nuclear strike. We will have saved the lives of thousands of people – including the kids and teachers at Novyj Yena. And the column won't find itself sitting in a tunnel watching the radiation levels rise.

'If we fail we'll be at Ground Zero at 11.00 tomorrow morning when the bombs cream in.'

He let it sink in. One soldier was nervously looking at his watch. The tent door was pulled back: Robbo's head appeared, the crush of men was so great that he could not get inside.

'Finished next-door, sir,' he said.

'Very good, Sar'nt-Major.'

Robbo's head disappeared.

Nick said: 'I don't feel able to order any one of you to come with us, but Mr Pendred and I and Sar'nt Noon are going, whatever happens. The sergeant-major wanted to, but I've ordered him to remain with the convoy. I want to take as many of you as are willing to go. I want to go with as much firepower as I can. We'll have Milan. We'll have Starstreak. We'll move up under cover of darkness and be in there before they know it. If anything gets in the way, we'll have the power to deal with it.

'But if any of you wants out, I'll understand. Some of you have wives and kids. You may have other reasons just as compelling. Anyone who wants to go with the column can leave the tent now. Nobody will say anything, now or at any other time.'

Some men looked round uneasily; most stared thoughtfully, as if preoccupied, at their feet, or at a point somewhere beyond Nick's ear. Nobody moved. Then two men, both married with small children, moved at exactly the same moment, muttered something under their breaths and crawled their way to the tent door. A driver from 5 Platoon, Gates, soon to be married and with only another month to serve, followed them. He was going into his dad's television repair business in Walsall, Nick remembered. Blushing, he brushed past his mates and crawled out into the darkness.

Nick looked at the floor to avoid meeting the eyes of the men as they left. He could hear others leaving . . . he could not blame them. He revolted, inwardly, at the thought of trying to force them to stay.

He stared fixedly at the ground.

The tent fell quiet.

'I think that's it, sir,' said Staff Beckwith.

Nick looked up. Five, perhaps six had gone, but Doran was there with the bulk of his lads, Staff Beckwith with his mechanics. Collins, Corporal Willis, Whitby, Hoddinot . . . Holmes the shaved Rottweiler, the Ugliest Man in NATO, and Sykes – Sykes was there, as miserable a bugger as ever was, but he'd not go to Colly after this, not while Nick had a breath in his body. Leech was there, Nick noted in some surprise, a fag cupped in his hands, a cynical look on his face, but staying nonetheless.

Nick said: 'OK, let's get going. Will the nearest person to the door go and fetch Sergeant Noon from the command vehicle.'

'And see you come back with him,' said Staff Beckwith.

Nobody laughed. Silence fell on the tent.

Noon flicked open the catches. Bedded in green baize was a tripod, slimmer than the mounting for a machine-gun. He took it out and set it up.

He opened a second package, the foam-protected tube from Munro's Bergen. He slid out a slim pencil of metal. It had protective lens caps and optical sights.

'Laser designator,' said Noon, cradling it in his arms, showing it round like a vacuum-cleaner salesman.

'It creates a laser cone over a target. It could guide a camel through a needle's eye, or a rat up a drainpipe. It will draw a missile down it. That's what it was made for.'

The men watched keenly, displaying the soldier's eternal

fascination with new kit. Noon again reached into the bergen. He produced the transmitter and handed it to Willis.

'Seen one of these?'

Willis shook his head. 'I'll hack it, don't worry.'

'Piece of piss. I'll give you a quick cadre later. That's it, then.'

He turned to Nick.

Nick said: 'We move into position and lock on the laser. We then signal *Revenge*. It will take her four minutes to launch her missile, and a further six minutes for the missile to come in on a curved trajectory and home in on the laser cone. Questions?'

Staff Beckwith said: 'What sort of missile is it?'

'Sergeant.'

Noon said: 'Conventional phased munition. A booster rocket will fire once it comes down to ground level, and that will drive it down into the ventilation shaft, down through concrete, steel . . . you name it. Sections of the rocket will explode at different levels, blasting out each floor of the bunker.'

'How do you know it'll work?' asked Beckwith.

'It worked three weeks ago on an identical bunker in Siberia. It'll work. All it needs – all I need – is fifteen minutes' line of sight on that ventilation shaft, so I can guide it in.'

'Would this be a good moment to mention gunships?' asked Leech.

'Shurrup, Leechie,' said a voice.

'It's just I've got a phobia about them,' said Leech.

'With some people it's spiders or snakes, but with me it's gunships.'

'I've got a thing about them as well,' said Nick grimly. 'I've also got Starstreak, and I won't hesitate to use it.'

'You're crazy,' said Brigite. 'It's cumulative stress distorting your judgement. You've got hardly any chance at all of pulling it off. You're working on the basis that everything will go right for you – evading the patrols, getting through the minefields, getting into your position and holding it for fifteen minutes against attack by troops and gunships, sending the message successfully . . . It only needs one thing to go wrong and you will all be dead.'

'I suspect we'd be dead anyway. There's no such thing as a clean, surgical strike. Everything within a radius of 40k is going to be like the inside of a nuclear reactor.'

'That's a comfort to us in our tunnel.'

'The tunnel's your best chance,' said Nick. 'It's your only chance.'

They were in the cab of the ambulance. Outside, men had finished digging out the vehicles, clearing the drifts, turning half the vehicles and pointing them back up the gully. In the tents men were gulping down a final meal. In the past hour soldiers had cleaned and oiled rifles and machine-guns, checked their kit. Milan and Starstreak had been broken out, assembled, and tested.

The wind had died, the snow was falling gently. Jamie had tried to make Worembrand take a picture for next year's battalion Christmas card.

'Have you written to your family?' asked Brigite.

'No . . .'

He did not know if any of the men had written. He would not know what to say.

He thought of Emma. He pictured her, for some reason, sitting over a log fire, eating scrambled eggs after a day's hunting with the North Shropshire.

Now it was midnight, and the column was preparing to move: half of it down the gully, on the last lap to the valley floor; the other half back up to the plateau, a thief in the night, a murderer creeping into 101 Regiment's backyard.

One tent remained standing: the assault group would have a final briefing once the column had departed.

Nick stood by Robbo's command vehicle. Robbo was in the cab; Gates was his driver.

'The last met report says the snow will clear in about another two hours. Go slowly. You shouldn't have any problems. Find the rail line and follow it. You can manage that, can't you, Gates?'

'Sir.'

Robbo said: 'It's gutted me, has this. It should be Mr Pendred.'

'I need Mr Pendred with me. I need *you* to command the column. That's the end of it.'

In truth, Robbo was ill, anybody could see it. His voice was thick, his movements slow. 'Exposure to some extent. More seriously, exhaustion,' Brigite had reported to Nick. Robbo's determination to do as well or better than any of his lads, relentlessly, day after day, had taken its toll.

'These lads,' he had once confessed ruefully to Nick,

'they have a pint of beer, their head hits the pillow and they sleep like a baby. It takes a bottle of scotch to put me out like that . . .'

Jamie skied down the column.

'They're ready to move off.'

Checking the column should have been Robbo's job.

'Cheers, Sar'nt-Major,' said Jamie.

'Good luck, sir.'

'See you in a few hours, Gates,' said Nick unnecessarily, with forced friendliness, determined to imply no moral censure.

'Sir.'

'Bye then, Robbo.'

Robbo nodded. The window closed. The command vehicle moved slowly forward, its lights on, its European flag and Union flag illuminated by the lights of the vehicle behind it.

Nick and Jamie watched the vehicles file past. The ambulance was in the centre, flying the column's UN flag.

A figure waved from the rear window. It kept on waving as the ambulance jolted past.

Jamie waved back. Then the ambulance was hidden by the vehicle behind it. The column was swallowed by the darkness. He and Nick turned away.

'Sar'nt Doran!'

'Sir!'

'Staff Beckwith!'

'Sir.'

'Get the men into the tent.'

* * *

For some time the figure kept on waving, and sobbing. Brigite, by the stretcher, looked up from Munro and smiled wearily, sadly.

Munro was conscious, his face frozen with pain. In another hour she would risk giving him a further one-eighth grain of morphine. In the meantime he was a soldier and must suffer.

Worembrand was also a soldier who was having to suffer. The ambulance reeked of blood. His duvet was stiff with frozen blood. He sat in his dossbag, cold and savage. That the buggers were out to get him was not new; that they were out to get him with nuclear missiles was a new twist entirely.

SIX

Slopes of Mount Kirovsk, 00.30 hours, 9 November

'101 Independent Rocket Regiment,' said Noon. 'Commander Colonel Vasili Aleksandrovich Kvatov. It has ten SS-27 *Satan* rockets, each with a yield of ten megatons. That means each rocket has the destructive capacity of ten thousand Hiroshimas. Each missile is in its own launch silo, and the silos are dispersed over an area of twenty-five square miles. Each silo is controlled from the command bunker *here* . . .'

He had drawn a sketchmap of the objective on a sheet taken earlier from the ambulance. Red, blue and green chinograph lines showed the rocket silos, the airfield, the guard company barracks, the command bunker.

Using a radio aerial he drew a circle on the map.

'101 Regiment has a strength of four hundred men. Two hundred and fifty of them are in the guard company. These men have probably never even seen a rocket. Their job is to protect the silos and patrol the wire and the minefields.'

Staff Beckwith said: 'Hold twenty-five square miles with only two hundred and fifty men?'

Nick said: 'These installations were built with war

405

against NATO in mind. All the protection is against missiles and planes. Nobody imagined that rocket silos deep inside Russia would be subjected to ground attack.' He nodded to Noon to continue.

Noon said: 'What the major says is correct. The guards are thinly dispersed. They are not highly motivated. Many of them are conscripts. They spend most of their time worrying about their pig farm, which is the biggest on the Kola peninsula. I'm not joking. If this turns pear-shaped, there'll be roast pork tomorrow and crackling that glows in the dark . . .'

Nobody was laughing. Nick saw a look, a shadow, flicker over the faces of the young soldiers crammed into the tent.

'Get on, sergeant,' he said curtly.

Noon said: 'Spetznaz: Russian SAS. 101 Regiment has recently been joined by a company of the Vilyandi Spetznaz regiment. They've about a hundred men, thirty per cent officers. They're organised in three reconnaissance platoons and one signals platoon. They're evil buggers, and they'll be probing out further than the guards.

'You know about the gunships. If the weather moderates, they'll be flying.

'Now the static defences. First a restricted zone: ten kilometres across, cleared of all vegetation, and regularly patrolled. That's here, running right round the plateau . . .'

Again, he pointed with the radio aerial.

'Then there are two fortified lines, and inside them we find a minefield, then the wire – a high wire fence like the old Inner German Boundary, enclosing an area of low wire entanglements. All of this is mined and booby-trapped with anti-personnel mines, anti-tank mines and spring guns.

'Finally, ground surveillance. Microphones and seismographic equipment capable of identifying a solitary man on foot anywhere in a ten-mile final perimeter round the command bunker. This equipment is re-sited on a regular basis. Any questions?'

Nick looked at the faces of his men. The shadows of doubt were evident now. More than one of those present, he guessed, was wishing he was with the column, wishing he had not felt impelled to play the hero.

'Remember that most of this,' he said quietly, 'will be buried under new snow. Perhaps all of it will be buried under snow. It's entirely possible that once we get through the anti-tank lines we will stroll through the minefield, right up to the wire, without anybody noticing.

'Remember what's at stake. Remember we have surprise on our side. We have HMS *Revenge* to back us up. We have the Snow Leopards. We have Milan 5 and Starstreak.'

He wanted to say that he was proud of them; that they were the best company in the best line regiment in the British Army. He believed it to be true, and wanted to say it.

But they were little more than a platoon in strength. And they were intelligent, and professional, and knew the odds.

And this was not an inter-battalion sportsday.

He looked at his watch.

'All right,' he said, 'let's get moving.'

* * *

The Russian MT-LB led the way, with Staff Beckwith driving, Noon in the turret, Jamie and five men in the back. Behind, just close enough to see them, came Nick in the command vehicle, followed by the four other Snow Leopards of the assault group.

Nick hoped the MT-LB would give them a few seconds' element of surprise; give the Snow Leopards a chance, if they stumbled into the enemy, to fan out into line and attack.

By 02.30 they were in the first RV. Nick conferred with his commanders. The drivers rested, closing eyes that were weary from straining to see the faint convoy light of the vehicle ahead.

At 04.30 they were in the second RV, a snow-filled depression on a hill plateau just short of the restricted zone. They drew the vehicles up in a tight group and switched off the engines. They ate chocolate, munched nuts, and drank from their flasks.

Nick and Noon left the vehicles and crawled forward to the ridge of the depression. The men crawled into dossbags to shiver until their return.

Nick focused his binoculars, pointing them over the ridge, but could see nothing in the blackness.

Less than seven hours to H Hour. He experienced a moment of panic, a sudden sick churning in his stomach. He longed for a slug of vodka, but did not dare risk it.

And when thyself with shining foot shall pass
Among the guests star-scattered on the grass

And reach the spot where I myself made One . . .
Turn down an empty glass!

Shining with radiation, like Noon's pork crackling.

The wind was losing its force. The snow had almost stopped. Three hours to dawn.

They crawled back to the vehicles. One sentry was out: Hendry, the youngest member of the company. Three months ago he had been a boy soldier, a Junior Leader newly arrived from UK. Nick had looked in on his eighteenth-birthday bash in Rheindahlen. Innocent, unworldly, Hendry had gone to his party at the Cherry-Ripe Club carrying his presents and cards from his folk back in Bridgnorth. Birthday cards with pictures of sportscars and fishing-rods from his younger sisters, a card with a picture of Lake Ullswater from an aunt, a travelcase and camera from his Mum and Dad. '*Happy Birthday, Mark* . . .'

The lads had bought him a tart for the night, but he was legless when Nick looked in to buy him a drink, and a corporal was slapping his face vigorously to try and bring him round.

'It's OK, Hendry,' said Nick, cautiously, as they approached the vehicles.

'Sir.'

They brushed themselves off, and climbed into the back of the MT-LB. Jamie and his five men were asleep, huddled together like rabbits in a burrow. By them lay their rifles, each with two magazines taped back-to-back for a quick change. Every inch of space was filled with armaments –

hand-held rocket launchers, ammo boxes, grenades lashed to crude, improvised crucifixes to prevent them from sinking and exploding uselessly under thick snow. In the driver's compartment Beckwith snored at the tillers.

Nick arranged his feet gingerly between a box of belted ammo and a pile of grenades. Noon poured two cups of thick sweet tea from a flask.

'When the storm hit,' he said quietly, 'they would have suspended patrols. Those close to base would have scuttled back to their bunker. Some outlying patrols would have gone to ground. Yesterday they started moving again. The patrol we bumped into was trying to re-establish surveillance of the western valleys. Today they'll be sending out work parties to re-site the ground surveillance and check the minefields. We need to reach the wire by 07.00.'

Nick nodded.

'How good is your information?' he asked.

'It's from a guy who served as a conscript here three years ago. Now he works for a merchant bank in London. SIS has been treating him to a holiday on the shores of Loch Long for the past month. I've talked to him, so's the boss.'

'It must be nice,' said Nick, 'on the shores of Loch Long.'

'Bit quiet for me,' said Noon. 'Nothing to do in the evenings.'

Nick drained his cup. He looked at his watch, the seconds ticking by.

He would let the men rest for another five minutes.

'You married, Sergeant?'

'Separated.'

According to army psychologists, a soldier placed in a classic SAS four-man unit rapidly developed a loyalty towards his unit that exceeded his loyalty to his family, his regiment, or his country.

Noon said: 'I've two boys. Eldest's sixteen, going for a Junior Leader in March. His mother says she'll kill him first, but she won't stop him. He's a tough bugger, a hard nut.'

'Takes after his dad.'

Noon nodded without smiling. He poured the last of the tea. He said: 'I'm jacking it in after this. They can RTU me back to the gunners or chuck me out, but I've had enough. That Russian lad was trying to hide under a rock. A poor sodding conscript. He couldn't understand why we wanted to kill him, but in the end he had the guts to fire back. I'd have been proud of him if he'd been mine.'

'You said it was an accident.'

'No,' said Noon, 'we had to kill him.'

Nick looked at his watch again. 'H Hour,' he said. 'Will it be missiles, or will they use bombers?'

'Stealth bombers from Siberia. Nice and clean.'

Jamie's body suddenly twitched, his head jerking up, his eyes opening in alarm, then blinking in confusion.

Nick said: 'Jamie? You take the command vehicle. I'm travelling ahead from now on.'

Noon said: 'Two hours to the start-line. Time to send Wildcat.'

* * *

Nick opened the cab of the command vehicle and shook Sykes. Sykes woke reluctantly, rubbing his eyes, slowly pulling his legs out of his dossbag.

'Sorry, sir . . .'

He stuffed his sleeping bag on to the rack behind him.

Jamie had gone round the other side of the vehicle and clambered into the co-driver's seat.

Nick leaned in and said: 'Anything happens to us, just go like hell for the command bunker, and get Noon and the laser into position. That's all that matters. That's all that's important.'

'Yes . . .'

Jamie yawned and shivered.

'You all right, Sykes?' asked Nick.

'Sir.'

What the hell, Nick wondered, was Sykes doing with the assault group? Who, in the entire regiment, had less reason than he had to go the extra mile?

Pride, perhaps. Sykes had been called many things in his army career – rogue, thief, drunkard, lunatic – but nobody had ever called him a jacker. Sykes never packed in, never gave up, never backed down.

Through the windscreen the faint convoy light was illuminated on the MT-LB. Nick said: 'See you both at the start-line.'

He ran forward and jumped into the back of the MT-LB. In the command vehicle Sykes pushed the ignition. The cab gently started to warm up.

The assault group moved off.

Two hours to the First Defensive Line, three hours to the light of day, six hours to H Hour.

SEVEN

Revenge was down among the dead men, down among the bones, proceeding at a steady walking pace above the cold slimy oil-shale, walking in the company of ghosts.

She had left the Clyde at the beginning of October, and now she was sharing a home with Clydesiders from the past. The *Empire Howard* lay eighty leagues north-by-north-west, the cruiser *Trinidad* twenty leagues due north, the *Edinburgh*, long since dispossessed of her golden cargo, lay five leagues to the east.

Since landing the SAS team at Kirkenes, *Revenge* had been prowling her dark Arctic territory, along the Murman coast from Kildin Island to the White Sea, north to Bear Island, and back to the mouth of the Kola. All the time her ultrasensitive voice-recognition signal was alert for the sound of Russian hunter-killers that might be out and about.

But *Revenge* was alone. Nobody, her captain said sadly, was coming out to play.

So she patrolled quietly along the seabed, her radio receiving antennae stretching up to float like a drift of seaweed, waiting for a signal from Norwood.

* * *

It came at 05.52 hours.

'XO and WEO to the wireless office, XO and WEO to the wireless office,' said the calm, quiet voice, little more than a whisper, penetrating into every corner of the submarine.

Three minutes later the Executive Officer and the Weapons Engineering Officer were in the navigation centre, opening a safe within a safe. The outer combination was known only to the XO and one other officer; the inner combination to the WEO and the Captain. Each safe contained information needed to verify the signal.

The XO looked at a card and said: 'My half authenticates.'

The WEO said: 'My half authenticates.'

'Authentication time?'

The time was written down. The cards were locked back in the safe.

Six bells sounded. The electronic chimes floated into Captain Andrew Rashleigh's dream, then floated out again. It was Easter Monday and he was at the North Cotswold point-to-point, and his sister-in-law's horse Cambrian Boy was winning at 8-to-1, and he could see it coming into the straight, he could see the jockey's yellow shirt with magenta cross, he could hear the commentator shouting . . .

'Sir? It's *Wildcat*, sir,' said the Executive Officer.

Rashleigh's eyes opened.

'Authenticated?' he said.

'Authentication time 5.58, sir,' said the Wireless Executive Officer.

Gifted with instant wakefulness, Rashleigh was already on his feet and reaching for his pullover.

'Bring the missile to condition 1 SQ.'

A king in his floating castle, he negotiated the spiral staircases with practised ease. In the control room an officer was already testing the hover-system values, checking the ship's balance and trim. *Revenge* had started to drift to a standstill. Rashleigh stared for a few moments at the data on-screen, then said:

'Stop engines.'

'Stop engines.'

'Hover in auto.'

A crewman said: 'Hover hull-valve open, hovering in auto, computer one.'

Hull valves began to open and close, drawing in and expelling hundreds of gallons of water, holding the ship on an even keel. On the screens wheeling dots of light spun in opposite directions, then slowed and became stationary.

In the inky depths of the Barents Sea, *Revenge* had undergone a metamorphosis: from a moving vessel, a living creature of the deep, into a launch platform as static and steady as a rock.

Rashleigh moved next-door, to the missile control centre where the WEO was feeding target information into his computer. Beside him a rating pressed a keyboard to display a mass of missile data: power, battery, gyroscopes, alignment.

'Missile spinning, sir,' said the rating. 'No defects.'

The WEO slipped on a combination headset and swung down the mike. 'All positions, WEO on the net,' he announced.

Rashleigh passed on, down another spiral staircase, through the junior recreation rooms and the library, past the engine room, forward through the ship until he reached security zone. He placed his palm on the pad and the door clicked open, and he passed through into the missile chamber, the room known as 'Sherwood Forest', where a double row of sixteen missiles, as tall and straight as young birch trees, sat under massive cantilevered hatches.

Here was power to kill a billion people.

The WEO's assistant was checking the onboard computer of the last missile. This was *Wildcat*, smaller than the gleaming white Tridents – a kitten of a missile, they joked, but lethal enough. The successor to *Tomahawk*, its non-nuclear payload could flatten six city blocks. The television camera in its nose was linked to an onboard terrain contour matching system that could take it to within fifty metres of its target.

The WEO was irked that it could not get closer. In Baghdad it could find its way round the city streets and in and out of the supermarkets, but on the flat snow-covered taiga it had trouble finding good radar signatures and, to the WEO's annoyance, it had to be nudged the final distance by men on the ground.

The AWEO finished his checklist. Rashleigh, as he always did, double-checked for himself. While he did so, the AWEO turned to a dial on the chamber wall, and adjusted it until the pressure in the tubes was balanced with the water-pressure outside the hull, so that the hatch would swing open freely on command.

Rashleigh nodded. The AWEO spoke into his mike, telling the WEO that the missile was ready to fire.

On the ship's intercom a voice said: 'Executive Officer to Captain. Weapons System is 1 SQ. Weapons System is 1 SQ.'

The missile was prepared, the systems were ready.

The red lights in the chamber turned to white, marking the ship's official transition from night to day.

06.30 hours. The land force would be in the restricted zone. He wondered what the devil they'd done with the female nurses, and the children they'd picked up on their travels.

EIGHT

Murmansk valley, 06.45 hours, 9 November

Houses appeared in the headlights: concrete blocks with sharply sloping tin roofs, behind them an open-cast mine of some kind, a wheel and gantry shaped like a huge, weird snow-sculpture. There were lights in some of the houses. Doors opened. Figures emerged, miners like grizzly bears in their fur coats and fur Balaclavas, preparing for an early shift. They looked in amazement at the column of vehicles, flags flying, that slowly descended from Mount Kirovsk.

'Any chance of a brew, sir?' said Gates, speaking loudly. The sergeant-major had not spoken for the past hour, and he felt uncomfortable.

Robbo said: 'Not yet. Follow that track down through the trees. Keep your eyes peeled for the railway line.'

The track ran down through stunted birches, alongside the course of a frozen stream. Several times they were slowed by huge drifts; on one occasion they came up against a vertical wall of snow, ten or twelve feet high, that even the Snow Leopards could not climb.

Robbo left the cab and went to recce a path round the flank. Private Best, co-driver of the second vehicle, hobbled up to the command vehicle.

'Anything left in your flask?'

Gates shook his head. Best looked at his watch, then hobbled back to his cab. Gates checked the LodeStar reading with the map: they were half a kilometre from the valley floor. It was still dark. He could scarcely distinguish the sergeant-major ploughing back through the snow.

Robbo got back into the cab. He had found a place where they could cross the drift.

An hour later the ground levelled, and they emerged from the trees. Before them, bisecting the track, was the Murmansk-St Petersburg railway line. It was still some time to dawn, but there were ripples of white light in the northern sky. In the distance, across the flat smooth snow, were buildings and what looked like grain silos. The lights of a tractor or oversnow vehicle of some kind were bobbing slowly towards some farm buildings.

The snow had stopped, and the wind was falling.

Gates pulled off the track. The other vehicles followed, and pulled up next to him. He turned off the engine for the first time in eight hours. Beside him, in the sudden silence, Robbo was breathing with difficulty. His face was ashen. He was sweating.

Gates said, 'You OK, sir?' and when he got no reply he thought for a moment, then left the cab. After hours of fuggy warmth the cold stunned him. Four soldiers, the designated sentries, had left their vehicles and were looking round for Robbo. After a moment they selected their own positions, threw their mats down on the snow, and lay on them facing outwards. Childs, the man injured on the raid on the farm, was in the turret of his vehicle, setting up the column's one remaining machine-gun. One or two men were stretching their legs; most preferred to stay huddled in the cramped warmth.

Gates walked past four vehicles until he reached the ambulance. He opened the rear door and told Brigite that he was no doctor, but he thought she ought to look at the sergeant-major.

Brigite looked startled, then fumbled her way into her camouflage whites, grabbed her bag, climbed down into the snow, and plodded with him back to the command vehicle.

Robbo had suffered a heart attack at some point, she guessed, during the past two hours. His irregular heartbeat indicated a bloodclot affecting his heart's electrical conducting system. He urgently needed to be in a coronary intensive-care unit, but at least he was alive. Fifty per cent of heart attack fatalities occurred in the first fifteen minutes.

'I can give him a drug to steady his heart rhythms. He might survive.' She reached for her bag. 'Who's the next in command?'

Gates looked at her, confused. There was Corporal Kelly, he said, from Sergeant Doran's platoon . . .

'He's the senior NCO?'

'Well, not quite,' said Gates.

The rear door of the ambulance jerked open in a flurry of snowflakes. Worembrand looked up wearily. He had his Leica out and was cleaning the lens, clinging to normality, to sanity. He was beyond protesting at the way people kept opening doors and clambering in and out for no fucking

423

purpose whatsoever. Brigite was standing looking in. Gates was beside her. They were staring at him.

Brigite said: 'The sergeant-major has had a coronary. It seems that you are now the senior British officer.'

They stood looking up the railway line, to where it curved into a plantation of firs.

Brigite said: 'At least we've only got 4k to go. How worried are you about motorised infantry coming down from Novyj Yena?'

Corporal Kelly said: 'We can't fight them, ma'am. We've just got to fly the flags and hope for the best.'

'Sergeant?'

Worembrand said: 'What?'

'What action do you suggest we take if we run into Russian troops?'

What action did he suggest? He could have cried.

'Well?' she said irritably.

'If they're between us and that tunnel,' he said, 'we've had it. They won't attack us, but they won't let us through either. They'll just be typical fucking foreign bastards and keep us sitting there while they scratch their arses and think about things.'

'So what do you suggest?'

'I suggest,' said Worembrand, 'we get on the radio and call Narvik, NATO, Petersburg, Berlin, the BBC, CNN, the Save the Children Fund, the *Daily Telegraph*, the *Sun*, the *Express* . . .'

'We can't do that. For heaven's sake, didn't you listen back in the tent . . .?'

Worembrand turned back towards the ambulance.

Brigite said: 'Sergeant Worembrand!'

He stopped.

'Take this vehicle. Travel a thousand metres ahead of the column. You will act as a forward screen, to give warning of any danger. Break radio silence if necessary, to warn us of any armed forces, hostile or otherwise. Corporal Kelly?'

'Ma'am.'

'Get the sentries in. Get the children back in their vehicles. We move as soon as the sergeant-major is in the ambulance. We may have to scatter and leave the railway line, so make sure every driver has the map references of the tunnel.'

'Ma'am.'

'Sergeant Worembrand?'

'Yes.'

'I will lead the column with Corporal Kelly. We will try to work our way round any obstruction you warn us about. We will not stop under any circumstances. I suggest you do not stop either. If we are separated, and you do not get to the tunnel, try to get your vehicle under a bridge or against the west wall of a low building by 11.00, and take cover in the back – not in the front cab. You understand?'

Worembrand nodded. He turned away, this time towards the Snow Leopard, which he noted was being driven by Mason, an idiot, the most stupid man in the regiment.

'Sergeant Worembrand!'

Christ almighty . . .

He turned back.

'Get your NBC suit from the ambulance.'

He pulled it from under the rack and unzipped the protective bag. The best Nuclear-Biological-Chemical warfare protection suit in the world, they said, but soldiers always boasted about their bits of kit being the best in the world. They were always suckers for smooth-talking Ministry of Defence procurement boys with their flash videos. Worembrand had worn a Noddy suit only once in his life, on exercise in Berlin, and it had rained a teeny, tiny, drizzly rain, and the rain had seeped into his best-protective-suit-in-the-world-bar-NONE and soaked him. But they never claimed it kept out the rain, of course. Just the nuclear fall-out and the poisonous chemicals and the killer microbes.

He swore foully.

Anneliese said: 'Max, please. Do your best – for the rest of us.'

Munro said: 'Let us down and I'll personally chop your balls off.'

'Now, you be quiet,' said Anneliese. 'You've been a good boy up until now.'

Worembrand picked up the camera he had been cleaning, and slung it round his neck. He looked at his camera cases, hesitated, then glanced at Anneliese. She was watching him. The door jerked open. Four men stood outside. They were carrying Robbo on a stretcher. Brigite was leaning over him, holding his wrist, shielding his head from the drizzle of snow.

'Clear a space,' said a young soldier curtly.

Worembrand grabbed his NBC suit and jumped down. He hurried away to the front of the column.

The soldiers lifted Robbo's stretcher and tried to slide it into the right-hand runners. There was not enough room.

'What's all this?'

'Sergeant Worembrand's boxes,' said Anneliese.

Without a word the young soldier began to chuck Worembrand's camera cases, his duvet, his Lufthansa bag and his dossbag out into the snow.

NINE

The Russian radio operator emerged from the tent and stumbled a few metres to relieve himself away from the wind. He felt ill, something more than the usual permanent hangover, a virus perhaps – with luck the flu virus that was filling the hospitals of Kandalakša and Arkhangelsk. There had been a dozen cases at 101 Rocket Regiment. The victims had been put into isolation in the warm sanatorium at base.

As he emptied his bladder he thought longingly about a warm bed, a dry warm bed, pushed up next to a radiator so hot you couldn't touch it, so hot you could smell the blistering paint.

But he did not really think he had the flu, and it had always been against the code of a Red Army soldier to feign illness. You could steal food, sneak girls into barracks, concoct alcohol (a man's got to live), but you did not *shirk military duty*.

All he was suffering from, he decided, was vitamin deficiency. His fingernails were falling out. Everybody's fingernails were falling out. In the summer they had gone on trips to find berries along the riverbanks – bilberries,

429

whortleberries, and cranberries – and crammed them into their mouths, exulting in their tart freshness.

But now it was November, and already their fingernails were falling out and their gums were sore.

He would have given a lot for a bowl of berries, but his breakfast – safely warming under his armpits – was dried salmon strips. 'Squaw Candy' the Americans called it. In Alaska they used it to buy themselves women for the night, so the radio operator had been told. Dear God, when had they last seen a woman in the Khibiny Mountains? – apart from the lesbians nesting in the radio room who were as sexually attractive as an old wolverine bitch with rabies and were, anyway, the officers' property.

The radio operator had pin-ups over his bunk, raunchy photographs of non-Russian womanhood from the Polish Army magazine *Infantryman*; and he had a girl at home to lust over (home was an Arkhangelsk suburb; he was a city boy) but love by letter, as the old Red Army saying had it, was like lunch by telephone.

He buttoned his trousers and limped back towards the tent. He had slept in his boots, and the paper he had used to line them – three days ago, before they set out on patrol – had crumpled uncomfortably under his toes, but he was not hauling his boots off, not out here. He passed the cab of the patrol vehicle and nodded a greeting to the sentry who sat staring out over the tundra. The sentry should have been outside in the cold, but he was a poor sort, a miserable bugger who couldn't be bothered to do anything right. He had been a doghandler until three weeks ago, when a deserter from the motor pool had killed his dog near the Murmansk road.

The radio operator was almost back to the tent when he heard the sound of a vehicle approaching. It was coming from the west, and he looked round and hesitated. Intelligence had told them that rabble from Murmansk, conscripts gone berserk, might make their way up from the valley floor – though why conscripts scrabbling to find their way south should want to venture into a Rocket Regiment defensive zone, Intelligence did not say.

He could have crawled back into the tent, into his sleeping bag, but a sense of duty prevailed. He took his gun from the rack and walked back to the BMD. He pulled open the cab door. The ex-doghandler looked at him angrily, then also heard the vehicle, and reached shamefacedly for his rifle.

They peered forward. White ripples in the northern sky lent a faint, ghostly luminance to the snowscape. After a few moments the familiar silhouette of an MT-LB appeared, negotiating its way carefully through exposed rocks.

'Patrol,' said the ex-doghandler. The radio operator nodded. It must be the patrol that had gone out the previous day, and had been reported out of radio contact. As he walked gingerly back to the tent (perhaps he would take his boots off after all; the paper wedged up under his toes was like some horrible Chinese torture) he wondered, with professional interest, what had gone wrong with the MT-LB's radio this time, and whether they would be able to fix it. For months they had been cannibalising old equipment to keep their sets in working order.

Behind him he heard the sentry give a cry of puzzled

interrogation. He looked round. The MT-LB was clanking to a halt. Two faces were just visible in the cab. The ex-doghandler was not looking at the cab, though, but at the turret gun. It was slowly swivelling. In a split-second of understanding the radio operator knew that something was disastrously wrong. He opened his mouth to shout to the ex-doghandler to take cover, but his words were lost in the deafening crack of bullets. The ex-doghandler jerked backwards, head over heels into the snow.

Now the turret gun was swinging rapidly, and figures were tumbling out of the rear doors, fire pouring from their automatic rifles. He threw himself sideways and rolled over, clutching his RPK automatic, crawling away until a bullet thudded into his leg and he collapsed and lay still. He heard a sudden, isolated scream that competed for a moment with the sound of the guns, then the scream was cut off, but the guns did not stop. He raised his face, looking round wildly for a way to escape. He saw four men standing round the tent, calmly emptying their magazines into the canvas.

He saw two men throw themselves against the patrol vehicle's side, then swing round the back to spray the interior through the open door. He felt a brief satisfaction that the patrol vehicle was empty, that there was nobody in it to be killed. Then he caught the eye of a man by the tent who was in the process of wrenching off an empty magazine and slamming in a fresh cartridge, and he saw the rifle rise and the flash of yellow flame.

'Stop firing!'

Silence fell.

Nick looked round: at the sentry lying in a drift of snow, at the body of the man he had just killed.

Two soldiers, Hendry and Leech, jumped down from the back of the BMD.

'Clear, sir,' said Leech.

He turned, heart pounding, to the tent. It had half collapsed, and was flapping and twitching in the stiff wind. Three soldiers stood with their weapons trained on it.

Nick approached it cautiously. He used his rifle barrel to push back the canvas doorflap. Suddenly, from within, there came a long cry of terror and pain. Instantly the soldiers were firing again, walking slowly in on the tent, their rifles pumping a stream of bullets into it.

Nick shouted for them to stop firing.

Over the tundra he could hear the sound of engines: Snow Leopards converging in a pincer from either flank.

He crouched by the entrance and, with his rifle barrel again, flicked the tent flap aside.

Blood dripped from the canvas, from the clothes hanging to dry. It dripped down the sides of the stove, and down the central pole. It dripped, black in the dim light of dawn, from the bodies of the dead men.

Noon said: 'Excuse me, sir,' and Nick stood back. Noon crawled in and started to go through the bodies, rummaging for maps and notebooks.

Nick turned away. Jamie was jumping down from the turret of his Snow Leopard.

'We've spotted the First Defensive Line,' he said. 'It's

433

about twelve hundred metres ahead. I've left two men on skis. There's no sign of life. I doubt if they heard the firing, not in this wind.'

But the wind was dying, the snow had almost ceased to fall, and soon the gunships would be flying.

Nick told men to collect machine-guns, ammunition and rifles and sling them in the back of one of the vehicles. He walked over to the man he had shot, the first man he had, to his knowledge, ever killed, and retrieved his gun. Driven by a compulsion he did not try to understand, he turned the man over and looked at him. Mid-twenties, late-twenties perhaps.

'Sar'nt Doran!'

'Sir!'

'Get these two men into the tent, if Sar'nt Noon has finished.'

Noon emerged from the tent, his camouflage whites smeared with blood. He carried papers and a tin can.

'Look at this,' he said. It was a five-pound tin of ham bearing the grey EC Food Aid label.

Jamie had poked his head curiously into the tent. Now he was standing in shock.

'No, don't look,' he said, stopping Hendry.

'I know they're dead, sir,' said Hendry, aggrieved.

Jamie looked as if he might be sick. Nick told him to organise a fatigue party with shovels.

Noon was bearing his prize back to the command vehicle. 'It's proper cooked ham this,' he told Sergeant

Doran. 'It's not reconstituted stuff full of water.'

'Let's get on with it,' said Nick. 'We move in one minute.'

The two bodies were dragged into the tent. The pole was collapsed. Snow was shovelled over it.

War, Nick remembered, was the coward's art of running away when weak, and attacking mercilessly when strong.

TEN

Worembrand's vehicle turned a bend and there they were,
half a dozen army trucks at a forest crossing, straddling the
track. Thick firs on either side prevented any chance of an
escape. They were caught, they were done for; they were
already, in Worembrand's imagination, garotted and
swinging from the nearest tree.

'There's a gap on the left,' said Mason. 'I can just get
through, if them buggers'll move.'

'I've seen it. Don't stop,' said Worembrand. 'Whatever
you do, don't stop.' His hands gripped the dashboard.

The Russians, some of them sitting on their vehicles,
some of them crouched round a fire, were staring at the
Snow Leopard. As they drew closer, a soldier climbed on
to the cab of the first vehicle and waved for them to stop.
Others unslung their rifles in a mechanical, routine, but to
Worembrand seriously threatening movement.

'It's a bit tight,' said Mason, 'as the actress said to
the . . .'

'Just shut up and keep driving, and smile at the
bastards.'

437

'But if they don't move, Sar'nt . . .'

'They'll move. They always move. Oh Christ, smile, smile!'

They were almost level with the first Russian truck. Soldiers were forming a line across the gap.

Mason said: 'You haven't told the convoy.'

Worembrand pressed the button on the RT and said: 'Zero Bravo to Zero Alpha. Zero Bravo to Zero Alpha. We're in trouble: the line's blocked. The line's blocked by infantry . . .'

Soldiers were aiming their rifles. Some sort of NCO was waving his hands and shouting. They were almost on top of them.

He dropped the RT handset and yelled: 'Drive through them, don't stop! Jesus what the fuck do you think . . .'

Mason was trying to swing the Snow Leopard into the wood. The trees were too dense. He swung the vehicle back. Soldiers were crowding in front, dodging about, their faces a few metres from the windscreen. He threw the caterpillar tracks into reverse and the Snow Leopard skidded sideways to a standstill.

'I'm sorry, Sar'nt, but bloody hell . . .'

Worembrand moved like lightning. He was swinging out of the cab before the first soldier reached it. He held up his camera. He bellowed: 'Associated Press, Reuters, the *Sun, Der Spiegel*. Who speaks English? English! Somebody has to speak English!'

Then he was down amongst them, pushing them back and crying in mounting rage: 'OK against the trees. Don't start grinning! Who told you to grin? You're supposed to be vicious soldiery out for pillage and rape, you silly sods!'

The soldiers fell back.

'Right now, hold it, HOLD IT, you revolting bastards, you stupid turds, you bloody awful foreign shits . . .'

The moment printed itself on his mind. He could smell cold fresh snow and acrid woodsmoke, and the resin of pines and food cooking over a fire. Christ! In this weather! No NATO ration packs and primus stoves for these boys! Through the lens he could see the ragged uniforms under the fur coats, the blankets round the shoulders, the thin, dirty, not unfriendly faces of conscripts . . . the casual, clumsy, dangerous way they cradled their Kalashnikovs.

He hopped from place to place. He knelt to get a low angle. He snapped and shouted, 'Eurekaaaa!' He grabbed a soldier and prodded him closer to another soldier. The soldier looked round in confusion, as if wondering why he had been picked upon. When Worembrand snapped, and shouted 'Eurekaaa!' for the fifth or sixth time, one or two tentatively mumbled 'Eureka' back, and Worembrand yelled angrily: 'I thought I told you not to smile!'

Suddenly there was a shout. An officer was walking towards them through the trees – a headquarters unit, hidden away, Worembrand guessed; piggy officers messing away from the ranks to gorge on the last tin of bully beef. The soldiers called back to him, amused, offering some sort of explanation.

Worembrand backed towards the cab. 'Thank you,' he said, 'for helping me to bring your agony to the notice of

the world. No longer will they call this the Forgotten War.'
He opened the cab door.

A soldier, an NCO of some kind, called out to him in a
stern voice.

Worembrand called back: 'You want a print? Don't
worry. I'll do you a print the minute I get back to the
darkroom,' a promise he always made, but prided himself
on never *ever* having fulfilled. As the officer entered the
clearing, he slumped in his seat and said:

'Go, you stupid fucker. Go! GO!'

Mason revved the engine and released the brake. The
Snow Leopard jerked forward.

In a final burst of inspiration Worembrand opened his
door and pointed back the way they had come, and yelled:
'Watch out for Kate Adie!'

Soldiers fell back on either side. The officer was
questioning the NCO, soldiers were waving: bored, weary,
hungry men who were grateful, Worembrand knew, for a
moment's diversion.

He fell back in his seat, his head thumping. After a few
moments Mason said coyly: 'You'll have to take my picture
next time, Sar'nt.'

ELEVEN

Mount Kirovsk, First Defensive Zone, 08.10 hours, 9 November

The golden eagle soared over Mount Kirovsk, over the plateau with its scattered, scrubby trees, its missile silos, railway line and forest tracks. As the sky lightened, it drifted down over the two defensive circles of concrete pillboxes, the snow-smooth minefields, and the inner circle of wire.

It saw, without interest, two groups of vehicles stationary in the snow, out beyond the First Defensive Line. It watched an arctic hare dash across a clearing, and it began to drift lower, wheeling westward, knowing through instinct not comprehension that it should not throw a shadow over its prey.

Then it saw a small pack of wolves out on the tundra, and with an infinitesimally small use of energy it continued its flight westward to investigate. The wolves were loping with some speed, as if they were following a scent.

Another eye looked down on Mount Kirovsk. A NATO observation satellite had been in geosynchronous orbit for over a month. Its camera lens featured state-of-the-art

441

technology, but was not as sharp as the eyes of the golden eagle, and it did not pick up the white arctic hare, or (for some time, at any rate) the white, camouflaged Snow Leopards, hull-down in two depressions in the snow. But it zoomed in, briefly, on the pack of wolves, now feasting in what seemed to be a small encampment some two kilometres to the west. And, as the light grew stronger, it made out the Russian vehicles that were now travelling with 'B' Company.

They had crept into position in the hour before dawn. Nick had three vehicles. Away to the left – some fifteen hundred metres – was Jamie with the main force.

'Stand by!'

'Sir.'

Light was spreading, a butter-yellow glow in the eastern sky. Standing in the command vehicle turret, he could now clearly see the scrubby treeline, still in shadow, four hundred metres ahead. Somewhere among those stunted birch and fir trees lay the first belt of defended outposts: dug-in concrete strong points ringed with wire and mines, each pillbox covering its neighbours with interlocking fire.

He sought them out with his binoculars. He looked for evidence of newly-dug snow, for the rising cloud of a sentry's breath. He listened for the clank of metal, the murmur of conversation.

All was still.

He looked at his watch. It was 08.15. According to Noon, stealth bombers were already airborne from Siberia.

'Milan crew, take post,' he said into his intercom.

The two-man crew slipped out of the back of the command vehicle. Bent double to avoid being seen, they carried the launcher a few metres from the Snow Leopard and bedded it in the snow. They slid the long, smooth missile casing into place.

The gunner peered into his sights.

Nick wondered what the Russians in the pillboxes were doing; if they were asleep or awake, eating, writing home, playing music, watching television.

In the Russian army, reveille for platoon commanders was 05.50, and for the men 06.00, followed by compulsory physical exercises for an hour.

That, at least, was how it was supposed to be – how it used to be in the days of the Red Army, in the days of professionalism and pride.

'These will be conscripts,' Noon had said. 'They're rubbish. They don't waste the elite platoons on this sort of duty.'

The gunner was focusing his electronic eye on the woodland edge, and checking the image on his computer screen. All they needed now was the target.

Again Nick scanned the forest edge. Sentries would be looking out from snow trenches, crouching by their machine-guns. In the pillboxes the conscripts would be looking forward to another day of boredom, another day of discomfort, another day nearer home.

His heart was thumping; he could feel it pounding in his ears. He was suddenly short of breath. A soldier's entire life was a preparation for the moment he went into battle. Not for an antiterrorist patrol in Ulster, a skirmish with

Kurdish freedom militia, or a drugs patrol in Hong Kong. These were not what justified years of field training and staff college. A soldier prepared for the clash of infantry and armour. The conflict of men and arms.

The radio buzzed, twice, each time for a split second.

'Two-One ready, sir,' said Collins.

This was it, he thought, the point of no return. Then he remembered the stealth bombers with their deadly nuclear cargo. The point of no return had passed at midnight, when 'B' Company had turned back from the Murmansk valley.

He looked down into the cab. 'Send,' he said.

Collins pressed the 'send' button on the inter-company radio.

From over on the left there came the roar of engines. Nick swung his binoculars. Jamie's Snow Leopards emerged from dead ground, six of them strung out in a line, racing towards the woods, their machine-guns sending bullets ripping into the trees ahead, smoke billowing from their grenade launchers, the sudden crack of a light mortar lobbing high explosives along the woodland edge.

It was almost as if, thought Nick, in a bizarre moment of fantasy, they were in Pasvik National Park, putting on an entertainment for a visiting NATO major-general.

'Sir!' Collins yelled, pointing.

There it was. The first reaction of a startled, disbelieving Russian sentry: a belt of tracer snaking out of the scrub to fall in a fine spray fifty metres to the right of the advancing Snow Leopards. A moment later a *Sagger* missile streaked out across the open ground.

'Seen?' Nick called down to Milan crew.

'Seen,' replied the gunner. 'Target registered, co-ordinates stored.'

The *Sagger* exploded in a black cloud. Snow and earth shot up into the sky. Two Snow Leopards raced out of the smoke unscathed, zigzagging now to confuse the enemy's aim.

'Send!' Nick shouted down to Collins. He did not dare let Jamie's group go in closer. They were the decoy, designed to puzzle, and confuse, and distract.

Jamie's vehicles halted, circled and raced back to cover, their turrets swinging to rain tracer fire on to the birches behind them, vanishing into the smokescreen that rolled gently down towards the Objective.

'Missile firing ahead!'

This was it: a flash of light and wisp of smoke from the covering Russian bunker, the real target, which was at last opening up in support – dear God, they should have been court-martialled, the time it took them – a *Sagger* flying aimlessly across the front towards Jamie's group.

'Four-fifty metres, half right,' said Nick into his mouthpiece.

'Seen,' replied the Milan gunner, swinging the launcher on its tripod.

'Fire when ready.'

Milan gunners were steady men, men with a pulse rate that never raced, men who knew what it was to guide a £250,000 missile to target in front of a dozen NATO generals and Allied chiefs of staff when they knew the War Office would not sanction the cost of another 'live' missile firing for the next six months.

'Locked on. Firing,' said the gunner.

A loud hiss. The missile shot up into the sky at one hundred and eighty metres a second, its gold and titanium guidance wires snaking out invisibly behind it, its spent case rolling back into the snow.

'Missile gathered,' said the gunner, as the blip appeared on his screen. Gently he brought it round in a half-circle, in towards the computer locked-on location of the smoke from the *Sagger* launcher.

'Ten seconds to impact. Five seconds to impact. Two seconds.'

The missile exploded.

'Go, go, GO!'

Nick slammed down the armoured windscreen cover as Collins gunned the command vehicle up over the low ridge, the other two vehicles following. Behind them the Milan gunner was swinging his tripod to the first registered target, his number two sliding a second missile from its sheath.

Now they were crossing the open ground, their three machine-guns playing over the Objective, red dots ricocheting skywards, confirming the presence of either concrete or armour at the base of the trees. Beneath them, anti-personnel mines exploded with muffled bangs, springer mines sprang, sending steel fragments harmlessly into the snow to either side.

A huge bang on their left – the second Milan hitting home, he hoped.

They were almost there. Fire was coming from a communications trench to the right of the objective.

'Sar'nt Doran!' Nick shouted into his throat mike.

Doran's Snow Leopard headed towards it, rose and fell, plunging down on top of a machine-gun nest. Screams as men were crushed under tracks.

'De-bus!'

Men tumbled from the back of the Snow Leopards, shooting from the hip as they landed, running behind the vehicles, along the hard snow laid by the caterpillar tracks. Now the command vehicle was on the bunker, on the huge circle of blackened snow where the Milan's 3.9lb hollow charge had slammed into the bunker wall.

Nick dropped down from the turret. Collins was already out, and kneeling to fire smoke grenades in the direction of the strong point on the right. Three Russians were running from the communications trench, back through the woods, clumsily; they had had no time to fit snowshoes or skis. One of Doran's men threw himself against the back wall of the communications trench and took slow deliberate aim. Two short bursts and the figures fell.

Nick rolled a grenade down the bunker steps, and stepped back against the wall. It exploded. He threw himself down the steps. The grenade had not been necessary: the Milan missile had penetrated the bunker wall and thrown a tongue of flame through the interior. Charcoal figures lay as they had died: six, perhaps seven, men clutching at charcoal weapons. He looked round quickly, then ran up the bunker steps.

Jamie's Snow Leopards, followed by the two Russian vehicles, were coming in from the dead ground. A solitary Snow Leopard was bucking over the snow in the sunshine, heading towards the Milan team.

Doran told him that one soldier was dead: Whitby, the mess waiter. Nick tried to remember whether or not he was married, had children, but Whitby had only joined 'B' Company in September, so Nick hardly knew him. Two men were lightly wounded.

'Clear the communication trenches. Throw out a screen.'

'Sir.'

There was thin, sporadic fire from the bunker on the right. The defenders, he guessed, were in total confusion. The bunker on the left, hit by the second Milan, was silent. Noon had slipped out from the back of Doran's vehicle and was hobbling towards him, crouching to stay beneath the waist-high parapet.

'I told you,' Noon shouted. 'Bloody rubbish.'

Nick nodded. The Russians' response would have earned them a bollocking from NATO Northern Command's General Hoepner. From the open ground, the main assault group was coming in.

Jamie was jumping down from his turret, a broad grin on his face. 'Well, that was a piece of piss—' he started, but Nick cut him off.

'Get those claymores out. I'm moving in one minute. Staff Beckwith!'

'Sir!'

Beckwith and his lads were standing like a gaggle of hens, grinning at each other, slapping each other on the back, telling each other that this was one for the bloody book; this was one for the regimental bloody records.

'Get the Russian vehicles backed up. Get men in the turrets in Russian caps.'

'Sir!'

Beckwith yelled to his lads, his face purple with excitement. Vehicles began to manoeuvre. Nick climbed on to the roof of the bunker. Noon joined him, climbing stiffly, wincing as he used his frostbitten hands.

Nick said: 'I'm worried about gunships.'

Noon nodded and looked at the sky. It was azure blue. The sun was rising, for the first time in a week, turning the snow-wreathed pines to glittering candles of white and gold. The wind was dying.

Noon pointed: 'That's the supply track to the next defensive line. The only way to move fast is to stick to it. They'll be rushing their reserves forward now. The advance platoons will be in position before we can overrun them.'

'OK, get back under cover.'

The assault column was re-forming. Men were pulling back from the communication trenches, climbing back into the vehicles. Behind them Jamie and his men were setting booby traps – claymore mines activated by tripwires.

Beckwith had already moved one of the Russian personnel carriers fifty metres up the track.

'All right, let's go,' said Nick. 'Mr Pendred!'

Jamie left his men and came running up.

'You know what to do. Follow us, about a hundred metres behind. Get your best LAW man on the front vehicle. When we're in sight of the position, fire. Make sure you're close. Make sure you miss.'

Jamie grinned. He was on a high. They were all on a

449

high – except for Noon and Doran.

Nick said: 'Jamie, I'm not joking. Make sure he fucking misses.'

His nightmare was to go down to friendly fire, to suffer for being too clever by half.

'He'll miss – he always does.'

'OK, get your men mounted up.'

Jamie turned away. Nick said: 'Jamie, if we're killed, do what Sar'nt Doran suggests. If he's killed, it's all yours.'

Jamie looked shocked for a moment. He nodded, then ran down to his vehicle, calling Corporal Leech to get the last of the men into the wagons.

Nick jumped down from the bunker and hurried up the track towards the Russian armoured personnel carrier. Looking back he saw a young soldier come out of Jamie's wagon and climb on to the roof, a light anti-tank weapon slung over his shoulder. It was Cole. Nick had trained him to fire the LAW on West Lavington ranges two summers ago. He hoped, as he ran up the track, that he had trained him well.

Willis pulled him up on to the vehicle and handed him a hat. Grey fur, the inside crusted with frozen sweat: dead man's sweat. He jammed it down on his head.

'OK, let's go.'

After five hundred metres, a solitary Russian stumbled out on to the track, frantically waving. He must have fled from one of the bunker positions. He thought they were friends. He was gasping, almost crying with relief as they came up the track towards him. He was overweight; he was unarmed. Lance-Corporal Holmes raised his gun.

'No,' said Nick, leaning over to wave to the man to get out of the way.

The man dived to one side. As they roared past, he jumped up and waved his fist at them in rage. Then he saw the Snow Leopards and dived back into the snow.

'Pillbox ahead. Half left five hundred metres.'

'OK, Staff,' said Nick, then shouted to the men clinging to the roof: 'Hold tight!'

In the cab Beckwith hauled on the tillers, and spun the vehicle round in a tight circle until it was facing back down the track, the machine-gun in its turret aiming towards Doran's Snow Leopard that had just come into sight.

'OK, now fire!'

They fired back at the Snow Leopard, and in return a LAW boomed from the first vehicle, and its rocket scorched past them and exploded, covering them in earth and snow.

'Fucking hell,' said Willis, startled.

Men in the pillbox were also firing, and Nick saw with relief that they were firing to right and left of them, giving them supporting fire, aiming at the Snow Leopards that had come to a standstill.

Now they were heading backwards into the Inner Defensive Belt, and the Russians were letting them through, letting them reverse past the machine-gun nests and rifle pits to the pillbox itself.

'De-bus!'

They dropped from the vehicle. A Russian NCO called to them, pointing to a trench. They ran towards him. He shouted angrily, trying to send them back. At ten metres

Nick shot him. Two men, who were kicking open ammunition boxes, stood petrified for a second, then grabbed for their rifles. Sykes caught them with a single burst. Holmes and Willis ran along the forward trenches, lobbing hand-grenades as they went. Men died – or crawled from their rifle pits and melted into the trees.

Nick was at the bunker. This time there was a bend in the stairway to stop grenades being rolled in through the door. An officer was emerging, the blue band round his cap denoting a guards regiment, the four pips of a major. For a shocked moment he stared at Nick – but he was dead before he had time to reach for his pistol.

Another grenade. Nick flicked his safety catch to automatic, pointed it round the corner, and fired the rest of the magazine. As the ricochets died down he looked inside at the bodies of men who, seconds earlier, had been trying hard not to kill him.

The command vehicle and Doran's vehicle were already up to the pillbox. Nick ran to the back of Doran's vehicle and opened the door. Noon was at the radio.

'I'm sending the warning code. We've got fifty-six minutes to get into position.'

Fifty-six minutes to cross the belt of minefields, to crash into the compound, to reach the Objective and to call up the missile. He scrambled into the command vehicle and yelled at Collins to move out. Doran's vehicle, Noon safely in its rear cab, was already manoeuvring to follow him.

'Sunray to Two-One. We're going right. Push on up the

main drag, and pin down anything that comes at you. Don't cross the open ground. Be prepared to swing right and support us.'

'Roger, Sunray,' replied Jamie.

Looking back, Nick saw him standing in the turret of his Snow Leopard, nosing slowly up to the smoking blockhouse at the head of his column.

Nick turned and looked up the tank track, through the trees.

Skull-and-crossbones signs, vivid red, were nailed to posts, tied to birches and firs. Helpful signs, keeping them out of harm's way: pointing them towards the open drag, directing them into the killing grounds.

Minefields are not meant to be crossed. Minefields are meant to squeeze attackers into gaps. Minefields are clearly marked 'Here lies danger'. No signs point the other, inviting way, to say 'Here lies death'.

Ahead of them now, glimpsed through the firs, the path led up a slope to a distant clearing where the sun sparkled on the crisp fresh snow. This was where 101 Regiment's machine-guns, anti-tank guns, rockets and artillery fire-plans would be targeted – where men from the guard barracks would even now be tumbling into machine-gun nests, manning mortars, preparing to rake the long, upward-sloping drag with fire.

On the intercom came Noon's voice.

'Swing right and follow the depression.'

'Hard right,' said Nick. Collins hesitated. Nick yelled

453

'Collins!' and Collins yanked the wheel violently round. The vehicle spun on its tracks, jerked forward, smashed its way over a skull-and-crossbones sign and bucked into the minefield.

'Oh Christ, oh Jesus Christ,' Collins was saying, sweat pouring from his forehead. He knew the safety factor that allowed them to cross the minefield. He knew that the six pounds per square inch pressure of the Snow Leopard's tracks made it the lightest over-snow vehicle in the world, exerting only seventy-five per cent of the downward pressure of the Russian troop carriers. He knew that four feet of fresh snow had fallen in the last three days. He had been told how a squadron of Sand Leopards crossed a minefield on the Turkish-Iranian border three months ago without a single vehicle lost . . .

He had been told all this, and had said, 'Bloody magic, sir.'

Now he expected to die.

'Oh Jesus . . .'

The tops of pines splintered, birches crumpled under the bonnet. The vehicle spun as the tracks slewed on slippery bark. For a moment Collins lost control of the wheel, and they slithered sideways down a slope and thudded into a snowdrift. Suddenly anti-tank mines were exploding under the snow, almost inaudible against the roar of the engines.

'Head north. We're drifting too far east . . .'

In Doran's wagon, Noon was plotting their course on his LodeStar-linked computer.

'Keep heading for the ridge. In fifteen hundred metres

we come out of the trees opposite the perimeter fence. Before then you may see the radar tower. If so, head directly for it.'

Nick acknowledged, switched frequency, and listened to Jamie – now spreading out his six Snow Leopards for a race up the drag to draw the enemy fire. Jamie's voice was cool, competent: he might almost have been enjoying himself.

Nick's eyes were on the fresh snow they were crunching under their tracks, trying to spot where it lay thinnest, where the mines were, just below the surface. Would he hear the one that killed him, or left him crippled in the mangled wreckage?

If it happened, Doran would not stop. Noon would not let him. The missile was poised beneath the Barents Sea, the stealth bombers were circling over Khibiny. Noon was the ball and the compound was the try-line. Nothing else mattered, not Nick and the command vehicle, not Jamie and the main assault force, even now risking themselves in the killing ground.

'Engine exhaust up ahead!' yelled Collins, and Nick grabbed the intercom.

'There's a track ahead with troops and vehicles. What is it?'

Noon said: 'There should be no track before the wire.'

'Which way do I go?'

'Keep going straight ahead. We're only seven hundred metres from the compound. It must be a new flanking approach to the main drag. It must be a column heading down from the guard barracks . . .'

A mortar bomb exploded fifty metres to their left, a ranging shot. Ahead, through the trees, a line of men were throwing themselves belly-down into a snow bank and opening fire.

'We're seen,' said Nick into the intercom. 'They'll be reporting our position . . .' Then, 'Straight at them!' he shouted to Collins. He clambered up into the turret. The soldiers were targeting him, but the Snow Leopard was a living creature, tossing and swaying, and he made a poor target. He swung the twin machine-guns and squeezed the triggers, traversing across the enemy line, hot cartridge cases cascading down around his feet. An RPG rocket launcher boomed, and the rocket cracked past his ear, then they were on top of the position and he swung his guns to the right to sweep up the firing line, while Doran rolled up the left.

Then they were through, and into another belt of woodland.

'Two hundred metres ahead,' said Doran.

'I see it.'

A track, diagonally across their route. Sweeping down it, across their path, came a troop carrier towing a line of skiers. As the Snow Leopards crashed out of the trees, out of the minefield, the skiers turned their heads in astonishment. They were still staring helplessly back, as their vehicle swept them round a bend.

'Sunray to Two-One. They're trying to work round your left flank. We're at the compound. Break off, pull back, and follow our tracks through the minefield.'

'Wilco. One Section break off!' yelled Jamie.

The last of 4 Platoon melted back through the scrub; a burst of hot fire, and then they were gone. Only five men and Corporal Hoddinot remained in the forward position, dug into snow scrapes on the edge of the drag, covering the platoon's withdrawal.

'Watch out for your left,' Jamie said. 'That's where they're coming from. Two more minutes. Give it everything you've got, then bug out. I'll leave somebody down at the junction. OK, give me some cover.'

He ran, bent double, back down the track. The Snow Leopards were under trees next to the break in the snowbank where Nick had burst into the minefield. The last of 4 Platoon was clambering aboard. He detailed a vehicle to wait for Hoddinot then climbed into the turret of the forward vehicle.

'Corporal Leech! Mount up!'

Leech and two soldiers emerged from fire positions, hauling their machine-guns. Already Jamie, in the first vehicle, was swinging through the gap.

'Two-One to Sunray. We're coming to join you.'

Opposite was a ditch filled with new snow, and behind it the high perimeter fence. Up the slope Nick could see a goon tower and some kind of command post: the main entrance to the compound. Three or four guards stood looking at them. One ran back into the guard hut.

'Sunray to Two-One. We're going through the wire

now. All right, Collins. Straight through.'

Collins said: 'Hang on tight, sir.'

He revved the engine and let out the clutch and slammed on the accelerator. They skidded on the hard-packed snow of the run, then piled into the soft snow in the ditch. The fence vanished as the tracks threw up a blizzard of flying snow. They hung, suspended, as Collins cursed and wrenched at his gears, then they lurched upwards and hit the wire. It sprang apart, a concrete post snapped. They were through.

Behind them Doran's vehicle tried to follow but foundered, with its spinning tracks digging it deeper into the ditch.

'Sunray to Two-Two. De-bus.'

Doran's men ran towards them, laden with machine-guns, ammo boxes and Milan tubes. They clambered on to the command vehicle. Noon pulled himself up by the turret, next to Nick, grinned, and pointed through the trees.

A wooden tower. The outline of a concrete building. The aerial farm and radar station. The Objective.

TWELVE

Icicles, stubby and stunted, black with dust. Chisel marks in the rock, not made, if Worembrand was any judge, by happy construction gangs fed on orange-juice and rump steak. Above the hand-hewn walls his torch showed the smooth circular designs left by mechanical cutters in 1972, when the line was electrified.

The tunnel, the MoD map said (and for once he had no reason to suppose the bastards lied) was half a kilometre long. Cold and dark as death. A wormhole carrying the permafrost deep into the mountainside. A bolthole, personally chosen for Sergeant Worembrand by the best tactical brains in ACE Mobile Force, Narvik. One thing about joining the army: they bugger you about, but they look after you.

Mason was still in the Snow Leopard's cab. Looking back, towards the tunnel entrance, Worembrand could see him, his face faintly illuminated by the green dashboard light. He was running the engine to keep warm. He would not be able to do that if they moved into the bowels of the tunnel, not unless they wanted to die of asphyxiation before the radiation got them.

* * *

As they had emerged from the pine trees, a gunship had roared and bucked down on them from Mount Kirovsk, a bird of prey falling on a dormouse. Mason had raced the Snow Leopard the last few metres into the tunnel entrance and slewed to a standstill, a manoeuvre he was getting used to. Outside, the gunship's rotors had screamed for a moment then faded away, presumably to beat up the column, if it could find it.

'Right, carry on into the tunnel,' Worembrand had ordered, faint with relief.

'How far, Sar'nt?'

'How the hell should I know?'

'Can't go any further without a recce. Might not be able to get out again.'

'Get a torch and recce four hundred metres.'

'Can't leave the vehicle,' said Mason. 'Staff Beckwith'd go bananas.'

In Worembrand's view, a small pile of radioactive dust could not, with any effect, go anything or anywhere. 'Don't argue,' he said. 'Do it.'

Mason shook his head in disbelief, marvelling that he should be asked to commit such a crime. He was in his mid-twenties and believed himself wise to the ways of the world.

'More than my job's worth. He'd have me back in a rifle platoon before I could say "cat". Bloody hell.'

Worembrand had recced. He had plodded down the line, stumbling on concrete sleepers, waving his torch, listening to strange subterranean roars that occasionally echoed from up ahead. Every fifty metres, a shallow hole had been hacked in the tunnel wall, presumably for railway workers to shelter in when trains passed. He squeezed into one, and its sharp edges tore his camouflage whites. He foully cursed the sloppiness of the tunnel workers. His plan, in so far as he had a plan, was to find himself a hole in the tunnel side and sink into it like a slug. The heatball – for he had no doubt there would be a heatball; the very fact that ACE Mobile Force planners had chosen this tunnel for its safety guaranteed that there would be a devastating, deadly heatball – might then, with luck, roll through the tunnel leaving him unscathed.

Now he was terrified that his Noddy suit would be snared on a sharp protuberance, and radiation would pour into him till his teeth turned green.

He dimly remembered the advice given to young soldiers by old soldiers, on what to do in the event of nuclear attack. Loosen your clothing, they said, then lean forward and sit with your head down between your knees.

Then kiss your arse goodbye.

Darkness lay ahead. The tunnel curved, and there was no sign of the northern exit. If he continued he would lose sight, behind him, of Mason and the Snow Leopard.

He would be alone, in the dark, deep inside a hill inside the Arctic Circle.

He sat down on a small block of concrete, overwhelmed by despair.

There was no way that this was supposed to happen.

Nothing was supposed to go wrong the way this had gone wrong.

He was cold. Intensely cold. He shivered convulsively.

After a few moments he stood up and plodded back down the line to the Snow Leopard, and climbed into the cab.

'Move forward two hundred metres.' Mason hesitated, looked at him doubtfully.

'What about the others?'

'From two hundred metres we can post a sentry – you – who will be able to see back to the entrance.'

'I've been thinking about that helicopter,' said Mason. 'It saw us take shelter. It'll come and get us.'

'Perhaps it will forget,' said Worembrand, 'or attack the column and then be satiated like a lion. Perhaps it will go to the other end of the tunnel and wait for us to pop our heads out. Move.'

'I don't know.'

'I'm a fucking sergeant. Fucking move.'

'You're only a photographer,' said Mason wisely.

'Move this vehicle or I'll have you up on so many charges you'll pray for a bomb to put you out of your fucking misery . . .'

Mason looked helplessly into the rear-view mirror, out at the grey-white, empty taiga at the edge of the pine forest. But there was no help for him there. He slowly let out the clutch.

After what might have been two hundred metres, they

stopped. The entrance to the tunnel was a distant circle of light behind them.

Mason said, upset: 'Did you say I had to get out? How long's first stag?'

Worembrand said: 'Turn off the engine.'

They sat in the darkness. The fluorescent controls glowed faintly. A small red light pulsed on the battery-operated radio.

The cold seeped in. Moisture on the cab roof turned to ice.

'I'm bloody gutted by all this,' said Mason.

Gutted by all what? Deadly radiation? Temperatures of five thousand degrees centigrade? The peculiar taste of the high-calorie fudge bars in the twenty-four-hour ration packs?

'I was fit enough,' said Mason. 'I told Staff Beckwith I was fit. A touch of exposure – what's a touch of exposure? Nothing at all. I could have gone with the lads. I wouldn't have let the platoon down. Why wouldn't they let you go?'

Worembrand thought of saying that his press pictures were wanted urgently by the Outside World, that he had a duty to Mankind – but he could not be bothered. There had been one terrible moment, just before the column divided, when Chard had called, 'Sar'nt Worembrand!' and Worembrand's bowels had dissolved in expectation of having a rifle thrust into his hand. But Chard had only said: 'Give Major Sendlinger and the sar'nt-major all the help you can. Whatever happens remember the children are the priority. Good luck.'

At least he had not told him not to slouch.

* * *

Mason began to whistle gently between his teeth.

'Stop that fucking noise.'

Mason stopped breathing. Worembrand listened to the silence. After a while he wondered, fascinated, if Mason was ever going to breath again.

Mason made a sudden shooshing noise as he exhaled breath.

Worembrand clicked on his torch and looked at his watch. He got out of the cab, went to the rear of the vehicle, climbed in, turned on the emergency light, and struggled into his NBC suit. As he pulled on the trousers he gagged at the smell of charcoal, the sweet perfume of the chemicals. He steeled himself, and pulled the thick hood over his head.

He clambered out and swayed slowly back to the front of the vehicle, then continued onward past the cab, plodding along by the side of the track.

Mason watched his torch beam until the line curved and he was lost to sight.

Some time later he switched on the radio, but was too far into the tunnel to pick up a signal.

He found a CD – Collins's CD of Madonna's *As I Grow Old* – and put it into the player.

The music thudded and echoed in the tunnel.

Worembrand, far ahead, a black rubbery spider lurking in his cold and rocky hole, heard it distantly, amplified and distorted through the ear-filters of his Noddy suit. He could now add earplugs to the list of things he needed but did not have – food, warmth, a BA club-class ticket to Hanover, an Airbus to use it on, and an air-hostess saying

'Welcome aboard, sir' as she poured him a large Bacardi.

He closed his eyes. When he opened them he could see nothing but a dim dark haze, even when he clicked the torch on. It took him a moment to realise that his gasmask goggles were freezing over, covering him in a thick icy curtain.

He closed his eyes again.

At 10.05 the column reached the tunnel. The noise of six engines rumbled down its length, but he did not hear – or, if he did, he took no notice.

Mason said: 'I think perhaps he's gone to stand guard in case a train comes.'

'Is that what he said?'

'No, ma'am.'

'Well, what did he say?'

'Nothing, ma'am.'

'Did he have a rifle?'

'I don't think so. He might have had a pistol.'

'All right, into the back and get your NBC suit on.'

'Ma'am.'

She looked up the tunnel, then walked back to the ambulance. Men were draining fuel from the vehicles into jerrycans, and dumping them outside, well away from the tunnel entrance. Kelly and two men were running out an aerial extension.

'As fast as you can, Corporal!'

'Ma'am.'

They had been forced to take a five-kilometre diversion through the forest to avoid the Russian infantry. Then they had stopped, still deep in the birch trees, when the gunship was sighted. Brigite had been about to give the order to move forward, gunship or no gunship, when the helicopter had suddenly wheeled and screamed its way back up the side of the mountain.

She climbed into the back of the ambulance. Robbo lay, grey-faced, breathing in short gasps, staring up at the roof.

Munro said: 'Hello, doctor. Have you worked out what will happen to us if a train comes? It would be a shame to survive a nuclear holocaust and be run over by an intercity express.'

'Sergeant Worembrand has posted himself further up the track.' She peeled back the thermal blanket and bandages from his feet. The white blotches were spreading, covering the toes.

'Well?'

'I don't know . . .'

She was an allergy specialist, not an expert on frostbite. She examined the wound in his thigh. It was healing well: he was suffering from severe exhaustion but he was young; his blood was thick.

She zipped the blanket and turned and examined Robbo.

'Sar'nt-Major? Sar'nt-Major?' she said, gently. Robbo showed no sign of recognition. He was fighting a lonely battle of his own.

'We're going to have to get him into a suit.'

'Don't bother. If the radioactive dust gets through the filters on these vehicles, it will get into a suit, no trouble.'

'That is not what Nicholas said.'

'Ah, well. It's one expert against another, in that case.'

'Can I leave you? I need to see Anneliese and the children.'

'You go to the children.'

'He's very ill. There's nothing I can do.'

'I'll look after him.'

She rubbed her eyes, wearily, then looked at Munro, thinking that perhaps it would be for the last time.

She said, reluctantly, knowing the futility of her question but unable to resist asking it: 'Will Nicholas make it?'

Munro said, after a moment: 'He'll have got past the two defensive belts.'

'Then?'

'I don't know. He's only got thirty-five men, even if they are Royal Mercians.'

'Don't be sarcastic.'

'I wasn't. As line infantry go, they're the best there is.'

'I think so,' she said quietly.

The children were spread between three vehicles. In one they had put on NCB suits and sat in two rows, hooded, silent, still. Their heads turned as she opened the rear door. Through their goggles they looked at Brigite with huge eyes. The soldiers had given the children all their remaining raisin and chocolate bars. In this vehicle the food lay in their laps, uneaten. A tub of appleflakes had rolled down on to the floor.

She told them to take off their hoods. 'We don't need to wear masks,' she said confidently, 'not unless we go outside – and nobody's doing that.'

In the second vehicle children were crying. The Polish

nurse with them was exhausted and fretful. She had tried to make them wear NBC suits, but they had panicked and refused. She had not taken them out to relieve themselves, as she had been instructed. A soldier sitting by the door had a look of fixed horror on his face.

Brigite calmed them as best she could, told them not to worry about the suits, told them they would soon be on their way again . . . would soon be in Norway. She promised them a trip to EuroDisney if they were good. The crying slowly stopped. Not, she suspected, because they believed they would ever go to EuroDisney, but because somebody was speaking to them with authority, and because they were Russian, and knew that crying was a waste of valuable energy.

Anneliese was teaching her children to play Bunnies. They sat facing each other, waggling their hands at their ears. They were all wearing NBC suits but without hoods or masks.

'You all all right in here?' asked Brigite cheerfully.

Lara said: 'We're not all right, we're truly wonderful.'

Inga said: 'That was not what she meant.'

'We're fine, aren't we?' said Anneliese. She was sitting with one arm round Misha and one round Kaka. They both nodded doubtfully.

'I'm Chief Sneak,' said Lara, 'and I'm going to be really tough. OK, let's get on with this. We were talking about the penalty for doing it wrong.'

'The forfeit if you get caught out,' said Anneliese, 'is to eat a *whole* raisin-fudge bar.'

'Not exciting enough,' said Lara. 'I propose ten minutes in the tunnel without a Noddy suit.'

'You think you are clever and sophisticated,' said Inga. 'Is anybody laughing? I'm not laughing. Kaka is not laughing.'

'Piss off, Inga,' said Lara. She was improving her language skills all the time.

Brigite said to Anneliese: 'I must go.'

Anneliese nodded. 'Can I have a word?' she asked.

She climbed outside with Brigite. Soldiers had finished draining the fuel and were dispersing to the vehicles. Corporal Kelly was checking up and down the line.

'No sign of Sar'nt Worembrand, ma'am,' he said. 'I sent a couple of men looking, but they couldn't go far.'

'Poor Max,' said Anneliese, shivering.

Kelly went to the command vehicle. Anneliese waited until he had walked away. She said: 'I just wondered . . .'

'They'll be going in to attack now.'

Anneliese's face was a pale smudge of reflected light from the tunnel entrance.

'I think it's going to be OK,' she said. 'Do you think it's going to be OK?'

'Yes,' said Brigite gently. 'I'm sure it's going to be OK.'

Anneliese nodded. She turned and opened the rear door. Two soldiers helped her back into the vehicle. She said: 'OK, kids, do we let the soldiers join in? The soldiers are called – what are you called, soldiers?'

'That one's Phil,' said Lara, 'and that one's Darren.'

* * *

Brigite had posted two soldiers to sit by the rear doors of each vehicle. On her command they were to lock the doors, and not open them again without a direct order.

She went to the command vehicle. Corporal Kelly and a signaller were by the radio sets. She pulled the rear door closed behind her.

Kelly said: 'Excuse me, ma'am,' and reached past her and locked it. He had taken three NBC suits from their bags.

'Did Sar'nt Worembrand have his suit on, ma'am?'

She said she did not know. Kelly called Mason on the intercom. Mason said yes, the sergeant had been all togged up.

'A brave bloke,' said Kelly. 'I'd be worried if I thought we didn't have somebody up the tunnel. It's surprising how folk turn out.'

Brigite spoke on the inter-company radio. She ordered rear doors to be locked in all vehicles.

'OK, get me Narvik.'

'Ma'am.'

It was 10.15. There was no longer any point in concealing their position.

The signaller was saying: 'Hereford, this is Matchmaker . . .'

They were linked from Hereford to Narvik in twenty-eight seconds. Brigite was looking at her watch, counting them as they passed.

'Terrier. Send. Over.'

'Matchmaker. Sunray speaking.'

'Hold on.'

A few seconds. Another voice.

'What is your position, Matchmaker?'

She gave the position. 'We have six vehicles and twenty-nine personnel, including sixteen children and two Polish nurses.'

'You are all inside the vehicles?'

'One sentry is posted to stop trains coming through the tunnel.'

'There are no trains in your area.'

'Have I time to bring him in?'

'Only if you have radio contact.'

'Do you know what has happened to "B" Company?'

There was a moment's pause, then the voice said: 'The satellite shows them still moving. Can we have a list of personnel with the convoy and personnel with the assault group.'

'Of course.'

'If things go badly, we estimate it will be sixty-four hours before we can risk sending in choppers to rescue you.'

Three minutes later the printer suddenly began spewing personal-letter faxes that had been locked on the satellite ever since 'B' Company closed its radio link. There was nothing they could do with them; no way to get them to the other vehicles.

There was a letter from Ingrid. She and Lawrence were planning to get married. All three of them had been miserable before, argued Ingrid, but now she and Lawrence

471

were happy, and Brigite was free. Ingrid knew that Brigite would want them to be happy, would find happiness herself one day.

Brigite read the fax twice. It seemed to her that Ingrid and Lawrence were people she had known long long ago. Why on earth should either of them be writing to her now?

THIRTEEN

Radar station, 10.30 hours, 9 November

The radio room was empty. The signallers had escaped out of a window, and were now scrambling away through the snow. Nick ran up to the second floor. A metal ladder was in the corner, beyond the banks of listening devices. He led the way up on to the concrete roof, out into the sunshine, Noon and Willis behind him.

This was the spot Munro had chosen, had selected months before from the KGB agent's information, from a virtual-reality projection of the Russian site blueprint. A flat concrete roof with a low parapet. They threw themselves down and crawled to the edge.

And there it all was. Exactly as Noon had drawn it, on that ambulance sheet pinned against the wall of the tent, at the briefing in the gully.

Every defence they had smashed through, every bunker and mine, every strand of wire, existed to protect this square mile of road and silo complex.

It was laid out like a sand-table model in a Sandhurst lecture room. A large clearing among the pines, a railway track, a two-storey administrative building, the guard company barracks, an airfield with a single long hangar and a line of snowploughs parked along its edge. Eight hundred metres away, at a point where all the tracks converged, was a low, squat concrete block, solid and massive, ringed by a wire fence and the grass mounds that held the ventilation shafts.

The command bunker.

Nick said: 'You all right?'

Noon said: 'If it fucking works.'

Willis was on his knees, screwing the low tripod. Noon was taking the guidance system from its protective sheath. It slid home with a smooth click. Willis fitted battery leads. Noon lay down carefully on the concrete, swung the tripod, and pointed it at the grass mound nearest to the command bunker. He looked through the telescopic sights, adjusted the tripod, tightened the screws.

Nick looked at his watch: twenty-five minutes to H-hour.

'Got it,' said Noon, pressing a switch. He turned and pulled his laptop out of his Bergen. Two soldiers had come on to the roof and were lying with their rifles pointing out over the parapet. Noon tapped out a code, cursing suddenly as his frostbitten fingers stumbled. He cleared the screen and started again. 'If I fuck it up once more,' he said, 'it closes down on us.'

Nick's radio buzzed.

'Gunships coming in, almost on us,' said Jamie's voice.

Noon said: 'Completion code *Riga Mortis* sent and acknowledged.'

Revenge had been at action stations for more than four

hours. Bacon rolls and coffee had long ago been taken round by the cooks, who were now taking round sandwiches and cans of no-alcohol beer.

At 10.35 the fax machines started printing out the four-page newspaper condensed from the *Daily Telegraph* and sent every morning to Royal Navy ships worldwide. At 10.36 the fax was suddenly cut. The operator buzzed the Wireless Officer and told him a priority signal was coming down from the satellite.

Captain Rashleigh, in the command centre, read the two words, *Riga Mortis*, and opened the sealed completion code envelope. He said: 'Weapons Engineering Officer, prepare to fire missile.'

'Acknowledged. Preparing to fire missile.'

'Status report, Nav Centre.'

In the navigation centre, where *Revenge*'s position was being monitored using an inertial navigation system, and where truncheons hung on the walls for use should anyone be found tampering with key equipment, the Navigation Officer reported: 'Fishing vessels still approaching 14 degrees by 9 nor-nor-west, estimated distance seven hundred metres. Satellite estimates speed fifteen knots.'

'Thank you,' said Rashleigh tersely.

In the missile control centre the WEO was now kneeling by yet another safe, his number-two weapons officer by his side. From the back of the safe he took out what appeared to be the butt of a revolver. It had a red trigger, and was linked by wires to the back of the safe.

'WEO to Captain. Standing by.'

'Status report, XO.'

Seated next to Rashleigh, the XO said: 'Weapons system is still 1 SQ.'

Rashleigh said: 'Nav Centre, tell me about the fishing vessels.'

The Navigation Officer said: 'About a dozen. Japanese. Five hundred metres to port and closing.'

The fishing vessels would have to take their chance.

'Weapons system is still 1 SQ,' repeated the XO.

'Acknowledged,' said Rashleigh. It was forty-five seconds since *Riga Mortis* had been received. 'The Weapons Officer has my permission to fire.'

'The Weapons Officer has your permission to fire,' repeated the XO.

Rashleigh took a red-painted key from round his neck and walked to the overhead firing board. He inserted the key and turned it.

In the missile control centre the WEO and his number two saw the red panel printed with the message 'Captain's Permission To Fire' turn from red to green.

The WEO said into his intercom: 'Captain's permission to fire. Roger.'

A panel displaying the words 'Missile Prepared' had switched from orange to amber.

The missile hatch was now open.

The WEO pulled the trigger.

It rose from the sea in a sheet of flame. It sent a massive wave crashing over the Japanese fishing vessels. It turned over the Kola peninsula and disappeared, travelling at 800 mph, causing klaxons to scream and lights to flash on every missile-warning screen between the Murmansk coast and Norway. Its estimated journey time was 14.3 minutes.

Jamie's Snow Leopards were clawing their way through the gap in the perimeter fence. The first gunship was moving up, hovering over them. Two other gunships were further back, following the path the column had made through the minefield, combing the trees for targets.

From the radar station roof Nick watched in horrified fascination. He could make out Jamie in the turret of the lead vehicle, aiming upwards as he fired off both barrels of his twin machine-gun. He could see the red flashes as the bullets bounced off the gunship's belly. He saw a Milan missile streak up into the sky and explode harmlessly. He saw the gunship turn and dip its nose, pointing its firing pods downwards.

In the trees beyond, flares of yellow light sprang up, bursts of crackling sodium, as the Russian troops marked their positions for the aircrews.

They were closing in. On the ground, and in the air, they were closing in.

The gunship hovered, leisurely, registering its target. Over the intercom Nick heard Jamie's voice calmly say, 'Milan team, get out now. Milan team, get out now,' and saw figures drop and roll in the snow. A single missile shot from the helicopter's pods. The Snow Leopard fourth in line, crossing the ditch and nosing through the perimeter fence, exploded, its petrol tanks igniting, flames soaring from the turret hatch, smoke billowing from its engine louvres.

Nick stared at the wreck, at the two Snow Leopards behind as they wheeled back from the burning shell and sought to make another gap in the fence.

The gunship veered away in a gust of wind, then swung back to take up position again.

Nick clattered down the stairs and ran outside.

Doran had thrown his eight soldiers out in a protective screen, a light machine-gun on each flank, each man hastily digging a fire position. Already mortars were opened from the woods, seeking them out. A soldier was firing bursts of tracer into the trees.

Doran said: 'We can't hold this place, sir. Not with fourteen men.'

'Mr Pendred's coming up . . .'

Nick flinched at the buzz-saw roar of the gunship's nosegun, the hiss of another anti-tank missile, and the explosion that followed. The gunships were now visible over the treetops. 'We're next,' he said. He grabbed the Starstreak gunner and shouted, 'Sykes!'

The gunner carried his launcher, Nick and Sykes each carried two missiles. As they crawled out on to the roof, a mortar bomb slammed into the earth next to the building and the concrete shook. Somebody screamed in pain.

Sykes slid the missile into place. The gunner raised the launcher to his shoulder and began adjusting the control dials, tracking the gunship through his sights.

The gunships would think they only had Milan. They would be careless, perhaps, confident behind their armour plating, as they had been in Afghanistan before the mujahideen were equipped with *Stinger* heat-seeking missiles.

Nick said: 'Fire when ready.'

Four Snow Leopards were out of the trees. Men were de-bussing, doubling up the slope to the radar tower, laden with weapons and ammo. Already the first men were passing through Doran's line, throwing themselves down in the snow, facing back towards the enemy. Jamie and Doran were huddled together, working out the best way to form a defensive ring with fewer than thirty men.

Now the gunships were coming.

Nick said: 'Ready?'

The helicopters were approaching in arrowhead formation. They were ignoring the Snow Leopards and aiming for the building.

'Keep coming, keep coming . . .' Nick heard the gunner whisper.

The leading gunship was dipping its nose to angle its missile pods. Nick looked up at the titanium shield, the armour-plated bubble-glass, the black-visored gunner. The missile pods were pointing down, down . . . almost directly towards him.

'Fire now!' he shouted.

As he spoke the gunship's nose-gun barked and bullets ripped chunks from the concrete. Beside him, the gunner's head jerked back in panic.

'Fire!' bellowed Nick again, and the gunner steadied the launcher and fired, and at the same moment the gunship's rocket pods flashed and four missiles smashed down into the building with a thud that sent Nick tumbling over, with

Sykes on top of him, clutching his leg.

Nick staggered up. The gunner was crouched, balancing expertly on his haunches, pointing his launcher skywards, while the gunship wheeled to escape the missile.

'Gathered,' said the gunner as the missile appeared on the screen that filled his eyepiece. The helicopter tried to gain height, its rotors screaming. It fired off heat flares, it twisted and turned, but the gunner just swayed gently back and forth on his heels, and the Starstreak missile homed in, and its six-pound warhead exploded, blasting off a sidewing. The aircraft hung for a moment, then plummeted down into the minefield.

'Reload,' said the gunner. The other gunships were peeling away, gaining height rapidly. When they came in again, they would be wary and much higher.

'Keep them up there,' said Nick. The gunner nodded, looked at Nick for a moment with glazed eyes, then turned to where Sykes, his leg soaked with blood, was crawling towards him, dragging another missile. Sykes tried to pass the missile over; he could not do so. His gloves were torn and his bare skin was bonded to the metal. The gunner tried to pull his hand gently away, but Sykes screamed. Then Sykes himself lifted the missile and threw it forward into the gunner's arms so that his skin was torn away from his hand. He yelled – but noiselessly in the rattle of gunfire and shriek of mortars.

The gunner slid the missile into the launcher. Nick crawled away, across the roof, to where Noon still lay, his eye clamped to the sights of the laser. Willis, beside him, was dead. Looking down over the edge of the roof, Nick could see the remains of Jamie's platoon pouring fire down the slope at ski-troops who rose and fell, fired and rose again, skirmishing forward in text-book fashion, while their supporting vehicles hosed the heights with their turret guns.

Four Platoon was pulling back, but carefully, coolly: Jamie establishing new fire positions before bringing his men back through. Five minutes and they would be back up against the wall. On the other side of the radar station, he knew, Doran and his men were fighting with their backs to the building. Looking to his left, he saw a group of figures – Spetznaz, he guessed – crawl up to the Snow Leopards; and a moment later the twin machine-gun in a turret swung round and opened up on 4 Platoon's flank. And the guard regiment was closing in. And still the bombs rained down, the din so continuous now it was impossible to identify one sound among the many.

'I don't know if we can do it,' said Nick. 'I don't know if we can hold them off.'

'Seven minutes,' said Noon, his gloved hands holding the pistol-grip. The smooth plastic shaft seemed inert, dead, its thin, high-pitched whine lost in the rage of battle. Only its green eye blinked to show it was working – projecting a vast laser cone over the ventilation shaft.

Enemy ski-troops were almost at the top of the slope, their vehicles close behind keeping up a constant fire, their turret guns sweeping from side to side. A Milan flashed from the left of Jamie's line and drew a storm of concentrated fire. Nick saw the gunner hit, saw him roll away, saw the number two take over and gather the missile on to the target. Then he too was hit, and the missile flew between two Russian troop carriers and exploded in the trees.

'I'm going down. I'll leave two men.'

Noon nodded, his eyes fixed on the laser sights. Nick told the two soldiers on the roof to give Noon covering fire. It was a gesture; that was all. If a mortar hit or a gunship missile slammed into the concrete roof they could not protect him.

He ran towards the metal stairs. At the edge of the roof, the Starstreak gunner and Sykes were tracking the movements of the gunships, firing when they came close, keeping them out beyond Starstreak's 5000-metre range. As Nick passed, Sykes clapped the gunner on the shoulder with a raw, bloody hand and mouthed the word 'Loaded'. Nick stumbled, caught by the weapon's back-blast as another rocket shot skywards.

Doran's men were dug in by the entrance. Four Platoon was struggling back over the crest and falling back through them. Jamie yelled 'Now' and Doran nodded and gave an order, and his men started to lob grenades over the crest.

Jamie was pouring sweat, his face black with smoke. He grinned and said: 'Hello, Nick.'

Nick pulled him down into a snow scrape and yelled: 'Sar'nt Doran!'

Doran ran over, bent double.

Nick said: 'The men in the woods are the fire support group pinning us down. The assault group's coming up the slope. Put most of your men against the east wall. Don't waste ammo on the woods. I want six men for a counter attack . . .'

Doran looked at him blankly, and Nick realised the nonsense he was talking, the futility of his words.

Jamie said: 'If you're thinking of the depression on the west side, Nick, they're already there.'

Suddenly there was a drop in the noise level. The Russian mortars had ceased to fire.

'This is it,' said Doran. 'They're coming in.' He turned and ran back to his men.

Nick said: 'Jamie, get up on the roof.'

Jamie started to move. A line of Russian troops came up over the crest, firing from the hip. Behind them appeared the turrets of their supporting vehicles. Jamie threw himself forward and aimed his rifle. Nick looked round and saw a machine-gun. He scrabbled towards it, grabbed it, swung it round, and was about to fire when the missile came in, low over the trees and the radar station, seeking its final flightpath.

Its sound was a massive sigh, a rush of wind. Its descent was like nightfall. It seemed to Nick that, as it fell, all firing ceased and a silence and stillness settled over the compound. It travelled too fast for the human eye to register, but he thought he saw a shimmer in the air over the ventilation shaft, a tongue of flame and a puff of smoke as its booster rocket fired, pile-driving it downwards. Some of the Russian troops stopped, aware that something had passed over their heads, looking round for the source of the disturbance in the air. Then the bunker roof burst upwards like a volcano, and the guards' barracks imploded.

Every window in the admin block smashed. The earth heaved. The snow moved like Pacific rollers, huge ripples radiating out in circles, snaking up the slope, covering the line of troop carriers in white foam, covering the Russian troops slithering back down from the crest.

Already a huge column of black smoke was blotting out the sun.

Far above, the satellite eye was sending its images, a hundred frames a second, in a priority stream to Narvik and to Moscow.

And again the bunker threw up huge chunks of concrete and twisted metal, for now the missile was driving down through its many floors, its phased munitions exploding in sequence, burning down to the control centre where the screens were blank and Colonel Kvatov and his officers sat in the darkness under three thousand tons of concrete and steel, looking upwards, listening to the hammer blows . . . waiting.

Northward over Khibiny the stealth bombers turned away, slowly wheeling homeward across the White Sea.

They dressed the wounds of the injured, and dosed them with morphine. The walking wounded sat on the roof, in the sunshine that slowly reappeared through the brown haze. In the back of the command vehicle two of Staff Beckwith's lads dug out a stove and made tea. Nick drank it, and with the warmth and the smell of thick, sweet liquid, he found himself weeping tears of shock. He coughed and walked over to the edge of the roof. The column of smoke was still rising from the bunker. By the parapet, Holmes was wrapping bandages round Sykes's hand.

Next to them the Starstreak gunner, still keeping a wary eye on the distant helicopters, said: 'We could use this bugger in support company, sir.'

Sykes said: 'You can fuck off. I'm a driver.'

The Russian troops were keeping their distance. They could, if they so wished, wipe out the radar station with mortar fire. Nick watched them through his binoculars, hoping that no enterprising captain or (more likely) gunner would think to do so.

The gunships remained, dots in the sky, for a little while, then moved off to the north, towards Murmansk.

Soon after they had disappeared, helicopters appeared from the south and landed on the airstrip. From the roof they saw men from the helicopters conferring with men on the ground.

Staff Beckwith brought round more tea. After a further ten minutes a vehicle came slowly up the slope, and Nick saw the blue hatbands of Federation Army officers.

'Aren't you going to go down?' asked Jamie.

'I don't think so,' said Nick. It seemed to him that the sun gave out a faint warmth, although that was, he knew, illusory. It was still pleasant to sit on the concrete, his back against the parapet.

The Russian officer said, in English: 'Do you want your

wounded taken to Arkhangelsk?' and Nick said: 'Thanks, but I think we'll hang on.'

Sykes said: 'I don't mind going to Arkhangelsk, sir.'

Nick said: 'We'll hang on, Sykes.'

The Russian officer nodded coldly.

'Have you many dead?'

'Six.'

Whitby, who had died at the outer fence. Willis who had died on the radar station roof. Two men who died in the first Snow Leopard hit by a missile. Two men from Jamie's platoon, killed on the slope.

Fourteen men were wounded, nine of them severely, but Nick was not handing them to the Russians.

The Russian officer went. An hour passed. The wounded were carried from the radar station into the three undamaged Snow Leopards, where they could be kept warm. It was almost one o'clock when Nick heard, with sudden relief, more helicopters, this time coming from the west. They came in slowly: three Navy Sea Kings from Nyrud. They circled the compound, the smoking ruins of the command bunker and guards barracks. On the radio he directed them to land in the clearing by the gate, near to where the column had crashed through the wire. It was the closest level ground to the radar station. There were still several hundred Russian troops in the compound area and, whether Federation or Red, he did not trust them a single centimetre.

* * *

The petty officer in flying overalls came up to where Collins was lying with his back against the radar station door.

'I'm looking for Captain Chard,' he said, reading from a flimsy.

Collins said: 'Major Chard.'

'It says Captain here. Anywhere about, is he?'

FOURTEEN

Malaya Sopcha railway tunnel, 13.30 hours, 9 November

They had found Sergeant Worembrand. They had found him covered in frost like a thick spider's web. They had prized him out of his hole, ice cracking on his frozen NBC suit, and carried him to the daylight, and pulled off his hood.

'Oh, Max, Max,' sobbed Anneliese, her face pebbled with frozen tears. 'Are you all right, Max?'

Worembrand blinked in the sunshine.

'This man's a priority,' said the RAF medical auxiliary, 'after the sergeant-major. Excuse me, ma'am.'

And Worembrand was casevac-ed, with Company Sergeant-Major Robson and Major Munro, in the first chopper to land at Malaya Sopcha, taken out ahead of the other exposure cases, ahead of the children and the nurses. He was wrapped in a thermal blanket and carried gently to the RAF rescue helicopter, and wedged, curled-up, in a seat because there was only room for two stretchers. He was borne up in the air, into the bright blue sky, and looked down, as in a dream, at the group of vehicles that had now backed out of the tunnel . . . at the children waving goodbye.

Soon they were crossing the Murmansk valley where, down in the winter sunshine, silly bastards were still killing each other. Then they soared over the western hills where the column had first been buzzed by gunships. Somebody brought him a hot breakfast of scrambled eggs and chipolata sausages, and rolls that had been baked that morning in Nyrud, and a mug of steaming coffee. Tears formed in his eyes. He tried to lift his fork but his nerveless fingers were useless, and it was the RAF orderly who patiently carried the food to his mouth, and held the cup to his lips.

At one point in the journey he looked out on a golden gleam, a sparkle of water, and there below were the Verchnetulomskoje lakes: remote, clean, peaceful in the sunlight.

After that he started to develop terrible pains in his hands and his feet, and he gave a cry of distress; and the orderly gave him an injection and he drifted into sleep. He woke in bed in the NATO wing of Narvik general hospital.

The next day, when he woke, he asked about his camera cases, and the nurse promised to pass the message. Instead of camera cases he got Anneliese, who sat by him holding his hands and saying 'Oh Max' in a dark, tragic Germanic sort of way. She finally admitted that his camera cases had been thrown wantonly out of the ambulance, and were somewhere in the Murmansk valley.

So it had all been in vain. He felt nothing, and calmly slurped up his Horlicks.

When he next awoke, the nurse and doctor were grinning,

and said: 'The sergeant-major's going to be OK.'

He closed his eyes.

His door opened, but he pretended to be still asleep as Nick and Brigite quietly entered and stood by his bed.

'Silly bugger,' said Nick: the man who had very nearly killed him.

'Oh, come on. What he did was incredible.'

'A lot of men did incredible things.'

'You perhaps? Yeah, well, you're supposed to be a hero. It's what you're paid for.'

'He's a soldier.'

'No, he isn't.'

'Well no, he isn't, but he's supposed to be.'

From all of which Worembrand, snoring gently, looking at them through slitty eyes, divined that Chard the Hero was now screwing the lady doctor.

They were turning to go. What a fearful couple they were, spreading death and destruction, disturbing honest people's lives.

He said, suddenly, 'Trying not to slouch, sir,' then closed his eyes tight. When he peeped they were by the door, looking at him.

It must be the drugs, he decided. That or he was going mad.

He did not want to talk to Chard – or to Brigite. He just wanted to go home to Rheindahlen.

Brigadier Grenfell was unhappy. He was under orders to debrief 'B' Company, and to do it with tact and sensitivity. Four doctors had arrived from the British Army Psychiatric

Unit, Woolwich, and had explained about the traumas that could result from operational experiences; the research that had been done since the Gulf war. Grenfell was no wiser. Nobody had indulged soldiers like pop stars when they went into action on the Somme, or in the Western Desert. 'These days,' he said in the mess bar, 'a chap nicks his chin shaving, and they're calling in the shrinks.'

For once he and Nick were in agreement.

'I'll shoot the first trick-cyclist that comes near my men,' Nick had said, when the subject of counselling was raised, and Brigite had said, irritably, 'Oh for Christ's sake, grow up . . .'

But several of the men who returned from Mount Kirovsk were having nightmares, developing illnesses that were not related to their wounds.

Nick's nightmare was not of the men in the tent, or in the pillboxes, or of the men who died in the compound.

He was dreaming, every night, of Colonel Kvatov, deep in the command bunker, trapped, awaiting death. He had obtained Kvatov's file. He knew Kvatov was born in October 1951, at Tulchin in the Vinnitskaya Oblast of the Ukraine, the son of Aleksandr Yakovich, a serviceman and poet in the Great Patriotic War.

He knew that Kvatov, like his father before him, had been a patriot. An old-fashioned patriot, out of tune with the times. And there was something else about Kvatov that he knew, or suspected.

'You'll never discover the truth,' said Brigite. 'Nobody will ever tell you the truth.'

'I can ask,' said Nick.

'Yes,' said Brigite ironically, 'you can ask.'

One night she insisted that he go out with her. She took him to a hotel in Narvik where Staff Beckwith and his lads, and Sergeant Doran's lot and Jamie's platoon were waiting. They cheered and carried him through the bar, until the manager threatened to call the police.

It was nearly midnight when Nick said: 'Where's Sykes?'

'Waiting for his court martial,' said Leech, reserved, not as warm as the others. 'The Monkeys took him off this afternoon. Thought you'd have known that, sir.'

Nick phoned Military Police and got the OC out of bed. He described, briefly, the part Sykes had played at Mount Kirovsk.

The OC said Mount Kirovsk was nothing to do with him.

Nick said: 'Private Sykes is to be released immediately. Any further action regarding the damaged vehicle will be taken by the commanding officer First Battalion Royal Mercians. The charges are withdrawn. To arrest a soldier without reference to his commanding officer is mindblowingly incompetent. I'm sending a truck for him now.'

The OC Military Police said he could send a fucking army but Sykes stayed where he was.

Nick phoned the main NATO number and said: 'General Hoepner. *Now*. I want to speak to him directly, I do not want the Chief of Staff. This is Major Nicholas Chard, First Battalion Royal Mercians.'

'Oh my God,' murmured Brigite.

'Hang on a mo, sir,' muttered Staff Beckwith.

Leech said, uneasily, 'He's all right where he is. Never you mind about Syco.'

Twenty minutes later, two MPs brought a bewildered and suspicious Sykes to the bar. Everybody cheered. A game of rugger started. The owner said he was definitely going to call the police, and did. They escaped just as the police cars arrived. Nick dispersed his men expertly through the backstreets, and it was Brigite who got caught. They let her go when she said the hooligans were French ski-chasseurs she had never seen before in her life before they picked her up outside the Pizza Grill.

It was disgraceful childish behaviour, stormed Brigite, and he agreed. He said: 'Never mind that. I want to talk about you and me.'

'There is no you and me.'

'There's nobody else but you and me,' he said, and she paused, impressed by his romantic imagery.

She said: 'You are just glad to be alive. A month with me, and you'd wish you weren't.'

He wanted her because they had shared an experience that nobody else shared, at least not on the same level of responsibility, and because she, uniquely, understood what he went through.

'I'm finished with the army,' he said.

'You love the army,' said Brigite.

'I've been *used*.'

'Lovers,' she said, 'are always used.'

She left Narvik without saying goodbye, in the late morning, while Nicholas was waiting to be debriefed by the final committee. By Terrier.

He told them how 'B' Company fought its way into the compound. How they had held the radar station. How Willis died helping Noon with the laser. How they barricaded themselves in after the missile attack, waiting for the mortars to open fire again.

He spoke for an hour. Afterwards he said: 'I have a question.'

'Yes?' said Hoepner.

'I was told by Major Munro that Colonel Kvatov was threatening a nuclear strike on Riga, in retaliation for the death of his daughter. I watched the silos. No attempt was made to fire a missile. Even when Colonel Kvatov knew he was under attack, even when he knew we were inside the compound and had taken the radar station, the silo covers remained closed. I should like to know if he ever threatened Latvia at all. I should like to know if there was ever a threat of a nuclear strike by the Feds.'

'Why should we tell you there was, if there wasn't?' asked Grenfell.

'Why not? Everything else I've been told since this job started has been bullshit.'

Grenfell's eyes bulged.

General Hoepner said: 'The stealth bombers were real enough.'

'And the rest?'

495

'Kvatov was demanding that Third Shock Army restore the honour of the army, he was demanding an invasion of the Baltic states, he was refusing to decommission his missiles.'

'Internal Russian politics.'

'Ten ICBMs?'

'The SAS hired out – did we charge by the day or the week?'

Hoepner stood up. He said: 'Congratulations, Nick. You did a magnificent job. You can feel very proud of yourself and of your men.'

'You did bloody well, Nick,' said Biggin. 'Leave it there.'

'Yes, congratulations,' said Grenfell awkwardly, adding with an effort: 'You can feel pleased with yourself.'

Nick said: 'In some ways I am. Misha is responding to a new French drug, and Lara is going to Berlin, to the Fleishner allergy clinic, although I fear Berlin is an unfortunate choice, bearing in mind her career ambitions.'

Grenfell looked at him blankly.

Hoepner said: 'Thank you for coming to see us. Enjoy your leave.'

Jamie and Anneliese walked in the short November afternoon, through the dead leaves, in a park overlooking the harbour. Jamie said that on winter afternoons in Shropshire they would go into Ludlow for afternoon tea with cakes. He urged her to write to Wolfgang, to let the chap down gently, but she said she had to go back to Hamburg, sort things out. She and Wolfgang were buying a flat together, after all, and he had gone to Dresden (she had since learned) to rescue Erike's cat. Anyway, she must see her parents. Well, then, could he come too? No he could not! Not this time. Not yet.

'Writing's so much kinder in the long run,' said Jamie.

She kissed him, in the sunshine, and told him not to worry. She would join him in England in a week's time. They went to the Atlantic Ocean Hotel and ate hot lobster for lunch, with a bottle of champagne. She was flying to Hamburg at 18.30. They had the afternoon ahead of them. 'I love you,' said Anneliese, when she had drunk some champagne. 'I love you, Jamie.'

'Yes,' said Jamie, who knew that she did.

Worembrand was by the air terminal newspaper stand when Doran approached him and boomed: 'Well well, look who's here.'

Worembrand ignored him and waved a bar of Swiss chocolate at the kiosk assistant. Doran hit him very hard across his back. Worembrand yelped in outrage and self-pity.

Doran said: 'Bloody well done. Come and have a pint. We don't give sweeties to fuckin' heroes.'

Worembrand tried to dig his heels into the marble floor, but Doran dragged him effortlessly into the bar. Half a dozen lads were waiting for the British Midland shuttle to Birmingham. They smiled and cheered, and in no time at all forced him to drink three litres of Norwegian lager, and after a while he started to tell them about his youth, as a young army photographer, when he quaffed ice-cold tiger beer in Singapore (this before his Bacardi days), and took his turn with the Thai International air hostesses known as SBFMs or Small Brown Fucking Machines . . . Yes, he'd lived, he'd had his day and, no, it certainly wasn't over yet. Bloody hell it wasn't, sonny.

'Another scoop of ale for my friend!' boomed Doran. 'This man is the bravest man in Norway . . . mind you, that's not saying much,' he added conversationally to a party of Norwegians standing at their elbow. 'The country's full of fucking pinkos . . .'

Anneliese came in.

'Max? For God's sake, we've been looking everywhere . . .'

He was going back to Germany in style, in a Luftwaffe executive jet. He sat by a window and Anneliese sat on the other side, and they were the only passengers. The sun was sinking over the cold North Sea as they headed down the Kattegat. The young Luftwaffe attendant said to Anneliese: 'I've had six generals in my cabin since I last saw you.'

'You'd rather have me, though, I'll bet.'

'Any day,' said the attendant wittily. 'Any time, any place.'

'I don't suppose,' said Anneliese, 'I can have a Luftwaffe Good Morning breakfast?'

'At 18.00 hours? I think we can do better than that.'

He shot Worembrand a thoughtful look. He wished that Worembrand was somewhere else. Worembrand knew this, but it did not make him uncomfortable. He was used to people wishing he were somewhere else.

* * *

Now they were over pink clouds, and Max was on the phone to Werner, confirming his decision to purchase fifty per cent of the Cherry-Ripe Club. Werner said he had made a wise move. Max had a flicker of anxiety, but decided he was a match for Werner any day of the week. Somebody else could be the next Beverley Goodway. It was only fair to give up-and-coming photographers a chance in life. There were, for that matter, enough nipples to be seen in the Cherry-Ripe on a Thursday (*Hausfräulein* talent contest!!!) night to satisfy the most indolent of voyeurs.

As for the army, he was finished with it. 'I'm not saying you didn't do your best, Mal,' the Head of Army Photographic (PR) Section had told him, 'but you're asking me to clear your chitty for a giant teddy bear that cost eighty-five ecus, and all I'm seeing here is seventeen snaps of Russian soldiers with their mouths open.'

'They were shouting,' said Worembrand, 'Eureka!'

'Unusual in a civil war, I'll grant you, but I don't know who's going to be interested. Can you explain why, in the caption?'

Over the corridor, Anneliese sat staring out of the window, deep in thought. She was a pretty girl, thought Worembrand, still sentimental on Norwegian lager. Pretty, warm and affectionate. She reminded him of those SBFMs in the mystic East – though she wasn't brown, of course.

Anneliese took her tiny laptop out of her bag, and opened it and switched it on. She looked at it for quite a long time. Below, now, the lights of Kiel were on the horizon. 'Dear Jamie,' she wrote. She stared out of the window again. Then she wrote: 'I think that this is the hardest letter I have ever had to write . . .'

The attendant brought her a glass of wine on a tray. He stopped smiling when he saw the tears coursing down her face. He put down the wine and turned back. He said curtly to Worembrand: 'Do you want a drink? Tea? Coffee?'

Worembrand said: 'A large Bacardi, with not too much ice.'

Nick went to Hereford, and dined with the Commandant, 22 SAS Regiment. He went with Munro and Noon to an SAS pub in the Black Mountains.

Munro said 'You ought to think of joining our lot,' and Noon said 'I'll second that.'

Nick was aware that he was being paid a great compliment. He was not tempted.

He had been confirmed as OC of 'B' Company. As Major Chard, he would take his men to join the United Nations Bosnia Brigade immediately after Christmas.

'They're getting you all out of the way,' wrote Brigite, cynically, in a letter from the Kurdish refugee camp where she now worked.

In another letter she wrote: 'I saw you change a great deal. I watched it happen. Perhaps I changed, as well. Not enough, though. Be lucky.'

Nick supposed Germans wrote this sort of stuff.

Now it was almost Christmas, and he was in the pub near

Leintwardine, ordering drinks at the bar, waiting for Emma. In a corner Jamie was sitting with a schoolgirl from Ludlow, an eighteen-year-old with long legs and clear grey eyes, who had asked for gin and tonic. Jamie was showing her the personal radio that had, he said, saved his life out there in the Russian snows.

'Curiously,' he told her, 'I didn't feel a thing at the time, I was too busy getting my men moving, getting some fire down on the buggers.'

The girl looked at him with admiration. Nick ordered drinks, and thought sadly of the wreath left in St Martin's churchyard, Hereford, by Toby Fuller's girl, with its inscription:

> To the world you were a soldier,
> But to me you were the world.

He looked out of the window. Emma's car was pulling into the car park. Northwards, fifteen hundred miles beyond the dark December loom of the Wrekin, new snow would be falling on the compound of 101 Rocket Regiment, and the wolves would be turning away to the richer pickings of Murmansk.

More Thrilling Fiction from Headline:

—— STEVE MARTINI ——
PRIME WITNESS

THE STUNNING NEW COURTROOM DRAMA
FROM THE AUTHOR OF *COMPELLING EVIDENCE*

**'MR MARTINI WRITES WITH THE AGILE EPISODIC
STYLE OF A LAWYER QUICK ON HIS FEET' JOHN GRISHAM**

'Steve Martini seems to have hit the nail right on the head' *Irish Times*

'A real page turner' *Sunday Telegraph*

PRIME WITNESS

In the space of five days the rural college town of Davenport is
rocked by four brutal murders: two couples – undergraduates – their
bodies are found tied and staked out on the banks of Putah Creek.
Then two more bodies are discovered. This time the victims are
Abbott Scofield, a distinguished member of the university faculty,
and his former wife Karen.

The police suspect Andre Iganovich, a Russian immigrant and part-
time security guard, but Paul Madriani, hot-shot Capitol City lawyer,
thinks there is more to the case than meets the eye.

Forensic reports on the physical evidence suggest lingering questions
about the Russian's involvement in the Scofield killings, and Paul
becomes increasingly convinced that the second murders are the
product of some copy-cat killer – a cold and calculating murderer
who has taken the lives of the Scofields for reasons that Paul is
determined to uncover...

'Prime is indeed the word for this involving read' *Publishers Weekly*

'Nice insider touches, and a hard-punching climax' *The Times*

Don't miss COMPELLING EVIDENCE and THE SIMEON CHAMBER
also available from Headline Feature

'The best debut, in my opinion, is *Compelling Evidence*' John Grisham

'Compelling indeed. This is a terrific debut' *Sunday Telegraph*

'A tense and gripping story, which held me to the end' *Books*

'A sensationally good courtroom thriller' *Los Angeles Times*

FICTION/THRILLER 0 7472 4164 3

ABOVE THE EARTH, BELOW THE EARTH, THERE'S NO DEATH MORE HORRIFYING

GARY GOTTESFELD
ILL WIND

When a massive earthquake uncovers a large Indian graveyard in Beverly Hills, forensic expert Wilhelm Van Deer – known as 'the Dutchman' – is confronted by more bones than he can cope with. But he soon realises that some of the remains are not as old as they should be, nor the manner of death as straightforward as first appears.

Digging deeper, he comes across weird underground passages and strange paintings of giant centipedes. Somehow these discoveries are linked to mysterious deaths that occurred over twenty years earlier, but there are powerful anonymous people now determined to keep their dark secrets buried for ever.

When the chilling murders begin anew, the Dutchman sets out to catch a maniac – an elusive psychopath obsessed with a grotesquely unusual method of killing...

FICTION/THRILLER   0 7472 4168 6

A selection of bestsellers from Headline

NIGHT OF THE DEAD	Mike Bond	£4.99	☐
SPEAK NO EVIL	Philip Caveney	£4.99	☐
GONE	Kit Craig	£4.99	☐
INADMISSIBLE EVIDENCE	Philip Friedman	£5.99	☐
QUILLER SOLITAIRE	Adam Hall	£4.99	☐
HORSES OF VENGEANCE	Michael Hartmann	£4.99	☐
CIRCUMSTANCES UNKNOWN	Jonellen Heckler	£4.99	☐
THE ASCENT	Jeff Long	£4.99	☐
BRING ME CHILDREN	David Martin	£4.99	☐
THE SIMEON CHAMBER	Steve Martini	£4.99	☐
A CALCULATED RISK	Katherine Neville	£4.99	☐
STATE V. JUSTICE	Gallatin Warfield	£5.99	☐

All Headline books are available at your local bookshop or newsagent, or can be ordered direct from the publisher. Just tick the titles you want and fill in the form below. Prices and availability subject to change without notice.

Headline Book Publishing PLC, Cash Sales Department, Bookpoint, 39 Milton Park, Abingdon, OXON, OX14 4TD, UK. If you have a credit card you may order by telephone – 0235 831700.

Please enclose a cheque or postal order made payable to Bookpoint Ltd to the value of the cover price and allow the following for postage and packing:
UK & BFPO: £1.00 for the first book, 50p for the second book and 30p for each additional book ordered up to a maximum charge of £3.00.
OVERSEAS & EIRE: £2.00 for the first book, £1.00 for the second book and 50p for each additional book.

Name ....

Address ....

....

....

If you would prefer to pay by credit card, please complete:
Please debit my Visa/Access/Diner's Card/American Express (delete as applicable) card no:

Signature .... Expiry Date ....